I0621617

The 24th Province

By Barry Phillips
Copyright © 2015 by globalwarmth publishing

Cover Illustration Copyright © 2015
Cover design by @JesseDeanRivero

Library of Congress Cataloging-In-Publishing Data
Phillips, Barry D.
The 24th Province
By Barry Phillips (1st edition), 2015
ISBN-13: 978-0692508725
Topics: Fiction, Christian, Suspense FIC042060

Published by globalwarmth publishing
10654 County Road 494, Tyler, Texas, 75706
e-mail: 24thprovince@gmail.com
blog: http://24thprovince.tumblr.com/

TABLE OF CONTENTS

Chapter 1 - Dengue
MONDAY 10:20am August 7th
Dibutunan, Aurora Province, Philippines

They bear no malicious intent, selecting victims based merely on proximity. The nearest creature with blood in its body becomes their prey. And, as blood-sucking day feeders, they are not particular about the species they feed upon; mammals, birds ... even reptiles become quarry. But humans are clearly their favorite source of blood protein. Human blood contains supplementary nutrients due to our position atop the food chain, and human skin is thin and easy to penetrate. Today had been a blissful feast for the rapidly expanding horde of bloodsuckers.

Reno West was visibly frustrated by the rising cloud of mosquitoes hovering in the intimate space she reserves for only her husband, Tom. Despite long sleeves, long pants, and an unhealthy slathering of DEET, Reno was bitten several times in the last hour. She was instructed by their missionary host to pack long sleeved shirts that "breathe" due to the tropical heat. So she brought cotton, linen, and rayon shirts that proved to be a pitiful barrier to the hostile masses of hungry mosquitoes that normally feed through the thick hides of livestock.

"Angie, honey, would you please spray some of this on my back?" Reno asked as she removed a red canister with a pump spray top from her backpack and held it up. Angie Ampatuan brushed away two mosquitoes from Reno's shirt, and then she scratched Reno's horribly itchy back from the top to the bottom with her beautifully manicured fingernails. Reno briefly froze and moaned with relief as Angie scratched her back. Angie smiled and continued to soothe the itchy bites on Reno's back before emptying the remainder of the canister of toxin on Reno's shirt.

"You're a Godsend, Angie! I don't know what I'd do without you." Reno said without taking her eyes off of the child she was examining. The ten years old patient had been suffering from fever, body aches and vomiting for more than three days. The child's fever had worsened overnight and her mother was alarmed. The tourniquet test revealed what Reno had suspected, another case of dengue.

"*Walang anuman, po*" answered Angie, teaching Tagalog to Reno as she had earlier requested.

"What does that mean?" asked Reno as she drew a vial of blood from the whimpering child's skinny arm and placed it in the Styrofoam cooler with the other vials of blood.

"Don't mention it." Angie answered, as she turned to the child's mother and gave her instructions for the medicine that Reno had prescribed. The young girl, wearing an undersized dress with all the color washed from it sat motionless, hanging her head in exhaustion. Her mother grabbed her hand and pulled her out of the small beige plastic chair. Angie then motioned for the next patient to join them. She introduced the mother and her twelve-year-old son to Reno as Irene and John Mark.

Despite nine years of medical practice in Charleston, South Carolina, Reno had never encountered a single case of dengue fever. An occasional infected tourist might bring the virus to North America from the tropics, but it rarely spread because it requires the aedes mosquito, which is found only in tropical climates. But the remote village of Dibutunan was now thick with aedes mosquitoes that hovered around Reno like a thick fog. Heavy rainfall from Tropical Storm Isang, which lingered just off the coast of central Luzon for almost a week, produced a mosquito population explosion. The entire month of July had been a banquet for them, and they were now so plentiful that they had to share their prey with one another. Reno didn't like being shared.

Angie Ampatuan had perfect teeth and a radiant smile. And when she smiled, everyone smiled with her. Even the suffering patients managed a smile for her. Members of the mission team imagined that Angie was barely a teenager, but she was twenty five years old and had already graduated from nursing school. She was graceful and petite, weighing less than ninety pounds. To say that she was petite would be an understatement; Angie was diminutive. She was a kilo of sugar in an eight-ounce bag. She dressed plainly and never wore, nor needed, makeup. After listening to Irene for a moment Angie said, "The same symptoms, ma'am; his mother says he has fever, body aches and vomiting."

Reno examined the boy's gums and discovered that they were bleeding. He was limp and listless. "We don't need any blood from John Mark", she said flatly. "He'll need to keep all the blood he can." Reno looked at John Mark with a concerned look. "He needs to be transported to the hospital in Cabanatuan as soon as possible. He needs to be hydrated and receive some fresh blood."

When Angie told Irene that the diagnosis was dengue and that John Mark needed to be transported to Cabanatuan the young mother dropped to her knees and wept. History told her that less than half of those who were brought to Cabanatuan ever returned. And her family didn't have the money to pay for his transportation or treatment. She knew how serious John Mark's condition was, and that there was absolutely nothing that she could do about it.

"It's okay, sister" Reno whispered, "I will pay. *Bayad ako.*" With that news, Irene jumped to her feet and hugged Reno, weeping loudly. She continued to hold onto Reno for more than a minute. There was no time to waste. John Mark needed treatment immediately. Sixteen suspected cases of dengue had already been diagnosed today, and it was not yet noon.

Reno could be mistaken for a Filipina because of her olive-colored skin and dark black hair. She remained slender and muscular by working at the gym and running every day. And she was grateful that she had prepared physically for this trip because the conditions were brutal. Reno always avoided junk food. Her motto was, "If there's an advertisement for it, don't eat it." She didn't suffer from jet lag from the transpacific flight; she managed to sleep soundly as her teammates tossed, turned and ambled around muttering to themselves during the weird hours of the night. Reno didn't realize it yet, but her conditioning would serve her well in the days to come.

Russian roulette is a potentially lethal game of chance. A single bullet is placed into the chamber of a revolver, and then the chamber is spun. The "player" then places the muzzle of the pistol against his/her head and pulls the trigger. The odds are in the player's advantage, as only one of several chambers will fire the weapon. And it's much the same with mosquitoes during a dengue outbreak. Most have not been exposed to the dangerous dengue virus and their benign bites are simply a nuisance. But the "loaded chamber", that singular mosquito that has recently fed on the blood of a dengue victim, can bring dread to an entire community.

Reno had been to Guatemala on a medical mission, so she thought she was prepared for third-world conditions, but she discovered otherwise. Antibiotics easily solved the bacterial and fungal infections she encountered in Central America. But in the Philippines she was combating a very different life form. Viruses don't respond to antibiotics. Instead of fighting the beast itself, she could only combat its symptoms. And the symptoms of dengue, the poorer cousin of malaria, are many. Some are mild, such as a low grade fever or headache. But some symptoms, such as bleeding, abdominal pain, or difficulty breathing indicate a serious condition that could lead to death. Practicing field medicine without proper diagnostic equipment frustrated Reno. All of the blood samples were sent to the regional hospital lab in Baler, which was an hour and a half away. The results of the lab work wouldn't be known until the following day. Field medicine, she once told her husband, is "like putting a Band-Aid® on an axe wound."

"Rod, I hear someone calling you on the radio!" Sean exclaimed as he carried Pastor Rod's backpack to him. Sean was a veteran of many trips to this region. He'd been to the Aurora Province so many times that he'd lost count. And he'd gained sufficient command of the language to communicate without an interpreter. He handed the backpack to Pastor Rod who fumbled around in the bag before locating the two-way radio that was borrowed from the local military detachment in Baler. Dibutunan had no cell signal, so the military two-way radio was their only communication out of the area.

Rod made sure that the huge radio was on channel seven, as he'd been instructed, and pushed the button to talk.

"This is Pastor Rod, can you hear me, over."

Angel Tolentino laughed when he heard Rod speaking into the radio as if he was in a 1970's combat movie. "There's no need to use formalities, Pastor, we're the only people on this channel. I just answered your cell phone, sir, and I have your wife on hold. I'm going to hold the phone up to the radio so that you both can talk."

"It must be an emergency," Rod said to no one in particular. "She's never called me during a mission trip before, and it's nearly midnight back home." Unsure what the news might be, and not wanting to alarm any of the others from Eastside Christian Fellowship, Pastor Rod retreated to the shade of a huge acacia tree across the road from their medical tent to speak over the radio.

"Hey, baby. What's up?" Rod began when Gina answered. He released the talk button to listen.

"Have you seen the storm that's headed your way?" Gina said excitedly. "It's a monster! The Weather Channel has been talking about it all evening and they say that it could even be bigger than Typhoon Haiyan, that storm that wiped out Tacloban City in the Philippines in

2014." Gina added with emphasis, "It's almost as big as the Philippines now!" Angel released the talk button.

"When and where is it forecast to make landfall?" Rod asked calmly. Rod was smiling and Gina knew it. He loved huge storms. In 1989, the South Carolina National Guard near Beaufort had turned Rod back as he drove into Hurricane Hugo with his camera gear. He had hoped to get onto Hunting Island, but never got close to the coast.

Angel pressed the talk button. "It will hit Luzon sometime before dawn on Thursday the 10th. The Weather Channel has the landfall directly over Baler! We're talking about a Category 5 Super Typhoon, Rod." Angel released the talk button.

"It's only Monday here, Gina. We have a couple of days to find a place to hunker down. Pastor Mark will make sure that we're safe. I'm sure he's been through many of these ..." Gina cut him off, clearly agitated, saying "Nobody's been through a storm like this one before, Rod! Get the team inland. Or better yet, get back to the hotel in Manila while the weather still permits you to travel.

"I know you're excited about this, Rod, but this one scares me. Please remember that you're responsible for the safety of the team." Gina paused for a moment as Rod considered what she was saying. "Tom West called me about an hour ago about the storm, and Sarah Turner freaked out when she saw the evening news at dinnertime. She wants me to call her back tonight to let her know about your plans." Angel released the talk button.

"Plans?" Rod asked a bit puzzled. "I just now found out about it, Gina. When we wrap up our medical mission here in Dibutunan this afternoon, we will return to Baler. I'll go to an Internet café and check out the storm. And while I'm there I will send a group message to all of the families to assure them that we'll be safe."

"Has the storm got a name?" Rod asked. He knew even tropical storms were named, so if this beast was already a typhoon it surely had a name. *"Kiko"* was the reply from Gina.

Angel pressed the talk button for Gina as she started speaking again. "And Kiko will be ripping apart the Philippines as we attend our Wednesday evening prayer meeting, Rod. We'll all be praying for you!" Gina began to cry. She knew Rod would do the right thing, but she also knew Kiko was no ordinary storm. She didn't like Rod's 'hunker down' mentality. She wanted him to get back to Manila before mudslides closed the roads. "Call me tomorrow, Rod, OK? Even if you send me an e-mail, I still want to hear from you over the phone again before the storm. Alright?" Angel released the talk button.

"Sure thing, baby. I'll plan to call you around 7:00 tomorrow evening. That's your time, OK?"

"Thanks, Rod. Please let everyone there know that we're praying for them. We'll plan to hear from you soon. Goodnight, honey."

Rod felt funny hearing "goodnight" as he put away the radio because it was just lunchtime in the Philippines. He felt the eyes of the team members follow him as he walked back across the street towards the medical tent. They knew from the length of the conversation that something was up. And considering that the call was made to their "emergency" phone number, they knew that an explanation was forthcoming. He smiled and asked Anna, the unofficial team mother, to gather the team together. Dr. Kemp was in the middle of a tooth extraction, and said that he would join them in five minutes. Ashley Ross, his office assistance, was the only member of the team that was not a member of Eastside Christian Fellowship. She remained with Dr. Kemp until the extraction was completed.

Pastor Rod gathered the team into a semi-circle and said, "Gina called me a few minutes ago." Rod tried to speak in his most authoritative voice. "She said that we have a huge storm bearing down on us. The Weather Channel is reporting that the Philippines will be whacked by a super typhoon early Thursday morning. And, as of this moment, it is headed straight for Baler. I believe we'll need to tear down our tent and bring all our gear with us when we head back to Baler today. We might not make it back here tomorrow."

"Let's plan to examine our last patients at 2:30. I know it's going to be tough for you to turn away people who are hurting, but we need to shut things down so that we can pack up our equipment. Some will be left out no matter when we stop." Several of the team members glanced at the growing number of patients seated near the medical tent. "We'll need your help with that," Rod said, as he looked at the Filipino members of the team. "We should be able to pack up everything before 4:00." Rod paused for a moment expecting questions, but everyone was still waiting for the rest of the plan. "We'll go straight to the Internet café near the church in Baler to find out more about the storm. We won't have a plan to present to our families until we discuss things tonight. When you talk with your families, please let them know that we'll share our plans with them around 10:00 Monday night *their time*."

Reno spoke up. "Okay, I'll need some help selecting patients who have the most severe symptoms. I can see only a dozen more before we close up, so let's chose them wisely. Kelly – I'll need you and Angie to tend to all the others. Both of you are medically trained, so I'll trust you to give them whatever medication you think they need before you send them home."

"We may be tested in the coming days, so let's remember to be patient with one another and lift each other's burdens." Rod clapped his hands, and then said, "We're ambassadors for Christ. Pour out His love on these people before we leave."

Very few places on Earth can compete with the landscape of the Aurora Province in the Philippines, particularly the mountainous section between Baler and Dibutunan. The mountains are green and lush with coconut palms, banana trees, cacao, ferns and thick vegetation. The ocean offers every shade of blue and green: azure, emerald, sapphire, jade, indigo, lime, cobalt and turquoise. The rock outcroppings, white sand beaches and caves hidden along the ocean cliffs add a mystical character to the magnificent scenery.

Andy Campbell, the father of the youngest team member, arranged for the team to be flown by helicopter directly from Manila to Dibutunan. He had a connection in Manila who 'owed him a favor'. The ride saved them a full day of travel, and the team was left speechless by the splendor of the Aurora province, which was especially spectacular when viewed from the air.

Despite the urgency to find out more about Typhoon Kiko, the team asked to stop several times on the drive back to Baler. The massive blue and white waves crashing on the long stretch of beach near Ampere proved irresistible. Nothing the team could do at this stage could change the course of events in the coming days. This was a time to laugh, splash in the surf and revel in the splendor of God's magnificent creation. The air was pure, the skies were clear, and there was no indication whatsoever of the horrors that lay beyond the horizon. They all knew that a storm was coming, but none of them could imagine the sense of dread that would soon envelop them.

Chapter 2 – China prepares for Kiko
MONDAY 3:45pm August 7th
Zhanjiang, China

The Director of China's Meteorological Administration was assured by his staff that the predictions regarding Typhoon Kiko were reliable. It was apparent that a massive super typhoon, unprecedented in strength, would hit just north of Manila in the pre-dawn hours of August 10th. Not many years ago such information would have been considered dubious, but the art of weather prediction had grown into a reliable science.

Meteorology has been known as an inexact science. Trustworthy predictions of a typhoon's future strength or path have long been considered to be capricious. But the sophistication of computer modeling has reinvented the art of weather forecasting. National meteorological agencies now share monitoring data with other nations. The United States, Japan, Korea, Taiwan, the Philippines and China reciprocally share monitoring information gathered from buoys, satellites, ships and weather balloons. But it was still too soon to provide a high level of confidence regarding Kiko's landfall in southern China. All models pointed to landfall somewhere between Hong Kong and Shantou sometime late Friday afternoon, August 12th. Some, but not all of the models, indicated that Kiko might also make landfall in China as a Category 5 super typhoon. Civil defense authorities were alerted.

The Chinese response to the news about Kiko was both immediate and organized. Hourly television and radio broadcasts provided clear instructions regarding preparation for the storm. Coastal residents were given 72 hours notice to evacuate to their designated inland shelters, which would be opened immediately. Compliance was not optional. Authorities permitted each family member to carry a single backpack, but nothing more. Pets needed to be delivered to designated "care areas." The government wanted to avoid large numbers of hungry feral animals wandering about in the post-storm debris. Private vehicle owners were ordered to secure them at inland storage warehouses. Public transport buses provided free rides to evacuation shelters. Anyone who remained behind after the 4:00pm deadline on August 10th would be detained, fined, and placed in jail. No excuses would be accepted. The government of the PRC had no plans to pluck ignorant fools from rooftops as the Americans had done in the aftermath of Hurricane Katrina.

Community civil defense coordinators would ensure that every building was secured and shuttered at least 24 hours before Kiko's arrival. Shelter managers were tasked to provide a three-day supply of clean water, food, toilet facilities, and beds. Generators were tested and a sufficient supply of diesel fuel was delivered to each shelter. Shelter security teams would prevent the chaos happening outside from being replicated within the shelters.

Frenetic activity was quickly underway at all coastal ports. China's container transport system facilitated its rapid economic growth. Nearly three *billion* tons of cargo is shipped each year from China's ports – more than 2,000 of them. Port authorities safely harbor most of the ships, but many vessels are safer at sea than anchored at port during a super typhoon. Docks are battered by ships during typhoons, so authorities ordered hundreds of ships to leave before Kiko's arrival. Smaller vessels navigated their way to major inland waterways and anchored far upstream from the coast. But the captains of larger vessels eagerly headed to the low side of Kiko while there was still time to do so. At 14 knots, there was still enough time to escape the leading edge of the storm by sailing south. Safe waters were only two days away in the South China Sea between Vietnam and Borneo. Ships were loaded, offloaded and fueled with a sense of urgency. Sea captains knew to get underway at once when large storms loomed, otherwise options evaporated quickly. They could all see that Kiko was no ordinary storm.

Ships need to maintain a safe distance from other vessels as well as from the shore during typhoons. And the weight from cargo can actually help stabilize ships against the waves. An empty ship is in danger during a typhoon. Ballast water in the base of the hull provides some stabilization for an empty ship, but the water causes a terrible roll as the water shifts. An experienced freighter crew could survive a typhoon at sea, and tell exaggerated stories to their grandkids. But without some weight, the repeated impact of the hull slamming through the troughs could smash apart any ship. Each captain was given his orders, and an unprecedented flotilla of vessels departed China's ports. The magnitude of this massive exodus was staggering, but also mystifying.

The flurry of activity in the ports at Zhanjiang, Xiamen, Hong Kong or Shantou made sense. But the number of vessels departing from Shanghai Harbor, the world's largest cargo port, made no sense at all. Shanghai is a safe, deep-water port located much too far away from the forecasted landfall area to be impacted by Kiko. Evacuating vessels from the port in Shanghai due to a storm headed for Hong Kong would be like moving ships away from Newark, NJ because of a hurricane headed to Charleston, SC. It didn't add up. And it captured the attention of Jim Adams, an intelligence analyst at CIA headquarters at Langley, Virginia.

Chapter 3 – It doesn't add up
MONDAY 1:30pm (EST) August 7th
Langley, Virginia USA

"What have you got, Jimbo?" asked Roger Lane, the Deputy Director for National Intelligence. Roger was 'pudgy' but always impeccably groomed. He cancelled a lunch date with his wife to meet with Jim Adams to discuss some data that Jim considered odd. Jim was Roger's physical antithesis. He was tall and lanky and was born without the 'fashion gene.' Even by appointment, few intelligence analysts would get even a brief opportunity to share their thoughts with a person at Roger's pay grade. But Jim Adams had a nose for data anomalies, and he'd been right every time he hoisted a red flag. Jim's instincts were keen. He didn't have to put together the whole puzzle, that wasn't his job, but Jim could easily identify pieces of the puzzle that didn't fit. And he believed that he'd uncovered something that was amiss.

"I've got three things that I believe are related, and I pray that I'm wrong. First, the Chinese have sent more than seventeen hundred ships to sea to keep them safe from Typhoon Kiko when it impacts the South China coast on Friday. That's highly unusual. Normal pre-typhoon evacuations number less than two hundred ships. And most of those vessels would head inland on the major waterways, not towards open sea" Jim began.

"Kiko is no ordinary storm, Jim." Roger explained. "I spent most of the morning dealing with contingency plans for our operations in the Philippines. The embassy is closing today, and they may not reopen anytime soon. It's headed straight for Manila and it will be a mess there for weeks."

"Yeah, there's no question about it. No amount of preparation can prevent massive damage from a storm as strong as Kiko. But that's what makes it weird, Roger. The Chinese response to Typhoon Haiyan in November 2013 was nothing like the activity we've seen with Kiko. And Haiyan was the strongest typhoon *ever to make landfall.* So I don't understand the unusual activity at the ports. Especially Shanghai; the impact from Kiko will be slight there and there's no need for the maritime precautions."

"So what can it mean, Jim? Are these military vessels?" Roger asked.

"Yes, far too many. That's actually my second concern. The *Liaoning*, the first aircraft carrier commissioned into the Chinese Navy, is already in the South China Sea. The South China Fleet is mostly still in port, but satellite imaging indicates that they are preparing to launch the 2nd, 5th, 10th and 18th Escort Task Groups. That includes two Luyang class destroyers, one Luhai class destroyer, three frigates, and replenishment ships. But here's the odd one, Roger. The 18th Escort Task Group includes a Yuzhao class amphibious transport dock. The only reason that they'd need an amphibious transport dock is if they intend to go ashore where there is no dock." Jim continued as Roger examined the report that he'd been handed.

"We've detected unusual activity with both brigades of marines, particularly the 1st Marine Brigade based in Zhanjiang. They've loaded up amphibious tanks and mechanized infantry vehicles, which are also amphibious. And their Dragon Commando unit has gone underground; we track several key members of that unit and none have been seen in over a week." Jim paused as the waitress delivered their drinks.

"And these are *marines*, Roger. They are the tip of the spear. These are the troops that China would use to lead any amphibious operation. I'm convinced that none of this activity at the 1st Marine Brigade has anything to do with civil defense plans for Kiko."

"I'm sure that our Pacific Fleet is tracking all this, Jim. Three of our battle groups are already in the western pacific. We outgun them on the high seas; there's simply no way they can contend with the firepower we can deliver." Roger added, "Not to mention the submarines tracking all this activity in the South China Sea. They'll be there all the way through Kiko."

"What's your third concern?" Roger asked. He checked for messages on his cell phone as the waitress delivered their food – two Rueben sandwiches with potato salad.

"This is an eerie thing, Roger. The Chinese word for "relief" is "fúdiāo". It's an uncommon word for Chinese mariners to utter over the radio, but we've logged the use of this word more than 600 times *this week*. It's a noun, Roger, which might mean "comfort" or "solace". And it is being used to describe their cargo. I'm convinced that this is an organized operation, but I can't connect the dots."

Roger added, "We know that they consider most of the South China Sea as their sovereign maritime territory. But the common wisdom in Washington is that a planned, direct military confrontation with the any of the claimant nations over disputed territories would be foolish. China has too much to lose economically by engaging in a war. An embargo would be placed on their ships, they would suffer through tough international sanctions, and their financial assets would be frozen worldwide."

"China is building a military base on Mabini Reef, which is clearly within the Philippines 200 mile territorial limit. They have guns and radar equipment on Mischief Reef. Anti-aircraft guns and an airstrip are now on Cuarteron Reef. They have high-powered naval guns on Fiery Cross Reef. Gaven Reef has now become a harbor for their naval patrol boats. Subi Reef now houses troops, has a helipad, and is armed with several naval guns. It's all in the report, Roger."

"And they'll continue to push the limits with their neighbors, but they don't want combat," Roger replied. "Their brand of bully diplomacy will continue unless we assert ourselves in the region. You've come up with some interesting stuff, here, Jim. I'll read your report and share it with my staff. I'm sure I'll have more questions in the next day or two. In the meantime, know that my door is always open to you." With that, Roger excused himself and walked to the cashier's counter to pay for their meal. He hadn't touched his sandwich, so Jim asked the waitress to put it in a take-out bag. He hoped that Roger was more alarmed than he demonstrated during the meal. Jim was almost certain that the Chinese were going to seize more of the South China Sea through force in the coming days. But, this time Jim was *wrong*.

Chapter 4 – Sleeper cells awaken
Tuesday 6:00am August 8th
Pantabangan Road, Nueva Ecija, Philippines

It was insidious, as two to three hundred men were inserted into the Philippines each day. They all arrived at various airports on different flights for diverse purposes. Some arrived as well-dressed businessmen into Davao City or Manila. Others came as tourists to Cebu or Clark wearing tee shirts and sandals and carrying only backpacks. They arrived from Hong Kong, Beijing, Kuala Lumpur, Bangkok and Singapore; an unnoticeable handful on every flight. No anomaly was detected by immigration authorities. All of them came as part of a devious master plan, each knowing exactly where they would go and what they would do once they arrived. Training had taken place for many months, and the equipment and supplies for their missions were all in place and ready. All they needed was a super storm like Kiko for cover. But even in their wildest imaginations, they couldn't have hoped for better concealment than amidst the chaos and confusion caused by Kiko.

Mao Zedong devised a three-stage insurgency doctrine requiring the use of highly trained and motivated revolutionaries to instigate chaos at the onset of an uprising. His strategy was formulated, however, for an internal rebellion, not an invasion. The cell groups for Operation Zhi, as the operation had been named in Beijing, were modified to create havoc, *and* to suppress any initial counter response. Super Typhoon Kiko would provide the chaos, while small groups of commandos disrupted key elements of Philippine infrastructure.

At dawn on Friday, one full day after Operation Zhi began, the "chaos" units would assist with the arrival of Chinese marines and Special Forces. The world would still be awaiting news of Kiko's devastation, wondering why more communications from the Philippines were not forthcoming. The international press would be muzzled by teams specifically assigned to intercept them. All communications, incoming and outgoing, would be jammed. It would be no secret to other governments that something more than Typhoon Kiko had happened in the Philippines, but the deviousness and swiftness of Operation Zhi would make an immediate response improbable. As classified meetings took place overnight in Washington to discuss response options, the "chaos" groups would secure selected port facilities and airfields for the arrival of reinforcements already underway.

The propaganda war would also begin during this phase. A small army of political officers would arrive in phase 2 to take control of all international aid extended by the world to the suffering Filipinos. All aid would be carefully repackaged in bags, pre-printed in Tagalog, with the message: "Please accept this small gift from the People's Republic of China. Our prayers are with you, neighbors, during your time of suffering. " The "prayer" part of the message was included because they knew that Filipinos are people of faith. Most Filipinos would be under a total communications blackout and would have no idea that they were being invaded. And their frustration at their own government's lack of response to Kiko would make them even more receptive to the generosity extended by the Chinese. Carefully crafted messages had been prepared to present to the Filipino people. The message dismissed the notion of invasion. It was a suspiciously worded narrative that explained their large presence as "relief" that the Philippine government would be unable to render.

The narrative extended to the international community was similar in nature. It stated that the Philippine government was a failed state, unable to respond to the great need of its people during this horrific calamity. The People's Republic of China, acting on behalf of the humble and embattled Filipino people, had helped restore order amidst the chaos caused by Kiko. Corrupt Philippine officials, according to their narrative, would not be able to siphon aid away from the suffering masses as they had during Typhoon Haiyan/Yolanda. The People's Liberation Army would make sure that every Filipino, no matter where they live, would receive adequate food, shelter and clothing during this time of misfortune. There would be no mention whatsoever regarding the continued suppression of communications, sequestering of news teams, and a growing number of armed Chinese soldiers arriving at ports around the nation.

And the PRC news to its own citizens was one of benevolence. The commentators would speak of Filipinos as their "little brothers" who needed help in the wake of a terrible tragedy. It was a message of compassion and concern. It was a message designed to instill pride and make every citizen of the PRC feel good about their national character.

Chinese spies were positioned surreptitiously throughout the Philippines for many years in preparation for this event. They had become captains in industry and leaders in high profile businesses. Filipino sympathizers, disgusted with government corruption and the unequal distribution of wealth, had also been recruited to participate. Some were high-ranking military officers while others were elected officials at virtually every level of government. And they would all play an important role in the days to come through intimidation, misinformation, and disruption of response plans. They would help discredit the existing government, emphasizing that it was "a failed state" and, in turn, they were promised positions of power in the transitional government.

Each cell group commando was a highly conditioned athlete, adept at hand-to-hand combat. They were the elite of the Chinese Special Forces. Few in the world could shoot with their accuracy. And none could be more ruthless in accomplishing their mission; especially the group headed by Captain Peng Bo Rong, who was cruel to his own men and without mercy to his enemies.

Captain Rong's reputation as judge, jury, and executioner was well earned, and he earned the nickname *Judge*, which he relished. He'd spent his entire lifetime without friends because of his cruelty, and most of the soldiers under his command kept their distance from him for good reason. He wasn't without a sense of humor, but his humor was dark and perverse and elicited awkward laughs. Judge could laugh with a fellow soldier one minute, and then beat him into a coma the next.

Judge leaned hard into a sharp left curve on a new Yamaha Seraw 250 dirt bike as he entered the mountainous section of the Pantabangan Road leading to the Aurora Province. The bike was powerful and agile and would draw little attention because of its plain styling. The early morning mountain air was cool. If stopped for any reason he was prepared. He had a valid Philippine driver's license, the motorcycle was properly registered, and he was carrying nothing but his wallet and cell phone. He carried only small bills, the equivalent of only $45, so that even if he was searched nothing would trigger concern.

But the van that followed him was anything but nondescript. Five heavily armed Chinese commandoes carried weapons and ammunition needed to secure the dock at the Baler fish port. They remained ten minutes behind Judge, who planned to notify them if he encountered any military roadblocks. A large truck carrying uniformed soldiers passed them in the opposite direction just ten minutes earlier, which put them all on high alert.

Three heavily armed vans used the alternate route that twists and turns from Cabanatuan through the small mountain town of Villa, which virtually disappeared under a massive landslide several years ago. The Villa road is sparsely populated and more susceptible to landslides than the Pantibangan Road. But Judge wanted his men to become familiar with both roads; he had to deliver an entire regiment of infantry and their equipment to the base of the Sierra Madre Mountains in Nueva Ecija to prevent the escape of Philippine soldiers from Fort Magsaysay.

Their intelligence officers explained that they would pass six platoon-sized military camps on the road to Baler. Judge sped past the first checkpoint without seeing a single soldier; there were only signs on the side of the hill to indicate the unit's designation. He used his cell phone to call the driver of the van behind him and said simply, "One clear" when the driver answered. In less than two hours they would all be at the beach "resort" that had been rented for their rendezvous at Diguisit. The resort owner was a Chinese businessman who frequently arranged travel to Baler for Chinese tourists. Hopefully he wouldn't consider it odd for 21 young men to be traveling together without female companions or children. They had been briefed that the resort owner spoke Mandarin, so they would need to speak carefully once they arrived. "Two clear" spoke Judge just two hundred meters past the second military encampment. Ten minutes later, as he sped past the third camp he called to confirm, "Three clear." Just like the others, there was no sign of a uniformed soldier.

There was little forward visibility due to the turns and twists in the road, so any surprise roadblock would appear without notice. On a long, steep uphill climb he noticed a Philippine flag atop the hill and saw Philippine military uniforms milling about near two barricades, one blocking each lane. The military checkpoints were initially established to prevent easy movement of rebels from the New People's Army, the military branch of the Communist Party of the Philippines. Aurora was a hotbed of activity during the 1970, and 1980's. The NPA retreated further into the mountains once cell phones were introduced to the province in the mid 1990's. By then the military checkpoints were familiar sights to the people coming and going from Aurora. But rarely would you actually see the soldiers.

Judge downshifted and weaved through the barricades, slowing only as much as necessary to navigate his way through. Nobody was actually manning the barricade; they were simply there. There were no second glances or close examination. Nobody even looked at him directly, so he continued past the checkpoint and stopped several hundred meters past it, out of sight.

"Don't stop. Don't roll down your window. Move slowly past checkpoint four. There are soldiers, repeat, there are soldiers, but nobody is manning the barricade. Call me after you clear." Judge waited at the top of the ridge, looking backwards for any sign of advancing traffic. There was none. He hoped that the heavily tinted windows on the van would prevent the soldiers from noticing that all the passengers were male Chinese nationals.

As the van neared the checkpoint, a lone soldier held his hand up to signal the driver to stop. The driver rolled down the window as they approached. The soldier asked for a ride to the Baubo checkpoint, but the driver did not understand him and replied in Chinese. The front seat passenger smiled at the soldier and also spoke to him in Chinese. The soldier smiled back and waved them through the checkpoint. He would get a ride from the next vehicle. *Too bad*, he thought, *this van had air conditioning.*

After passing through the checkpoint, the driver contacted Judge as he had been ordered to do and told him that they had been stopped. Judge was livid because his order not to stop had been disobeyed, but there seemed to be no damage. He would deal with the disobedient driver later.

The Baubo military detachment was the last they had to pass before reaching Baler. The motorcycle raced past Baubo, and the van followed a few minutes later. Thirty minutes later the men were standing barefoot on the beach at Diguisit. They looked like tourists as they walked in along the beach with their pants rolled up. All were joking and laughing except for Judge. He would have no peace until the remaining vans arrived safely.

Intercepted communications made it clear that all twelve of the TA-50 fighters recently acquired from South Korea would be moved from Villamor Air Base to the international airport in Davao, far to the south of Kiko's reach. Additionally, most of the C-130 airlift fleet would be there too. And recent information suggested that the helicopters that could not be properly placed in hangars would join the other aircraft in Davao. There would be no chance for the evacuated military aircraft, parked neatly in rows, as trained commandos swooped in on them. Just one experienced mortar team could take them out, one by one, walking down the entire row of aircraft. It would be like shooting fish in a barrel.

Teams would secure the Ninoy Aquino International Airport in Manila at midnight, just hours before the arrival of Kiko. Power would be out, and all communications would be suppressed at the start of the operation. They didn't want to destroy anything unnecessarily, as the facilities would be needed later. It would be foolish to destroy what, in a few short hours, would belong to the People's Republic of China. Teams would arrive at the airport in Philippine National Police vehicles wearing PNP uniforms. Snipers would make sure that they arrived unimpeded. Teams would quickly overwhelm airport security using jeeps that would emerge through holes cut in the perimeter fence, facilitated by total darkness of the power outage. Suppression teams would prevent access to the airport from every direction. Additional suppression teams would be located in other locations around Manila: Pasig, Mandaluyong, Makati, Pasay, and Paranaque. Their task would be to thwart any military movement towards the airport.

Similar activity would take place at Clark Air Base. The objective at the former US airbase would not be to engage the fairly large contingent of airmen and soldiers, but to secure the runways, control tower, and hangars. With communication suppressed, the advantage would be on the side of the aggressors. Commandoes would be placed at key intersections and atop selected buildings. They would be totally unexpected in the midst of typhoon strength wind and heavy rain. Reinforcements would arrive in 24 hours, when all hope for the Filipino defenders would dissipate.

The port at Subic would also be seized. Subic served the Americans well during the Vietnam War, and it would soon serve the PRC as the primary staging area for their military equipment. Kiko would damage some of the facilities at Subic, but its location on the west coast of Luzon would protect them from storm surge. Ships sent into the South China Sea from Chinese ports would converge on Subic in the hours after Kiko exploded back into the South China Sea. In a daring display of seamanship, the captains of hundreds of vessels would arrive at the port as directed by the government of the PRC.

Judge gathered his men together for a briefing after the three remaining vans arrived at the beach resort. The tinted windows prevented prying eyes from seeing the weapons hidden inside the vans, which were moved next to their rooms and carefully guarded. Judge explained that they would need to move inland to safer accommodations as Kiko approached. Staff Sergeant Li, who was fluent in Tagalog, was sent to look for safer accommodations further inland, yet close enough to secure the fish port when the winds subsided.

The fury of Kiko would be a footnote on the events of the coming days. The terror of war would, like a demon in a horror movie, return once again to haunt the people of the Philippines.

Chapter 5 – Mission on hold

Tuesday 9:00am August 8th
Baler, Aurora Province, Philippines

"Hey Gina, sorry for getting back to you so late, but the Internet café just opened up," began Rod.

"We're all worried sick," Gina interrupted. "Have you been watching the news?"

Rod said, "We have only a few minutes to talk, so let me explain our situation. We held a team meeting last night to discuss options and have decided we're going to hunker down a few miles inland from Baler. Ramada Community Church in the town of Maria Aurora has agreed to accommodate us. They have filtered water, a restroom, and the building has withstood previous storms without any damage."

Gina was furious, but held her emotions in check. She couldn't imagine that they were actually going to stay in the path of the storm. "Are you far enough inland to escape storm surge? And is it elevated so that you are not flooded?"

"We've been assured that it is the safest place to be in the entire region. We'll be fine there", said Rod.

"Kiko has shifted a little bit south, Rod. It's no longer headed directly at Baler. It's still going to hit somewhere between where ya'll are at and Manila. The sustained winds are now at 200mph – have you been watching the Weather Channel?"

Rod laughed. "The Weather Channel isn't available here, Gina, but CNN is providing updates every hour or so. We'll watch the local news tonight at 6:30 to find out what the local media is saying."

Rod continued, "We prayed about it as a team, then discussed all options, including a swift return to Manila. We know that there's an element of danger in staying here, but Kiko is really not an unusual occurrence here; they've been through these many times here in Aurora." Rod was speaking partly out of ignorance and partly from information he'd obtained from a quick search of the Internet. Super typhoons had, indeed, ravaged the Aurora Province in the past. But Baler had been spared the brunt of those storms. Most had come ashore in sparsely populated areas in the northern region of the province near Casiguran. And the loss of life had been minimal.

"We're here on a medical mission, Gina. We have doctors, nurses and medicine with us. We're going to be needed here after the storm hits. We came to serve the people of Aurora and the Lord has put us here at just the right time. After the storm we'll be able to continue our mission. That's what we've been called to do, honey. We're all going to be fine, so please stop worrying; we'll keep you updated as best we can." Rod paused.

Gina said, "Just keep your cell phone charged up – I'm sure we'll be calling you frequently."

"Sure thing, baby. We know that we won't have electricity for at least a day or two after the storm, so I'll be conserving the battery. But I'll contact you via Skype as soon as the electricity is restored. If the cell towers are not damaged you'll be able to call or text me anytime. They are looking for a generator to hook up at the church; if they get one I'll be able to keep my cell phone charged up."

Once again Gina protested. "You'll be home before the power is restored there, honey. We're already hungry for information and we'll all be going crazy if you lose communications there. The team families are terrified that you're sitting in the path of a raging monster."

"We have to trust that the Lord will take care of us, Gina. That's what we do as His people – we trust Him. We know that God is with us in every circumstance, and this is an opportunity to live out our faith. We'll come back with some extraordinary video and pictures and share our experiences with the church when we get home. I know it's hard not to worry, especially when you don't hear from us, but just know that we are firmly in God's hands." Rod knew that he could do nothing to comfort his wife, but her faith in God would provide the peace she needed.

"I wouldn't do anything to jeopardize the safety of the team, Gina. You know that. We've all agreed to batten down the hatches and ride this thing out. I know this isn't the news that you wanted to hear, but it was the best decision. If we left later today for Manila we could be cut off by landslides in the mountains or stopped by flooding in Nueva Ecija. It's clear here right now, but the weather could change at any moment. If Kiko shifts south and heads towards Manila we might actually be in a safer place here than in Manila.

"Okay, listen baby; I'm going to have to go. Manny is back with the jeep, and we're going to check out the shelter where we'll stay for the next few days. We've got to bring all of our stuff there tomorrow. And we'll probably do some local medical ministry there until the storm hits. I miss your smile, Gina. So keep smiling, we're going to be fine here."

Gina began a reply, but Rod interrupted, "Okay baby. I really have to go. They're all headed outside now. Everyone seems to have been able to contact someone from home, so I believe that we're set for now. I love you. I'll talk to you again soon. Bye-bye." The electricity was out before Rod finished. Gina never heard him say, "I love you". Rod walked out of the Internet café and was surprised how hot it had become in just a half hour. The team was already loaded into the jeepney, and Pastor Rod climbed aboard.

Manny suggested that the team should visit the sights before the storm hit. Even though the team had only been in Aurora for three days, it would be best if they took their R&R day before the storm. With Kiko arriving on Thursday, there would be no possibility for the team to go sightseeing on Friday as planned. Fallen trees would block the roads, and flooding or landslides would likely prevent them from seeing the sights. And the ocean would turn from the beautiful aquamarine color to a murky, brackish brown from all the mud that would be washed into the sea. Manny was right. If they would have any opportunity to look around, today was it.

Pastor Mark suggested that they go to the beach at Diguisit for a picnic lunch. They could swim there and explore the tidal pools. After they scouted their new accommodations they could spend a few minutes at the largest banyan tree in Asia. They had seen pictures of the thick gnarled branches and large tunnels inside the tree. The newcomers on the team were eager to see the sights and quickly agreed with Pastor Mark's suggestion.

Sister Marilou and Sister Angie were dropped off at the market to buy the food they would cook at the beach. The jeepney continued to the church to pick up pots and pans, plates and eating utensils. And nearly a dozen church members had been alerted by text messages and were already waiting for them. With all of the people and picnic supplies there was little room inside the jeepney, so the Filipinos from the church were all "top-loaded".

There seemed to be no community preparation whatsoever for the impending storm. Maybe there were things happening behind the scenes, but it was clearly invisible. Shopkeepers were conducting business as usual. None of the storefronts were boarded up, through some stores had folding metal doors designed to secure the contents at night. Driving rain might permit some water to seep in, but the doors, when padlocked, would hold securely in high winds. Banners and billboards remained hanging over the streets and on the sides of buildings. Perhaps they had experienced so many storms that they could secure everything in little time. Or maybe they responded to so many false alarms that they no longer reacted until the last minute. Nobody seemed to be concerned about loose items that might become missiles in the fierce winds that were coming. Even coconuts – why wouldn't the plantation owners lighten the load at the top of the trees just to prevent the trees from snapping in half or being uprooted? There was absolutely nothing in the behavior of the local people that indicated a deadly super typhoon was bearing down on them.

By the time that everyone was aboard, more than thirty people were in and atop the jeepney as they headed to the beach for their picnic. Filipino jeepneys are among the most practical vehicles in the world. They are extended WWII jeeps that have long benches down either side in the back for passengers. They can navigate difficult roads and carry heavy payloads. The church jeepney was designed to accommodate twenty Filipinos inside, which equates to about a dozen Americans. They were dangerously and comically overloaded as they headed to the beach.

A uniformed guard stopped them at the entrance to the beach resort, explaining that the entire resort had been rented out for a private affair. The public was not invited at this time. The resort was large, yet only four vans were visible. Perhaps others were on their way. Manny backed the jeepney onto the road and drove to the small resort next door just meters away.

Pastor Mark admired the four brand-new vans parked next to the cabins at the neighboring resort. All had good clearance, a wide wheelbase and black tinted windows. There are no restrictions regarding window tinting in the Philippines, so black tinting is not uncommon. The vans appeared to be the newest model of the Honda Odyssey. The deep blue color looked almost black as they sat in the shade. Four expressionless Chinese men stared back at Pastor Mark as he examined their vans from the fence of the resort. Filipinos are genuinely friendly people; smile at them and they will smile back. But there were no smiles returned to Pastor Mark. Three of the men turned away and scurried inside the closest cabin. The remaining man glared back with a fierce look in his eyes. Pastor Mark returned to the group to help cook their lunch of grilled tuna, eggplant and rice.

Even though they had been together for only three days, there was a remarkable camaraderie that was evident between the Filipinos and Americans. They teased one another and everyone laughed easily. Despite the jet lag, they played "Fast Scrabble" and learned new card games the previous two nights. Reno seemed particularly close to Angie; they spent most of their free time together and sat next to one another wherever they went. Angie spoke good English, which made conversation easy. And her nursing background allowed them to work side-by-side during the day.

The team teased Tyler because of his antics. He never met a mirror that he didn't like, and considered himself a 'ladies man.' He was tall and lean, almost skinny, and sported a comical haircut with dirty blonde bangs that often covered his eyes. He became infatuated with Angie, who was more than decade older than him. Even though she looked like a young teenager, Angie was mature in so many ways. She was also spiritually mature and showed grace to Tyler by humoring him. She wasn't leading him on, but she didn't roll her eyes or say anything to hurt Tyler's feelings as he openly flirted with her.

Marilou Marcos coordinated all of the logistical concerns on the Philippine side of the team. She shopped for the food, arranged the cooks for each meal and made sure that someone was assigned to wash dishes and clean up. She hired a laundry lady to wash, iron and fold clothes. Marilou took care of communication, transportation food and lodging. She even organized snacks and activities in the evenings. Anna Dean did the same thing for the Americans. She was in charge of the budget, kept all the receipts as money was spent, and she relied heavily on Marilou's help. And she liked Marilou enormously. They met and became immediate friends on a previous trip. Their friendship continued online with frequently messages sent to one another over the Internet.

Marilou was married, but her husband of three years worked as a computer programmer in Saudi Arabia. He arrived for a visit just as the team was returning home last year, and Anna met him briefly. He seemed distant and cold and Anna gave Marilou some space after he arrived. Anna had no boyfriend and wasn't looking for one, but Marilou, ever the matchmaker, made a point of introducing Anna as "available" to the young men in the church. Ashley called the pair "Maranna" because they could always be found together.

You wouldn't have known that a super typhoon was bearing down on them as they played in the tidal pools and climbed on the rocks.

And for a brief while everyone seemed to forget that they were in the crosshairs of a deadly storm. Nobody noticed the wide, semi-circular clouds high in the atmosphere that clearly indicated the approach of a powerful low-pressure system to experienced weather watchers. Dark, low clouds would soon arrive from the northeast, just above the treetops. Heavy squalls of rain and wind would signal to the locals that the typhoon reports were, in fact, real. But for now the sun was shining and life seemed perfect.

A group of young men stood on one of the rock outcroppings looking back towards the beach in Baler. They pointed and talked, and none of them joked or laughed. They seemed to be concentrating, as if in a business meeting. The stern faced man was not among them. They seemed clearly different than the average tourist found at the beach. All wore long pants, none of them swam, and they didn't seem to be enjoying their time together.

Manny Angara approached the group of men, who looked warily at him as he approached. He was simply extending a greeting, but they wanted no part of it. None apparently understood English or Tagalog. They made no attempt to reciprocate his attempt to communicate. They looked at each other, nodded at Manny, and then turned to walk back towards their rented resort. Manny was a bit puzzled by their behavior and tried to dismiss it. They must be from a big city, thought Manny. City people just don't quite know how to respond to genuine hospitality or kindness from strangers.

Manny couldn't get the odd behavior of the Chinese guys out of his head. He thought it curious that none could speak English or Tagalog. They didn't even seem to have a translator with them. He wondered what sort of business they could be discussing at this out of the way beach resort in the path of an approaching super typhoon. And as he looked at them, he noted that they were also watching him. How strange.

Chapter 6 – Something's happening
Tuesday 7:00pm August 8th
US Embassy, Roxas Blvd, Manila, Philippines

Some revelations bring joy, and some deliver dread. And as the staff gathered in the situation room at the US Embassy in Manila, the latter heavily covered the assembly like a wet quilt. In less than thirty-five hours, a typhoon of unimaginable strength would rip Manila apart. And, under ordinary circumstances, the staff would be encouraged to go home and prepare their homes and families for the extraordinary tempest. But today's events were anything but ordinary. Roger Lane, the Deputy Director for National Intelligence was connected via a secure audio-video link. With him was the lanky, unshaven Jim Adams, who had called the ambassador's office to ask if there was anything amiss. There was.

Ambassador Stephens began the teleconference without small talk. "Let me fill you in on what we know so far. We've lost two of our operatives in the past 24 hours, and five others can't be reached. Mac Villanueva was dispatched to investigate a cell of Chinese operatives in Zambales. He was assassinated in traffic about three blocks from his house early yesterday morning. Two men on a red Honda XR200 dirt bike killed Mac from very close range while he was trapped in traffic at a stoplight. He was boxed in and had no place to escape and never had a chance to respond. They didn't miss even a single shot – he was hit seven times, three in the head from a 9mm, and four body shots from a .45. The culprits wore helmets with tinted facemasks and they disappeared in seconds. We have only shell casings and ballistic evidence. We're checking now to see if there are any security cameras in the area that may have footage."

"When you say that he was investigating a "Chinese cell", sir, what does that mean?" Jim interrupted.

Jason Brock, the field agent's supervisor replied, "A group of Chinese men moved into an apartment next to one of our administrative officers' apartment in our Zambales detachment. They drew suspicion because they came and went at all hours of the day and night, none apparently holding down a job with regular hours. And they all had expensive toys. There was never a woman with them and it seemed odd that none of them ever brought along a wife or girlfriend. So he set up a surveillance camera. What happened next is what brought Mac to the scene."

"One of the men at the house was Paul Chang," Jason explained. "We identified him using facial recognition software from the captured video uploaded to us. He's an experienced commando from the Dragons. He's been used in clandestine operations throughout Southeast Asia. He's an explosives expert and is the best at what he does. He's fluent in Tagalog, Thai, and Vietnamese and blends in well wherever he goes. If he's here, something is going to be blown up."

"A simple hunch about this group has now turned into something big. Big enough to cost the life of our most experienced field agent." Jason Brock was pained as he spoke those words because he was quite fond of Mac. "We had very limited resources assigned to this effort as it was based on only a suspicion," continued Jason. "We were only in our third day of surveillance when they all left in different directions – none of them have returned. We finally raided the house this morning to see what evidence we could find and there was not so much as a fingerprint available. It's rare to find even two Chinese agents in one location for more than a moment, yet we had a houseful of them, perhaps as many as twenty coming and going from this place. It's not typical behavior for the Chinese; they like to hide in the shadows. It's like they didn't care if we saw them."

Jason spoke for a minute about his friend, Mac. "He was, perhaps, the best field agent in the country. We worked together on several assignments and I know how cautious he is, or was. Mac clearly didn't know that they were onto him, but someone obviously knew who he was. He wasn't careless – he had uncanny situational awareness and nothing escaped his notice."

Everyone assembled for this teleconference knew that the group that killed Mac was extremely well organized, very well trained, and were supplied with real-time intelligence. "We've uploaded the photos and video to see if we can identify anyone else. We don't have much to go on, guys; we're essentially running in the dark right now. We've managed to keep this incident out of the press, but have notified the Philippine National Police and the National Bureau of Investigation. They don't know everything, but they do know that Mac was one of ours." Jason continued, "The reality is that we have little to give them because we're also in the dark. We stumbled onto this. Chang's face is the only break we have in this case. They are still examining the ballistics, but we don't expect any matches. We're going to need more resources on this one."

Two men on a single motorcycle arrived at a Chinese safe house on the outskirts of Davao City, not far from the airport. They would lead the assault on the Davao International Airport to destroy most of the Philippine Air Force. These men were the elite of the elite and were selected because of their uncanny intuition, a sixth sense that few people possess. They instinctively knew when things were not as they should be. Their mission was vital to the success of Operation Zhi.

The two men noticed the safe house operator's eyes narrow for a split second. They both detected it at the same time. He had recognized one or both of them, and there's no reason that he should have. They'd never met before, but he showed just a hint of recognition, and that's all that it took. Neither of the men responded to what they had seen; both continued to greet the others in the room. But both knew that there was no time to waste – something needed to be done about him *now*.

They acted instantaneously and without mercy. One pulled a pistol from the small of his back and affixed a silencer. The safe house manager knew that he was their target, and accepted his fate. He made no commotion at all as he was ordered into the back room and was followed there by both men. He was totally complaint, obeying every instruction. The last instruction he ever heard was, "Now close your eyes."

He received two bullets to the base of his skull as reward for eighteen years of service to the People's Republic of China. He was in fact a traitor. For three years he had supplied information to his Filipino handler. The Chinese had been carefully monitoring his communications and believed that he could no longer be trusted. He was just another loose end that needed to be cleared up over the next 24 hours. The Philippine authorities wouldn't have time to connect the dots. By the time that they even realized that a dozen Chinese operatives had been killed, Typhoon Kiko and Operation Zhi would be upon them.

Two men unloaded large cardboard box from the back of a rental van in Paranaque City, just a mile away from the Ninoy Aquino International Airport. The box contained ten police uniforms and badges. There were two types: one for the airport security guards, and the other for the Philippine National Police. Ten men would come here to change into the uniforms and pick up their weapons, which were already inside the apartment. They would emerge as PNP officers, correctly wearing the uniforms. Badges would be pinned in the correct locations. Nametags were properly sewn in place. Rank insignia would be sewn or pinned on the uniforms, which had been perfectly tailored for each of the men. The uniforms were already pressed and folded, and even the shoes matched the uniform requirement. The men in the van left quickly to deliver boxes to other teams in the area. As Operation Zhi began at the airport, each man would look precisely like the people who guarded the airport. But for now only two men would remain at the apartment to guard the weapons and uniforms, which would prove to be essential in gaining the element of surprise.

Clandestine operations were taking place throughout the Philippines. Small pockets of men, all acting independently, prepared for Operation Zhi. They all knew that they would be operating without backup for at least twenty-four hours. There would be no forgiveness for miscalculations or errors in judgment. The People's Liberation Army would join them in less than a day when the full-scale invasion began. These men knew that they would be hailed as heroes for their efforts. They would help shape the new Chinese Empire.

Audio engineers in Beijing discovered that they could simultaneously eliminate noise in audio signals in every frequency range. The military quickly realized the potential of their frequency suppressors, and hired them to develop the technology into a battlefield weapon. The result was quickly classified and mass-produced. Just like electronic countermeasure equipment employed by the US Air Force since the late 1970's the frequency suppressors could effectively block all communications in a specific area. And, just like the US Air Force equipment, the higher it was positioned, the wider the resulting region. But unlike the US Air Force equipment, the Chinese had developed very portable units that could be placed in key locations and activated remotely. These devices were already affixed to communications towers, TV antennas, the tops of tall buildings and hilltops throughout the Philippines. Each commando cell also carried one, just to be sure that their enemies would be unable to communicate.

One of the men assigned to the commando team in Baler located new accommodations not far away from the fish port. He laughed as he signed the one-year lease, knowing that the contract was useless. The three small apartments were far enough inland to protect them from tidal surge, but close enough to the fish port to be there in just a few minutes. They scouted out the locations of backhoes, bulldozers and other heavy equipment just in case it was needed to clear landslides. They could allow nothing to impede the movement of their comrades once they made landfall after Kiko.

There was no need to review their plans; everybody on this team knew exactly what they would do, where they would be, and how everything would come together. They didn't need to risk exposure by talking about it, even in Chinese. Now was the time to prepare mentally. The men needed sleep. Once the storm started, there would be no rest until their mission was completed. They were all eager for Operation Zhi to commence.

More commandoes arrived every hour at the very airports that they would soon assault. They studied the terminal layout, the location of security cameras, and the number of armed men. Airport operations would cease by midday on Wednesday. So this was the last chance to survey the battleground. None of the men were viewed with suspicion. They arrived singly or in pairs. And they quickly vanished from the airport, many with video of the facility that had been obtained from concealed cameras. It would help with individual assignments the next evening. The men stayed close to the airports after being driven on a circuitous route to their hotels to make sure that nobody was following them.

In only 27 hours a horde of commandos would rise up and bring glory to the People's Republic of China. These men had been born for this day. And now, after years of preparation, the pain of physical training, and the endless classroom rigor they would finally have a chance to prove themselves.

Some men are measured by the life that they have lived, but these men would be measured by the death that they died. Every one of them was prepared to die for this glorious cause. They all knew that their sacrifice would make the Philippines an integral part of the People's Republic of China.

The average citizen of the PRC had been fed a steady diet of hatred for the leaders of the Philippines. They were angered by the brazenness of Philippine politicians, who claimed that Chinese ancestral maritime territory now belonged to the Republic of the Philippines. Arrogance dripped from their mouths like foam from a rabid dog as politicians declared that they would 'surrender every drop of Filipino blood' if necessary to maintain control over Chinese claimed territory. It seemed absurd to even suggest that the Philippines could fight and win a war against China; the mere notion was laughable. News reports throughout the PRC showed Filipino politicians continually poking their powerful neighbor in the eye rather than seeking diplomacy. China believed that it had shown enormous restraint regarding the disputed territories. But the time had come to show them that China could be pushed only so far. They would punish the Philippine leaders for their foolishness and arrogance. Filipinos would soon be liberated from the corruption and overindulgence of the powerful aristocrats who, for many decades had oppressed them.

Chapter 7 – Last Call

Tuesday, 8:00pm, 8 August
Baler, Aurora Province, Philippines

Super Sky Internet Café was dimly lit and loud. A narrow walkway separated two rows of computer workstations along either wall. Six workstations extended the length of each wall, but only eight of the twelve worked properly. There were no headsets available, which meant that everyone in the establishment monitored every conversation. Reno felt uncomfortable talking to her husband, Tom, in such a non-intimate environment. She wanted to tell him sweet things - private things. But there would be no privacy in Super Sky. Privacy is much more an American concern than a Filipino worry.

Reno spent every available minute of her time with Tom; they truly enjoyed being together. The only exception was early in the morning when Reno ran, biked, or swam. Tom, although athletic, didn't punish his body like Reno did; his job at the hospital offered enough exercise during the day. Tom was always tired when he got home from work. And he needed to leave for work just as Reno called. He knew that they would need to keep the conversation brief.

Reno hated Skype even in the best of conditions. It was awkward enough to arrange a time to speak, but she thought that the whole process was too complicated. The person being called had to install the application and approve you as a 'contact' before any call could take place. And today was especially bad for using Skype. She sat in a loud, public space and everyone around her passively monitored her call. The room was hot, with only one electric fan at the far end of the room. The computers were old and slow, and likely purchased new with Windows 95 installed. Reno had never experienced Internet as slow as Super Sky.

Reno selected 'Tom' after she signed into Skype and she could hear the application ringtone. As soon as Tom answered, Reno saw only her golden retriever, Lucky. Lucky sat in Tom's lap and barked at the screen when he recognized Reno. He couldn't stop barking, so Tom was forced to bring him into the bedroom and close the door. But Lucky didn't calm down; he wanted to see Reno as badly as Tom did.

Two groups of gamers on either side of Reno excitedly screamed obscenities in Tagalog that none of the Americans understood. Super Sky Internet Café was more distracting than Lucky's incessant barking.

Tom started the conversation, "Hey baby, you're fading in and out a bit." So was he. The connection was hanging on by a thread, which broke before they could converse. And they were both talking to a dead screen for a moment before they realized it.

Reno once again selected 'Tom' and redialed his number. She quickly explained to him, "Our mission trip has been put on hold while we prepare for the typhoon."

"You're still fading in and out," said Tom, "I missed that."

"Skype is ridiculous!" Reno replied, "We're packing everything up tonight and we'll be moving to a church in a town called Maria Aurora first thing tomorrow morning. We went sightseeing today and this place is absolutely gorgeous! Aurora is really amazing. We went to a stunning beach and stopped at two different waterfalls; you and I need to come here alone sometime." Both Sean and Kelly looked at Reno and smiled as she spoke the words *alone sometime.*

Reno, now conscious that everyone was listening told Tom, "I love you, Tom. I'm not sure if we'll be able to stay connected for long, so I just wanted to get that out of the way."

"I love you too, baby. Stay safe and hurry home. I have a present waiting for you when you get home." Tom said, smiling.

Reno didn't realize he was being crude and replied, "How thoughtful! What did you buy?"

"I didn't buy anything, babe – you know what I'm talking about." Tom said grinning.

Other team members were now giggling, and Tyler turned to Reno and said, "Ya'll need to keep it rated "G", I'm just a kid."

Reno smiled and reprimanded Tom, "Don't embarrass me, Tom. Everyone in this place can hear you. Tyler seems worried that you might have just tarnished his virgin ears."

Tom smiled, but didn't stop. He knew Reno could handle the teasing. "It's the next best thing to heaven, baby, I'll gift wrap it if you like."

Reno knew to change the subject. "Has Mom called you yet? I know she's aware of Kiko and will be worried."

"Yeah" answered Tom, "She's called twice now. I told her not to worry, but she wants to hear it from you."

"Please call her if you have a chance in the evening." Reno answered. "She's on the west coast, Tom, so it is only 5:20am there right now. I could call her now, but would rather be poked in the eye with a sharp, flaming stick than talk to her after waking her at 5:30 in the morning."

Tom chuckled and replied, "When she calls back, and we both know that she will call, I'll let her know that we've talked and that everything is fine over there. And I'll tell her that you love her very much."

"She'll think I'm knocking on death's door if you tell her that. Tell her that I'm fine and that I'm too busy to call. OK?"

Tom began to speak again, but the electricity died and then returned to life. The computers beeped as they began to reboot. Everything was plugged directly into DC current, and had completely shut down. The routers and communications equipment started their slow boot process. Tyler spoke up, "This is like living in the dark ages. You'd think they would have an interrupted power supply or something in this place." Reno was embarrassed by Tom's remarks, but also from Tyler's insensitivity.

It took a full five minutes for the connections to be restored. The gamers, like a fetus connected to an umbilical cord, were unable to be disconnected from a device for even a minute. They quickly pulled out their cell phones and texted friends until their computers had fully rebooted. Reno once again called Tom on Skype, "What happened?" Tom asked as he appeared on the screen. He looked like the star of an action movie with his tanned skin, deep blue eyes, dimples and beard stubble.

"We just had another power outage." Reno explained. This wasn't our first power outage today. It was off for an hour around breakfast, and dropped off-line for a few moments at least two other times."

"I'm gonna let you go now, baby. I'm on shift in fifteen minutes, so I have to say goodbye," said Tom. "Call me again whenever you get a chance. Love you."

"Love you too, Tom. I'll be home soon. Please keep the receipt for my gift in case it's the wrong size, okay?" Everyone laughed as Reno said it, even the Filipinos playing games, who had been listening to their conversation.

The winds grew stronger outside, and the tops of the trees swayed. The weather was not yet dangerous, but strong gusts caused small branches to break and fly to the ground. Low, swirling, dark clouds had appeared several times throughout the day. And four or five fast moving rainsqualls quickly passed, delivered huge amounts of sideways rain.

Sean and Anna moved quickly to sit at a terminal that was vacated as one of the 'gamer' groups left the Internet cafe. The café became noticeably quieter. Reno got up and offered her computer to Kelly.

Rod planned to call Gina after he examined the storm online. He found what he was looking for on www.typhoon2000.ph. What he saw was frightful and he asked the cashier if he could print some pages to show to the team later in the evening. Kiko was growing, and was now larger than the entire island of Luzon. The storm's outer bands looked as if they should already be hitting Baler. Even though Rod loved big storms, the images of Kiko sent chills up his spine. Rod had never seen a storm like Kiko before because there had never been such a storm.

Rod then called Gina and just as she appeared on the monitor's screen, Sean screamed out loud from behind him, "You're kidding me! That's incredible! Wow! I can't believe it! How many months? When will we find out whether it's a boy or a girl?" Sean was standing with his hands over his head. His wife, Christi, could only see his midsection from the webcam and she asked him to sit back down. The other conversations all shifted to the news that Sean had just received. Sean was excited by the news of another baby. Their baby daughter, Hanna, was almost three years old and Sean wanted Hanna to have a baby brother. "Praise God!" he exclaimed.

Gina had already heard the news from Christi, but she was waiting for Sean to hear it from Christi before sharing the news with Rod. Gina heard Sean in the background and knew it was now permissible to talk to Rod about it. Gina was still worried about Kiko so she asked Rod, "Have you moved your stuff to the other church yet?"

Rod replied, "Not yet. We're moving our things there first thing in the morning. We'll be packed up tonight before we sleep."

Gina just wanted Rod and the team to get there soon. Reports of Kiko had moved from the Weather Channel to all networks. And it wouldn't be long before weather conditions deteriorated in Baler. Gina explained that Matthew and James had already caught the school bus and should now be in class. Rebekah missed her daddy and stayed home "sick" so that she could talk to him.

"Daddy?" she said as she stepped in front of the screen. "I miss you."

"I miss you too, baby girl. Why aren't you in school?" Rebekah looked at her mother for the answer. Both knew that she stayed home so that she could talk to Rod. Rebekah smiled as her mom, from off camera said, "Rebekah isn't feeling too good today." It was true. She was worried sick about her father and *needed* to hear his voice.

"Well I'm glad you're home so that I can see your pretty face. I can't wait to get home and give you hugs. If you feel better, maybe you should go to school later so that you don't miss the whole day."

Rebekah looked at her mom again and said, "Okay. I think we're going soon."

"Alright, that sounds good. I love and miss you both. I'll call again when I get a chance, but don't expect anything for a couple days after the storm – we won't have electricity. I'll keep the phone charged up, so you can text me or call this phone. International roaming isn't cheap, but we're still available here if there's an emergency."

Rod said his goodbyes and signed out of the computer. As he stood up he could hear Kelly Boykin say, "I miss you, baby." Some of the team members were surprised by it because they didn't know that Kelly had a boyfriend. He was a well-kept secret.

Ashley also had a boyfriend, Justin, and she opted to call him instead of her parents but her conversation didn't go well. In fact, it quickly turned into an argument. Her boyfriend had been bar-hopping with friends and he was now hung over. Ashley woke him up when she called and thought she heard a woman's voice. Since Skype supported video she asked Justin to hold up the laptop and scan the room so she could see for herself. He refused. Her boyfriend insisted the voice she heard came from the TV. She knew he was lying because the TV was visible behind him and it wasn't turned on. She closed Skype, abruptly stood up and walked towards the door muttering words that few missionaries ever repeat.

Anna Dean cried as she talked with her mom and dad. She really missed them and knew that they would be fine in her absence. She was so accustomed to caring for them that she felt guilty leaving them for the two-week trip. Her father was confined to a wheelchair after an industrial accent three decades ago and her mother now suffered from dementia. Neither of them could drive. Anna lived with her parents in order to care for them. Her father's insurance settlement with his former employer was substantial enough to hire all the help they needed, but Anna insisted that she care for them. She bought their groceries, shopped for them, prepared their meals, washed their clothes, and cleaned their house. She loved her parents more than she could express, and cried over the phone as she told them so.

As Ashley stormed away from her computer terminal she offered it to her boss, David, but he refused. There was nobody he needed, or even wanted to call. David had been sitting in the back of the jeep while the others called home. The clouds became faster, darker, and lower as he watched them. David was nervous by nature, and Kiko scared him. He did his best to disguise his concern, but his fingernails were already gone. He wondered why the rest of the team seemed so calm - they were in front of the largest storm ever recorded!

The two remaining groups of gamers were loud and obnoxious and Tyler couldn't hear what his mother was saying. "Would you guys shut up!" he yelled at the group to his left. They stared at him with blank looks on their faces for a moment, then burst into laughter and continued their game. The noise level upset him, but Tyler was already in a somber mood. Whatever was going on at home seemed to bother him. Whatever his folks told him wasn't good news.

The lights were still out when they got back to the church. Rod announced, "Please come inside for a few minutes. We need to talk about our plans for tomorrow." Rod was most concerned about their valuables. They would be leaving their belongings in the care of strangers at a church in another town.

"We'll need to secure our valuables in the morning. Put your cash, smart phones, cameras, computers- basically anything of value in your backpack. And you'll need to keep your backpack with you, OK?" Rod looked around and made sure he saw the heads nodding. "We trust the people of Ramada Community Church, and we don't want to insult them in any way. But let's not tempt anyone to do the wrong thing."

Rod continued, "We're gonna start early tomorrow. Breakfast will be served at six o'clock. We want to be on the road by seven, so we need to get our things ready tonight. We still have a full day of ministry activities planned so let's get rid of the distractions and plan to make a difference for Christ."

Tyler was unaccustomed to boundaries. His parents didn't tell him when to go to bed. They didn't tell him when to get out of bed, what to eat, what to wear, or when to do his homework. He felt the weight of all the rules that Pastor Rod seemed to be making up. He didn't find Filipino food particularly appetizing and he didn't like being told to eat it. While in Dibutunan he wore his shirt unbuttoned and open in the front and was frustrated that Sean had the audacity to ask him to button it up. Tyler was accustomed to pushing boundaries, but he wasn't accustomed to anyone pushing back. He sulked into the back room of the church where he slept. He was irritated at the entire world.

The motors from the electric fans began to hum, and the lights flickered on. Cheers erupted – the power was back! There was a steady breeze and it was raining outside, but the air was still thick and muggy. The electric fans made it so much easier to get some actual sleep, not just rest. This was going to be the last night they would experience good sleep, or even proper rest for that matter. Everyone found their assigned locations and prepared themselves for tomorrow's events. The men had to wait while the ladies took a "bucket bath" at the hand pump behind the church. Then the men would take turns pumping cold water from the rusted pump.

Reno and Angie walked by carrying shampoo and soap. They had towels draped over their shoulders and they laughed as they walked. Tyler began to follow them, and Sean grabbed him by the arm, smiling. "Settle down, champ." he said. But Tyler wasn't smiling. "Get your hands off me - you're not my dad!" he said, as he broke loose from Sean's grip. Sean let him go and headed for his sleeping bag.

Sean intended to recommend a more thorough vetting process for future teams. Sean argued with Rod about Tyler's participation when he found out that Tyler had signed up for the team. "We need to have better criteria for sending missionaries than their ability to raise money." Rod agreed, but pointed out that Tyler's parents were very big givers. "Relationships also matter." Rod argued. True. Sean hoped that none would be damaged because of Tyler's immaturity.

Chapter 8 – Burn Victims

Wednesday 2:40pm, 9 August
Maria Aurora, Aurora, Philippines

"Dr. Reno! We have an emergency here!" exclaimed Kelly. Two small kids were carried to Ramada Community Church on makeshift stretchers made from large rice sacks. Both were badly burned. Kelly was an experienced nurse and she knew an emergency when she saw it. She led Reno to where the children lay. Angie asked the man sitting on the examination table to return to the waiting area. Bones were visible on the man's toes, which were deteriorating from advanced diabetes. And even though the man needed immediate medical care, the burned children became their priority.

Their frantic mother, Melody, couldn't stop screaming, so Marilou took her aside to calm her while Angie and Reno examined the kids. Reno turned to Pastor Mark as he came to check on the situation, "Please get an ambulance here now!" Pastor Mark didn't speak. He fumbled for his cell phone and walked briskly to the front to find Marilou, who was still trying to calm Melody. He handed the phone to Marilou and told her to get an ambulance, and then he grabbed the mother's hands and said simply, "Let's pray."

Pastor Mark prayed fervently for the two children. He asked the mother for the names of the boys so he could pray by name for Reynaldo and Mark Joseph Santos. Mark knew their father, who was working abroad in Saudi Arabia. Or was it Kuwait? He wept openly as he prayed, "Lord, we need you now. You are the Great Physician, Father, and we know that you have the power to restore Mark Joseph and Reynaldo back to health." He hesitated as he wept, and was surprised to hear Manny take over, "Comfort this woman, Lord. Give her your peace that transcends all understanding. We're struggling to understand what has happened to these precious children, but we don't need to understand, Lord. We need *you*. Words can't provide comfort to this family, Lord, but you can. We ask you to heal these children and restore this family in the name of our Lord and Savior Jesus Christ. Amen."

In the examination room Reno was horrified by the extent of their burns. She expected to treat respiratory and urinary tract infections on this mission trip. She knew that she would encounter patients with allergies and skin infections, but Reno never expected to be the first responder to such severe burns. This was a church medical mission, intended to be a gesture of good will, not a trauma center! She cut away their clothes and Angie assisted. They knew not to peel off any more skin, and much of the boys' clothing had been burned into their skin. The horrifying extent of the burns became evident after they removed as much of their clothes as possible; fat and muscle were also burned, not just their skin. And it wasn't localized, it covered their entire bodies: head, neck, chest, back, stomach, arms and legs. Both children seemed short of breath. Neither was crying; they were clearly in shock. They would have been airlifted to a major trauma or burn center in the US, but Dr. Reno was now the best hope they had.

Mark Joseph had just entered first grade in June. He loved animals and he spent most of his free time playing with the neighbor's puppies. He always had a chicken, kitten, or puppy in his arms. When their sow had piglets, Mark Joseph selected one and named it 'Winnie'. He carried Winnie everywhere he went until the pig was too big for him to carry. He fashioned a leash from a discarded fishnet, and led Winnie proudly around his neighborhood. Other kids teased him, calling him "pig boy." But Mark Joseph didn't mind the teasing. He was indeed Pig Boy. But Mark Joseph's first love was not a barnyard animal; it was his little brother, Reynaldo. He loved his little brother intensely, and they were inseparable. And now, unfortunately, they lay together on makeshift examination tables struggling for their lives.

Mark Joseph had been playing with a kerosene lamp when it fell and shattered, spreading flames across the only doorway to their small nipa hut. Flames immediately spread to the walls, curtains, and bamboo bed. Mark Joseph ran towards the back of the hut to wake his younger brother, Reynaldo, who had been napping. There was simply nowhere to go, and they panicked. With only their hands they attempted to dig a small escape tunnel underneath the thatched *sawali* exterior wall. But the dirt floor had been packed down for many years and it was dried like brick. A wooden strip bordered the bottom of the thatched wall, and the boys found it impossible to dig enough to slide under the board.

They quickly ran out of time and abandoned their efforts to dig their way out. Reynaldo choked on the smoke, so Mark Joseph picked up his four-year-old brother and ran through the flames, screaming for help as he ran. They emerged through the front door with their clothes and hair aflame. It was a shocking sight to their neighbor, who had been removing laundry from her clothesline when the fire began. She saw the boys materialized through the fire, and she snatched two towels from her clothesline and raced to extinguish the flames. Melody Santos had also seen the billowing gray smoke and ran back to the house to see the horrific sight of her badly burned children positioned on the ground about thirty feet in front of their flaming house, their clothes still smoldering.

Dr. Reno and Angie wrapped them in moist bandages. They were not permitted to carry narcotics through Philippine customs, so Reno had no effective pain medication to administer the boys to help with their intense pain. They whimpered as their mother tended to them, whispering to them through her tears. Reno asked for help carrying the boys to the ambulance when it arrived and maneuvered into place to load up the patients. Tyler, Rod, Manny and David grabbed the ends of the examination tables and carried the boys to the back of the ambulance. They were a frightful sight; the boys were nearly naked with horribly burned flesh and scalp.

Tyler moved to the front of the ambulance and vomited as soon as they sat the boys down. The ambulance was occupied by a driver and one EMT who would treat the boys as they made their way to the regional hospital in Baler. Dr. Reno was shocked when the driver first asked to 'settle the matter of payment.' David Kemp stepped forward, announcing that he would take care of any payments. He jumped into the ambulance with Mark Joseph, Reynaldo, and their mother, and shouted, "*Let's GO!*" Melody cradled Reynaldo in her arms and sang softly to him. Manny and Pastor Mark also jumped in the ambulance, which raced away with its siren blaring and lights flashing.

The continued parade of patients seemed endless. Even though their medical mission was impromptu and unadvertised it was quickly inundated with patients. More than fifty patients sat quietly in the coliseum-style seating of Ramada Community Church when the burned boys arrived. Now there were more than sixty.

The rest of the afternoon seemed surreal to the Americans as they resumed operation and treated more patients. Brother Jun and Sister Marilou collected bio-data and medical histories as patients arrived. They used forms that a previous team had created to properly document patient information. Kelly and Ashley checked each patient's temperature and blood pressure and documented it on the form. The patients were then sent to the pastor's office for a "spiritual health check." Pastor Mike and Angel Tolentino tag-teamed their questions. But now that Mike was gone Angel asked the questions by himself.

"If you were to die today, do you know where you would go?"

"Why is that?"

"So salvation is based on your deeds?"

"Would you like to know what God's Word says about salvation?"

The examination room consisted of a library table covered with bed sheets, a battered plywood desk, three plastic chairs and an electric fan. A small, colorful plastic cabinet held their most prescribed medications. Sheets hung on a wire that extended from one wall to the other created a modicum of privacy for patients being examined. The electric fan was placed behind Dr. Reno. Angie explained, "Germs and viruses will blow away from you if the fan is placed behind you. That way you won't get sick."

It was mid-afternoon and Reno was mentally exhausted. She had seen three patients with advanced cases of cancer. All would be dead soon, and they would suffer until death due to lack of pain medication. One tuberculosis patient she had seen was also near death. His two sons carried him to the clinic sitting in a chair. A six-month-old baby whose skin was yellow was diagnosed with a severe liver condition. Reno treated a patient with a tuberculin tumor on his leg – a condition she had only read about in textbooks during her studies. Today made dengue look like a common cold. Secretly she wished for five o'clock, when Marilou would announce to the remaining patients that they needed come back on Friday after the typhoon had passed. Tomorrow would be spent staying safe and dry in the middle of a colossal storm. Or so they thought.

Pastor Mark returned on a motorcycle with an attached sidecar that Filipinos call a tricycle. Dr. Kemp and Manny remained in Baler with Melody Santos and her boys. He asked everyone to join him for a moment of prayer for the Santos family. But before he prayed he announced, "Mark Joseph, the elder of the two boys, died on the way to Baler. He was pronounced dead on arrival at the emergency clinic at Premier Hospital. Reynaldo is so badly burned that they believe he will also die from his burns. They are taking him to Cabanatuan by ambulance. Let's all pray for the Santos family."

Reno and Angie remained behind the curtain in the examination room. Their patient, a young mother, had come to get treatment for a skin rash, fever, and vaginal sores. Dr. Reno suspected that it was actually the secondary stages of syphilis and treated it as such. Angie explained, in Tagalog, what she was being treated for and the young woman wept as she left. Angie and Reno also wept. They hugged one another and cried loudly after hearing the news from the next room. Five o'clock couldn't come quickly enough.

Rob had good news to share with the team after the remaining patients had all been sent home. "Eternity was changed on this day for fourteen people who came here for treatment. They all acknowledged their guilt before God and each of them clearly understood that Jesus was the only remedy." The good news was met with subdued enthusiasm. Marilou and Jun clapped their hands, and Tyler said loudly, "Alright!"

They came here to wrestle souls away from the evil one, right? So why did it suddenly seem less important than Mark Joseph's death? They had all observed his mother's anguish and they felt helpless. They had witnessed a small child, in the midst of remorse and agony, step into eternity far too soon. Today would be impossible to forget. And tomorrow would be even tougher.

Chapter 9 – New information
Wednesday 4:35pm, 10 August
Langley, VA, USA

Jim Adams sprinted down the hall and burst into his office. Jake Wilson was already seated on a small, black, imitation leather sofa positioned across from Jim's desk. His notebook was open and he was on his cell phone. Jim didn't acknowledge him and went straight to the secure phone on his desk. He dialed Roger's cell phone number, which was busy, so he left a message, "Roger, this is Jimbo. We have some new information for you. I'm sending you an update on the secure system. Please call me as soon as you read it. Thanks." It was approaching five o'clock in the morning at Langley, and Jim hadn't slept the previous two nights. He was exhausted, even a bit irritable, but the adrenaline he felt from all the chatter they were picking up elevated his normal level of awareness. There was no question in his mind, or in Jake's that the Chinese were planning a military attack. The exact location and scope of the mission was uncertain, but an assault was clearly imminent.

After their previous meeting with Roger he assigned several additional analysts to carefully scrutinize what was taking place in the PRC. They looked closely for anomalies and unusual behavior. Signals intelligence picked up far more communications between military commanders than normal. More "crypto" assets were assigned to decode intercepted communications. And as Jack and Jim began to analyze the heavy flow of information, they quickly realized that they needed to elevate their findings – immediately! The puzzle pieces still didn't fit neatly together, but what they could see developing was frightening. What they had pieced together couldn't wait until later to be shared. They both admired Roger and didn't want to see him sitting in front of a Senate investigating committee explaining why he didn't know more sooner.

Traffic analysis detected unusual patterns in the military communications within the PRC. Units were being activated, and members within those units were making a flurry of calls to take care of last minute business before they were deployed. "The Russians warned Bashar Al-asaad that certain U.S. Army units were being deployed to the border of Syria," Jake explained. "As our troops were notified, they called the next person on the list of their 'recall roster'. That was detected first. They knew their mission was classified and didn't talk about specifics, but as they began to make arrangements for their kids, pets, rent, car payments, and other details a communications pattern emerged." Jake then explained, "We even went back and examined the patterns ourselves. It's easy to distinguish. And we now see that same pattern around each of China's major military bases." Jim already knew everything that Jake was explaining. Perhaps, he thought, he's practicing for the conversation with Roger.

"Let me share a couple things that I have, Jake", continued Jim. "An intercepted conversation from a mid-level Marine officer to his wife clearly says that he is deploying with his unit *to the Philippines*. The Chinese monitor all communications, and the major could be executed for revealing such information before an attack. And we recorded a Colonel trying to disguise the classified nature of his conversation by substituting words, but his message came through loud and clear: he is leading a brigade of marines *to the Philippines* in Operation Zhi."

"Operation Zhi is already underway," said Jim. "Three decrypted messages from their aircraft carrier, The *Liaoning*, explicitly stated that they were 'underway' and then 'in position' for Operation Zhi. Both of the intelligence analysts came to the same conclusion: the Chinese were about to seize selected islands in the disputed Philippine waters by force. It was logical. The Chinese made no claims to ownership of the Philippines. But they were progressively asserting their might in the South China Sea. They were going to "re-claim" the disputed territory by any means necessary. Even with so many indicators pointing to an operation much larger in scale than seizing a few islands, the analysts simply couldn't even imagine a takeover of the Philippines by China – it was unimaginable.

Roger stuck his head in the door and said to Jim and Jake, "I'll be with you in five minutes; let's meet in the conference room."

"Sure thing, sir. We'll be ready in a moment," said Jim. They picked up their laptops and notebooks and headed to the conference room to get things set up.

Roger walked in and asked, "Can we get the Philippine delegation in on this discussion?" Within minutes Frank Stevens, the U.S. ambassador to the Philippines, and his superintendent of field agents Jason Brock appeared on the huge conference screen. Ambassador Stephens made quick introductions of seven others gathered with them in the room. Jim felt momentarily self-conscious because he was, as usual, dressed down. He put on blue jeans and a polo shirt when he went home to shower and eat dinner. Even the Filipinos were wearing ties!

Roger quickly introduced Jim and Jake and asked them to share the information that they had uncovered. Jim Adams was the first to speak up. "How much information would be required before it is considered 'actionable'? Jake and I have spent the past three days analyzing intelligence information from various agencies that seems to indicate that the Chinese are preparing to invade the Philippines." The men gathered together in the embassy briefing room glanced at one another and fidgeted, but nobody interrupted Jim.

"You've all likely examined the report I sent to you. Large numbers of ships have put out to sea in advance of Typhoon Kiko. Many are now safely south of the impact area of the Typhoon, including their aircraft carrier, *Liaoning*. We have intercepted encrypted communications from the *Liaoning* that unambiguously state that they were 'underway' and then 'in position' for Operation Zhi. And we have other communiqués that link Operation Zhi to an invasion of the Philippines. We have satellite images that show heightened military preparations over the past ten days. Their senior battle staff convened last night for five hours, with the meeting ending well after midnight. That is unprecedented."

Jim and Jake took turns sharing specific analysis. They showed photos, diagrams, and maps, all which clearly illustrated the severity of the situation. Nobody interrupted until they were through with their presentation of the analysis. Jim ended emphatically, "During the time that it took to put this presentation together and deliver the information to you, we've uncovered the words 'Operation Zhi' *nineteen more times*. These come from intercepted, encrypted, classified military-to-military transmittals. There is increased chatter and every indicator says that Operation Zhi is already underway."

Roger butted it into the conversation. "Guys, listen closely. It's not our call regarding action. We collect data and turn it into useful information. I'll contact the Secretary of Defense and let him know what we've got. And I'm sure that we'll have an audience with the President sometime tomorrow. I'll make the recommendation that we move some assets around to better protect the Philippines."

Ambassador Stephens cut Roger off. "I have to contact our Philippine military liaison officer as soon as we finish this meeting. They are going to blame us for withholding information. Why didn't we have better intelligence about this before today?"

"I was just getting around to that, Ambassador. We have a great deal of coordinating to do. You should make the arrangements you need to make and I will take care of things on my end. There's going to be plenty of blame to go around if we're right on this, but it's not the time for that right now, Ambassador." Roger spoke bluntly.

"Don't misunderstand me, Roger. I wasn't blaming you. I know that you've done all you can, but there are some fingers that will also be pointed at me. I'm just preparing myself for the coming diplomatic storm."

"Right now, Ambassador, you need to be concerned about the real storm that's coming. Get your families to safety, evacuate them if there's still time. I know the weather is moving in, but get all of the non-essential personnel out now!" Roger was providing advice, not a professional mandate. Roger had no authority over State Department staff, but he knew that Ambassador Stephens would accept it as advice. Good advice.

"And if we're right on this," added Jim, "Kiko and the political fallout are the least of your worries. Events are in motion, but we have at least 24 hours – there's no way that they can move until the storm has passed. I don't think the Chinese, even as brazen as they are, would risk so many troops in the face of this monstrous storm. It would be disastrous. If we can quickly reposition assets from the Seventh fleet the Chinese may reconsider whatever they are planning. They have to know that we're already aware of Operation Zhi. And they are not stupid; they know that if they make a move against the Philippines we're going to respond. Not only us but Japan and the rest of ASEAN."

Ambassador Stephens explained, "Most government agencies here have been shut down all day. All remaining government employees were sent home at noon, because the Department of Transportation has ordered the Light Rail Transit Authority to shut down service at 3:00pm. Even here at the embassy we are running a skeleton staff. Manila streets flood even from a heavy thundershower, and the weather conditions have been deteriorating since noon. The roads are already flooding."

"Will you be able to reach everyone who needs to be contacted?" asked Roger.

"That's where I was headed - even during normal conditions it's tough to get things done here. Underlings here are simply not empowered to make decisions, so I'm quite concerned that we may have some issues getting the right people immediately involved." Ambassador Stephens continued, "It's now late afternoon on Wednesday here and Typhoon Kiko will keep all offices shut down until the weekend. It could be Monday before I get to speak to the right people. Civil servants here don't carry work home with them. And most won't answer their phone after work because they don't want to be dragged back to the office. We can send text messages, but there's no assurance that they will be read, or acted upon. The timing couldn't be worse!"

Jim Adams added, "It's not a matter of if they are moving against the Philippines. Everything clearly points to a military operation that is already underway. We need to find out where they intend to go, and get in front of it."

Roger spoke up again, "They've literally caught us with our pants down! Typhoon Kiko will prevent us from moving our assets into a proper defensive position until Friday. It would be imprudent to respond during the storm, so we're at a military disadvantage right now and the Chinese know it. If they move into the Philippines before we can intercept them, God knows how difficult it will be getting them out again. It will be tougher than getting fleas off a rabid street dog."

Ambassador Stephens, ever the diplomat, interjected, "You might not want to us that analogy again, Roger."

"I understand, Ambassador, I'm also still absorbing the gravity of the situation. I apologize if anyone may have taken offense to that remark."

"There are people that need to be alerted immediately," said Ambassador Stephens. "We need to make sure that the Philippine Armed Forces are prepared for this. They need to know that this is more than just a possibility – an attack is eminent."

"The chatter has become deafening in the past twelve hours. It's now coming in far faster than we can analyze it. At first we thought we were onto something, and now we absolutely *know* that a military operation by the Chinese against the Philippines is imminent."

Roger cut Jake off, hoping to put a swift end to the meetings so that they could activate a response. "I believe we're all in agreement, Jake. Could you and Jim provide us all with your briefing notes? I know that you've been racing against time without sleep, but we also need a formal report to provide to our Philippine counterparts so that they have the complete picture. Could you have that done within the next hour?"

"Yes sir," said Jim. "We'll just need to prepare a quick synopsis and cut and paste everything into the proper format. I'll send it as soon as we get it ready."

"Great! Then you two get some sleep. We're going to need you to be alert as things begin to unfold. You both look like horses that have been ridden hard and put away wet."

Roger then addressed Ambassador Stephens directly, "Ambassador, I'll make an appointment and meet with the Secretary of Defense this morning; we're going to get you the assets you need. I'm sure that this will also make it to the President's agenda today, and I'm confident that things will move quickly from our end."

"I need to alert the Armed Forces of the Philippines immediately," said Ambassador Stephens. But I need that formal report ASAP. Please call me as soon as you send it out, okay, Jim?"

"Yes, sir," Jim and Jake said in unison.

"And I don't think this needs to be said, but I'll say it anyway," reminded Roger. "What you've heard in this meeting is classified as 'TOP SECRET'. You cannot tell your families why they are being evacuated. You cannot talk on unsecured phone lines about this. Understood? We can't afford to provide the Chinese with any more advantage than they already have."

The meeting abruptly adjourned. Jim and Jake retreated to prepare the formal report and send it out as an encrypted file as quickly as possible. Roger called the Secretary of Defense to arrange a meeting. Ambassador Stephens began making preparations to evacuate all of the families of his embassy staff before Kiko arrived. And, in doing so, he failed to follow protocol. He called his wife at home on his personal cell phone and said, "Listen closely Lisa. I can't explain everything right now. Get your 'bug out' bags together because you and the kids will be leaving the Philippines immediately. Be ready in an hour, OK? A driver will come for you soon. I've gotta go – things are happening fast and I can't talk now."

His staff and family were in danger and Ambassador Stephens was nearly hyperventilating as he picked up his secure line to call the Chief of the Armed Forces of the Philippines. It was too late. All communications had been severed. The Chinese had been monitoring all communications from embassy staff, waiting for any mention of family evacuation. Immediately they remotely activated their signal suppressors atop buildings, billboards and towers around Metro Manila and every form of electronic communication immediately ceased. Electricity was already out in the entire Metro Manila area, and rain heavy rains flooded the streets. It would soon be dark, much darker than anyone could imagine.

Chapter 10 – No power

Wednesday 4:58pm, 9 August
North Luzon Expressway, Philippines

On June 10th, 1999 the entire island of Luzon lost power. There were rumors of a coup attempt to wrestle control from then President Joseph Estrada, but it turned out that forty million people sat in the dark and sweltering heat due to jellyfish. Jellyfish! A mass of jellyfish – some 50 truckloads of them – had been sucked into the intake pumps supplying water to cool the coal burning power plant in the town of Sual, Pangasinan. At the same time, another plant in Calaca, Batangas was taken offline because of a technical glitch; an igniter fan had failed. Four other independent power producers then 'tripped' in a chain reaction due to supply deficiency.

In May 2013 the National Grid Corporation of the Philippines (NGCP) explained that five power plants switched into emergency shutdown mode as another island-wide power outage affected Luzon. As before, a sudden 'supply deficiency' was deemed to be the problem. Around 3,700 megawatts went offline, causing a series of events that, once again, plunged much of the nation into darkness.

To say that the Philippine power grid is fragile is an understatement. The Department of Energy warned the public to "brace themselves" for rolling power outages in the summer of 2015. Inadequate power generation capacity combined with increased demand was simply more than the grid could handle. They needed 450-500 megawatts more than what was available and urged the public to conserve energy. Regions were forced to share power, with one region being shut off entirely so that the other could have electricity. Each region took its turn in the dark, except for Metro Manila, which was spared as much as possible. Previous administrations had learned that voices in Manila cry far louder than the voices in the provinces.

Chinese military planners took note of the fragility of the Philippine power situation and intended to take advantage of the weakness. If they could eliminate enough generation capacity, they could shut down the entire grid. They selected the 'jellyfish' plant in Sual, Pangasinan, as it had already proven effective in taking down the grid. They also selected the Malaya Thermal Power Plant in Rizal province; the

Ilijan gas powered Station and the Calaca coal plant in Batangas; five gas powered units in Santa Rita, Nueva Ecija; the Sucat thermal power plant in Muntinlupa; and the Kalayaan pumped-storage hydroelectric plant just south of Manila in Laguna. Seven three-man teams, only twenty-one men, would put most Filipinos in the dark at exactly 5:00pm on the eve of Kiko.

Paul Chang helped rig all of the explosives that would be detonated. Each satchel was packed with a synthetic explosive device developed by research chemists who had been hired away from the Institute of Chemistry, Chinese Academy of Sciences. They were brilliant researchers who had perfected molecular super assembly of hydrogen atoms. They assisted in development of hydrogen fuel cells, and they were experts in binding hydrogen atoms to highly electronegative atoms such as nitrogen. The Ministry of State Security, however, hired them to design an extremely portable hydrogen powered bomb.

These small devices could obliterate everything within three hundred yards, vaporizing everything within a hundred feet. The crater left behind would be deep enough to require extension ladders to inspect them after detonation. Paul Chang personally tested two of them, measuring every element of the blast using high-speed cameras, and was impressed with what he observed.

Fourteen such devices had been carefully assembled and were delivered by submarine to carefully selected Filipino agents posing as fishermen in the waters off Scarborough Shoal. They had no idea what they were receiving, but were being paid enormously for their efforts. The handoff took place on May 25th in calm waters at 10:00pm. Six black-clad commandos carrying sealed Styrofoam containers climbed aboard the first of the three waiting boats. Fifteen more commandoes emerged from the submarine wearing blue jeans, polo shirts, tennis shoes and sandals. All were armed with high-powered rifles and pistols.

Few boats in Philippine waters could match the speed of these three boats. Each fiberglass hull was designed for racing and was equipped with twin 557 horsepower turbocharged outboard motors. With calm waters they could easily reach 80 knots, allowing them to easily outrun the Philippine Coast Guard if it became necessary. Such boats would be quite conspicuous in Philippine waters, so they had been assembled and hidden in a "floating warehouse" that had been openly disguised as a fisheries research facility.

The submarine disappeared back into the black waters. The darkness of the new moon made the three boats invisible as they slowly headed for land. They remained close together, about fifty yards apart. Their low profile and shape made them almost unseen to radar, which is why such boats have been a favorite for Caribbean drug smugglers in the United States. Dim running lights allowed them to see one another, but they were completely hidden to the rest of the world. The only witnesses were U.S. Navy observers who monitored the submarine come to the surface to meet three waiting boats.

The U.S. Navy tracked the boats as they headed for the coast of Zambales. They created a radar signature only because they remained close together. As the boats came within five miles of the port In Iba, the U.S. Navy officials alerted the Philippine Coast Guard and port authorities of their arrival. Almost immediately, as if they had been listening to the call between the U.S. Navy and the Coast Guard, the three boats split up and raced in different directions. The monitors were shocked at their speed because they believed they were tracking fishing vessels.

Immediately one boat veered north and was later found beached in Masinloc. Blood was found in the boat. The other two boats sped south; and after dawn one was found on a beach in Cabangan, the other was beached in San Narcisso. None of the occupants were found, however six Filipinos were found floating in nearby waters – each had been shot in the head. All of the boats were empty and void of any registration information. Fingerprints were found, but they didn't show up in any database. Whatever or whoever the sub had delivered had made it safely into the Philippines.

Seven commando teams planted the explosive devices and took up positions far enough away from the blast radius to observe their work. They placed the devices near enough to their intended targets to completely destroy them. The team assigned to the Santa Rita gas plant had the trickiest assignment. The five gas generation units were spread out, so they opted to blow up the gas mainline, which would spread fire in every direction. The men steered their new van to the shoulder of the southbound lane expressway. Rain fell sideways and the wind was fierce. It was six minutes until five when they stopped the van to watch. The blast would soon launch a fireball high into the sky and send out a shockwave that would rock their van. The minutes seemed like hours as they sat and waited.

After only three minutes a vehicle with flashing yellow lights pulled up behind them. It was an expressway assistance vehicle patrolling the highway to assist stranded motorists and arrange tow trucks to remove disabled vehicles. Two men walked towards them wearing reflectorized orange raincoats. Both approached on the passenger side of the van, with water pouring from the hoods of their raincoats. The front window slid down and the passenger smiled and began speaking to them in Chinese. He wanted to stall them for three or four minutes before the blast, and then race away in the confusion that followed. But to his amazement, one of the men responded to him in Chinese.

"You cannot stop here," he spoke in perfect Mandarin. "Why are you stopped here?"

Traffic was heavy at this time of day, and cars were now slowing down to gape at them as they passed. The heavy rain slowed the traffic to the pace of a slow bicycle. The commandos seemed momentarily paralyzed, each waiting for the other to do something. They hadn't planned for this.

"We are lost. We were looking for directions on our GPS system to get off at the Valenzuela exit." The driver was clearly nervous. As both men leaned forward and peered into the van they spotted an Uzi submachine gun in the lap of the back seat passenger. As they spotted the weapon, both men glanced at one another, and one yelled, "Run!" They ducked down and ran back towards their truck. But they didn't make it; both were riddled with bullets as the backseat passenger climbed from the van and sprayed them with bullets. Their blood mixed quickly with the rain puddles and created huge crimson pools that enveloped the dead men.

People stared from their vehicles in disbelief. Motorists and their passengers gawked at them. Some were pointing at the dead men while others took out their cells phones to call authorities or text for help. But communications had already been severed. None of their calls succeeded. Bus passengers took pictures and video of the van and the dead men using their cell phones. A few dozen passengers on a Z-Liner bus alongside them strained to look into the van's dark tinted windows. With no discussion, the rear seat passenger in the van pressed the detonator button on his remote control. The percussion was delayed by two or three seconds, and their van was rocked by the blast. A huge fireball leapt into the air and a mushroom-shaped cloud of smoke billowed skyward. The bus passengers scurried to the other side of the bus to see the horrific fireball.

The commandos hurried to get off the expressway. They had to pass through a tollgate in order to leave the expressway. Why hadn't that occurred to them before now? Long lines of cars were stacked up at each tollbooth at this time of day. The commandos couldn't risk being pinned in the traffic, so they quickly discussed their options. They drove on the shoulder for ten minutes, enough to get in front of those who had witnessed the shooting, and then they abandoned their van on the shoulder of the road and ran quickly across a field into a huge community of squatters. It was an impulsive move, but improvisation was their only option at this stage. They climbed onto the first passing jeepney and passed the fare forward to the driver. The jeepney stopped too frequently to escape; they knew they would be caught if they remained aboard.

One commando spoke in clear Tagalog, asking the driver to stop. They had traveled less than two kilometers, but it was far enough from the expressway to blend in with other pedestrians. They swiftly stepped from the jeepney carrying only their concealed pistols. They walked directly to a new Toyota Highlander SUV parked on the side of the road with its engine running. The driver didn't have time to protest. One commando yanked the driver's door open and shot him in the forehead and then tossed his lifeless body into the road. All three men jumped into the vehicle and they sped away. As quickly as they appeared, they vanished in the stolen van. Very few people remained on the street in such foul weather, and those who were outside were fixated on the massive plume of smoke rising up from the nearby Santa Rita power plant.

A bystander who spotted the murdered driver tried to call for help but discovered that cell phone communications were now as dead as the driver in the puddle. The prepositioned communications suppressors had been remotely activated at the moment the power went out. Phone calls from frantic witnesses to the expressway murders were cut off before they could report the crime. Local officials could hear and see the blasts, but no coordinated response could be organized. Each of the communities located near the targeted power plants thought that their 'accidental' explosion was an isolated event. Little did they know that similar explosions were taking place simultaneously around the entire nation. The first shots had been fired in the war to liberate the Philippines.

Chapter 11 – Bombs!

Wednesday 7:00pm, 9 August
Manila, Philippines

"The airport is closed and you won't find any restaurants open in this weather," said the desk clerk to his three Chinese guests who were headed out of the hotel lobby. "Our dining facility serves some of the best food in Manila, so there's no need for you to get wet to find a great meal."

"Our manager insists that we meet him tonight. We tried to talk him out of it because of the weather, but he is resolute," explained the only one of the three who spoke English. "It's not far away from here, so we won't be worried about flooding."

"We have a service, sir. We can take you there and pick you up later – door-to-door. You won't have to worry about parking or ..."

"Thanks, but the boss is sending a car to pick us up, and I think that van may be ours."

The men wore suits and ties when they had checked into the hotel and had worn them daily. But today they wore khaki pants and polo shirts with casual leather shoes. They carried what looked like oversized gym bags and the desk clerk joked as they headed to the door, "You're not checking out are you?"

The young Chinese man flashed a smile, turned his head and answered, "Not today." The men got drenched from the blowing rain as they ran to the waiting van parked under the overhang near the entrance to the hotel. The sliding side door opened on the van and the men scrambled aboard. Three others were already inside. The door slid shut and the van drove slowly to the far end of the parking lot and stopped. It remained there for fifteen to twenty minutes. The windows were tinted black and it was now dark, so nobody outside the van could know what was taking place inside.

They removed two satchel bombs from a small leather duffel bag and set the timers for midnight. One would detonate in Camp Crame, the national headquarters for the Philippine National Police. The other would destroy Camp Aguinaldo, the headquarters for the Armed Forces of the Philippines. It was inconceivable that the military and police camps were located in the center of a major city. When traffic was snarled neither the national police nor military would be unable to move troops or equipment from either facility. And the commandos thought it ludicrous that they should be located directly across the street from one another. How convenient! How absurd!

One of the men wore a perfectly fitted PNP uniform and another was clad in an AFP Army Jungle Digital Camouflage uniform. Both of them had the name "Lim" embroidered above the front, left pocket. Filipinos have a mixed heritage, and an officer with a Chinese surname would attract no attention at all. Both wore the rank of captain. And both spoke fluent Tagalog. They would carry the satchels into the camps and conceal them. They had studied satellite photos of the grounds and knew where they would get in and out of the walled fortresses. The satchels were watertight, so they could easily leave them outside in a trashcan, or place them on the roof.

The rain and wind would help conceal any noise they might make, and these two men were better trained than ninjas. The satchels were strapped to their backs as they quickly scaled the walls to get into the camps. Their mission was to plant the satchels in the center of each camp to maximize carnage. They could easily have parked the van along the roadside and destroyed much of both camps. It would have been less risky and quite easy. But the prime targets at the camps were the senior officers who lived near the back of the camps.

Both men were dropped off in the rain just two blocks north of the camps. And within ten minutes the first bomb was securely hidden. The bomb within Camp Crame was placed inside a gym locker and a padlock was put in place to keep it secure. The gym was closed but the door remained unlocked. Lim 1 secured the satchel and returned by scaling the same wall he climbed over to get in. He was invisible the entire time. He walked to the designated pickup site and climbed into the van.

The bomb planted in the AFP camp took longer to situate. Lim 2 was able to remain in the shadows after gaining access to the camp, but an unexpected flurry of activity made it difficult for him to move. He spied a flagpole to the side of a darkened building near the center of the camp. The top of the flagpole was indiscernible in the darkness, and Lim 2 thought it a perfect place to hide the satchel. He affixed the bomb to the ropes and hoisted it to the top. Ten minutes later he sat in the van on his way to their hotel. The men changed clothes and left the wet clothing under the seats of the van.

They carried their bags back to their rooms, all of which were near the top of the building on the street side. They would now become a suppression team, preventing any military movement towards the airport. Their comrades across the street would also assist with suppression support. The remote controls for both satchel bombs sat on a computer desk in Lim 1's room. Both teams sat silently in the dark, peering out the windows, eager for the culmination of this mission. Untold anguish would be unleashed on Manila in less than four hours.

Two more satchels were already positioned at the Davao International Airport. The raiding party was eager to begin; the entire Philippine Air Force was laid out in rows right in front of them. Many of them would be destroyed by the two satchel charges. Then mortar teams would destroy the remaining birds. The operation would take less than fifteen minutes, and escape was highly likely. The team was in high spirits, knowing that their efforts would help keep their liberation of the Philippines brief.

The facility at Clark Air Base is a sprawling 230 square miles, but the portion that contains the runway is much smaller. The runway was designed by the Americans to accommodate B-52 bombers and is capable of landing any size aircraft. Two members of the invasion team enjoyed their hotel stay in one of the finest rooms within an area known as the 'Clark Freeport'. One man needed to remain in the room to protect their satchel, but the other was free to swim in the hotel pool or hang out at the hotel bar; one of them was always in 'party mode.' The other one, however, remained in the room at all times to guard the satchel. Both men had carried this satchel since they climbed from the submarine seventy-five days ago. But this evening it would finally be detonated. And they were glad to unhand it. They carefully placed the satchel in their room's air conditioning vent, drew shut the curtains and checked their weapons.

Filipinos accept power outages as Americans accept taxes; they are unavoidable, but necessary. The power companies had convinced the public that it was necessary to shut off the power for a full day to perform 'routine maintenance.' Customers are grateful when a month passes without a 'scheduled' outage. Filipinos are also accustomed to poor service from their communications providers, so it wasn't odd at all that the electricity and cell phones were out - especially in weather like this.

Seven of the fourteen bombs had already been detonated as they destroyed the power grid. Little was known about the extent of damage or whether any coordinated response by Philippine forces had begun, but it was clear that they had succeeded in knocking out power to every corner of the island of Luzon. Two more bombs were now planted at the PNP and AFP headquarters in Manila. Two more were positioned inside Davao International Airport. And one bomb was now sat inside a hotel vent at Clark Freeport. The remaining two bombs were not yet in place, but would soon be positioned inland from the seaport at Subic.

Chinese terror cells emerged from hiding like a deadly virus. And like a virus, the only protection from them would be distance and shielding.

Chapter 12 – We're all guilty
Wednesday 7:00pm, 9 August
Maria Aurora, Philippines

The wind howled outside Ramada Community Church. Coconut palms were no longer swaying; they were bending and flapping. Banana trees could not stand in this wind; rain had loosened the soil around their shallow roots, and the wind easily blew them down. The sound of coconut fronds whipping in the wind made it difficult to hear voices inside the church. Falling branches and coconuts became missiles and frequently shook the church as they hit. It was difficult to carry on a conversation, but Pastor Mark decided to conduct their 'normal' Wednesday night prayer meeting.

Filipino pastors typically defer to their missionary guests when it comes time to preach or teach. Pastor Rod was given the opportunity to deliver tonight's message, so he decided to speak from the heart on a topic that concerned him.

He was concerned that many of his Filipino counterparts practiced and taught a very legalistic faith. They felt that you couldn't be a *real* Christian if you smoked cigarettes, or if you drank alcohol, or if you gambled, or if you even attended a cockfight. Pastor Rod wanted to set the record straight; *real* Christians are sinners who have been saved by faith in Jesus Christ. He wanted for them to understand that God's grace comes through faith, not our goodness.

Pastor Mark Santos started off with a prayer and then led the group as they sang *"Kay Buti Ng Dyos."* The words were printed in magic marker on a large poster board, and the Americans tried to sing along. It was easy for Sean and others who had been to the Philippines many times before; they sang the same song on each previous trip. Sean even knew what all the words meant. But the 'first timers' just clapped their hands and swayed to the upbeat melody. They all enjoyed the passion with which Filipinos worship.

Pastor Mark spoke loudly, almost yelling in order to be heard. The noise outside had become deafening. The roof bounced from the wind and the rain pounded hard on the windows and tin roof. Water now dripped into buckets stored in the kitchen for this very purpose. The church could not afford a generator, so the only lights came from flashlights and cell phones. Sister Marilou attempted to light candles, but the wind, even inside the church, quickly blew them out. After a lengthy introduction by Pastor Mark, Rod walked to the small wooden 'portapulpit'. He had no notes, and he couldn't read well in the dark, so he planned to speak from his heart.

He began, "This topic makes many Christians uncomfortable. But it's a message straight from the heart of God. Not long ago I watched the host of a 24-hour news network interview several people who identified themselves as Christians. Several states had passed laws to protect religious groups from discrimination by the government. But this news agency evidently felt the laws were really designed to deny services to gays and lesbians. The network clearly had an agenda. So they visited a small, conservative community in South Georgia to ask business owners if they would provide their product or services for a same-sex union. 'You mean, like a gay wedding?' one asked the interviewer."

Rod continued, "Every single one of the self-identified Christians said that they would refuse to bake a wedding cake, deliver flowers, or cater the event. Every one of them! They explained that it was because they were Bible believers and followers of Christ. They view homosexuality as heinous sin. And, listen closely now, the reason they view homosexuality as a serious sin is because it's not *their* sin."

A huge crash against the side of the church sent three men to the window with their flashlights to see if they could identify what crashed into them. It sounded like tin from a neighboring roof that had been ripped apart. Rod paused and waited for them to return.

"It's easy for us to condemn others for sins we don't commit. Murder is a big sin because we are not murderers. Rape is a big sin because we are not rapists. Theft is a big sin because we are not thieves. But lying is a minor sin because we lie. Do you understand what I'm saying here? God doesn't assign a point value on sin! All sin is repugnant to God because he is pure and holy and perfect. We don't get to add new sins to his list or subtract anything from what scripture defines as sin. And we don't get to assign arbitrary point values to sin. God does not assign a point value to sin. There are not 10 point sins, 25 point sins, and 100 point sins. To God, sin is sin. And all sin separates us from him. And please pay attention to this: we are not the judges of other people's sin, God is!

"Do you think those so called Christians that were interviewed would serve heterosexual couples who have been living together? Of course they would! That's hypocrisy, folks. Sex, when it's outside the confines of marriage, whether heterosexual or homosexual, is sin *as defined by God.* The very word 'sin' is not part of a non-believers vocabulary. So we should expect non-believers to act like they're non-believers. To them, everything is relative because right and wrong are not based on God's rules, but their own. So if we refuse service to everyone guilty of sin we would have NO customers!"

"We're all guilty. Romans 3:23 says clearly, 'ALL have sinned and fall short of the glory of God.' Every single one of us is guilty!" A huge crash and the sound of breaking glass filled the room. Once again, several people went to investigate. "I am guilty. Pastor Mark is guilty. Reno is guilty." Rod was yelling now to be heard at all. "And it's our sin that separates us from God. Romans 6:23 says, '*For the wages of sin is death, but the gift of God is eternal life through Christ Jesus.*' It's because we're sinners that we all need Jesus. We diminish the value of Jesus and what he did on the cross when we forget about God's grace.

"When a woman was caught in an adulterous affair, she was dragged into the street to be stoned to death. When they asked Jesus to participate he said, '*Let he who is without sin among you cast the first stone.*' They dropped their stones and walked away. They knew that they were also guilty. And so are we.

"Galatians 2:21 says, '*For I do not set aside the grace of God; for if salvation can be gained through works, Christ died for nothing.*' We're not Christians because we are *good.* We are Christians because we place our faith in Jesus, who is perfect. When we start pointing our sanctimonious fingers at others, we're not serving Christ; we're doing Him a disservice. We are also sinners who have been saved by God's grace.

"So can you really point your finger at a brother or sister and suggest that they are not *real* Christians *because they smoke*? Not without sinning in the process. The Bible doesn't address smoking as sin. Sure, you can say that smoking defiles your body and that your body is a temple for the Holy Spirit. But eating junk food does the same thing, and I don't hear anyone saying that people who eat junk food can't be *real* Christians. You tread on dangerous ground when you make yourself the judge of others, and unless you are without sin, you need to keep such judgment to yourself!"

A coconut fell from a nearby tree onto the roof and it resounded like canon fire. Some of the girls screamed. So did Tyler. It was quite difficult to hear because of the howling wind and pounding rain. It was hard to concentrate; there was too much anxiety in the room because of Kiko. Rod planned to include the need for repentance, but the noise made it impossible to continue. He smiled at them and said, "Let's all pray silently."

They weren't going anywhere after they finished the service. The church was their shelter for the night, so they stayed in their chairs and shouted over the storm to one another. All were all wide awake because of the ferocity of the storm, which continued to intensify. The conversations became intensely personal over the next couple of hours. Reno cried and hugged Angie as the youthful Filipina explained the depth of her family's poverty. Reno couldn't imagine having to forage for her next meal, eat a beloved pet, or beg. She loved Angie's humility and knew that Angie felt uncomfortable relating her family's situation. Flashlight batteries were dimming, and some of the cell phones had been turned off to conserve the remaining battery for later. Everybody was concerned about the strength of Typhoon Kiko. It was still offshore and more than 100 miles to the southeast. How much stronger could it possibly get?

Chapter 13 – No Way Out

Wednesday 7:20pm, 9 August
Manila, Philippines

Emergency evacuation protocols for 'non-essential' personnel and the families of the embassy staff had to be improvised. The established process, which is rehearsed at least twice each year, requires telecommunications. But with no way to contact families, Ambassador Stephens began to panic. He forgot to take his hypertension medication, and his high blood pressure began to show.

"Forget the damn procedures, Brian. We're not going to reach anyone on the phones right now. We need to send vans to pick up each family and bring them to the airport!" Ambassador Stephens was unable to reach his wife, Lisa. As the wife of a diplomat, Lisa knew that Frank's work demanded much from him. But she was frustrated, even angry, that he wasn't home with her and their two sons, Austin and Jeffrey. The family's backup generator worked fine, so they still had lights and air conditioning. But every TV station was dead, and they couldn't pick up anything on the radio. And even the Internet was dead. Lisa planned to give him an earful when he got home. Why would he choose to leave them alone in the middle of a super typhoon? And why did he need them to pack their bags to leave in the midst of this massive storm?

"See how many vans or SUV's are here from the motor pool. We'll need drivers too. Get the roster, Brian, and supervise the pickup process. I know you'll get this done. Get the families to terminal three at the airport. Start with Lisa and the boys. I'll have a plane arranged to depart at 9:00pm. You get on the plane with the others, OK? Anyone not on the plane will be left behind, got it?"

Brian Roberts was the Ambassador's personal assistant. They met in Washington, and then Brian was selected as part of Frank's staff in Tanzania, and later in Kuala Lumpur. Brian was the only person that Frank Stephens had ever met who had a photographic memory. It wasn't just a great memory; lots of people had the ability to recall details that most people overlook. But Brian could recall *every* detail of conferences, telephone calls, or situations. Brian was also persuasive and could get things done. He was the perfect person to run interference for Ambassador Stephens. But there were quirks that accompanied his brilliance. He needed to be reminded about personal hygiene. So Ambassador Stephens' wife, Lisa, arranged barber appointments, dry cleaning, and simple things like shoe shines for Brian. He was like an uncle to their two boys, and Lisa knew that Brian was largely responsible for her husband's success.

"Jason, is your car parked here?" Ambassador Stephens knew whom he could count upon, and Jason was indispensible.

"Yes sir, I have the issued SUV."

"Grab your wife and get to the airport. Any U.S.-based carrier will provide us with an aircraft. Delta should have at least a couple on the ground. Have them fuel it up and ready to taxi at 9:00, OK? Show them this," he said, presenting Jason with a shoulder bag containing a standing executive order, memorandums of agreement, authorization codes, and all the instructions necessary for reimbursement. "I'll see you there in an hour."

Few staff members remained on duty at this late hour. Those who had cars were responsible for bringing their own families to the airport. Brian didn't need to write down who they were, he remembered their names and he knew which homes they needed to visit with vans. He reproduced copies of the staff roster with their home addresses. The roster was classified, as the embassy didn't wish to share home locations with just anyone. He planned to drive one of the vans and pick a family who had no transportation. Then he would retrieve Ambassador Stephen's family. Brian gathered the drivers together and handed out addresses and maps. Those who could drive themselves would be encouraged to do so. Those without suitable transportation would need to climb into the waiting vans immediately. There was no time to waste.

"Where will you be, Ambassador?" Brian needed to know what to tell Lisa.

"I'm going to Camp Aguinaldo to alert the AFP," answered Ambassador Stephens.

"There's no way that you can make it to the camp, then back to the airport in an hour, sir; especially in this weather," said Brian, who fiddled with two sets of van keys. "Why can't you just inform General Mariano, our military attaché? He lives in Pasay on our way to the airport. He's our proper channel, sir." Brian was right, General Mariano was the person he would contact under ordinary circumstances, but today was anything but ordinary. What if General Mariano wasn't home? What if he *was* home? There's nothing he could do to communicate the situation to headquarters. The leadership at Camp Aguinaldo needed to hear it directly from Ambassador Stephens.

The remaining security detail was told to lock down the embassy and remain on high alert. People ran from room to room to make sure that nobody was being left behind. The nasty weather outside heightened their state of panic. A team was assigned to incinerate all of the highly classified documents. They didn't want the Chinese to learn more about the American intelligence operation in the Philippines than they already knew. It would take days to gather everything that needed to be destroyed, so Ambassador Stephens provided them with a pre-planned priority list for destruction of all the necessary information.

Ambassador Stephens then jumped into the passenger seat of his SUV. His driver, James Ibale, waited with the engine running. James was skilled enough as a driver to get them out of any situation. And he could get them to Camp Aguinaldo despite the flooding in Manila. They normally traveled with a full security detail consisting of five SUV's and eighteen men. But Ambassador Stephens insisted that all the remaining vehicles be used to ferry embassy staff and their families to the airport. The guards opened the gates as James roared from the embassy compound. Blue lights flashed on the dashboard as they quickly performed a U-turn across the median and headed north on Roxas Boulevard. Ambassador Stephens turned on his mobile radio and tried every channel. There was no signal. He knew what that meant.

"What do you mean there are no planes here? This is an international airport, for God's sake! We have a crisis situation and require an aircraft now!" Jason flashed his embassy credentials a second time, but he received the same answer from the senior security agent on duty. What he knew about the impending Chinese invasion was classified "TOP SECRET" and Jason wasn't at liberty to share it with the security team at the airport, even though they needed to know.

There wasn't a single airline representative available at the airport. But even worse, there wasn't a single *aircraft* at the airport. All operations had been suspended at Ninoy Aquino International Airport at noon. All aircraft had been moved to other airports in order to protect them from the storm - every last one of them. The decision of what to do next rested entirely on the shoulders of Jason Brock. It was clear that there was no way out from Manila by air, so he decided that the embassy staff and families would need to drive together in a caravan to Clark Air Base. Clark is far enough inland to hangar aircraft from the winds. He knew that they had at least two refurbished C-130's there, and he was certain that he could make arrangements for the embassy staff to be evacuated from there. And he was pretty sure that the C-130's were the same aircraft used to fly into hurricanes to measure them.

Brian was the first to arrive at the Manila International airport with Lisa Stephens and her two sons. They were cramped together with five other people that they'd picked up. Jason met them at the curb and explained the situation regarding the plane. Jason quickly agreed to arrange airlift from Clark, and sped away from NAIA, drifting around the tight left-hand curve, his tires squealing as he left. The remainder of the staff would travel by motorcade to Clark. It would be safer that way. It was time to stick together.

The drivers struggled to find the homes contained on the list of addresses. Finding an address in Metro Manila is often impossible. It doesn't matter what the map or GPS says, streets are often unmarked and house numbers non-existent. And their GPS systems were suddenly useless; all frequencies, even from satellites, were jammed. The embassy drivers drove up and down the same streets several times. They knocked on doors and asked for help from neighbors. It was beyond difficult, and some families simply had to be left behind – everyone had been told that the plane would leave precisely at 9:00pm.

Brian greeted each of the vehicles as they arrived at the airport and arranged them into a convoy. He waited until 9:05 before leading the convoy to Clark. Some of the staff and their families demanded to know what was going on. They complained, stating how reckless it was to be out in this weather. What could possibly be more dangerous than driving around in a CAT 5 typhoon? Brian refused to provide them with details; he explained that they wouldn't be doing this if it were unnecessary. He didn't want to create any more fear or panic than they now felt. He asked all of the drivers in the convoy to turn on their emergency flashers, and then he climbed into the lead vehicle, a new black SUV belonging to the embassy, and slowly left the airport with blue lights flashing from his dashboard.

Ambassador Stephens did not arrive at the airport, and was not part of the caravan. Perhaps he'd spot them as they drove north on EDSA, the main thoroughfare through Manila. Their emergency flashers would surely catch his attention. But Frank Stephens and his driver, James, did not reach Camp Aguinaldo. The stress of the situation overcame Frank, and he suffered what appeared to be a heart attack.

Ambassador Stephens slumped forward in his seat and was caught by the seat belt harness. James immediately stopped in the center of the road and administered first aid. He made sure that the Ambassador was breathing and that his heart was beating before driving to the hospital.

The ambassador was still breathing, yet unconscious when James arrived at Chinese General Hospital emergency room. James explained who his passenger was and the emergency room staff immediately loaded him on a gurney and whisked him to the intensive care unit. James was filled with anxiety. He knew that it was a matter of utmost urgency to get Ambassador Stephens to Camp Aguinaldo, even in the midst of Kiko, but he didn't know *why*.

After an hour and a half of splashing through Manila streets and driving up on sidewalks, the caravan finally arrived at the North Luzon Expressway. Police officers stood in front of every tollbooth, routing all traffic back into Manila. There were very few people driving at this time, yet some had decided to evacuate Manila and were desperate to go north. Brian rolled down his window to speak to an officer that was frantically signaling for him to turn left across the median and head back south. Rain flew sideways into the window.

"I am Brian Roberts, Executive assistance to American Ambassador Stephens. We have been ordered to evacuate all non-essential passengers to Clark Air Base."

"The expressway is closed, sir. No traffic is allowed to enter. I'll need you to turn around." The officer continued to motion them to a U-turn lane in the median.

"Is there a problem with the road? Or is it just closed?" asked Brian.

"The road is passable, sir, but we have been ordered to close it to traffic," said the officer.

"Well, you have your orders. And I understand that. But I also have mine. I have to deliver these families to Clark tonight. So either shoot me or get out of the way." Brian put the SUV in gear and roared forward. Eleven vehicles following behind him did the same. Nobody made any effort to stop them or gave chase. They had no way of knowing that shooting had already begun at Clark Air Base. The U.S. embassy staff would soon find themselves in the center of bedlam.

Chapter 14 – AFP Alerted
Wednesday 11:20pm, 9 August
Manila, Philippines

Ambassador Stevens awakened slowly, and his face looked confused as he tried to comprehend where he was. Powerful sedatives clouded his mind, but he soon discovered that a male nurse was pushing him on a hospital gurney. James Ibale walked alongside the gurney and met his eyes as they opened. Instant panic overtook Ambassador Stephens when he realized that he had not yet been able to contact the Armed Forces of the Philippines. He quickly removed the oxygen mask from his face and discovered that his tongue wasn't cooperating with his brain. The nurse stopped and tried to refit the mask onto his face, telling him, "Relax, Mr. Ambassador, I'm taking you to a private room – you're going to be okay." Ambassador Stephens resisted the mask and tried again to speak.

"James, the car…Camp Aguinaldo." He flopped back to the gurney, frustrated that he wasn't making sense. He was groggy and knew that he couldn't slip back into unconsciousness. He tried to sit up, but James helped the nurse return him to a prone position on the gurney. Looking at James again, he forced himself to sit up again, accidentally tearing the IV tube from his arm. He took off the mask and took three deep breaths. Then he spoke quickly.

"James, this is urgent. We need to talk somewhere alone for a moment. I'm going to share something with you that is highly classified." Frank Stephens was desperate to share the news of the Chinese invasion with the AFP. He was wearing only a hospital gown, his hair was disheveled, and he was now wide-eyed. James had never seen the Ambassador like this, as Lisa was meticulous in the details of his clothing and grooming. Even his eyebrows were carefully maintained. "We need to be alone, NOW!"

Ambassador Stephens knew that James was not cleared for TOP SECRET information and intentionally avoided certain conversations while James was driving. But there was simply no choice; even though James was not cleared to receive the information he was about to share, he was the only option to alert the AFP. Ambassador Stephens could be fired, fined, and even jailed for intentionally providing TOP SECRET information to James. Even for accidental disclosure the same held true. But James was trustworthy, and Ambassador Stephens knew that he would do the right thing.

James turned to the nurse and asked, "Where can the Ambassador and I be alone for a moment to talk?" The nurse pointed to the door at the end of the hallway, which would be Ambassador Stephen's room, the best in the entire hospital. Top-level politicians, corporate executives and the ultra rich enjoyed this hospital suite. It was furnished more lavishly than most luxury hotel suites.

"It's the door on the right, sir." The nurse replied. He looked at James and said, "But please be quick, I'll need to get his IV started, and make sure that he's back on oxygen." The nurse expertly wheeled the gurney into the room and put into position. No accidental bumping into doors or other furniture. The nurse was an expert driver, just like James. He locked the wheels in place and said, "I'll be back in five minutes, or you can find me in the hallway – I'm not going anywhere."

"Thanks," James and Ambassador Stephens responded simultaneously. They waited for the nurse to close the door and move away from it before talking.

"Are the cell phones working, yet?" asked the Ambassador, and James nodded in the negative. He knew that the Chinese were already jamming all of the broadcast frequencies, and that all communications were out. He wanted desperately to call Lisa to check on her and the boys. He needed to know if they made it onto the plane with the other staff members and their families. It was best that he didn't know that they hadn't. In fact, his family was just now arriving at the Santa Rita natural gas plants that had been bombed.

As soon as the nurse stepped out the door Ambassador Stephens began to talk quickly. He reached for James and brought him close as he spoke. "I need for you to *go right now* to Camp Aguinaldo. Insist on seeing whoever is in charge there. Tell them who you are, then let them know that we're about to be attacked by the Chinese." James stepped back in shock. His face was filled with terror. "Tell them that all communications are being jammed by the Chinese. We have evidence that their military fleet is in motion – their ships are already on their way here. We've intercepted communications that speak of 'Operation Zhi,' and it is already underway. They have an aircraft carrier already positioned in the South China Sea and it will arrive here as soon as this storm clears. Tell them they need to mobilize the military NOW to repel this invasion."

James stood with his mouth half open. He was visually stunned by what he heard. Usually he was able to piece things together before they were announced. He normally picked up portions of people's conversations while driving and was good at assembling the pieces. But this information came as a total surprise. His feet wouldn't move. He wondered whether he needed to write down details or whether he could remember everything that Ambassador Stephens just told him.

"James! Did you hear me? You need to go *now*! Tell them where I am; they can confirm it with me if they want. But they need to know it *now*."

James turned and sprinted from the room. He knew Ambassador Stephens well enough to understand the gravity of the situation. In the last sixty seconds he had inherited a great burden. *What if they won't listen? What if they don't do anything? What if I can't get there through the flooding?* His mind raced as fast as his legs. He reached the SUV, put it in gear and raced from the hospital parking lot. The wind howled, and heavy rain covered the windshield even with the wipers at full speed. The ambassador's vehicle was armor plated and heavy, which helped maintain traction in the flowing water. The engine was powerful and the tires were new. If anything could get through this weather, it was this all wheel drive SUV. James almost missed a turn because all of the usual landmarks were hidden in the darkness. With the power out, Manila was an eerily different place.

All of Manila was now flooding, and James struggled through the deepening waters. Fortunately the drive to Camp Aquinaldo wasn't far from the hospital. Even with traffic he could have made it in 25 minutes. And now, as the only vehicle on the road, the trip took longer than normal because of the floodwater. At times James was unable to discern where the road began and ended. He used the buildings on either side as landmarks and positioned himself between them to navigate his way through the deepening waters to Camp Aguinaldo. The main gates at Camp Aguinaldo were closed and locked when James arrived. He honked the horn, holding it down until a guard finally appeared at the gate.

James jumped from the SUV; while its lights flashed blue and the emergency flashers blinded everything nearby, James showed his embassy identification to the guard, who appeared unimpressed. The guard seemed irritated that the driving rain was wetting his legs, which were not protected by his poncho. James spoke to him in excited tones.

"I'm delivering news from the U.S. Ambassador and I need to speak to the commanding officer immediately. I have urgent intelligence information that I need to share." Water was blowing off James' face in streams as he stood facing the guard, who still seemed reluctant to open the gate.

"Open the damn gate you fool!" He couldn't remember being this irritated and his words reflected his anger. James stood incredulously in the lights of his vehicle watching the motionless guard process his next thought. Then he turned and jumped back into the vehicle and continued to honk the horn until a second guard appeared. This time he shared the news with them both, "The Chinese are attacking the Philippines! It's already underway. They are using this storm as cover for their assault. And you two imbeciles will be blamed when people ask why we didn't defend ourselves. I need to speak to the commander now! You can visit the U.S. Ambassador at Chinese General Hospital if you want verification." The two men looked at one another and spoke inaudibly as they opened the gate and allowed James to drive into the compound.

One guard pointed towards the back of the compound; the base commander would be located there. James quickly drove to where the guard had pointed and he ran into the building hoping to find the commander. But what he found, instead, was the duty sergeant, who brought him to a young Lieutenant who brought him to speak with a sleeping Captain. Until the Captain heard the entire story, he wasn't willing to wake his supervisor to move the matter forward. James was then introduced to a Major who wanted to hear the whole story. James lost his patience and began to scream, hoping to attract the attention of someone higher than the next peon in the chain of command. It worked! A general officer emerged from a room at the end of the hall and walked briskly towards them. And before he even reached where James was standing he spilled out everything that Ambassador Stephens had told him. Finally! The alarm was now sounded!

Ambassador Stephens was unable to maintain his sleep, even with the heavy doses of sedatives given to him. He was groggy and worried about his family. He hoped that they were out of the way of the storm and the impending invasion. He wanted to talk to them, but knew it was a futile thought. He worried what the Chinese would do to him if he were captured. He then smiled as he thought of James at Camp Aguinaldo. He was confident that James had made it there and that the AFP was now responding.

The commandos watched James arrive at Camp Aguinaldo from their upper floor hotel rooms. And they became concerned by the sudden flurry of activity taking place in the camp. Two vehicles quickly roared out of the camp and headed south on EDSA. The commandos realized that they could no longer wait any longer to detonate the devices placed inside the two camps. A slightly early detonation would change nothing. They quickly flashed signals to one another from the upper floor rooms of their hotels. They braced themselves for the shock of the explosions. They gathered together on the bathroom floors to prevent any flying shards from the explosion. The earth shook, and flying debris peppered everything in the vicinity. The percussion of the blast imploded the windows at both commando positions. The elated commandos quickly took up their sniper positions at the broken windows. James and the news he delivered were vaporized. The battlefield in Manila had quickly shifted into the favor of the People's Republic of China.

Chapter 15 – The monster grows
Wednesday 11:50pm, 9 August
East coast of Central Luzon, Philippines

Kiko had become a monster storm with record winds of 202.5 mph. No storm in recorded history could match the ferocity of Kiko's current winds. Maximum wave height was estimated at 55 feet. Stunned meteorologists marveled at Kiko's continued intensification. Until now, Typhoon Tip held the record low sea-level pressure at 870 millibars, and its wind speed reached a record 190 mph. That was thirty-eight years ago in the open Pacific. Yet Kiko already exceeded Tip's speed by 12.5 mph and the pressure was still falling at 860 millibars. And in only four hours Kiko would make it into the record books as the strongest storm ever recorded at landfall.

Storm chasers from around the world gathered in the Philippines to get in front of this massive storm. Some were thrill seekers, but most wanted to document the storm and turn it into a payday with startling video images. Kiko was a dream storm for these demented people. They would film unimaginable devastation. They would film dead bodies floating in canals or hanging from trees. They would shock their audience with videotape of people with grotesque injuries: impaled by debris, bones producing from their bodies, or severed limbs. Hordes of the walking wounded, staggering zombie-like in shock would punctuate their reports. A crying mother frantically searching for her children would wrench the hearts of viewers. And if they added naked victims, whose clothes had been ripped off by the vicious wind or rushing water, their documentary would gain additional viewers. Heart wrenching stories would emerge from the rubble, and heroic tales of rescue and courage would soften the documentaries from the harsh reality that Kiko was basically a heartless monster.

Several storm chasers traveled north of Manila when the initial forecasts pointed towards landfall in Baler. Landslides and flooding trapped them along stricken roads. They would have to settle on a different aspect of the storm than they'd planned. Most of storm chasers, however, chose to hunker down in Manila and move to high ground to obtain video. They purchased executive suites at posh hotels with backup generators and the promise of electricity and air conditioning even after the storm. They also carried extra provisions for after the storm. They had no charitable intention; they just wanted to guaranty themselves a sufficient supply of beef jerky, granola bars, liquor and coffee when nothing else was available. They had all been through this before.

And at this late hour, Kiko was already spanking Manila. Windows shattered from the fierce wind. And when the windows broke ceiling panels and other loose items took flight. Deep water flowed in the streets. Tree limbs littered the landscape and large sheets of tin flew at dangerous speeds throughout the city. Wind speeds in the eye wall were as high as an F5 tornado, and unprecedented amounts of rain had already fallen. And soon it would get worse. Much worse!

The outer rain bands pounded the entire eastern shore of Luzon, especially to the north. Twenty-foot waves crashed over the seawall in Baler, flooding hotel lobbies, restaurants, kitchens and the first floor of every home and business. Panic set in as authorities realized how much they had underestimated the power of the Kiko. The forecasters had done their job well. They were emphatic about the strength of Kiko and made sure that nobody remained ignorant of the storm's strength and location. Local governments forced evacuations and set up thousands of inland shelters to get people away from the coast. Despite their best efforts, all the preparation in Kiko's direct path was futile.

Severe flooding filled the provinces of Bulacan, Pampanga, Tarloc, Zambales, and Pangasinan. Dangerously high water levels at dams throughout Luzon forced operators to open the floodgates, releasing torrents of water onto downstream communities. The gates of Angat, Ipo, Ambuklao, Binga, and Magat Dams were opened up because water had breached the spilling levels. And the worst of the rainfall was still on its way. Water poured into the La Mesa reservoir from open floodgates upstream on the Angat-Ipo-La Mesa water system, putting incredible stress on the dam. The La Mesa dam spilled over the top at levels unseen before. Engineers cautioned that the dam might rupture, in which case tens of thousands of people might drown. Water poured into Quezon City from the north, and the city filled up from lack of drainage. There was clearly big trouble ahead for much of metro Manila - far more than they realized.

Chapter 16 – Midnight attacks
Thursday 12:00am, 10 August
Davao City, Philippines

Two gigantic explosions ripped through the Davao City airport precisely at midnight. Two fireballs shot high into the air and a dual mushroom cloud climbed into the night sky. Amid the confusion that followed nobody quite realized what was happening, especially the Armed Forces of the Philippines. Many were sleeping; others were frequenting local bars. But very few were on duty when the mortars began to rain down on their aircraft, conveniently parked in straight rows on the ramp. Within minutes every aircraft at the airport had been rendered inoperable.

The commandos didn't need to completely destroy the aircraft; their mission was to prevent them from being airborne for at least the next 72 hours. This airport would soon be under full Chinese control. In fact, the entire nation of the Philippines would soon be liberated if things went well. Security at the airport did not return fire; they were in total disarray. The bombs obliterated much of the potential resistance, and the remaining force remained fragmented and confused. They couldn't even tell where the attack was coming from. The commandos worked efficiently in the darkness and quickly completed their mission. After the last aircraft was burning, they promptly ran to their waiting vans and drove swiftly away from the airport.

Their success could not have been any more complete. There was absolutely no resistance. The fight was over by the time that security forces realized that they were the victims of an orchestrated attack designed to destroy the Philippine Air Force. They were vanquished, and burning aircraft littered the flight line. Secondary explosions resounded throughout the complex. The airport was totally demolished, and the perpetrators quickly vanished into the surrounding countryside. Communications were suppressed, and there was no way for a resurgent security force to request backups, establish roadblocks, or intercept the commandos as they fled.

One squad of elite commandos remained behind to quell any opposition, positioning themselves near the dock to thwart any effort to follow them. With RPG's and large caliber weapons they could repel even a large, organized response. But no resistance came. The team members quickly retreated to waiting boats, and they moved hastily into the depths of the Davao Gulf. They would soon return with tens of thousands of Chinese marines.

Two uniformed men stepped out to meet the PNP vehicle carrying the first commando team as they arrived at Ninoy Aquino International Airport. They were instantly killed; they never even suspected that they were confronting an enemy. Four Chinese commandos leapt to the ground and quickly hid the bodies. Four men remained at the checkpoint as thirty-four commandos wearing Philippine National Police and airport security uniforms sped to the curb of the departure and arrival gates at terminal one.

They arrived at the curb in new white PNP trucks. Six commandos who were fluent in Tagalog jumped from the bench seats in the back of the trucks and pounded on the doors, demanding access. The lights were out in the entire arrival terminal, but they could make out the figure of a lone security guard walking towards them. The howling wind made conversation impossible through the closed door. So the guard opened the door wide enough to find out what they wanted. He never had the chance to utter a word. He dropped like a sack of rice after being hit by two bullets to his head from a silenced pistol. The commandos used his body to hold the door open, and more men raced into the terminal, each going directly to his assigned location. The police trucks drove quickly away to fetch additional teams.

An identical scenario took place simultaneously at terminal three. The commandos were able to clear the departure and arrival gates without firing a single shot. The first opposition came as they approached the customs area in terminal three. Four armed customs agents positioned themselves behind cement pillars and hid behind newly installed passport scanning machines. But the large number of well-coordinated aggressors quickly overwhelmed them. The gunfire lasted less than two minutes and was inaudible beyond the confines of the airport. Kiko provided perfect cover with its wailing winds and thunderous rain. They encountered even less resistance inside the terminal than they had imagined.

The remainder of the airport fell quickly into enemy hands. Their jeeps rolled rapidly through sections of runway fence that had been removed. Snipers were quickly positioned on the rooftops of the terminals. Men moved into position near each of the aircraft hangars. More men promptly arrived, signaling by flashing their headlights, and situated themselves to prevent any counterattack. Some situated explosives around the airport perimeter. They positioned their heavy weapons in locations that would be protected from aerial assault. Large bulldozers rumbled onto the runways after making their way through the perimeter fence. Teams moved to every side of the runway. They filled sandbags and fortified their positions to shield themselves from the counterattack that they knew would come. They streamed in like picnic ants, covering the 'sweet spots' that would be used to defend the airport from any counterattack.

Twelve of the fourteen bombs had now been detonated. The bomb at Clark failed to detonate and another was being held in reserve to crush any counterattack that might be mounted against their forces at Subic Bay. Kiko had provided all the cover they needed; the winds howled and the pounding rain was deafening. People were shut tightly in their homes with the windows and shutters closed, oblivious to what was happening around the nation. The military response from the Armed Forces of the Philippines was disorganized, late and futile. The People's Liberation Army would soon flood into the Philippines and overpower any remaining opposition.

Chapter 17 – Chaos
Thursday 12:45 am, 10 August
Maria Aurora, Philippines

Conversation was impractical; the howling wind, pounding rain, and variety of unidentified objects crashing into Ramada Community Church made it virtually impossible to carry on a conversation. The missionaries yelled over the storm until their voices strained and their throats hurt. And around midnight they simply surrendered and sat in stunned silence in awe of the power of the storm. The light from Pastor Rod's small solar lantern waned, and the tiny gas lantern burned dimly. They glanced at one another as the church shook from a particularly massive impact or when the roof lifted and chattered in the wind. Kiko raged outside like an angry beast, yet the eye of the storm was still three hours from landfall a hundred miles to the south.

As they sat in the dark Pastor Rod wished that he was filming the rain and winds, but there simply wasn't enough light for his small camera. The battery, which he intended to use for pictures in the aftermath, faded quickly. Rod loved big storms, but Kiko now satisfied his craving to be in the midst of a super storm. He had experienced enough of God's power in the past four hours to fully sate his appetite for more. He imagined himself standing in the driving rain, watching branches fly by in the distance. He didn't imagine himself cowering in a darkened building as rain flew through shattered windows and stung his face. He wished that he were sitting on his sofa at home watching Kiko on the Weather Channel. He hungered to go online and see Kiko's current location and intensity. From the strength of the storm, Rod guessed that it had accelerated towards Luzon and was now making landfall quite close to Baler. He was wrong. The worst of Kiko was yet to come.

Reno and Angie embraced one another as they sat on the floor against the center wall of the church. They didn't need to speak to share their concern for one another. Angie was clearly frightened by Kiko; she had experienced many typhoons, but never anything like this. She screamed as objects hit the church, and her tears were real. She wept out of worry for her family, particularly her younger sister, Sophie. Sophie was only six and clung tightly to Angie whenever she was around. Angie, without fail, brought Sophie a small gift every single day, even if it was only a peso candy. She loved Sophie like a mother loves her child, and she wanted to hold and comfort her baby sister at this moment. Their home in Baler was inadequate for a storm like this. As the church was being battered, she knew that her family's home might not withstand the wrath of Kiko. Angie knew her headstrong father well; he would insist that they take shelter at home - *he* would keep them safe.

Reno's mind was on her husband, Tom. She smiled as she remembered his simple marriage proposal. There was no ring, and his proposal was entirely spontaneous. He didn't get on one knee and recite some rehearsed line. His proposal wasn't the least bit traditional. They sat at a corner table in Dimarzio's Pizza, a crowded establishment with an unpleasant odor when there was nothing baking. But the food was delectable! And between bites of his Italian sausage calzone Tom looked at her and said simply, "I want to be with you for the rest of eternity." That was it. Reno said simply, "I accept." Instead of Champagne, they celebrated with two 'skunky' Dutch beers from heavy green bottles with clamped ceramic tops.

Marilou never stopped being a good host. First it was bananas. Later she handed out saltine crackers. Then she brought around juice and served it in small colorful plastic cups. Next she delivered slices of pineapple. Pineapple season peaked in early June, but fresh ones could still be found at the local market. Marilou liked it when the American visitors ranted and raved about local produce, and they *always* raved about the fresh pineapples from Aurora. She smiled at each person as if she was an airline stewardess as she brought them chunks of pineapple presented in small plastic cups with metal forks. Marilou, if she was a flight attendant, would still serve her customers during severe turbulence. But her expression changed abruptly when the roof began to lift.

The roof groaned loudly, and then it separated from the building on the side facing the wind. It flapped for five or six seconds before coming apart from the church entirely. It crashed into the darkness amidst screams and the angry howl of the wind. The kerosene lamp blew out, and only a dim glimmer remained of the solar lamp. Pastor Rod pulled out his cell phone and turned on its light. It wasn't much, but in the total darkness it was enough for everyone to see. Pastor Mark and Pastor Rod shouted for everyone to move close to the interior wall and listen to them. The team needed to move to more secure shelter, and Rod decided that they would all walk to the small Bible school dormitories only fifty yards away.

"We'll need to move quickly because it's dangerous out there. If we go to the downstairs dorm we'll have concrete over our heads." Pastor Rod shouted loudly and hoped that everyone heard what he had said. "Pair up! Everyone needs to have a partner. Nobody goes alone, OK? Grab your stuff and let's try to stay close together."

Before everyone could pair up Pastor Mark grabbed Tyler and said, "Tyler and I will go first and shine a light back towards you from the door." Tyler had a strong pen light and Pastor Mark's cell phone had a strong light and a good battery. Without any additional words Pastor Mark and Tyler slipped into the darkness. They illuminated the white, horizontal rain as they trudged towards the dormitory. At first they walked on wet gravel, and then the water became ankle-deep. And before they arrived at the dorms the water had become knee deep. They stumbled for five minutes, fighting the wind every step of the way, and finally they arrived at the steps to the dormitory. The door was unlocked so they opened it and stepped inside, startling seven students who huddled against the back wall. Pastor Mark stood in the doorway and focused the beam to his light towards the church. He waved it in a large semi-circle, signaling that they had arrived.

Sean knew that Kelly would need extra help and quickly volunteered to be her partner for the trek to the dorm. Kelly had difficulty breathing when she did anything strenuous. And the walk to the dorms would be a struggle in this wind. They put on their backpacks and joined arms before stepping into the black night. Neither of them had a light, so they shuffled in the darkness, taking baby steps. Directly behind them were David and Ashley. Dr. Kemp felt responsible for bringing her here, even providing the funds for her ticket, and he wouldn't be able to face Ashley's parents if something happened to her. Anna and Marilou followed them by ten feet. Reno and Angie were next out of the door followed by Manny and Jun. Pastor Rod wanted to make sure that everyone made it out safely before he left the church. Finally he and Angel locked arms and stumbled towards the light.

The march to the dorms was chaotic; they staggered, stumbled and fell as they fought through the storm. Ashley lost her backpack on the way, but Reno stumbled over it and picked it up. A huge palm frond ripped through the space between David and Anna, missing both groups by mere inches. Lightning flashes provided an occasional peek of the terrain in front of them. Ashley hit her shin on an object beneath the water and it hurt unbearably. Angie's knee was scraped from a stumble, and something struck Pastor Mark's hand, causing a deep cut on his left palm. When Pastor Rod and Angel arrived they quickly shut the door behind them, but the noise barely diminished.

"Where's Anna?!" Reno was quick to notice that Anna and Marilou were not inside the dorm. Pastor Rod's heart fell and he raced to the door and opened it. "We need a light here!" he exclaimed. He called into the darkness, "Anna! Marilou! We're over here!" Their strongest lights were now scouring the darkness as they hoped to get a glimpse of either girl.

"Tyler, hold this light and shine it back and forth, don't stop until I get back, OK?" Rod prepared to return to the church to find the two lost girls. He turned to Sean and asked, "Would you come with me?" Sean was already standing in the doorway and eager to return. They left their belongings and hurried into the darkness holding the best flashlights available in the group. They called out to the girls as they fumbled their way through the darkness. Kelly, Manny, and Jun joined Tyler at the door, shining light into the darkness and shouting into the darkness that screamed back at them. Manny began to pray out loud, and the entire group joined him, each calling out to God for the safely of their two sisters.

Reno tended to Angie's knee while Dr. Kemp treated his assistant's injured shin. Nobody noticed that Pastor Mark was bleeding profusely from his hand. He took off his shirt and used it to wrap his injured hand, and then he sat with the others against the wall. There was nothing that could be done at this moment that hadn't already been done. Ashley took two pain relievers and lay down with her leg elevated.

Angie didn't wince as her wound was cleaned and bandaged. She softly asked Reno a question that had crossed both of their minds, "What if we can't find Anna and Marilou?" She and Reno had followed them out of the church and she couldn't remember seeing them, not even once, on the walk to the dorms. Had they wandered off in the wrong direction? Were they back in the church? Had they been hit by debris and injured? The range of possibilities flashed through Reno's mind.

"I'm sure they're okay, Angie," Reno replied. "They probably just got lost in the dark." Their eyes met in the dim light, revealing their worried faces. Neither of the girls believed that their friends were okay.

"I hope you're right," Angie answered. Then both women joined the others in praying aloud for the safety of their teammates. Angie's prayer focused mostly on her family and her precious sister, Sophie.

Pastor Rod and Sean returned to the dormitory after nearly thirty minutes. They looked exhausted and frightened, and Rod quickly asked, "Are they here?" The result of their trip was quickly revealed. Ashley and Kelly began to wail loudly. Even though everyone prayed aloud, the prayers were imperceptible over the storm. Tyler and Manny remained in the doorway and shined their lights into the darkness. They continued to shout the names, "Anna! Marilou!"

Sean and Pastor Rod looked at one another and finally Sean spoke up, "We have another problem. The water outside is rising and it is nearly to the entrance of our door. It's more that waist deep now and it is flowing. And it's saltwater!"

"What! Saltwater?" Pastor Mark asked, standing, still holding his wrapped hand. "That can't be! We're almost ten miles inland."

"We're certain. You can come to the door and check it yourself." Pastor Rod invited Manny and Pastor Mark to double check what they already knew.

Pastor Mark took three steps towards the door, and then collapsed. The loss of blood from the wound on his hand made him dizzy. Reno saw his injured hand for the first time and quickly grabbed her medical bag. She cleaned the wound and carefully stitched his hand in the dim light of a kerosene lamp. Pastor Mark was conscious, but unable to stand. He leaned against the driest wall and asked, "Where do we go when the water starts coming in this door?" It was a good question. Considering that two members of their team were lost on the short walk from the church, the only viable option was to climb the stairs to the second floor of the dormitory. The roof was gone, so the risk of flying debris was a concern, but they could escape the rising water.

Manny and Tyler climbed up the stairs to make sure that the upstairs room was suitable for their next evacuation. Ashley was inconsolable. Her despair was complete. She was injured, wet, in the center of a massive typhoon that was still gaining intensity, her teammates were missing, maybe even dead and they were now being forced to leave the safety of their shelter to escape rising seawater. Could anything possibly be worse? She would soon find out that things could be far, far worse.

Chapter 18 – Embassy staff panics
Thursday, 1:00am August 10th
Manila, Philippines

The U.S. embassy caravan crawled slowly north on the expressway. The elevated highway exposed them to the full force of the wind, lifting their vehicles as the current sheared upward towards the elevated road. The powerful impact of the wind slammed directly into the passenger side, lifting and rocking the vehicles as the drivers fought to keep them centered on the dividing line of the two northbound lanes. The distance from the tollgate to the Clark air base passenger terminal was only fifty-six miles and normally took just over an hour to drive. But in the midst of Kiko's fury they could manage no more than fifteen miles per hour.

Brian Roberts drove the lead vehicle with Ambassador Stephens' family. He struggled to see the road as horizontal sheets of rain shielded his view of the highway. Water no longer puddled on the road due to the vicious wind, which whisked them away. The flat plains of Bulacan offered no shielding whatsoever, and the fierceness of the wind coming off the rice fields became too much for their vans, which lifted and slid to the left. And as much as Brian hated to abort their trip to Clark, he knew that he was responsible for the safety of the embassy staff and their families. They needed to leave the expressway.

Jamie Stephens sat in the front seat with his mother. He was the first to notice lights in the distance and asked, "What in the world is going on up there?" Flashing lights came slowly into view, blue, red, and yellow. And the bright glow of a massive fire appeared behind the flashing lights.

Lisa turned to Brian and asked him, "What do you think, Brian? What could that be?" It was still too far away to see anything but the glow of the fire and the flashing lights. Sheets of rain, parallel with the ground, obscured their vision.

"I'm not sure. It has to be something really bad for them to be out in this weather. That's some sort of petro-chemical fire, nothing else would stay lit with this amount of rain." The horizontal rain pounded with the force of a fire hose. Brian was right about the petro-chemical fire, but it wasn't an educated guess. He had passed this place many times before and his keen memory stored away images of the natural gas power plant. They all strained to see what lay ahead.

As they inched forward the largest van in their convoy suddenly lurched to the left and lifted completely off the ground, flying into the median, driver side down. Jeffrey watched out of the back window and had seen it coming – the van had been struggling to remain upright. As Brian saw the lights from the van disappear from his rearview mirror he stopped immediately.

Jeffrey screamed, "The van with the Andersen family flipped over!" His closest friend, Dylan Andersen, was in that van! Jeffrey wanted to jump out and run to help his friend, but Lisa knew that it was too dangerous to leave the vehicle, so she warned the kids, "Stay inside. The men will help them into other cars."

Brian backed the SUV as near as possible to the flipped van. The other vehicles also gathered alongside to help block the wind. Two people clamored from the capsized van, and then fought against the wind to get reach the SUV behind them. Lisa said, "Open the door; we can take a couple more with us." They could squeeze in more passengers - this was a matter of life and death. The door swung open and a woman carrying a child struggled up the embankment towards their vehicle.

"How many more are in the van?" asked Brian.

"There are nine of us altogether" replied Sandy Andersen. She carried her daughter, Becky, with her, but her two oldest children were still in the van. "Nobody is injured, but we're all shook up." Sandy counted as each of the remaining passengers climbed into other vehicles. Her husband, Dennis was the final passenger to leave the disabled van and he gave a 'thumbs up' as he climbed into a Toyota Land Cruiser.

Brian began the slow slog towards the commotion ahead of them. They could see giant orange flames fanned sideways by the typhoon. Flames leapt all the way across the freeway, and their concern heightened as they approached the flashing lights. As they arrived at the sign for the Santa Rita exit they could make out the silhouettes of police trucks and armored military vehicles. And as they edged forward they found themselves facing dozens of men with automatic weapons leveled at them.

At first Brian thought that the men might be Chinese soldiers, but it was only his imagination playing tricks on him. Philippine soldiers, confused over what to do with traffic, provided different hand signals. Due to the black window tinting, they couldn't see anything inside the vehicles. One soldier motioned for them to move forward and two others signaled them to remain where they were. Half of the vehicles in the caravan had flashing blue lights on the dash, which generally indicated some kind of authority. Brian opened his door, and placed both hands where they could be seen. The men signaled for him to move towards them. He closed the door and struggled against the powerful wind to reach the soldiers.

Brian produced his embassy credentials and explained that he had Ambassador Stephens' family and most of the U.S. embassy staff with him. It was such an odd place to be, rather than in the security of a strong building in Manila, and the soldier in charge wanted answers. "Why are you out in the storm at this hour?" he asked. Brian asked him to step aside from the others so that he could provide him with the honest answer. These men needed to know what they were facing.

"The Chinese are planning to attack the Philippines, and we believe that they are using this storm as cover for an invasion." Brian hoped that the officer understood his English.

"They've already hit us here, sir," replied from the station commander. "The fire you see came from an attack on the gas power plant here. Chinese infiltrators who detonated this bomb shot two men. We have eyewitnesses who saw them shoot the men and detonate the bomb."

"And this is no ordinary bomb, sir. The crater is more than twenty meters deep and hundreds of meters wide. It wasn't a conventional weapon, but we have no equipment to measure radioactivity. You may all be in danger here." The Captain did not seem surprised in the least by news of a Chinese invasion. He and his men had already come to that conclusion.

"Where should we go?" asked Brian. "It's too dangerous to continue on the expressway. Is there any place nearby that we can shelter for the night?" Brian suspected that it was too late to escape the country before a full-scale invasion. Clark would be a priority target for the Chinese. He didn't want to place the embassy staff or their families in any more danger. He would find safety from Kiko tonight and worry about the Chinese in the morning.

"Tabang Elementary School is being used as a shelter. It's very near, and there is room there. We rested there earlier this evening. I'll have Corporal Mendez accompany you. He'll take care of you." He then spoke to Corporal Mendez in Tagalog and pointed to the lead vehicle.

Corporal Robert Mendez opened the back door and squeezed into the passenger side with the others already seated there.

Corporal Mendez directed Brian to pull off the expressway and turn right. They felt the intense heat from the burning power plant as they passed near the flames. After nearly a mile, Brian turned left and moments later they arrived at the school. Corporal Mendez jumped out of the SUV and provided parking instructions for the other drivers. He ran to the nearest door and disappeared inside. Moments later he emerged and signaled everyone to join him.

As Lisa Stephens, her sons, and the remaining passengers stepped in the door of the school office they saw two-dozen soldiers rolling up their sleeping mats and gathering their belongings. Corporal Mendez informed them that the U.S. embassy staff and their families would be taking their place in this room. Two kerosene lamps lit the room and the floor was dry. Three small windows on the same wall as the door were still intact. The soldiers were courteous and helped everyone get from their vans to into the school building. Corporal Mendez had been tasked to ensure that they were comfortable and safe. And he had succeeded in the second half of that order.

They were all physically and emotionally exhausted. The small children fussed and whined as they were told that the floor would be their bed for the night. Walt Summers, known to the kids as 'Uncle Walt' showed them how to make pillows from clothes in their bags. He hit his head when the van flipped over on the highway and the dried blood all over his face made him look like he had just stepped out of a zombie movie. Within a few minutes everyone laid down to rest. The wind outside of the school office was violent and seemed to be gaining strength. Brian sat next to Lisa on the floor to get her opinion on their next move.

"Lisa, can I talk with you for a few minutes?" Brian was very close to the Stephens family and didn't need formalities. Most of the staff referred to Lisa as Madam Ambassador, a title that she accepted, but never really liked.

Lisa wasn't worried. She was frightened. She knew that the Chinese soldiers would be looking for the entire embassy staff. "Sure Brian. Where do you think we should go from here?"

"That's what I wanted to talk to you about," Brian answered. "I think that continuing to Clark may be a mistake, considering the explosion here. Whatever kind of bomb was used to hit this power plant was massive. I think Clark may also be under attack. I think we need to hide someplace that has no strategic value to the Chinese."

"Where's that?" Lisa hadn't considered hiding, but maybe they needed to get out of sight if they couldn't escape.

"If we stay off the expressway and head northeast on the secondary roads we can cross the Sierra Madre Mountains into Aurora or Isabela. There are some small communities there that won't be part of any invasion plan. We may be able to remain there until we can communicate to the outside world and get help."

"Excuse me," interrupted Corporal Mendez. "I apologize for eavesdropping, but I overheard you say that you would like to go to Aurora. My uncle is the mayor of a small town called Alfonso Casteneda on the way to Baler. He could easily hide your staff and families there."

Brian was shocked to hear that he'd been overheard revealing TOP SECRET information. He spoke loudly over the storm, but didn't realize that his voice had carried that far. He didn't even know that Corporal Mendez spoke English. He wondered if anyone else had listened to what he had said. He hadn't yet shared the news with his own staff. He reasoned that it really didn't matter at this point. The Chinese were already invading the Philippines and the news would be on every news network in the next day or so.

Brian signaled to Corporal Mendez to come close. "What you just heard is TOP SECRET information, understand?" Corporal Mendez nodded. "I've already explained the Chinese attack plans to your commander, so your senior leadership here knows what is happening."

Corporal Mendez stood up and Brian said to him, "We accept your offer to go to Alfonso Casteneda. We can warn other military units on the way as we travel. Please get permission to travel with us." Corporal Mendez opened the door and the howling wind quickly filled the room with a slight mist. Everyone looked towards the door as Corporal Mendez exited to speak with his commander about plans to travel to Aurora.

Brian looked at Lisa and smiled, "Well, I guess that's settled. I've been through Alfonso Casteneda before and it's perfect. It's in the middle of nowhere and surrounded by mountains. I believe it's a safe place for us."

"We'll need to let them know to tell Frank and James where we're at. Otherwise he'll never find us." Lisa worried that her separation from Frank might be much longer than hours or days. She had no way of knowing that Frank was in the Chinese Hospital in Manila or that James had been vaporized in a massive bomb explosion at Camp Aguinaldo.

Corporal Mendez returned, dripping wet, with the same Captain who they had encountered on the expressway. They escorted Brian to a remote corner of the room and asked him to repeat everything he knew about the Chinese invasion. Brian told him about the communications jamming in Manila, the intercepted communications, unusual numbers of ships headed to the Philippines, and the intelligence information that had been reported by Roger Lane and Jim Adams.

"Corporal Mendez now reports to you, and he will do whatever you need him to do. We will send an armed escort with you as far as Alfonso Casteneda, and they will alert our detachments along the way. Your military escorts will continue to Baler to alert our units there. Corporal Mendez will remain with you until you release him back to this unit." He stood almost at a full attention as he spoke, and when he was done Brian thanked both men.

"I have a question for you, sir," Brian asked of the station commander. "One of our staff members, a man named Jason Brock may have passed here about an hour ago. Did you encounter him?"

"Yes, he arrived in a vehicle like yours, with blue flashing lights and told us that he was headed to Clark on official U.S. business, so we let him pass." The Captain added, "We advised him not to go there because we have seen no traffic coming from that direction."

Brian said, "Thanks. If Ambassador Stephens comes this way, please let him know that the rest of us will be in Alfonso Casteneda."

"Of course, sir. If there is anything you need, Corporal Mendez will make it happen."

Brian then turned to Corporal Mendez and said, "I'll need you to be fresh in the morning. Why don't you get some sleep here with us? We'll leave as soon as it is safe to do so."

"I'll be back in thirty minutes, sir. I just need to arrange our escort vehicles for tomorrow, with your permission, of course." Corporal Mendez was perfect for his new assignment.

Within minutes Brian, Lisa and the entire staff were sound asleep on the damp floor. They would be more comfortable on this night than in the nights to come. Corporal Mendez returned just twenty minutes later to find everyone sleeping. He joined them on the floor and also fell quickly asleep.

Chapter 19 – Landfall

Thursday 3:41am 10 August
Infanta, Quezon Province, Philippines

Kiko took the long route to shore. It sprung to life as a tropical disturbance in the central Pacific as just another cluster of rain hugging tightly to an area of low pressure. Dozens of storms spontaneously generate in this vicinity every year, and most evaporate into mere rain showers along a trough of low pressure. Kiko didn't draw any additional scrutiny than storms that preceded it until it approached Guam. And, just like David Banner transforms into the Incredible Hulk, Kiko suddenly became a monster. Kiko transformed from a tropical storm on Saturday night into a deadly CAT 4 typhoon by mid-afternoon on Sunday. The rapid intensification took place just south of Guam, and unexpected damage that took place at Andersen Air Force Base at the northern end of Guam caught the media's attention. What would Kiko do next? Where was this killer storm headed?

The initial forecasts projected landfall at the northernmost tip of the Philippines in the Cagayan province. Then, as high pressure built to the north, the strengthening steering ridge changed the forecast for Kiko to make landfall further south in Isabela. A day later Baler, in the Aurora province was in the crosshairs. Then the city of Infanta in the Quezon province became the target. Kiko traveled in an arc, traveling from 12 degrees north to 17 degrees north, then back to 14 as it traveled westward. The long arc brought the monster into Manila from the northeast, without losing any of its punch by traversing over land like most typhoons that approach Manila over land from the Bicol region. Only a small sliver of Quezon province and Rizal stood between the ocean and Manila.

Infanta, Quezon is a beach town. It isn't near the beach; it is *on* the beach, with homes and establishments constructed atop the heavy dark volcanic sand just above the high tide line. Small, colorfully painted outrigger fishing boats normally sat in the sand in front of the homes, but they had been removed from the water entirely because of Kiko. Large groups of men hoisted the boats onto their shoulders the previous morning and carried them almost 100 yards inland. They tied down the boats to prevent them from blowing away in the heavy winds that Kiko would bring. The coastline bent and curved with the terrain, and mountains surrounded Infanta to the west and north. Ordinarily this town was an idyllic place to live or visit, but today was anything but ordinary.

Just as an angry bull would charge a matador, Kiko headed straight at Infanta. It destroyed Polilo Island as it approached landfall in Infanta. Three intense hours of roaring wind uprooted even the most stubborn coconut palms, heaving them in twisted piles throughout the town of Infanta. Every roof lifted off and splintered into shards of metal and wood. They bounced and rolled through the small town of Infanta in the intense wind. Most buildings, even those constructed more than a half mile inland, shredded into sections. Some obstinate pieces still held in place, but flapped and fluttered in the vicious wind. Everything became missiles, and the fools who remained behind to protect their homes from looters were bombarded with rubble. Even the fools themselves became missiles, lifted into the air by 205 mph winds and hurled at their neighbors.

And with a final heave of strength, the powerful typhoon blasted ashore unleashing a fifty-foot tidal surge on the entire town. Nothing remained anchored as the tidal surge ripped apart the small wooden structures. As the water surged into Infanta, every remaining shred of rubble became part of a dangerous, swirling soup of spinning annihilation. Concrete pilings snapped and ripped apart, dragging steel bars that extended from either end. They quickly joined the powerful torrent to make the devastation complete.

Seawater poured inland for more than an hour, filling Infanta like a basin. The waters were without mercy or remorse. The flowing blanket of water swirled until it reached a height of fifty feet on the side of the mountain, and then it began to recede quickly towards the sea carrying trash, debris, and dead bodies; some intact and others torn to pieces. The winds quickly died, like a powerful wind-tunnel fan had been unplugged or switched off. A waning quarter moon appeared brightly overhead, illuminating the debris that now flowed backwards towards the Philippine Sea. It looked like a living organism as it twisted and turned, with spiraling arms that breached the surface as it swam. A sudden silence eerily replaced the deafening howls of the wind, but there wasn't a soul alive in Infanta to witness the calm of the storm's massive eye. Everyone who remained in Infanta had perished. Later counts would reveal that an estimated 6,300 souls perished, and another 2,600 were reported as 'missing'.

Stars twinkled brightly in the clear skies of the storm's massive eye. Birds circled in the night sky, hoping that the storm would dissipate before they lost the strength to continue their flight. The ever-present mosquitoes were gone, as were gnats and other small flying annoyances. Rats and snakes shared the safety of floating debris. They were normally mortal enemies, but all creatures instinctively recognized a 'survival truce' as they clung to the pieces of floating wreckage. The slurping, sucking sounds of the water was unheard by human ears.

At least eight thousand people were killed in the great hurricane of 1900 in Galveston, Texas. It was the deadliest hurricane in U.S. history, killing, by some estimates as many as twelve thousand people. Those who survived the storm spent many days performing the gruesome task of removing bodies from the rubble and burying them. The surviving residents of Infanta would share the same experience as the Galveston residents who returned to find that their town had completely vanished. They would find no landmarks, streets, buildings, or trees. They would find piles of stench-filled rubble containing dead fish, seaweed, pets, livestock, and rotting human corpses.

The moon and the stars quickly disappeared as the backside of the eyewall cloud began to punish Infanta. All the debris loosened from the front side of the storm quickly took flight as the ferocious winds returned, this time from the south instead of the north. Predators quickly kill their prey and devour them. But Kiko was no predator. Kiko killed its victims, and then it killed them again and again. The devastation in Infanta was complete. And other towns up and down the eastern coast of Luzon were also being punished by the enormous storm. If God uses storms to gain our attention, Kiko was the ultimate attention-getter.

Baler is located exactly forty-three miles north of Infanta. Kiko's eyewall extended thirty-eight miles from tip to tip, so Baler was only twenty-four miles north of the eyewall. People who know much about hurricanes and typhoons know that they are first cousins. They both spin counter-clockwise, and both tend to travel generally westward. So when a massive storm makes landfall, the region to the north of landfall takes what is called a 'right punch'. The right side is the most powerful side of the storm, and the right punch can cover a very wide area. And Kiko packed a particularly powerful right punch. The Aurora province, immediately north of Infanta, took Kiko's right punch on the nose. The town of Dingalan experienced a thirty-foot tidal surge, destroying most of the town and killing hundreds of residents. A twenty-five foot storm surge demolished the small villages of Dicapanisan and Dibut in the municipality of San Luis, and all were feared dead. And a wall of water twenty feet high emerged from the sea in Baler Bay and raced inland. Rice fields, only a few feet above sea level were quickly inundated with the massive flood of seawater.

Rivers already swollen from the heavy rainfall spilled over their banks. The flooding quickly widened, filling low-lying areas first, and then spreading over the entire inland region. The rivers normally flowed with crystal clear water, but they were now muddy brown and spreading sewage and garbage as they over spilled their banks. People would soon suffer from dysentery, leptospirosis, hepatitis A, cholera, and typhoid fever. And the standing water would breed more dengue and malaria mosquitoes. Kiko delivered the first wave of death. The Chinese Liberation Army would bring the second wave. And disease would bring the third wave of casualties to the people of Aurora.

As the floodwaters rose, the Aurora province was pounded by CAT 4 winds and massive amounts of rain. Multiple mudslides added to the anxieties of the people in Maria Aurora and Dipaculao. Several homes in the town of Diteke were buried deep under watery mud, and a school that served as an evacuation center in the community of Wenceslao was covered by twenty feet of mud and rock.

Tornadoes typically form when cold dry air mixes with warm moist air. Such atmospheric conditions are rare in the Philippines, so tornadoes are also rare. But small tornadoes are often a byproduct of strong typhoons. They typically occur near the front right quadrant of the typhoon after landfall. And Kiko turned into a tornado factory, with many of them touching down in the Aurora and Quirino provinces. Most people don't need to see God to know that he exists; his creation is evidence enough. And tornadoes don't need to be seen to know that they happened. The evidence is clear from the path of devastation on the ground. Tornadoes were the best explanation for the horrific sound and violent, roaring winds that ripped though Maria Aurora. And it would be evident from the path of destruction that would be visible only after daylight when the winds subsided.

Manila did not receive the deadly storm surge. Infanta was sacrificed as it shielded the Metro Manila area from the massive wall of seawater. Infanta was, in essence, gone. But it wasn't long after Kiko made landfall that Antipolo, Makati, Quezon City, and Manila experienced the eyewall winds of the strongest storm ever recorded. Urban damage is much different than what is experienced in the provinces. Huge steel billboard frames buckled in the wind and toppled into buildings. Cranes overturned. Air conditioning units were ripped from buildings and hurled into others. Windows burst from the force of the wind, and small projectiles flew through windows and ripped through interior walls. Floating garbage clogged the drainage systems, and Manila became a series of small islands as deep flowing water covered the city. The normally bustling streets were empty and dark. The howling winds shrieked even louder as the eye of the storm approached. Virtually every window-facing north burst or blew from its frame. And soon the southern facing windows experienced the same fate. Buildings shook from the impact of huge pieces of debris. Residents moved to the interior hallways of their buildings and huddled in the darkness. Minutes turned into hours. Their nervous jokes ceased, and all conversation ended as the noise from Kiko intensified. And then it stopped!

Only morons would move from the safety of a secure building to walk around in the serenity of the eyewall of a storm like Kiko, but the world is filled with such people. Shouts resounded from the street below. People could be seen dancing atop submerged cars with flashlights in their hands, believing that they had outlasted Kiko. More and more of them poured into the streets in celebration. Then Kiko answered their foolishness with an enormous roar, spitting metal, glass, wood, and plastic loosened by 200mph winds. Windows burst and damaged structures fell. Screams were unheard over the shrieking of the typhoon's winds. Kiko's strength had diminished from the strongest storm ever recorded to, *still*, the strongest typhoon winds on record.

Chapter 20 – Newsflash from Davao
Wednesday, 7:00pm August 9ᵗʰ
Charleston, South Carolina

Gina Franklin hurried home from church and immediately turned on the TV. The Weather Channel was still tuned in. She listened to the reporter's voice as she walked to the kitchen to make a quick sandwich for dinner. Matthew drove Rod's new pickup truck to the church to attend the youth group meeting and agreed to bring James and Rebekah home with him. They would eat pizza at the church, so Gina didn't need prepare any food for them. The phone rang as she opened the refrigerator door.

"Are you watching this on CNN, Gina?" Christi Turner saw the BREAKING NEWS banner appear across the top of her television screen and was horrified as she saw that the Davao airport *in the Philippines* had been bombed. She immediately called Gina.

"Just a minute, Christi, I'm still on the Weather Channel. What's happening?" asked Gina.

"There's been a huge explosion in the southern Philippines in Davao City. I'm not talking about a gas leak or something like a pipe bomb blast; what they're showing on TV looks like a nuclear explosion. Are you on CNN yet?" Christi Turner was glued to her television set and trying to listen to the commentators, read the scrolling news feed, and speak with Gina at the same time.

"They say it happened seven hours ago, Gina. Why would it take them so long to get this on the news?" Christi quickly looked at the other news channels and found that FOX News and MSNBC had also preempted their normal broadcasts to cover the unfolding story in the southern Philippines.

Gina glanced at the report on CNN as she scampered to her computer. "I'm searching for Davao now." Gina quickly pulled up a map of the Philippines. But Christi had already located Davao on the map told her where to find it on the map.

"It's way down south, Gina, right at the southern tip of Mindanao. They're saying that two simultaneous bombs hit the Davao airport around midnight. This was an attack! I thought Rod and Nathan said that the Philippine islands are safe." Christi was panicked even though she knew that Davao was more than 1,600 miles away from her husband and the mission team. She had already converted the kilometers to miles.

"Sean explained to me last year that Islamic separatists in the south have been fighting the Philippine government for decades. But I don't think they have those kinds of weapons." Christi stared at the aerial view of the damage from a satellite image being shown by CNN. Two huge craters, each the length of three football fields had destroyed the entire airport complex. All of the aircraft hangars were obliterated, the passenger terminals evaporated, and the control tower was completely missing.

"Wait a second, Christi" Gina said. "I'm on FOX NEWS right now and they said that it was more than two big blasts. They are reporting that all of the aircraft at the airport were also attacked. They say it was either rockets or mortars. Hold on … the Filipinos are blaming *the Chinese*!"

"What! Are they saying that the Chinese have attacked the Philippines?!" Christi and Gina both stopped speaking. They were watching different channels, and the Philippine attack was the only topic on the news. Christi said, "CNN just said that authorities in Davao discovered several sophisticated communications jamming devices. And witnesses claim that large groups of armed men escaped on boats." Christi stopped talking and began to cry.

Gina was trying to connect the dots. Why were no reports coming from Manila? Just an hour ago Kiko was the top news story, but they hadn't seen any new video from Manila since noon. "Maybe communications in Manila are also being jammed. I mean, there must be 200 news agencies there that are trying to outdo one another on their coverage of Typhoon Kiko." Gina spoke the words as the thoughts crossed her mind. Was this possible? It was clear to both women that something was terribly wrong. Every reputable news agency carried satellite uplink equipment, especially when they knew they'd have no reliable infrastructure to work with after the storm. Yet not a single video of Kiko's landfall in Infanta appeared on TV. And, even though it was now daylight in the Philippines, not one solitary image of Kiko's aftermath had surfaced.

Gina needed a few minutes alone to process the information she'd received, and the lack of information she craved. She told Christi,

"I'll call you back in a little while. I need to let the others know as soon as possible. All we can do is pray, Christi."

Christi replied, "I'll update the family members on . Call me back at eight, OK?"

"Sure thing, Christi. Thanks!"

Gina's phone rang immediately when she hung up. It was Alan Adams. "Gina, there's bad news coming out of the Philippines right now. CNN is saying that a large number of unknown assailants have attacked an airport in the southern part of the country. And they are suggesting that the attack came from a 'foreign nation', but ...." Gina cut him off.

"FOX News believes that it was an attack by the Chinese, who took out all communications as they attacked." Gina and Alan both remained quiet for a moment. They were thinking the same thing. *What about Manila? What about Aurora?* Gina began to choke up and needed to be alone for a while. "Listen, Alan, I can't talk right now. Christi is updating the families on , but we still don't have anything to share with them except what is on the news. I'll call you back in awhile, OK?"

"Alright," Alan replied. "I'll be up late, not even sure that I'll sleep tonight, so call me whenever you have the chance, okay?"

"I will, Alan. Thanks!" And, once again, the moment she hung up her phone it began to ring. This time it was her mother and Gina decided not to answer the call. She turned off her phone and plugged it into the charger. She would need it in the coming hours. She returned to her computer and listened to CNN playing in the background. Gina signed onto to see what Christi had posted. And as soon as she was logged in she found a message from Kelly's boyfriend, Mark. It contained a link to an article entitled, 'The Mysterious Silence." The article stated that the only news agency currently reporting from Manila was Xinhua News Agency from the People's Republic of China. All other news agencies remained silent, and the author of the article suggested that it was a 'forced silence.' Xinhua was providing coverage of Kiko, but they made no mention of the blasts in Davao City.

Another message appeared from Teresa Ross, Ashley's mom. She somehow managed to find a video of the storm from Aurora! And it was after daylight, so it was very recent news. An independent storm chaser going by the name of Disaster Bob travelled north of Manila to videotape Kiko's 'right punch' and ended up in the small coastal village of Dibut located just south of Baler. He managed to upload two reports to his blog site, 'disasterbob.tumblr.com.' The first was amusing, as he documented his preparation to film Kiko. He filmed himself, looking like a hippie from 1969, climbing several hundred feet up a mountain to the west of Dibut. He struggled and slipped and his climb was comical. After selecting a suitable place to film, he dug a foxhole and filled large sacks with the mud from the hole and stacked them around the entrance. Heavy rain filled the hole as he dug it. By the time he climbed into the hole it was completely filled with water. The report was whimsical and funny.

But Disaster Bob's second video was horrifying. Dibut is just around the corner from Baler Bay on the map and the video showed the village of Dibut before and then after Kiko arrived. Nothing remained standing! Every single building was entirely gone! Not a trace of the town existed except for the bodies of its people that floated in the surf and lay strewn across the wide, sandy beach. Disaster Bob was wide-eyed and looked like a wild man in the video. He explained to the audience that he intended to walk north to Baler within the next six hours and file a report from there. Gina bookmarked his blog site and returned to the sofa to watch the news.

Matthew opened the door and held it for his little sister, but tried to close it on his bother James before he could get in. Matthew spotted his mom weeping on the sofa. He suspected that she'd been given some terrible news and was almost afraid to ask why she was crying. Gina didn't want the kids to see the video from Dibut and glanced at the computer to make sure that it wasn't on the screen. She asked the kids to join her on the sofa and told them, "We still don't have any word from your dad or the team. I've tried calling them, but there's no answer. I'm just so worried about them."

Matthew tried to console her saying, "No news is good news, isn't that what they say? You know dad, he'll be fine. They moved away from the beach to high ground yesterday, so I'm sure they're fine." Rebekah hugged her mom and kissed her on the forehead like her daddy would do. Matthew hugged his mom and offered her some left over pizza.

Christi called Gina, who had been busy researching news stories about Philippines and posting the links on . Most of the news was now mere repetition of information that had already been shared. And none of the stories were about Kiko. Christi asked Gina, "Did you watch the videos that Teresa found?"

"Yes! I don't know what to say. That second video was horrifying."

Gina paused and Christi cried into the phone as she spoke. "That's only a few miles from Maria Aurora, Gina. You know that, don't you?" Christi wept, unable to speak.

"I looked at it on a map of Aurora – they are only a few miles apart. I can't get those images out of my head. I'm as frightened as you are, Christi, and I don't know whether I should be more afraid of the storm or the bombings." Gina looked up and saw Matthew turn around and return to his room. She knew that he'd overheard her comment to Christi. He needed to know the truth soon, but Gina didn't want to alarm him unnecessarily. She would wait until she had more news to share.

Christi blew her nose into a tissue, then said, "Tyler's dad called me a few minutes ago. He said he tried to reach you, but couldn't get through. He's going to have his friend with the helicopter fly up and get the team. He said he'll keep trying to reach his friend, and as soon as it's safe to fly they will all return to Manila with him. He'll let you know as soon as it's arranged."

Gina replied, "Maybe you should post that on so the church will know what's being planned. That may be the first good news that the families have heard. Do you and Hanna want to come spend the night here? I have no plans to sleep and can use the company."

Christi quickly replied, "I'll be there in a half hour. Thanks so much! Is there anything you want me to pick up on the way?"

After a moment's pause Gina said, "A fifth of Jack Daniels® would be nice." It was intended as a joke, but Christi took it seriously.

"Is there anything else?" Christi had written it down.

"I don't need anything, Christi. The bourbon was a joke, by the way; I guess it wasn't funny. I've got everything you need here, but you may want to carry along your laptop so we can both search for news. I've got pillows, blankets, and whatever else you need – hurry over." Gina felt blessed to have a friend as close a Christi. Even though they were a decade apart in age, they were as close as sisters.

Gina walked into Matthew's room and sat next to him on the bed. Matthew had the Weather Channel displayed on his computer screen. He was clearly worried about his father and the rest of the team. Gina began, "I don't know if you've heard the news from the Philippines, but CNN and the other news channels say that the airport in

Davao City was attacked with two huge bombs. Some reports say that it's part of a foreign invasion because they destroyed all the military aircraft that had been moved there to protect them from Kiko. One network is even saying that the Chinese are invading the Philippines."

"I know, Mom. We were all watching it on the big screen at the youth group meeting. Do you think they're safe from the storm in Aurora?" Matthew fidgeted with his cell phone. He had just watched the two Disaster Bob videos. His eyes watered up and he said, "I don't want to lose Dad."

Gina hugged him and they both wept. "Neither do I, honey. Your dad is a survivor. He's also a thrill seeker and I know he loves every minute of this storm. I don't think he knows anything about the bombs, but that happened 1,600 miles away. Our mission team traveled there with medical supplies, nurses, and doctors, and God has put them exactly where they need to be. We just have to trust that God will protect them and bring them home safely. In the meantime they have a mission to do."

"I don't want James or Rebekah to know anything about this tonight, okay?" Matthew nodded in agreement. "I want them get some sleep. We may have good news to share with them tomorrow, you never know." The doorbell rang and Gina kissed Matthew on the forehead, just like Rod would have done. "You get some sleep too. I love you."

Gina closed the door to Matthew's room and hurried to open the front door for Christi and Hanna, and she was surprised to find Tom West at the door. "Hi Tom, please come in. I was expecting Christi, she's on her way here now with Hanna."

Tom had not seen any of the news reports yet. A Filipina nurse at the hospital told him that the Philippine Islands were under a full-scale attack by the Chinese. She knew that Reno was there on a mission trip and she wanted to make sure that Tom was aware of the situation in her homeland. Her account was embellished with exaggerated facts, and Tom was alarmed. He was unable to find a news report on his car radio on the short drive from the hospital to the Franklin's home. He tried to reach Gina on her cell phone, but she had turned off the ringer. Tom said simply, "Fill me in."

They walked into the living room and Gina turned on CNN to see if there were any new details. Gina told Tom everything she knew about the attack, but she didn't share anything about Disaster Bob's video. While she was explaining the communication jamming equipment that had been found the doorbell rang again. She excused herself to answer it. Christi and Hanna entered carrying a bagful of warm Krispy Kreme® donuts.

The first thing Christi said when she saw Tom was, "Did you show him the Disaster Bob videos?"

Gina replied, "We haven't gotten that far yet." There was still no video of Kiko appearing on CNN or any of the major networks. Gina returned to the topic of the signal suppressors. "The Philippine military discovered several devices in Davao that were used to prevent communications. Some of the analysts believe that is also the case in Manila. That's why we haven't gotten any video of Kiko as it came ashore. It's nearly 8:40am there now and not a single daylight image of the aftermath has surfaced, except for these." Gina clicked on the bookmarked link and showed him the first video, telling Tom as it played to brace himself for the second one. Christi and Gina both cried as the second video began to play, and Tom was crying before it ended.

Tom responded in the only way that he could think of. "Let's pray," he said. And for the next twenty minutes, with CNN playing in the background, the three missionary spouses prayed for God to deliver their loved ones home safely.

Tom got up to leave and said, "Please call me if you hear anything. I'll be checking on for any updates." He walked to the door, still wiping tears from his eyes. Reno was his life. She was his eternity. He couldn't imagine life without her, but there was now a chance that he may never see her again. Tom continued praying in his car as he drove home.

Hanna and Rebekah always enjoyed sharing a bed together. After twenty minutes of laughter they settled down and slept. Then Matthew joined his mother and Christi on the sofa for a night of Krispi Kreme® and non-stop news. But any real news was still almost ten hours away.

Chapter 21 – The search
Thursday, 7:50am August 10th
Maria Aurora, Aurora Province, Philippines

Pastor Rod stood in the doorway as the first light began to appear over the eastern horizon. He hoped to see Anna and Marilou huddled together in the distance, waving to him to signal that they were safe. The floodwaters were still far too deep to venture out, so all they could do was peer into the distance, scouring for any sign of the girls. Every team member crowded near the doorway or peered from a shattered dormitory window hoping to see Anna and Marilou. But what they saw disheartened them.

Every coconut tree within sight had been uprooted or snapped in half; not one remained intact. Whole trees and branches floated by, creating logjams as they clustered together against fences or other obstacles. Pastor Rod tried to imagine the speed of wind capable of snapping trees in half and ripping them entirely from the ground. Ramada Community Church looked like the aftermath of an airstrike. The roof and doors were gone. All the windows had been shattered and the paint looked as if it had been sandblasted from the cement blocks. Evidence of the wind was now also floating in the water.

The floodwaters flowed swiftly towards the sea. Garbage and bits of buildings swirled in the water. Plastic pails, motorcycle tires, and unidentifiable pieces of floating wreckage showed the power of the flowing water. The current rippled as it flowed along the edge of the dormitory building, creating a gurgling sound that was now audible above the sound of the dying wind. All eyes peered into the water and any objects above it, but Marilou and Anna could not be seen. The team shouted their names, "Anna!" "Marilou!"

"What's that?" Tyler yelled as he pointed to a huge object floating near to the dormitory. Nobody responded. They all gazed through the early morning light as the bloated carcass of a huge water buffalo floated by. The floodwaters carried it quickly, its legs appearing and disappearing as it rolled in the swirling waters. Its giant horns emerged from the water as it rolled, then they vanished beneath the dark water. Within minutes the carcass of a dog swirled by in the fast flowing water. The entire team felt the same sickness in their stomachs as they thought of the two lost girls. *How could they possibly have survived the rushing waters and fierce winds?*

The howling wind subsided, yet strong gusts continued to spring to life, banging the remaining tin that miraculously held to the roof against the dormitory wall. Periodic downpours replaced the heavy sheets of rain. Absent the strong winds, it was now possible to step outside, but there was no accessible place aside from the top of the staircase. As the rain subsided the team members surveyed the flowing waters looking for any sign of Anna and Marilou. Nothing extended above the water line aside from logjams or trees that had snapped in half. There was no sign of life in any direction. And even though they didn't expect a reply, they called into the floodwaters, hoping that the two girls who vanished in the night would reappear.

And although he didn't want to admit it, Pastor Rod was frightened. He wanted to believe that they were safe, but he knew in his heart that the two missing women were likely dead. The ferocious waters had risen too quickly for the girls to escape. And he knew that they would have had difficulty surviving the ferocity of the winds if they remained above the water. The debris that pounded the church and the dormitories would surely have pounded the girls. And even the best of swimmers couldn't have survived rapid floodwaters in the blackness of night. As the waters flowed back towards the sea, Pastor Rod hoped to see Anna and Marilou float by, hanging onto a coconut tree that had been blown down by Kiko. He prayed out loud as he watched the waters swirl by, tears streaming down his face. Others joined him in prayer. They all knew that the outlook for the girls was grim.

Pastor Rod didn't have time to plan their evacuation from the church the night before. In their escape they left behind their purified water, and they had all become parched. They all thirsted, but not one asked for anything to drink. Aside from water that fell onto their faces, they had nothing to drink since the juice that Marilou had provided to them the night before. Rod turned to Sean and asked, "Do you think the water container with the purifier is still floating inside the church?"

"I sure hope so. The Sawyer filters can make nasty pond water cleaner than bottled water from the grocery store. We're going to need some soon." Sean was eager to do something, he felt so helpless. He added, "I'll check as soon as the water level drops."

"I'll go with you," said Pastor Mark. "I'm ready now." Pastor Mark surprised the others as he turned toward the water and stepped from the stairs into the murky flow from the upstairs balcony. He quickly discovered that the water was more than seven feet deep. The current was much stronger than he anticipated, and he was promptly taken towards the church even though he attempted to swim back towards the dormitory. He swam as hard as he could towards the church, and was able to grab the railing for the back porch and pull himself inside. He made it look intentional, but it was a close call. If he had missed the porch, he would have been swept downstream in the rushing torrent. The porch was elevated so he was able to stand up, but the waters came up to his chest. He looked around for a few minutes and managed to find the water filter floating in a corner. He emerged a few moments later and, smiling, he held up the blue water can. Through hand signals he indicated that the girls were not there.

Reno carefully monitored the depth of the waters, measuring the rate of decline as the water subsided. She timed six inches in twenty minutes. Then ten inches in thirty-five minutes. Soon the water was down by more than eighteen inches. David Kemp decided that it was worth another try to step into the water. The flow was still steady, but not as strong as when Pastor Mark had climbed into the water. Dr. Kemp lowered himself into the flowing water. It was chest deep and he was able to walk, but the flow made it impossible to navigate. The flow began to drag him downstream. He pushed with his legs and swam with his arms and was able to climb up the back stairs to Ramada Community Church. The water inside the church was now only waist deep.

David Kemp leisurely climbed the stairs and joined Pastor Mark on the second floor balcony in the back of the church. The team could have escaped the rising water on the porch the night before, but they would have been fully exposed to projectiles hurled by Kiko's brutal winds. They made the right decision by seeking shelter in the dormitory rooms. With no walls around them for protection, they would have been injured or killed by projectiles or blown into the water by the fierceness of the wind. The second floor balcony now provided a good vantage point to look for Anna and Marilou. David and Pastor Mark scanned the horizon, but they saw no sign of life.

The waters receded further, and the bottom became visible through the cloudy flow. The entire team would soon be able to step into the waters and look for Anna and Marilou. Pastor Rod was concerned that team members could be injured as they stepped though the water. Debris was everywhere, and littered the bottom of the water.

Sharp pieces of twisted metal, broken glass and jagged sticks could easily puncture their rubber shoes. And all of them had seen reptiles swimming in the water. Two giant '*bayawak*', a type of carnivorous monitor lizard, found refuge on the dormitory steps before being chased away by Manny Angara. And a Philippine cobra climbed into their shelter on the second floor of the dormitory in the darkness. They didn't notice it until after daybreak. And rather than risk getting bitten, they simply gave it plenty of space. If anyone was bitten they would have no access to a doctor or hospital, so the snake was permitted to share their shelter. They planned to move back downstairs as soon as the floodwater permitted them to do so.

Pastor Rod stayed with the remainder of the mission team until it was safe to leave the second floor of the dormitory. Then he went down the stairs to see if the downstairs could, once again, be inhabited. He knew that this place would be their shelter for the next day or two and the cement roof would protect them from more rain, which would surely come.

"Reno, could I ask you, Angie, Ashley, and Jun to remove the remaining water and mud from downstairs?" Pastor Rod knew that they considered him the team leader and expected for him to make team decisions.

Without tools it was difficult to accomplish much, so Brother Jun walked around the dormitory and picked up several pieces of wood. He demonstrated how he intended to use them saying, "We can push the water and mud out the door using these." He asked Angie in Tagalog, "Please find a bucket, a cup, or anything that will hold water, we will need it to rinse the floor once the mud is gone." Angel joined them and the mud was quickly removed using their makeshift tools.

The crew began to sweat in the heat and humidity. Reno asked, "Could we filter some drinking water? We'll need to find a clean container to hold the clean water." Angie quickly volunteered saying, "I saw some 1.5 liter bottles with caps inside the church kitchen. Let me check to see if they are still there." She walked slowly across the muddy path between the dormitory and the church, and soon emerged carrying three large empty 1.5 liter bottles. She picked up the container for their water filter and filled it in a deep puddle. Soon they had three full bottles of drinkable water. They shared the water and then they refilled the bottles. Muddy puddle water never tasted so good.

They were soaked just as much from their own sweat as from the floodwater. The dense humidity smothered them. They wanted to search for Marilou and Anna. Pastor Rod knew that they needed to remain busy to take their minds off of their lost teammates. They had learned to rely on God for answers, and they had been praying fervently. Where were the answers? Why wasn't God answering their ardent prayers?

The water subsided to the point where land replaced water dominating the landscape. Garbage was everywhere, and strange bits of items that had been snatched from homes by the raging waters. A broken guitar and a computer printer from the church could be seen sitting in the mud. Busted plastic chairs, curtains, pots and pans, a canister of propane gas, pictures in frames ... the landscape was littered with pieces of the past. A new reality covered the countryside.

Sean asked Pastor Mark, "Will you walk with me to look for the girls?"

"Of course", answered Pastor Mark. "Maybe we can send out three teams, each with a Filipino to translate. Jun! Angel! *Halika dito.*" As the men approached, Sean called Tyler and David to join them.

"Tyler, you, and Brother Jun can head back towards the main highway to look for Anna and Marilou. Pastor Mark and I are going to walk in the upstream direction as water flowed in last night. And Angel, if you and David could walk in the other direction, just in case they were swept downstream by the receding waters." Sean, as a staff member at Eastside Christian Fellowship, was second in command. People recognized his authority as one of the leaders of the team. He spoke to the men, saying, "Let's pray before we go." He led them in prayer, crying as he prayed, and they all wiped away tears after he said "amen."

"Let's take our time and look everywhere. We don't want to imagine that they might be trapped under debris, but make sure to look in the piles of logs and everywhere, okay?" Sean had faced the grim reality that the girls may be dead. The others knew it too, but nobody articulated it as Sean had done. Sean spoke up again, "Let's plan to be back at the church in about an hour and a half; has everyone got a watch or some way to tell time?" They nodded and each of the three teams trudged through the mud in their designated direction.

Pastor Mark had relatives that lived less than a mile away from the church. He knew this area well and had often visited as a child. He played in these fields, swam in the nearby river, and stole coconuts from the local plantations. He decided to go straight to his uncle's house to ask for their help in finding Marilou and Anna. They examined bushes and clumps of debris as they walked, finding nothing. There was a commotion near Mark's uncle's home, and they quickly joined his family outside the house.

Pastor Mark's auntie was wailing and crying, and unable to stand because she was so stricken with grief. The body of her daughter's closest friend had washed up against the edge of their home and was pinned by the waters to the wooden roof supports. She hung upside down from the rafters and was grotesquely swollen from the floodwater. The girl was more than just a neighbor; she was an extended part of the family, spending much of her young life in this very house. Pastor Mark climbed up the side of the house and helped lower the girl to the ground. They were grateful that her best friend, Mark's cousin, was in Manila and did not see her friend in this condition.

Sean wondered if either Anna or Marilou could swim. Neither of them was particularly athletic, and they would have faced incredibly challenging conditions. They would not have been able to see what was in front of them, next to them, or underneath them due to the blackness of the night. The winds were ferocious when they disappeared, hurtling dangerous debris through the air. It's unlikely that they could have remained together. The realization that he might actually lose one of his team members suddenly struck him, like flying debris. What would he say to Anna's parents when he returned home? How could he possibly face them? Her parents relied on her help and loved her above everything else.

Tyler and Jun walked to the highway south of the church. It was elevated above the surrounding terrain and people had gathered in small groups along the roadside. Jun asked if anyone had seen an American woman, and the answer was negative. They hoped that Marilou and Anna were together in one of the houses along the road. Most of the cement homes were intact. And even though they were missing the roofs they appeared as though they may have offered safety from the storm. Tyler was stunned when they came across three bodies laid out in the roadway. One was a small child and the others were either teenagers or young adults. He reached for his cell phone to take a picture and Brother Jun immediately chastised him.

"What's wrong with you, Tyler? These people are grieving, suffering and in pain, and you want to take pictures of them?" Jun was livid. He had seen Tyler's immaturity, but he expected better judgment from the teenager than this.

"I'm sorry," said Tyler. "I really wasn't thinking." Reaching for his cell phone was instinctive. It's what he had been conditioned to do whenever something unusual appeared in front of him. And this was the first time he had witnessed death up close.

Jun quickly turned away from Tyler and began to walk towards the river bridge. Tyler trotted up behind him and said, "I said I'm sorry." Jun wasn't interested in Tyler's apology; he just wanted to finish their search and return to the church. He wished he'd been paired with someone else.

David and Angel had been given the most challenging route. There was no road to walk on and the mud was thick. The current had created many huge debris piles, and some of them were so large that it was impossible to know what was contained beneath them. A horrible sight awaited them as they navigated around a massive pile of trees and rubble. Legs stuck out from the pile of trees! The two men accepted the grim responsibility of removing the body from the debris. They couldn't see the upper torso or face, but this clearly wasn't Anna. The body was swollen from the water, and had been battered, as it washed downstream. Gashes and abrasions covered the body, which was badly disfigured. Bones had snapped and the body was contorted. The men lifted branches and David used a huge branch as a lever to lift a large log that held the body in place. They finally freed the victim, and to their horror, discovered that it was Marilou!

David and Angel laid her atop the mud and adjusted her clothing that had been partially removed. They hugged each other and cried. Angel had known Marilou her entire life. He was friends with her older brother and teased her as she grew up. They needed help carrying her body, but where would they bring her? There was no reason to bring her to the dormitory, and the local cemetery was miles away.

"Should we bury her here?" asked Dr. Kemp. David was being pragmatic. He knew that the sight of Marilou's disfigured body would be traumatic for the others if they carried her back. "We can take pictures for identification; I could also take a hair sample that can be DNA tested." Local protocol could be abandoned during a crisis like this. The coroner couldn't possibly certify all of the deaths in person. Hundreds of bodies needed to be buried as soon as possible, and most would need to be buried where they were discovered; trees, flooding, and wreckage blocked the route to the cemetery.

Angel spoke softly, "I've known this sweet girl since she was born. I would like to bring her to her family." And even as he spoke he thought about her family's reaction to the sight of her battered body.

"There's no way we can return her to Baler anytime soon. And, think about this, Angel; would you rather see your sister this way, or learn that she died and was buried? Personally, I would rather know that my sister was gone than see her like this." David's observation struck Angel in the heart. He knew that David was right, but he loved Marilou's family. The Marcos family had fed him and purchased his school uniforms when he was young. Marilou's father helped him get his job as a security guard. How could he possibly bury her here in the mud?

Angel sat next to Marilou and hugged her lifeless body. He prayed out loud for guidance, for her family, and for strength. Tears poured in streams down his face. Finally he turned to David and said, "I agree with you. Let's bury her here, but let's agree not to tell anyone. I would rather her family hold out false hope that she's alive than know that I buried her here. They would never forgive me, David."

David thought for a moment before he answered. The thought of lying about her death seemed wrong. But he thought of her family's anguish and the distress that would result if they told the team of her death, and he decided to agree with Angel. "Okay. I won't say anything if you don't. We'll pretend that this never happened."

The mud was soft and digging was easy. Angel found a bucket that served as a shovel, and David found a piece of metal that helped loosen the soil. The grave was shallow, little more than three feet deep, but adequate considering the circumstances. They laid Marilou in the shallow grave and both prayed aloud, asking the Lord to comfort her family and forgive them for their deceit. They covered her with mud and placed two large logs atop the shallow grave to prevent any animal from digging up her body. They rinsed off in a nearby puddle, and trudged back towards the church.

They all craved answers. Why would God allow his children to suffer in this way? They were serving people who needed medical help. They came to serve the suffering and had become the suffering. What had happened to Anna and Marilou? What would they tell their families? And even though they searched for answers, God would not provide them with answers. Not today.

The mission team continued to search the surrounding region for the remainder of the day. At times the rain pounded down, and lightning accompanied some of the heavier rain. It became apparent that their search for the girls was futile. If they were alive they would be found and cared for by others. The survival of the remaining team members became the immediate need. Aside from a couple of snacks, they had no food. The heat and humidity were oppressive and began to lower their spirits. Their clothes were wet, as were the contents of their bags. Everything was wet, including cell phones, laptop computers, cameras … they hadn't prepared for this.

The team became more pessimistic as the day progressed. When the sun came up they were optimistic that Anna and Marilou would be found alive and healthy. The team had survived the storm and the winds and rain subsided early in the day. And as the floodwaters flowed back towards the ocean, they were certain that the worst was over. But the heat, humidity, mosquitoes, lack of electricity, and inability to find Anna and Marilou had cast a negative shadow over the entire team. They felt little comfort from God. Their faith was rigorously tested.

Chapter 22 – Miracle
Thursday, 1:00pm August 10th
Maria Aurora, Philippines

After several hours of searching for Marilou and Anna, Pastor Rod decided that the team needed to find food, rehydrate, and get out of the hot sun. They retreated into the downstairs dormitory room because the roof to the church was gone. It was small, crowded and hot. But they had drinking water and shade. Pastor Rod gave money to Manny and Jun and asked them to find food for their group. Surely someone had a pig, goat, chickens or a cow that had survived the storm. Tilapia that had escaped from local fishponds now skimmed through muddy puddles, and Reno, Kelly and Angie laughed as they chased them through the shallow waters. Papaya, coconuts, bananas, and other fruit lay on the ground aside the trees that produced them. Food would soon be coming, and for Tyler and Sean it couldn't come soon enough; they were famished.

Two women appeared at the gate of the church, carrying a small girl on a makeshift stretcher. They called out, and Angel quickly ran to assist them. The bed sheet they used to transport the girl was bloody and the girl wasn't moving. Reno quickly sprang into action. "David, please get my backpack for me – it's the red one on the end by the door. Have Rod and Ashley clear off a dry space where we can lay her down." She ran with Angie towards the women and asked questions as they traveled the last forty feet to the dormitory.

"How old is she? What is her name? How did this happen? How long ago? Who is the mother?" Angie absorbed all of the information and relayed it to Reno. The girl's name was Karen Coloma and she was seven years old. A huge tree branch fell on the girl about an hour before, and it took several men to lift the branch off of her. She had been knocked unconscious by the impact and hadn't moved since. She was breathing and her heart was beating, which was a miracle considering that her chest was crushed, her sternum broken and most of her ribs had been shattered. Miraculously her heart and lungs were still functioning. A huge cut, from the top of her forehead to her lips bled steadily.

Pastor Rod and Angel led the women away from the dorm and began to pray with them in the shade of a jackfruit tree that managed to remain standing. Its leaves were gone, but the branches still provided a bit of shade. The prayer was as much a distraction for the women as it was a plea to God for mercy. Karen was laid on the floor of the dormitory atop a damp blanket and Reno quickly stitched the facial wound to stem the flow of blood. She was certain that there was internal bleeding as well, but she wasn't prepared to perform any surgical procedure. All she could do was stabilize the girl, provide some pain relief, and pray. She gently rested her hand on the girl's broken body and prayed for a miracle. And a moment later, the girl began to cry softly. Her eyes opened and she tried to move. Reno expected Karen to be in enormous pain when she awakened, but there was no grimace on her face. Angie called for her mother, who quickly joined Reno and Karen.

"Angie, ask her if she knew her name." Reno watched incredulously as the girl's hands and feet began to move. The paralysis that Reno feared was no longer a concern.

"*Anong pangalan mo, Iha?*" Angie asked in Tagalog, and the girl answered quickly and politely, "Karen Coloma, *po.*" Angie asked her age, "*Elan taon ka na dao?*" They both smiled when the answer was provided in English: "Seven, *po.*" Karen was alert and responding clearly to questions. And, except for her shallow breathing, she didn't appear to be in any discomfort. Karen's mother stroked her hair and asked Angie if she could let her daughter drink water. Angie replied in Tagalog, telling the mother that water might harm Karen due to her internal injuries. Reno heard her say the word "hemolysis" and she gave Angie a 'thumbs up.' Water could dilute the blood, releasing the hemoglobin and hastening the effects of blood loss.

Reno studied the girl's face. She was smiling as she talked with her mother. She remembered seeing the falling tree limb, but didn't remember being hit. Karen had no problem moving her fingers or toes on command. The stitches had stopped the external bleeding, and God had apparently repaired the rest. Before Angie or Reno could do anything about it, Karen sat upright. It took no effort for her to do so and she still demonstrated no signs of pain. Angie sat next to Karen on the blanket and held her hand against Karen's damaged ribs. "Can you feel this?" she asked the girl. Karen nodded and answered, "*Opo.*" She felt Angie's touch. "Does it hurt?" Karen responded, "*Hindi, po.*" meaning "no, ma'am."

Angie was certain that she had just witnessed a miracle. Karen was all but dead when her mother laid her on the floor. And now she was sitting up and talking without any signs of pain. She watched Reno pray for the girl moments before she awakened and attributed Karen's new life as the direct result of Reno's prayer. Reno had seen other miraculous recoveries, but nothing like this. She examined Karen's chest and ribs and could no longer feel the fractures. She lowered her head, closed her eyes and spoke to God once again, this time thanking the Great Physician for what he had done to heal Karen.

Manny and Jun returned with two wicker baskets filled with fruit, meat, and fish. They had even found a few kilos of dry rice to cook. They would all eat soon. Tyler had been picking up dry wood and stacking it up to be used for a cooking fire. He had never been involved in scouting, yet he expertly sized and stacked small branches in places where they would continue to dry even though the rain came and went. Angel found two sheets of tin and leaned them against one another to keep their fire out of the rain. It wasn't raining, but they knew that more would soon come. Ashley found a knife on the church floor and she rinsed it off and began to slice papaya. Everyone seemed busy, including the woman who helped Karen's mother carry Karen to the church. She sliced garlic and onions to season the pork that was being prepared by Manny. The activity helped keep their minds off of their situation.

Angie thought of her little sister, Sophie, who was a year younger than Karen. She fought back tears as she thought of what Sophie must have gone through over the past 24 hours. Sophie loved Angie more than anything and spent more time with her than anyone else. Angie was Sophie's best friend, mother and sister all rolled into one. And now, as the storm waned, Angie thought of going home to look for her family. But she knew that the roads were impassable; she would have to wait another day or two to find out the fate of her family. Reno saw her deep in thought and approached Angie. "God's still on his throne, Angie. Everything will be fine." She knew what was on Angie's mind and she gave her a loving hug. Angie began to sob and Reno wiped her tears with her own blouse.

Several more patients came to the church for treatment before the food was ready. Reno reset a dislocated shoulder and broken arm. Dr. Kemp joined Reno in stitching wounds and dispensing antibiotic ointments. Most of their bandages were wet, but the medication they had carried with them remained sealed. Brother Jun took all of the available medical supplies and moved them under the overhang of the dormitory from the church. Miraculously, all but two of their blue plastic tubs of medical supplies remained in the church office during the storm. The lid on one of the tubs had remained sealed, so he was able to supply David and Reno with clean gauze and bandages. Pastor Rod helped him sort the medications into separate tubs after wiping them clean. Aside from tongue depressors, cotton swabs, bandages, gauze and some Tagalog Bibles, their equipment and supplies seemed to be intact.

The racket of distant chain saws was, for once, a welcome noise. It meant that the roads were being cleared, and that help would soon be able to reach this community. Pastor Rod was eager to return home to Gina; he supposed that buses, trucks, and vans would soon be able to navigate the road back to Manila. The entire team was weary of the heat, uncomfortable from the moisture and mosquitoes, and horrified by the fact that they could not find Anna or Marilou. They had enough medical supplies to last two or three more days. Pastor Rod prayed for Anna and Marilou every few minutes. He couldn't imagine going home without Anna. Her parents needed her. And Pastor Rod needed for her to be okay; it would be impossible to return to Charleston without her.

Chapter 23 – New reality
Thursday, 4:30am (EST) August 10th
Atlanta, GA USA

"I'm Trisha Handy in Atlanta and this is BREAKING NEWS from CNN. CNN has received evidence that points to the People's Republic of China as the culprit behind the two massive bomb blasts that ripped through Davao City Airport in the Southern Philippines just sixteen hours ago. Satellite images obtained by CNN show the assailants leaving the port at Davao City on what appear to be two large fishing vessels. And just six hours later these same boats joined together with a small group of Chinese military vessels that are clearly within Philippine territorial waters. CNN has confirmed that hundreds of Chinese vessels are converging on various regions of the Philippines just hours after Super Typhoon Kiko struck the island nation. Here's more from our correspondent, Tito Raza in Davao City."

"As you can see behind me, the Davao City airport has been shredded by two massive explosions around midnight last night. The initial speculation was that Islamic extremists were responsible, but new information places the blame clearly on the People's Republic of China. With me is Davao City Mayor, Raymundo Vicente. Mr. Mayor, what can you tell us about the two midnight blasts, and why do you suspect the PRC?"

"Thank you, Tito, for having me as your guest. As soon as we saw the magnitude of the blasts we knew that the weapons were far too sophisticated to have been detonated by terrorists. This is clearly the work of another nation, and we have only one enemy in the region, and that is the PRC."

"But what actually links these blasts to the PRC, sir?"

"We were able to find four communication suppressors that were hidden throughout our city. They were placed in elevated locations to maximize their range, so we searched in elevated places until we retrieved them all. We opened them up and sent high-resolution photographs to FBI and CIA laboratories in the U.S. for analysis. And U.S. experts have confirmed that the devices are clearly Chinese in origin. We also have eyewitnesses who have told us that they saw Chinese men retreating to their getaway boats. And we now have satellite images that show their escape boats meeting up with Chinese military ships."

"Let me interrupt for a moment, Mr. Mayor, so that we can show our viewers images that have been obtained exclusively by CNN that show the boats as they escaped from Davao City. An alert citizen who wishes to remain anonymous saw the blasts and captured this footage. You can clearly see these men are carrying automatic weapons as they leapt onto boats at Davao Harbor. And here, eight hours later, are the same boats as they join up with a group of Chinese military vessels near the coast of Borneo."

"I'm hearing now that the People's Republic of China has released a statement, so let's go now back to Trisha Handy in Atlanta to hear the statement released from Ji Man Feng, Chairman of the Communist Party's Central Propaganda Department. Trisha."

"Thank you, Tito, we'll return to you in a moment. The PRC has been implicated in the Davao City bombings and Chairman Feng responded with this statement: 'The People's Liberation Army is currently assisting many other vessels in bringing relief to the people of the Philippines in the wake of Typhoon Kiko. We consider Filipinos to be our friends and neighbors, and despite our territorial disputes, we do not wish any harm to our Filipino comrades. We categorically deny any involvement in the dastardly bombings in Davao City, and we offer our assistance to help the Filipino people in the aftermath of both disasters.'"

"The PRC is clearly denying responsibility for the bombings in Davao City. But this brief statement doesn't address the specific accusations levied against the PRC. There is no mention of the communications devices, satellite images or hundreds of their vessels converging on the Philippines. We have Mr. Jian Chan, the PRC Ambassador to the US, with us now. Thank you, Ambassador Chan, for joining us on short notice. You've heard the accusations against your country, and you have seen the statement released by your government. What can you add to this discussion?"

"Thank you, Trisha, for giving me a chance to respond to the false accusations being directed at the People's Republic of China. We are just as appalled at the horrible carnage in Davao City as the rest of the world. I have been in touch with our most senior leadership and have been assured that we are not involved in any way with what has taken place in Davao City. I believe that CNN is guilty of recklessness by accusing the PRC of involvement in the bombing without better evidence; it serves no purpose except to create more stress in an already tense situation.

"I would like to address your report that hundreds of vessels from the PRC are now on their way to the Philippines; that is true. Our port authorities asked the captains of hundreds of our vessels to seek shelter from Kiko in the open ocean rather than in port. If you look at the trajectory of the storm you will see that our nation is also a target for Typhoon Kiko. It will be a strong CAT 4 storm when it impacts our southern coast. Therefore, we ordered all vessels capable of avoiding the storm to leave port, as they would be safer in the open sea. These vessels have now been ordered to deliver assistance to our Filipino brothers and sisters in the wake of Typhoon Kiki, so they will offload any food, potable water, medical supplies, or other products that might be needed by the Filipino people."

"There are so many unanswered questions, Ambassador Chan. The CIA and FBI have said that the communications suppressors are of Chinese origin. And we now have satellite images that indicate that the culprits in the Davao bombing have met with several PRC military vessels in Philippine territorial waters. How do you respond to those charges, sir?"

"I have no information regarding the communications devices found in Davao City, so it would be inadvisable for me to address them at this time. I was informed that our navy has, indeed, intercepted two vessels that fled after the bombings in Davao City. Our navy has taken several men into custody and they are now escorting those boats back to Davao City. We are in contact with the Philippine Coast Guard as they return to Davao City."

"Can you disclose the nationality of those men, Mr. Ambassador?"

"I have been told that they are Filipino. We will have more details about the men when they are turned over to Philippine authorities."

"Why do you suppose, sir, that we are not hearing any news from Manila?"

"I'm not in the business of supposition, Trisha, I'm a diplomat. I would gladly share information with you if I had it. We're all eager to know what is happening in Manila after Typhoon Kiko. But I'm as puzzled by the silence as you are."

"Thank you, Mr. Ambassador for taking the time to speak with us. We appreciate your candor."

"Thank you, Trisha. I am pleased that you have allowed me to keep your viewers informed."

"Ambassador Chan has reported to us that PRC naval forces have intercepted the two fishing vessels that fled Davao City after last night's airport bombing. He admonished us for jumping to conclusions, and stated that he is just as baffled as we are regarding the silence out of Manila. Let's return now to our CNN correspondent, Tito Raza who is with Davao City mayor, Ray Vicente, Tito."

"Thank you, Trisha. Moments ago we witnessed six fighter jets roar by overhead. We believe that they are American F-15's or FA-18 Hornets. If they are F-15's they have likely arrived here from Okinawa. If they are FA-18's they are likely part of a nearby U.S. carrier group. Our video of the aircraft is now being analyzed and we will provide you with details as we have them. Let me return Mayor Vicente. You heard the statement from Beijing and the comments of the PRC Ambassador to the U.S.; that are your thoughts?"

"It's exactly what I would expect from the Chinese government. Our nation is under attack from a cowardly enemy that has killed an unknown number of innocent passengers, airport workers, and security personnel here in Davao. Just look at the result! Our Air Force was their target. They knew that Davao would provide a safe shelter for our aircraft as Typhoon Kiko approached Luzon. It was premeditated. Their commandos were in place before the aircraft even arrived here!"

"Once again, Mr. Mayor, I apologize for interrupting. But we just received information from our bureau in Atlanta that the aircraft we filmed just a few minutes ago are Shenyang J-15's from China, also known as the Flying Shark. It is a twin engine, twin tail carrier-based aircraft. This would mean that these aircraft have come from the aircraft carrier Liaoning. Why would the Chinese launch fighter jets over Philippine skies, especially in the aftermath of the bombings?"

"My God! They are firing rockets at the port! Turn the camera around! The J-15's have returned in single file from the ocean to the south and they are dropping bombs and firing missiles at targets near the docks in Davao Harbor.

"There's no doubt whatsoever regarding a PRC invasion of the Philippines. We see additional aircraft that have joined the attack, and we see absolutely no response. We see incoming rockets, but we do not see any outgoing missiles. From our west we see dozens of aircraft approaching Davao. They are not fighter aircraft; they look more like transport aircraft. Focus on the transport planes! Men are parachuting from the aircraft, hundreds of them! We can see …"

"You are watching a CNN Special Live Report from Davao City in the Philippines. We just lost our live feed from our correspondent, Tito Riza in Davao City. He was interviewing Davao City Mayor Ray Vicente when they spotted a group of fighter jets identified as Chinese J-15's. The aircraft flew quickly over the city, then returned from the south, over the ocean, and attacked an area near the port. Tito observed some transport aircraft arriving from the west and reported that hundreds of men were parachuting into Davao from these aircraft.

"Let's take another look at the video of the fighter jets and the arrival of the transport planes."

Gina Franklin sat on the edge of her sofa and stared at her television set in disbelief. She fell asleep on the sofa just four hours earlier, unable to keep her eyes open any longer. She woke during the interview with the Chinese Ambassador to the United States. But as he spoke she believed his words sounded more like an alibi than fact. And now that Davao City was being invaded by the People's Liberation Army, what did that mean for Rod and the missionaries in Aurora? Could they possibly escape from an island nation at war?

Gina's phone was in silent mode and it began to vibrate on the coffee table. Someone else was awake and watching TV. She didn't even check to see who was calling; instead she placed her face in her hands and sobbed.

Chapter 24 – Uneasy sleep
Thursday, 10:30pm August 10th
Maria Aurora, Aurora Province, Philippines

Reno normally slept soundly at night. Tom frequently teased her about how quickly she fell asleep. She would lie down while Tom brushed his teeth, and before he could return to the bed Reno would be comatose. Reno was a creature of habit, and her normal habits had been abandoned during the mission trip, especially since the storm began. Her normal diet, exercise routine, and devotional time had been discarded, and now her sleep suffered from it. When she wasn't slapping mosquitoes, Reno was praying for Marilou and Anna. She added Angie's family to her prayers, particularly her baby sister, Sophie. The winds had shifted and now came from the south, carrying heat from the rice fields of Nueva Ecija with them.

The howling winds were gone, and the pounding rain had vanished. In their place came penetrating heat and suffocating humidity. Reno thought about Betsy, one of the senior women in the church. Betsy was now eighty-eight years old and she still talked about returning to the Philippines as a short-term missionary. Betsy made the difficult trip to the Aurora province three times after her eightieth birthday, which is remarkable considering the heat, power outages, and physical rigor required of the team members; and she had managed quite well. Betsy planned to be part of this team, and Reno was glad that she had changed her mind. Although healthy for an 88-year-old woman, the escape from the church to the dormitory during Typhoon Kiko may have been too much for her. Reno loved Betsy and thanked God that she was home safe.

Reno was never more than arms length away from Angie when they slept, and she moved Angie's hair off of her angelic face. Angie looked like a child, especially while sleeping and Reno wondered how anyone so spiritually and emotionally mature could appear so much like a child physically. Angie had flawless skin, perfect teeth, and delicate features and Reno admired her, thinking that Angie was asleep. But Angie wasn't sleeping either. She rolled onto her side and smiled at Reno. And in that moment Reno felt all her anxieties vanish. She smiled back at Angie, then leaned down and gave her a hug. Reno wasn't normally a hugger. In fact, she felt uncomfortable when people in the church felt obligated to hug one another as they met. But with Angie, she wanted to hug her. She needed for Angie to know how much she meant to her. She wanted for Angie to feel loved.

Pastor Rod snored loudly, and Tyler snorted harmony with him. The entire team was restless, slapping mosquitoes and turning over on the hard cement floor every few minutes. Frogs croaked loudly in the darkness, and dogs barked in the distance. Reno could hear every minute noise, even Ashley's troubled breathing. Reno had noticed that Ashley was struggling at times to take in a full breath and she asked Ashley about it. Ashley dismissed it, saying that she had allergies, but Reno suspected that she was asthmatic. Three drunken fireflies bounced off the ceiling and walls, igniting like a small fireball every two or three seconds in a different part of the room. Reno could see them glow through her eyelids.

As they prepared for the trip, Tom had informed Reno that the team would be able to see a partial lunar eclipse in the Philippine sky early in the morning on the 8th of August. But once the team learned about Typhoon Kiko everything else was forgotten. Reno couldn't remember whether it was clear or cloudy on Tuesday night when the eclipse took place. She was disappointed that she'd missed it, more for Tom's sake than her own. Such things fascinated him, so Reno feigned fascination to feed his enthusiasm. She missed him. She knew that Tom was going crazy as he worried about her. She was eager to finish dispensing the remaining medications and return home.

Reno closed her eyes, hoping to sleep, but Anna and Marilou's disappearance haunted her thoughts. What if they were seriously injured and still alive? Maybe their injuries made it impossible to get back to the church. Hopefully someone found them and was caring for them. She wanted closure that would never come.

Reno heard a soft voice outside. It was a woman's voice and she was speaking English. Reno stood and walked swiftly to the door and opened it. The moon was bright and stars shone through silvery clouds. She didn't see anyone, so she stepped from the porch onto the gravel and walked a few steps towards the church. She heard the voice again, but it was more distant. It was clearly a woman speaking American English. She strained to make out the words as they faded into the night. She wanted to yell out, hoping that it was Anna, but she didn't want to startle those who had fallen asleep. She took several more steps towards the front of the church and stopped to listen.

This time the voice was louder, and seemed to grow closer. She could hear two women talking, and they were not far away. The moon was bright and Reno could make out the silhouettes of two people walking towards her. They were in the shadow of an ancient banyan tree, but Reno could see them trudging slowly, arm in arm. Two dogs barked loudly at the figures as they walked out of the shadows into the bright moonlight. It was Anna and Marilou! Reno ran towards them and called their names. Anna called out, "Reno, I'm so glad to see you." Anna and Reno hugged one another. Then Reno hugged Marilou.

"Where have you been? We've been worried sick. We thought we'd lost you." Reno could barely breathe. It had been nearly twenty-four hours since the girls had vanished and so much had happened during that time. Reno had witnessed a miracle early in the day as Karen Coloma survived impossible injuries. And now she had witnessed a second miracle; Anna and Marilou were alive!

"Marilou was hit by a palm branch as we tried to make it from the church to the dormitory and it knocked us both down. We tried to stand up, but the waters were flowing and the footing was difficult. We yelled for help, but I guess with all of the noise from the storm you couldn't hear us." Anna beamed at Reno and hugged her again. "We were quickly carried downstream and the waters got even deeper. It was pitch black and we couldn't see a thing. Marilou and I got separated and the wind was deafening, so even though we called out we couldn't hear each other. It was horrible! I've never been so frightened."

Marilou turned to Anna and said, "You should tell her now." Anna nodded in agreement.

"Tell me what?" asked Reno.

"God has his hand on you, Reno. I've known it from the first time we met. You don't just talk about God: you live for Him. While others *say* what they believe, you actually *do* what you believe. Are you following me?" Anna had not answered Reno's question, and Reno was now confused.

"What is it that you want to say to me?" Reno felt uncomfortable receiving praise for her faith, especially now. She wanted to bring the girls back to the dormitory so that the others could celebrate their return.

"Your faith is going to be tested, Reno. You'll soon face the most difficult decisions of your life. You're going to have an opportunity to take up your cross and follow Christ, and it will be most difficult. But you cannot fathom the impact of your obedience." Anna spoke with a smile, and placed her hand on Reno's shoulder as she spoke. Marilou stood a couple of paces behind Anna as she spoke.

Marilou then stepped forward, nodding and added, "God has chosen you to do a marvelous thing, Reno."

Reno looked at the girls in amazement. She studied them in silence for a moment, and then she became frightened. Neither of the girls were cut or injured in any way, and considering what they had both endured, it seemed impossible that they could suffer such turmoil without injury. Even their clothes had not been torn.

Anna looked directly into Reno's eyes and said, "Do what is right. You'll know what I'm talking about when the time comes." With that, Marilou and Anna turned and began walking back towards the shadow of the large banyan tree.

Reno called out to them, but they kept walking. "Where are you going? The rest of the team wants to see you!"

The two girls ambled slowly away together, arm-in-arm without speaking again. Soon they disappeared into the night. "Anna! Wait for me," Reno began to jog down the muddy dirt road to catch up with the girls. "Hold up! Wait for me."

"Who are you talking to?" asked Angie. Pastor Rod was a few steps behind her. His shirt was misaligned, with buttons placed through the wrong holes as he quickly got dressed.

Reno wasn't sure what to say. Did she just see Marilou and Anna? Or was she sleepwalking? Reno answered, "I heard voices, so I came outside to see who it was."

Rod asked, "So who was it?"

"I believe that I saw Anna and Marilou, but now I'm not so sure." Reno was confused. It seemed real. She even smelled Anna's perfume when she hugged her.

"What did they say?" asked Angie. Angie had grown up with many superstitions, and she paid attention to dreams, especially when sleepwalking. Her mother believed in the spirit world and even offered food to the spirits in exchange for protection.

"They said that God would test me, and they told me to do the right thing." Reno paraphrased what they had said, but it was essentially the message she had received from the two girls.

"What kind of test? Did they provide you with anything specific?" Rod was now asking the questions.

"No" answered Reno. "Anna said I would know what she was talking about when the time comes."

"I believe it was just a dream," said Pastor Rod. The girls aren't here, and I'm sure if they returned they would remain with us. I think the trauma of the last couple days has gotten to all of us. Come on, let's go back inside and get some rest while we can."

Angie held Reno's hand and walked with her back to the dormitory. Reno seemed a bit confused, which was unusual for her, and Angie seemed concerned. "I saw you get up and walk out the door, but I thought you were going outside to pee. I woke up Pastor Rod when you didn't come back." Angie let Reno step up into the dormitory first, and then followed her into the darkened room. It took a moment before their eyes adjusted to the darkness, and Angie and Reno returned to the place where they had lain before Reno went outside.

"I believe that you spoke with them," said Angie in a whisper. "I think that God sent them to you to prepare you for something."

"Let's hope that I was just overtired and was walking in my sleep. Thanks for looking out for me, Angie." Reno laid her head on a makeshift pillow made from her dirty clothes. She knew that there would be no sleep tonight, so she closed her eyes and prayed, asking the Lord for strength.

Chapter 25 – The phone call
Thursday, 10:30am (EST) August 10th
Washington DC

President Clover listened carefully to her foreign policy advisors, taking notes as she prepared to call PRC President Xi Huang. She would first convey, in the strongest terms possible, that the United States condemned the PRC military invasion of the Philippines. She would explain that America was bound by treaty with the Philippines to defend their long-term ally, and that the US would act in accordance with this obligation. President Xi Huang needed to know that the fight to regain Philippine sovereignty would not be limited to the Philippine islands; the Chinese mainland would be targeted and the Chinese people would suffer until they retreated entirely from the Philippines. And the Chinese economy, which had been so strong over the past three decades, would suffer from worldwide sanctions.

President Clover reviewed her notes, and asked, "What is our intention for Chinese vessels as we enforce a worldwide embargo?"

"We would escort them to the nearest friendly port, where we would detain their crew, sequester their cargo and impound their vessels." Dwayne McCloud, her senior advisor handed her a list of talking points. "You have to convince them that there is no other option; they will pay a price that is too high unless they withdraw from the Philippines."

"Make sure that they understand that the Joint Chiefs of Staff have already convened and have ordered a military response. They can see what we are doing from satellite images and will know that it isn't an empty threat." Dwayne believed he understood the Chinese well. He served as an intelligence analyst in the Far East division and specialized in Chinese affairs. He spoke fluent Mandarin and he had even served inside the U.S. Embassy in Beijing for a short period of time.

"It's getting late in Beijing, Madam President. We need to make the call now."

The diplomatic hotline always seemed awkward. Interpreters needed to be available before the call was placed, and each President would speak a complete thought before the interpreter would convey what was said. The calls were recorded so that they could be analyzed and the recordings were saved for legal reasons. This would be the most difficult call of her life. President Clover would threaten the President of the largest army in the world with war and hope that her words were fierce enough to change their course of action.

"President Xi Huang is on the line, Ma'am." She nodded and the speaker phone was turned on so that everyone present could listen in.

"President Xi," she began, "please accept my apologies for calling so late in the evening. My staff has been working diligently to prepare a suitable response to your incursion in the Philippines. I hope that we are able to come to an understanding."

"Madam President," began President Xi, "my line is always open to you at any hour of the day. I also hope that we will be able to arrive at a mutually agreeable understanding. Let me explain our situation. The government of the Philippines has, for a number of years, defied our demand that they recognize our sovereignty over the South China Sea. But instead of entering into dialog with us, they filed cases against the PRC in international courts and have decided to use the United Nations to claim our sovereign territory. When you poke a bee's nest, you will be stung."

President Clover countered, "We are fully aware of your position regarding claims to most of the South China Sea. The Republic of the Philippines has acted prudently by seeking third party mediation instead of seizing your vessels that flaunt her borders or destroying the artificial islands that you have built within their territorial claim.   You have bullied your neighbors for far too long, and your actions in the Philippines have crossed the line." President Clover was taking the long route to an ultimatum.

"We have no quarrel with the United States. In fact our working relationship has grown stronger over the past two decades than ever before. I respect your administration and believe that we can avoid military conflict with one another. Before we finish our conversation, I will offer you a proposal that I believe you may find acceptable. War between our two nations will prove to be very costly for the entire world. First, it will be costly in human lives; we are prepared to sacrifice millions of our finest men to defend our sovereign territory. I do not think America is prepared to do the same. The people of both our nations will suffer, but ultimately we will prevail. The reason we will prevail is not because our military is stronger; we know that America will inflict great damage upon us. We will prevail because the American people will demand an end to the war as hundreds of thousands of your sons and daughters return home in body bags." President Xi was correct in his assessment. The American people were weary of war, and would demand an end to such a bloody conflict far before one hundred thousand soldiers were killed. America had not been attacked, the Philippines had.

"President Xi, the Philippines is more than an ally to the United States, they are our friends. We have agreed to defend them against attacks such as the incursion that you have committed, and we will fulfill our mutual defense treaty obligations. Your military analysts can confirm that our naval forces are already responding to the situation. They are awaiting my orders to attack. And please understand, sir, that your invaders in the Philippines will not be our only targets. We will attack your home. We are also prepared to fight and die, if necessary, to remove every soldier of the People's Liberation Army from the Philippines. And the reason that we will prevail is that we possess a vast technological advantage, some of which you have not yet seen. If you chose war, sir, it will not be a protracted war. We intend to end it quickly." President Clover was perspiring. She was also bluffing and President Xi knew it.

"Please Madam President; we both have the technological capacity to kill every living creature on the planet. Neither of us wants to make such threats. But you must understand our resolve in this matter. America has been involved for more than 100 years in the Philippines and you have failed your Filipino friends. They are the poorest nation in our region and they suffer from an oppressive system that keeps the people impoverished. Our nation is determined to liberate the Filipino people as we reclaim our sovereign territory. We have controlled this region as our sovereign territory for many centuries; far longer than America has been a nation. The Law of the Sea Treaty, which permits countries to claim a 200 nautical mile territorial limit, was an invention of your country that didn't exist until 1994. We will not sacrifice what has belonged to us for many centuries because of a twenty three year old invention of American imagination. Consider this before you command your military to fight and die."

"You mentioned that you were prepared to offer a proposal that might prevent war. I am interested to hear it. But please know that it must include complete withdrawal of your forces from the Philippines." President Clover struggled to maintain her stance. She desperately wanted to see diplomacy prevail over combat. Wars result from failed diplomacy, and President Clover was glad that President Xi was willing to negotiate. But the type of offer that would be extended would soon stun her.

President Xi began, "In 1898 America purchased the Philippines from Spain for twenty million dollars. We are prepared to purchase the Philippines from America for $1.4 trillion. That is the amount of U.S. debt that we currently hold. It is an increase of *seven million percent* on your 1898 investment in the Philippines. That works out to nearly a 59,000 percent increase per year, which is not a bad investment. Here is our proposal: we will forgive all $1.4 trillion of your debt that we hold in exchange for your inaction. You can threaten us and impose sanctions, provided they are lifted in a reasonable amount of time. You can even state that you'll refuse to repay the debt so long as we remain in the Philippines. We will seek no redress for this in the international courts. America will be able to save face, your economy will blossom, and millions of lives will be spared."

The translator struggled with the words. The meaning of the words was quite clear, but the content amazed him. He had served as an interpreter for more than twenty years and had been privy to many strange political arrangements between the PRC and the U.S., but this was the most incredible conversation that he had ever been part of. Even President Clover was visibly stunned. She didn't quite know what to say after President Xi laid out his offer. But it did not include her one condition. She hesitated for nearly ten second before she spoke, "That's a most creative offer, Mr. President. But we don't own the Philippines and cannot sell the nation to you. And your offer still does not meet my one condition. You must withdraw your forces at once from the Philippines."

President Xi was quick to respond. "Spain did not own the Philippines either, yet you purchased the Philippines from Spain. I respectfully ask that you meet with your cabinet to discuss my offer; that is all I ask. Before you initiate any aggression against us, at least discuss this option for peace. I believe it is generous. Your economy will soar rather than plummet. Your people will flourish rather than mourn. And our nations can work together instead of tearing each other apart. You have my pledge that no unnecessary violence will befall our Filipino comrades. Our desire is to minimize casualties and damage to infrastructure. We want the Philippines to prosper, and we are prepared to make an enormous investment to secure them a better future."

"You have my word, President Xi. We will discuss your offer, but if my cabinet officers reject it, I'm afraid that we are left with only one option. Our forces will continue to position themselves for combat, but no shots will be fired until I give the order. Restrain your forces also, so that nothing escalates tensions before we speak again." Even as she spoke the words President Clover couldn't believe they were flowing from her mouth. She had just agreed to examine an offer that included $1.4 trillion in exchange for doing nothing. And she had agreed to contact her enemy before launching an attack against them. As she hung up the phone President Clover looked around the room. All seven others in the room looked at her in astonishment, including the interpreter. This was a very unexpected twist, and President Clover wasn't sure how to respond.

"I want to remind you that what you have just heard is classified TOP SECRET. You may not discuss this information with anybody without my consent. Understand? Let's get everyone into the Cabinet Room immediately. I want the recording of this to play to the other cabinet members. Do not make any copies. I want to use the original. Dwayne, I need you to secure the recording and bring it to the Cabinet Room as soon as you make a transcript of it for each of my cabinet. Thanks everyone, we'll meet again after the cabinet discusses our options."

Even her body language suggested that President Clover considered President Xi's offer viable. She knew that war would destroy her chance of reelection, and the offer placed before her would allow her presidency to thrive. It would allow America to prosper. She had always been an anti-war candidate and had marched against the Vietnam War during her college years. She was now in a position to bring her nation into a bloody, costly war against the largest military power on Earth. Or she could offer harsh alternatives to punish the Chinese incursion and gain her nation $1.4 trillion dollars. She was eager to hear what her closest advisors would suggest. Anything seemed better than war against China.

Chapter 26 – Helicopters
Friday, 4:15am, August 11th
Maria Aurora, Aurora province, Philippines

Activity normally begins early in the day throughout the Philippines. Vendors move through neighborhoods on bicycles, honking horns and ringing bells as early as 4:00am. Shortly after 5:00 the dawn light spreads over the eastern horizon with spectacular bursts of color: yellow, orange, red, pink, and grey. The length of days remains consistent throughout the year because the nation is situated near the equator. Farmers work in the cool of the morning, long before the sun peeks over the eastern horizon. Smoke wafts through rural neighborhoods, hanging in the air as wood fires are lit to cook rice for breakfast. The intensity of roosters crowing builds into a deafening chorus as the sun rises, making sleep impossible except for drunkards or foreigners.

But this morning was different. The vendors were silent. The farmers remained home. And even the sound of roosters was absent. And a peculiar noise filled the pre-dawn air. Whop-whop-whop-whop-whop; the noise was a distant and steady. There was more than one, and the noise grew louder. The missionary team was still sleeping restlessly, but the distant noise caught Sean's attention. He sat up and listened carefully. It grew louder. He could make out the whine of engines and quickly recognized the sound as helicopter noise. And they were coming closer. The moon had already moved beyond the western horizon and dawn was an hour away, so the night sky was as black as the bottom of the deepest ocean. Sean stepped from the dormitory room to look for the helicopters in the sky.

It took only moments before the mysterious aircraft loomed overhead; they flew directly over the church, whooshing by quickly and loudly. They flew dangerously low and fast without lights. Sean tried to count them, but he couldn't distinguish the sound of one craft from another. He estimated that it was more than a dozen, but he remained uncertain. Pastor Rod appeared at the dormitory door using his cell phone as a flashlight. He saw Sean and quickly joined him.

"What was that?" Pastor Rod knew that a cluster of helicopters had just flown by, but what he really wanted to know was why they flew so low and without lights. Sean was thinking the same thing. If the aircraft were part of a relief effort why would they be hugging the treetops and flying so fast in such a mountainous region? And why would none of them use navigation lights?   Jun, Kelly, and David quickly joined them outside.

David spoke first, "They were close! Why were they flying so low?"

Sean answered, "I don't know, that was really strange. Where could they be going with so many of them together like that?"

Rod responded, "I don't know where they're going, but they came from Baler. Maybe there's a navy ship off the coast. Maybe we should try to catch their attention the next time they fly by; they might be able to get us out of here."

"The U.S. Embassy in Manila knows that we're here; we registered our plans with them online, so maybe they *are* looking for us." David was thinking out loud. He didn't really suspect that the aircraft that raced by in the darkness were looking for anyone – they were in a hurry to get somewhere.

Sean spoke up again, "None of them had their navigation lights on. Maybe it was some kind of military operation."

"Who would they be fighting?" asked Jun. "There's no insurgency here in Aurora, at least not anymore." Aurora had once been a hotbed of activity for the New People's Army, but the peace and order situation in Aurora was now quite good.

"How can we get their attention? If we want them to find us maybe we should start a big fire or spell out something on the ground with logs or something? Kelly offered a couple of suggestions based on TV programs that she'd seen. But she was right. There was no way that a group of Americans could be located from the air unless they made an extra effort to be noticed. Dawn would come soon, and they would figure it out then.

Rod said, "Let's talk about it in the morning. We can still get a couple more hours of sleep, so let's figure it out once the sun is up."

"I don't think I'll be able to go back to sleep" said Sean. "That was just weird. It makes no sense at all. If they are part of a rescue effort, why are they flying at night, especially so low and fast without lights? I think I'll stay outside for awhile."

The others opted to return to the hard cement dormitory floor to rest for another hour or two. And Sean found a large dry rock to sit on in a clearing beside the church. Clouds covered most of the sky and he felt an occasional raindrop. Sean had always been filled with questions. Christi teased him about asking more questions than their baby daughter, Hanna. Everything to Sean was like a puzzle, and he would not be able to rest until he fit a few things together. He did not believe that the helicopters were rescue aircraft; the speed and manner of their flight seemed incongruent with what he knew of rescue missions. They were intentionally hiding in the sky by flying without lights. Why? Sean mulled it over and could make no sense of it.

Sean was startled by a low growl to his left. He shone his light at a lone dog that was snarling and showing his teeth. The animal was inching forward. Sean quickly picked up a large rock, but the dog didn't back off. So Sean threw the stone at the menacing cur, missing the animal, but startling it. He picked up another rock, and as he did he heard another snarl behind him. Three more dogs had circled around behind him, and they stood between him and the safety of the dormitory. He picked up two more rocks and began to shout.

"I need some help out here! Help! I'm being attacked by dogs!" Sean continued to yell for help, and he screamed at the dogs, hoping that they would scatter, but they didn't. They stepped closer as Sean threw another rock, this time hitting the closest animal. The dog yelped loudly, but rather than running away it attacked Sean. Sean's athleticism allowed him to deflect the dog's lunge. He surprised a second dog with a kick that sent the dog tumbling along the ground. Sean then raced towards the dormitory, but he stumbled in the darkness and fell. Two of the dogs pounced on him before he could regain his footing. One grabbed his left wrist, its teeth cutting deeply, the other biting and ripping the back of his bare leg. "Help!" Sean flung the dog that was biting his wrist to the ground and kicked him in a single motion. But the dog was undeterred and resumed his attack. As he reached behind him to grab the dog that had his leg, the animal let go and tried to get his hand. Sean spun and caught the animal under the chest with a deep swing of his right foot. And before the animal regained its footing two more dogs grabbed hold of Sean's legs. "Help!" Sean screamed once again.

Jun and Angel were the first to reach Sean, who was stumbling backwards as he grabbed, punched and kicked at the attacking dogs. Rod, Tyler and David were right behind them. The dogs immediately gave up the fight and ran towards the street when confronted by the group of men. Angel and Jun picked up rocks and hurled at the animals as they fled together in a pack, with one of the stones hitting its mark.

Six dogs ran out the front gate of the church grounds, and a seventh stood its ground near the church. David and Rod helped Sean stand up and limp back to the dormitory. Reno was already preparing to stitch him up. There was no arterial bleeding, which was good news as there was no place to get plasma or blood. But Sean's blood loss was still dangerous, requiring forty-one stitches in all. He received fourteen stitches on the back of his left leg, eight on the ankle of his right leg, twelve between his thumb and forefinger on his left hand and seven in the palm of his right hand.

The sun peeked over the horizon before Sean was sedated and resting. They had all heard about the pack mentality of dogs, but none of the missionaries had ever seen such a group of dogs before. Reno took Lucky to the Hazel Parker Park Dog Run in Charleston, where dogs were permitted to run around off leashes, and had never witnessed dogs form into packs. But just one day after Kiko, everything seemed to change. Sean, Ashley, Pastor Mark, and Angie were injured. Marilou and Anna were lost. Mysterious aircraft raced by in the darkness. They witnessed a miraculous healing and had survived a super typhoon. It was all getting too difficult to process, and Ashley began to crack.

Ashley felt horrible about talking to her cheating boyfriend, Justin, instead of talking to her family when she was at the Super Sky Internet café. She began to obsess about it, and was unable to stop thinking about anything else. She now loathed Justin, and she loved her brothers and her parents more than ever. What if she couldn't get home? What if she never spoke to them again? All of the anxiety came to a peak as Sean was carried into the dormitory, bleeding and in pain. The horror from the storm, the loss of Anna … it was simply too much to take and Ashley began to weep. It was more than mere weeping; it was howling, moaning, wailing, and screaming. Angie and Reno tried to calm her, but Ashley was inconsolable. Dr. Kemp was her employer and friend. He had invited Ashley along, and he felt responsible for her. He walked near to her and tried to put his arm around her; he just wanted her to know that everything was going to be okay. Ashley surprised him with a sharp uppercut, hitting him under the chin hard enough to make him wobble. He stepped back and stared at her in disbelief.

Ashley screamed, "It wasn't supposed to be like this! You tricked me with pictures of the beaches and the waterfalls, but this is what I get. Look at us. We are hungry, bloody, eaten by mosquitoes, sleeping on a damp concrete floor without electricity! We're like animals! I want to go home now. Take me home now! I didn't sign up for this!" Instead of slowing down, her rant intensified. "I'm going home. If I have to walk back to Manila I will walk, but I am leaving today!"

Pastor Rod took command and told her, "We're going to stick together, Ashley. You will leave when we all leave. The roads are closed right now, and we can't get back to Manila until they clear the roads. As soon as we are able to reach Manila we will all go. We're all ready to go home, just like you."

Sean spoke up. "Look at me, Ashley. If you wander off by yourself you are going to end up even worse. Those dogs tore me up!"

Ashley dropped to the floor and continued to wail. Reno prepared a syringe with a sedative; she knew that Ashley wouldn't take anything voluntarily, so she would need to surprise her with an injection. She nodded at Angie and Kelly, and all three women moved slowly towards Ashley, who was now pounding on the floor. As Kelly tried to hug her, Ashley struck out as she had with David. A vicious punch just missed Kelly's head, and Kelly surprised everyone by responding with a left hook that landed flush on the side of Ashley's head. Ashley was stunned and remained still and silent. Kelly asked Reno to hand her the syringe, and Reno placed it into her hand. Kelly injected the sedative into Ashley's left leg, then stood up and moved away from her.

As Kelly walked away, Ashley began to cry loudly. "I'm sorry, everyone. I'm really sorry. Why is this happening to me?" Her voice grew softer as the sedative took effect. She then cried softly over and over, "It wasn't supposed to be like this." Soon she was sleeping and she would remain so for another two or three hours.

Manny, Jun, and Angel found wood to start a fire to cook their breakfast. David and Rod stepped to the front of the church to discuss what was best for Ashley. Reno and Angie began to sort through their remaining stock of medications. Tyler tried to go back to sleep, and Kelly laid beside Ashley and hugged her. This day began crazily with mysterious helicopters and it was barely light and Sean had been attacked by a pack of dogs, Ashley had freaked out, David had been punched by Ashley and Ashley had been thumped by Kelly. But this day would end more strangely than it had begun. The weirdness was only beginning.

Chapter 27 – Baler invaded
Friday, 4:45am, August 11th
Baler, Aurora province, Philippines

The engines of three yellow Hyundai bulldozers growled loudly as they raced in the pre-dawn darkness towards the Baler fish port. Mudslides blocked three sections of the road, so Judge ordered his men into action before 2:00am to clear the road. This was the essence of his mission. Judge would be held solely responsible if men and equipment were delayed in any way, so he had prepared for contingencies. The mudslides were predicted, and clearing them was simply part of his planned mission. He would not fail.

As the engines sprung to life a lone security guard ran from his small security shed towards the equipment, putting on his uniform shirt as he went. But he never managed to catch a glimpse of any of the culprits. Judge waited for him outside the plywood door to the shed, and nearly severed the guard's head as he sliced the man's throat. The guard was pitched, like unwanted garbage, behind the shed next to the carcass of his useless guard dog.

Two commandos acquired a pickup truck before midnight and loaded four reserve barrels of diesel fuel in the back. The pickup truck passed two of the team vans and positioned itself behind the bulldozers. Judge stayed in the rear of the convoy to observe their situation. The hard-hearted Captain was quite familiar with Baler. He laughed while studying satellite photos of the streets of Baler on Google Earth. *Only Westerners would expose themselves to such scrutiny*, he thought. He knew every street name, the location of the police station, gas stations, where to find the local military detachments, and every possible route to leave town. He remained invisible under his full-faced tinted helmet as he scouted the entire region on his Yamaha 250 two days earlier.

The first mudslide was small, and the three bulldozers barely broke stride as they cleared the road. The first bulldozer removed a slice of the mud close to the side of the mountain, pushing the mud towards the left. The second bulldozer stayed near the center of the road and pushed the mud further to the left. The third pushed all the remaining mud off the road. The vans, pickup truck, and motorcycle easily navigated the shallow mud as they continued. As they neared the Aurora

State College of Technology, known as ASCOT, one of the vans stopped and four heavily armed men emerged from the third van. They would prevent anyone from moving towards the fish port. They selected the location because they could easily defend it. They enjoyed a wide field of fire from defensible positions that offered target triangulation.

The second mudslide was much larger. The two remaining vans moved several hundred yards back to protect the team as they worked, but it was unnecessary; nothing approached them from the rear. After forty minutes the road was cleared and all the remaining mud was expertly pushed aside. The bulldozers surged forward and the vans caught up quickly, taking their respective positions in the formation. Judge glanced at his watch; it was now 3:50. Boats would be arriving at the fish port in just another ninety minutes. They would arrive there with time to spare.

The third mudslide contained large boulders that had fallen from the side of the mountain. They needed to be moved far enough off the road to provide a wide lane for their comrades. The first bulldozer pushed the mud and rocks aside, but lurched to the left as the left track separated from the wheels. They maintained their own practice equipment and knew how to tighten the tracks, but they hadn't planned for one to break. The other two bulldozers pushed the first one off the road and it rolled to its side and slid down the hill. They didn't need it and could easily finish the job with the two remaining machines.

At 4:25 all seven vehicles arrived at the fish port. The bulldozer drivers quickly turned around to block the entrance with their huge machines. The vans sped to the buildings near the cement pier to clear them of any people. They found an elderly woman who used the building to sell snacks to visiting tourists and fishermen. Judge parked the motorcycle and walked to the buildings to see what his men had uncovered. He ordered Corporal Ling to execute the woman, and Ling hesitated. He protested saying, "I will tie her up and place her in the back." Judge drew his pistol and shot Corporal Ling in the forehead. "That is for disobeying my order not to stop at the checkpoint." Then he shot him again in the heart and said, "And this is for not killing this hag." He then shot the woman and went outside to watch the driver of the pickup truck maneuver his vehicle fifty meters past the entrance and park it sideways in the narrow road to prevent anything from approaching from the unpopulated south. They wouldn't need the diesel fuel. The two bulldozers were still more than half full and all the vehicles that would come ashore here would be full as they rolled onto the dock. And they wouldn't need Corporal Ling either.

Judge didn't know it, but his team was being observed. Rogelio and Aldrin Soriano lived on the beach near ASCOT. Their mother had taken their two younger sisters inland to escape the wrath of Typhoon Kiko. Their father insisted that the boys stay with him to help save their small boat, and he had perished in the process. The two young boys then climbed Ermita Hill and weathered the storm inside the public restrooms at the tourist overlook. They heard the bulldozers and stood at the edge of the overlook to watch what was happening. They were mesmerized by the effort of the bulldozer team as they expertly cleared the second mudslide. The lights on the equipment gave them a birds-eye view of the cleanup effort. But they knew instantly that the drivers were not Filipino. Filipinos would never push such an expensive and needed piece of equipment over the side of the mountain. Perhaps they were Americans, they thought, as they continued to stand on the ridge overlooking the fish port.

Li Heng brought the signal lamp from one of the vans and shined its bright light towards the open water. The high tide would arrive in thirty minutes, so it was time for the larger vessels to begin their approach to the port. And the first of the boats, as planned, contained a group of fifty well-armed marines that quickly fanned out to help secure the port. They unloaded crates of ammunition from the boat, and it quickly returned to the mother ship that was anchored just a few miles away in Baler Bay. The second boat arrived moments after the first departed. Its dark silhouette was now visible against the grey and pink of the early morning dawn. Two dozen four wheelers, like those used for recreation, were quickly offloaded along with more crates of ammunition. Each of the ATV's, known as 'silun' by the invaders, was fitted with machine gun mounts, and the guns were quickly attached in assembly line fashion as the next two boats arrived simultaneously on either side of the long cement pier.

Li Heng was responsible for the staging area at ASCOT, but he needed to return to the fish port every thirty minutes to guide the next group to the staging area. As he sat in the gunner's seat he observed two people atop Ermita Hill pointing at him as he went. It was now light, and the first glimpse of the sun was visible over the ocean. More people would see them soon; it was no big deal as there was nothing they could do to stop them. But when he got back to the fish port Li Heng chose to inform Judge that they were being observed from Ermita Hill. He didn't consider their observation to be a danger, but Judge thought otherwise, ordering Li Heng and two other men to go with him to "neutralize the threat."

Rogelio and Aldrin had seen the armed ATV's pass by below and they knew that the Philippine Islands were under attack. And they heard the silun climbing Ermita Hill they ran for cover. Without other options they climbed into the escape tunnel that had been built over five hundred years earlier so that villagers could escape from invading Moro pirates. They knew where the tunnel came out down below, but both boys had been too afraid to enter the tunnel until now. They heard local tales of ghosts, strange creatures, and other frightening things that awaited anyone who climbed into the tunnels and they wanted no part of it. But a couple hundred meters of steep descent in the darkness was now their only option. Aldrin, the older brother, climbed in first, and Rogelio hesitated, but followed him when he spied the two silun racing towards them. They also saw him.

The first five meters went straight down, and then they felt their way along a broad left curve for another ten meters before climbing downward again. Judge dropped a grenade into the hole and the percussion from the blast in the confined space damaged the boys' eardrums. Rogelio squealed in pain and grabbed his ears, but Aldrin was unable to hear him. Judge heard Rogelio whimpering and knew that the grenade hadn't killed them. He pulled his pistol from its holster and climbed into the hole after the boys. They couldn't hear him coming, but they saw the beam of his flashlight and hurried their pace towards the bottom of the hill.

Aldrin squeezed through a narrow portion of the tunnel, barely able to pull himself though, then he helped Rogelio through the tapered opening. The air was thin inside the tunnel and both boys struggled for breath in their fear and exertion. They had no light and felt around in the darkness as they climbed, face-down, for another six meters before arriving at a large landing more than fifteen feet wide. Aldrin carefully felt around to locate the next section of the tunnel. Just as he located it on the side of the tunnel at nearly waist level, a bullet whizzed by his shoulder and hit Rogelio on the corner of his shoulder. Rogelio cried out, and Aldrin grabbed him, pulling him into the side tunnel. He could feel his brother's blood, and he knew they needed to find help quickly. They couldn't remain hiding in the tunnel.

Judge was furious. He wanted to capture whoever had been spying on them. His black jumpsuit was torn on the left sleeve and was covered in mud. He had no time to finish this task; he had to return to the dock to make sure that everything was being offloaded successfully. He returned to the silun and sped down the hill alone, angry because he had failed to kill the boys and that he now wore a torn and dirty uniform. The other three men climbed aboard the remaining vehicle and returned to the fish port to complete their mission; they knew to keep their distance from Judge when he became enraged. The boys continued their journey to the bottom of the hill and emerged from the darkness completely surrounded by thick underbrush.

Aldrin took off his tee shirt and wrapped his brother's shoulder. The bullet had ripped off a small corner of flesh on Rogelio's shoulder, but the wound wasn't life threatening. Aldrin knew that his brother needed to lie down and rest so the bleeding could stop. He concealed Rogelio in branches and planned to run to Baler to alert the authorities and find help for his little brother. But with the Chinese soldiers positioned at ASCOT he needed to climb high in the mountains above them, or sneak to the ocean and swim to Baler. He estimated that the swim would take around an hour and the climb might take more than two, so he snuck down the hill to the edge of the road and hid himself. When he was certain that nobody was looking he scurried across the road and sprinted across the narrow beach into the water to begin his long swim towards Baler.

Aldrin's father was a fisherman and the ocean was part of his heritage. He had been swimming before he was three years old, and he was a powerful swimmer. He'd never swum as far as Baler, but was confident he could make it across the bay. He chose to use a breaststroke as it exposed only his head as he swam. He worried that his brother might try to move from his hiding place, but he had been emphatic to Rogelio – *just stay put!* Adrin had almost forgotten about Typhoon Kiko, but as he swam several hundred meters from shore, the enormous waves reminded him that these were not ordinary conditions. The waves sometimes crested and splashed water up his nostrils, and he fought for breath as they crashed over his head. Just as he was beginning to panic he found a large branch that was floating in the water and he held onto it. He continued to paddle his way towards shore and began to formulate what he would say to the first adult he could find.

Dozens of small vessels arrived at the fish port delivering more marines, more weapons, more ammunition, food, and medical supplies. Three light rocket artillery trailers arrived and were quickly connected to trailer hitches that had been installed on the vans. Judge acknowledged the captain of the final boat, who informed him that no additional assets would be offloaded at the fish port. All the remaining vehicles would be amphibious assault craft and amphibious tanks that would come ashore on Sabang Beach in Baler. It was now up to Judge to mobilize his deadly convoy to secure the beach for the amphibious landing.

Judge once again straddled his Yamaha 250 and sped towards the staging area at ASCOT. Staff Seargeant Heng was ordered to bring up the rear, making sure that nothing was left behind. As he arrived at the staging area Judge was provided with a bullhorn. He stood atop one of the vans and announced to the assembly, "We will travel in pairs. Gunners on the left will secure the left side of the road. Gunners on the right will secure the right. Maintain forty meters between each team. Our objective is to eliminate the police and army threat. We will quickly surround their headquarters and you are commanded to take no prisoners. We will search quickly through their records to learn the names and addresses of their officers.

Half of you will come with me to find and eliminate them; the other half will secure the beach for our amphibious landing. Understand that we may encounter security guards or even private citizens who have guns. Anyone with a gun is considered a threat and must be eliminated. Before we depart from Baler we will seize additional vehicles to carry our supplies, so look for suitable vans and trucks to confiscate after we have secured the beach. We will soon be in place to prevent the escape of soldiers from Fort Magsaysay into the mountains. The People's Liberation Army will prevail!" The soldiers cheered and started their vehicles. This was the day they had all been waiting for. They eagerly followed Judge as he had commanded with two silun at a time, side-by-side with forty meter spacing between them. Judge drove quickly ahead to scan for threats.

Judge placed both bulldozers at the front of the formation as they began their assault on the municipality of Baler. The drivers were instructed to push anything that blocked the road out of their way. Very few soldiers were assigned to the detachment at the end of Sabang Beach, and many of them had been redeployed to Metro Manila to assist with post Kiko cleanup. A couple dozen police officers with small arms would have no chance against this well armed, fast moving force. They knew where they were going, and the Philippine military and police were quickly surrounded and obliterated. Nothing in the Aurora Province could match the firepower that rolled towards the Baler public market. The convoy rolled past clusters of homes where groups of men and women gaped at them as they roared by.

Two officers standing on the corner near the Baler Museum watched the bulldozers and silun approach, and before either man recognized the threat they were dead from a single machine gun burst. Spectators came from their homes and businesses to see the approaching convoy, but after the gunfire they melted quickly away. Another officer was gunned down as he stepped from out of Gerry's restaurant. The convoy moved swiftly to the police station located in Barangay Suklayin and surrounded the building with machine guns. Five officers stepped from the building with their hands in the air, and all of them were summarily executed. Commandos quickly confiscated their three filing cabinets and loaded them onto a van. They located home addresses for other officers as they drove to engage the AFP. The convoy quickly turned around and drove another route back towards the beach. This time they were headed to the local military encampment. The military would likely be better armed and better prepared than the police had been. There would also be more of them. Judge approached their encampment from three sides and ordered his men to open fire. Return fire came from two windows in the central building, but the gun battle was over in less than a minute.

The commandos cautiously entered each of the buildings and found only six bodies. *If the soldiers were not here,* Judge thought to himself, *they knew we were coming and they will fight us when they have the advantage.* "Carry their files with us, let's find out where they live. We will go to their homes to kill them." Two teams sorted through the files and placed red stickers at various places on a large aerial photo of Baler. They wrote names and addresses next to each red dot. Judge would take fifty men and hunt them down. Everyone else secured the beach for the amphibious assault.

House-to-house searches require discipline and training because the fighting is on the enemy's home turf. They know the layout of the building, where to hide and how to escape. The men with Judge knew how to minimize their risk when gaining entry and searching a home. But at the very first home they searched one of his men was killed by a shotgun blast as he entered the home. Enraged, Judge ordered that everyone in the home be killed. After that, the 'red dot' homes were ripped apart from the outside, leaving little chance that anyone inside could survive. He divided his men into three teams, and forty-six 'red dot' homes were destroyed within an hour. When they finished, they met at the municipal building and returned to the beach together as a team. The first amphibious tank rolled onto the sand just as they arrived. On the top of the vehicle was a young boy who had been fetched from a branch as he floated out to sea. Aldrin Soriano was saved from drowning, but he was now in the grasp of the enemy.

They bounced up and down as they approached in the churning sea, looking like more pieces of debris in the ocean than an invading force. More than one hundred amphibious vehicles bobbed in the water for more than forty minutes as they made their way through Baler Bay to the beach. Li Heng and three other men placed the vehicles into position so that they could begin to move as a convoy after the last one arrived ashore. Citizens of Baler watched their arrival from safe distances, wondering why there was no opposition. And Disaster Bob was also watching their arrival, adding narrative as he filmed them come ashore. He had crossed from Dibut over the top of the mountain, hugging the beach so that he could film the ravaged coastline. Disaster Bob was able to capture Adrin's rescue from sea, and was witness to the first wave of Chinese marines to arrive on the Island of Luzon.

He felt too exposed to set up his backpack satellite uplink unit; he was as visible to them as they were to him. So he retreated back to the other side of the mountain towards Dibut. Soon he was completely out of sight. After setting up the uplink unit he placed his camera on a small tripod and filmed a short introduction to the video he would send. He began, "This is Disaster Bob somewhere between Baler and Dibut in the mountains of the Aurora province in the Philippines. Yesterday I witnessed astounding death and devastation, and today I have something even more shocking to share with you. As I approached the crest of the mountain walking towards the provincial capital I saw soldiers arrive on the beach of Baler in armored personnel carriers and tanks. You will see small four wheelers with machine guns mounted on them patrolling the streets of Baler. The uniforms are definitely not from the Philippines or America. I believe that the People's Republic of China has launched an invasion of the Philippines. I have no way to be certain, but I'm sure that someone out there can analyze this video and provide some analysis for my viewers. I'll post more updates later. This is Disaster Bob - I'm gone."

Bob transferred the video to his laptop computer and performed a few simple edits. The total running time for the video was 3 minutes and sixteen seconds. It showed Aldrin being rescued and several amphibious tanks and personnel carriers roll up onto the beach. But most of the video showed the ATV's with mounted machine guns moving around the streets of Baler. He then connected his laptop to the uplink unit and sent the video to his blog site. Within seconds, Gina Franklin was watching the video as she cooked dinner for her children. She turned off both burners to her stove and dropped to the kitchen floor crying. Matthew stepped from his bedroom with his laptop in his hand. He had seen the video too. Gina's cell phone rang; it was Ashley's mom, Teresa. There was no doubt about it now; Rod and entire ECF mission team was in danger.

Chapter 28 – Rumors
Friday, 9:45am, August 11th
Maria Aurora, Aurora

The '*bamboo telegraph*' refers to jungle news transmission, which is normally swift and accurate. And the news of soldiers and equipment coming ashore in Baler arrived swiftly in Maria Aurora. One of the members of Ramada Community Church shared news of the attack with Pastor Mark before the last marines had even arrived ashore. Sister Maribel was out of breath when she arrived at the church. She had to sit down and breathe for a few moments before she was able to speak. She stood up and became animated, waving her arms and shouting as she spoke. She provided details of all terrain vehicles with machine guns mounted on them, armored personnel carriers, amphibious tanks and hundreds of *Chinese* soldiers. Pastor Mark suggested that perhaps they were delivering relief supplies after Typhoon Kiko, and Sister Maribel again got loud. "They are killing all of the military and police! It's an invasion!"

Pastor Mark knew that Sister Maribel was sometimes prone to exaggeration and was a bit of a gossip. It was difficult to believe her words, but she was clearly affected by what she had been told. She urged Pastor Mark to hide the Americans to protect them. As she ran back towards the church gate to warn others, Mark returned to the dormitory to share the news with Pastor Rod. Considering the helicopters they heard before daybreak, the news was alarming. Mark asked Pastor Rod if he could speak to him alone for a few minutes. He was helping David hold a small child still while Reno stitched a wound on his foot. The child wasn't cooperating; he screamed and squirmed and had managed to kick Reno twice in the face. She smiled each time she was hit, but she was clearly frustrated with the child. Pastor Rod told Mark, "I'll be with you as soon as Reno finishes these stitches."

Rod rinsed blood from his hands and wiped them on an old shirt from his backpack before joining Pastor Mark. "What's on your mind, sir?" he asked. Pastor Mark chose his words carefully.

"One of my church members just shared some very disturbing news." Mark first established the source of his news. "She said that amphibious tanks, armored personnel carriers and hundreds of four wheeled vehicles with mounted machine guns have landed in Baler. She said that we're being invaded by the Chinese, and suggested that we hide you and the other Americans for your protection." Rod was stunned and didn't know what to say. He called to Sean and asked him to join them.

Rod repeated what Pastor Mark said and Sean stood astonished, his mouth partly open and his eyebrows furrowed. Pastor Mark jumped in, "Sister Maribel said that they are already killing police and military officials and she was concerned about your safety. Perhaps we should consider moving you into the mountains for safety reasons. They won't find you there – at least not today."

"Let's move!" Sean turned quickly towards the dormitory and shouted to the other team members, "Pack your stuff, we're leaving in five minutes. The Philippines is under attack; I'll explain as we go. Please hurry."

Sean returned to where Rod and Mark were still talking. Mark spoke first, "There's a remote village above Kadayacan; it's almost two day's walk from here, mostly uphill. I've been there before and can take you there. We will hike up to the Ilongot tribal village where my grandfather was born."

Rod was still not convinced that fleeing their shelter at the dormitory was wise. He interjected, "We need to get more information. Think about it; we are going to run into the mountains to hide based on a rumor from one person. I've seen it before; rumors run rampant in the midst of calamity."

"Pastor Mark, can you ask Jun and Angel to get more information about the Chinese invasion before we run to the mountains? I'll get everyone ready to move, but we need to be sure that we're acting on good information."

Reno approached Rod and asked, "Is Sean telling us the truth? Are we really being invaded?"

"We don't have all the facts yet, Reno, only a rumor. Jun and Angel are going to gather more information before we do anything. But we need to be prepared to move quickly, so please help the others get their things together. Tell them to bring only what can be easily carried – the route is uphill for more than a day."

"Why would we be in danger from the Chinese? We're civilians and have no intention of fighting back, so why would they target us? They might even be our ticket out of this situation." Reno wanted to be optimistic and at least present an alternative option. Hiding in the mountains might secure them for a period of time, but ultimately, *they would need to surrender in order to get home.*

"This isn't a permanent situation, Reno. All we're doing is buying time to think. It may provide us with options that we don't yet see. Let me throw all my stuff into my bag; I want to be ready when Angel and Jun return." Rod's heart was racing. He knew the adage – war is hell – and he believed it. Civilized men commit horrible, immoral acts during war. They dehumanize their enemies and slaughter them not as humans, but as: krauts, japs, chinks, zips, slopes, gooks, or ragheads. Every culture at war does it. So there was no reason to think that the Chinese wouldn't do so. Their largely homogeneous society has cultivated a racist culture, which would surely manifest itself in a conflict with any foreign ethnicity.

Rod trotted back to the dormitory to pack his belongings. Ashley sat in the corner, crying hysterically. Rod immediately walked to her, knelt beside her, placed his hands on her shoulders and said, "Ashley. Listen to me. We're all going to be okay. Get your things together because we need to leave here in just a few minutes. We have very little time, Ashley, and we need your cooperation." She didn't look up or acknowledge that he had spoken.

Angel arrived first, about a minute before Jun, and confirmed the rumor. "We've got to move now! ATV's with machine guns are parked on the highway by the Ramada road. We could see more of them coming from Baler. They are everywhere!" Angel was in good physical shape, but he was out of breath from sprinting nearly three hundred yards to deliver the news.

When Jun arrived he was also out of breath and spoke intermittently between breaths. "They are here! We saw them with our own eyes. It's no rumor! We have to go!" All of the ECF team members stood outside the dormitory in a narrow sliver of shade on the backside of the building, away from the road; all except Ashley. Rod returned to Ashley, this time grabbing her by the arms and standing her to her feet. Her head hung low and she didn't look up.

"Ashley, look at me!" She refused, so Rod grabbed her under the chin and yanked her face upward. She was startled by his roughness, and she looked at him with angry eyes. "This is life or death, Ashley. Either you come along with us now, or we'll leave you behind. We have no choice. You don't want to be alone as a woman in the path of an invading army – trust me on this. We'll look out for you. Grab your pack and come now." Rod let go of her chin and Ashley quickly reached down and picked up her bag. Her mind was processing the thought of being left behind as she moved. Rod walked towards the door and heard Ashley say, "Thanks, Pastor. I'm coming."

"We need to stay off the roads. We can walk behind the church towards the cemetery. It's wide open for much of the way and we'll be visible, so we'll need to stay low and move quickly. We can hide in the coconut groves after we cross a large rice field. We'll stay to the right of the homes there and cross the old Baler highway near the cemetery. From the cemetery we will begin our climb into the mountains. The first part is dangerous, but once we are in the hills we'll be safe." Brother Manny knew this area well. His grandmother lived in Barangay Uno and he used to play in the cemetery as a child. His family scolded him for 'disrespecting the dead', but he stopped only after they began telling him ghost stories.

Manny led the way, walking through the trees towards Cadilan. David and Angel looked at one another as they approached the huge pile of logs and debris where they had discovered Marilou's bloated body. They tried not to think about it, but the horrible memory of her corpse would haunt them forever, especially here in this place. They walked in pairs, staying close together and moving quickly. Kelly's weight and conditioning presented a problem. She needed to rest every five minutes or so, and her pace was much slower than the others.

Angel spoke up, "I'll stay with Kelly; the rest of you can go ahead. Please wait for us at the back of the cemetery and we'll join you there." Nobody protested; they knew that Kelly needed more time that everyone else and would expose the entire group if they waited for her. Kelly sat down, breathing heavily and thanked Angel between breaths.

"You're really an angel, Angel. I can't keep up. Thanks for staying with me. I won't be a burden; I just move a bit slower than the others." She was smiling at Angel, grateful for his gesture of kindness.

Rod turned to Angel and said, "We'll wait at the cemetery until you get there." He handed his plastic water bottle to Kelly saying, "Just a little at a time, Kelly. Stay hydrated, okay?" Kelly nodded and Rod rejoined Sean, who he had chosen as his partner for the long walk. They followed Manny as he stepped quickly forward.

Two sleek black helicopters roared by overhead from behind them, one following the other, just as the group approached the rice field. They were low and fast, just like the helicopters they had heard before dawn. And within moments the aircraft were out of sight. Their appearance created momentary chaos. Sean, Tyler, Jun and Angel dove for cover. Pastor Mark, Ashley, Angie, and Reno retreated deeper into the trees. It was clear that they were unprepared for aerial observation. They planned to stay away from the highways, where the enemy soldiers seemed to be concentrated. But in time they knew that the invaders would find their way onto the side streets and would secure each of the small communities. David turned to Kelly and gave her a 'thumbs up', "Thanks for slowing us down!" She smiled at him. Until this moment she felt bad that she couldn't keep up with the team, but *perhaps her incapacity served a purpose.*

Pastor Rod spoke before they continued forward. "When you see anything ahead of us, Brother Manny, raise your right hand and squat down. When you see him give that signal, do the same thing he does. If Brother Manny runs, follow him. If he lies down, do the same, okay? We need to become better organized." His pastoral training included spiritual warfare instruction, but did not include combat training. "We need to move through this open area quickly, so let's stay close to Brother Manny and move rapidly."

Kelly recovered and was ready to begin the trek across the open rice field with the rest of the team. Manny led the way, walking rapidly and bending down to keep a low profile. The others did the same, staying only yards apart. Kelly and Angel remained at the back of the group, which quickly separated from them. On level ground, a sprinter can cover two hundred meters in twenty-five seconds. But even the rice farmer who created this muddy, elevated path would have difficulty navigating the 200-meter distance in less than four minutes.

David's shoes slipped so much in the mud that he took them off. Ashley fell into the rice field water and needed help from Rod to get back onto the path. The team was unable to walk as pairs on the narrow path, and balance on the slippery mud was impossible. Even Manny slipped into the water several times as he led the team towards the rows of coconut trees on the other side. The water was deep because of Kiko, and the path was totally washed away in some sections. Tyler, who considered himself an athlete, was embarrassed after he fell for the third time. But it was Kelly who found the path most difficult.

Sean timed their trip across the rice field; Brother Manny was able to traverse the distance in eight minutes and thirty-two seconds. With the exception of Kelly and Angel, the rest of the team managed to climb into the cover and shade of the coconut grove in less than ten minutes. They laid down in the shade of the trees for a few minutes before Rod suggested that they continue their way to the back of the cemetery as planned. The team would rest there with better cover. Kelly and Angel were only halfway across the rice field as the team continued forward.

Without warning two helicopters returned from the west. They circled the field and hovered above Angel and Kelly. The pair stood still for a moment, and then waved at the helicopters. Their broad woven hats hid their faces in shadow, and it would have been difficult to discern that muddy Kelly was an American. Her size, however might betray her. Filipinos, particularly in the provinces, tend to be slender, especially farmers who labor under the hot sun day after day. One of the pilots turned on a loud speaker and spoke to them in Mandarin. They continued waving, as the lecture, whatever it was, continued. Then the helicopters turned and resumed their original course.

They had been spotted, and they tried to figure out the implications of being seen. Would soldiers be waiting for them near the cemetery? Would the helicopters return to capture them? Maybe they were returning to base for ammunition and would return to shoot them. So many thoughts flooded Kelly's mind as she struggled to negotiate the remaining seventy-five yards, and none of them were happy thoughts.

Kelly struggled for another ten minutes, falling twice and slipping with every step. She hugged Angel as he helped her onto dry land under the coconuts. Angel sat down in the shade and said, "We can rest here for a couple of minutes. The others have promised to wait for us." Angel admired Kelly's kindness and concern for her. And Angel admired Kelly's perseverance after witnessing her incredible struggle through the mud.

Kelly looked across the rice field towards the mountains. The setting was idyllic, and under normal circumstances she would be taking panoramic photos or video to share with Mark when she returned home. But she was now concerned about surviving so that she could return home. She spotted two more helicopters several miles away towards the beach. They were only dots in the sky, but she knew that they could arrive quickly if they turned her way.

"I'm okay, let's continue," she said. Angel helped her to her feet and they followed a muddy trail through the coconut grove left by their companions. Angel knew that Kelly struggled to push forward and wondered how difficult the next two days would be. They would climb to an elevation of six thousand feet, traverse ridges, enter back into a huge valley, and then climb up the other side of the valley. He knew that she would need help. Perhaps more help than he could provide alone.

Manny asked the team to remain hidden while he walked to the road near the cemetery. It was good that he took such precaution. Two of the silun were parked near Wesleyan University. The drivers were absent, but the gunners stood in the back, ready to fire. Manny moved towards a cluster of houses and walked into the first open door, pretending that he belonged there. A frightened young woman, perhaps twenty years old clutched her small daughter and cowered in the corner. Manny reassured her, "My name is Manny. I am from Baler and I'm trying to avoid the soldiers outside. I won't hurt you."

The woman responded loudly, "You've placed us in danger just by being here! They took my husband and my brother about an hour ago, and if they find you here they will also take you!"

Manny tried to soothe her fear. "I will only be here for a few minutes. As soon as I find a way to cross the road I will leave. I'm sure that the soldiers will move away, or take a lunch break. I won't let anything happen to you."

The woman covered her face and began to weep. Manny didn't want to know the details of her grief; he just wanted her to know that his presence would cause her no harm. He found a small gap between the boards of her house and peeked towards the soldiers. The drivers were still absent. Suddenly gunfire erupted inside the university. The soldiers leveled their guns towards the school and prepared to fire, but they were both dead before they could acquire a target. Two uniformed police officers armed with shotguns raced from the cemetery towards the downed men. The officers stripped the soldiers of their ammunition and side arms, then climbed aboard their four wheelers and sped to the entrance of the university. Three men emerged carrying weapons and quickly hopped onto the back of the vehicles. And as they sped north towards Dipaculao Manny motioned for the team to join him. They had a small window of time to cross the road into the cemetery.

As the team ran across the road towards the cemetery, three more uniformed men ran towards them. The Filipinos immediately recognized the AFP uniforms, but the Americans were unsure what to do. The men ran to where the dead soldiers lay and quickly moved them out of sight, away from the road. Then they ran towards the university to hide the bodies of the silun drivers. Manny moved through the maze of tombs and headstones at the cemetery. There was no scheme for burial in the Maria Aurora cemetery. Families dug wherever they could find enough space to bury their loved ones. There was no particular orientation for the tombs. They faced every direction, and navigating through the cemetery meant climbing over many of the tombs. The team moved quickly to the back of the cemetery and continued almost a mile into the forest on the side of the mountain. They found a heavily forested area that shielded them from the air and from all sides. Manny planned to return later to guide Angel and Kelly to their hiding place.

The Ilongot tribesmen were feared headhunters until the late 1960's. Few people ventured into their territory on purpose. And very few of those who gambled their lives by going into Ilongot territory ever came out. But times have changed. The tribesmen, once known for their fierceness as warriors, were now ardent followers of Jesus Christ. Every evangelist or missionary who visited Aurora made sure to bless the Ilongot people as they came. Yet they still aggressively protected their territorial integrity. Fifteen tribesmen quickly surrounded the missionary team as they lay on the ground recuperating from their dangerous trip through the lowlands. One of them, Bukhil, immediately recognized Pastor Mark. They were second cousins, and had spent years together as children.

"We need your help, Bukhil," said Pastor Mark, who was relieved to see his cousin. He knew that they were now under the protection of the Ilongot tribe. The Ilongot people take hospitality seriously. They would willingly sacrifice themselves to protect a guest, and Mark knew that the team was now secure. "We need to reach the village as soon as possible. Can we rely on your help?"

"Of course, cousin. What is happening below?" Bukhil knew that something was going on, but the bamboo telegraph somehow missed the people of Kadayacan. Mark explained what he knew to Bukhil, who assigned four of his warriors to accompany the team back to the village. Two men waited for Kelly and Angel behind the cemetery and the other two guided the first group to safety. Bukhil led his remaining men to strike terror in the hearts of the invaders. Pastor Mark's injured hand began to bleed again, and the wound had turned bright pink around the edges with infection. Bukhil glanced at Mark's hand and shook his head, and then he joined his men to prepare their battle plan.

Kelly and Angel were oblivious to the events that took place at the university. As they approached the highway there was no sign of trouble. They quickly crossed the road into the cemetery, and were met by the men assigned to escort them to the village. But before they had navigated the odd path through the graveyard, they heard gunshots coming from the road behind them. Instinctively they ducked behind the elevated mausoleums. A single silun driver had spotted them climbing over the graves and raced towards them. But without warning the silun was overturned by a board that had been placed across the road. A rope, hidden behind a roadside narra tree, yanked one end of the board as the four-wheeler passed over the board, spilling it onto its side. The two People's Liberation Army soldiers never saw their assailants; they were pounced upon with machetes while still rolling on the ground. Their assailants then righted the silun and headed north.

Kelly and Angel continued to move inland with their two Ilongot guides. As they climbed uphill, Kelly grew faint and struggled to breathe. And with no discussion, the two Ilongot guides hoisted her over the shoulders of one of the men in a 'fireman's carry' and they continued their climb for more than an hour with Kelly carried like cargo. The Ilongot warriors brought them to a small cave concealed by a heavy canopy of trees. And they got there just in time. Three helicopters unexpectedly materialized overhead just as Kelly was seated inside the cave, moving slowly as if searching the terrain below. They were invisible through the thick canopy of trees, but the helicopters sounded as though they were directly overhead, and the wind from the rotors made the trees above them sway and flap. They all moved deeper into the small cave and remained motionless as the helicopters navigated down the side of the mountain.

This was sacrificial love, thought Kelly. These men, total strangers, helped and encouraged her. They carried her. And they seemed willing to die in order to save her. To her, they embodied what every follower of Christ should be like. Tears ran down her cheeks as she quietly observed the men. She silently thanked God for providing these men. She focused on Angel for a moment and considered that he might, in fact, be a real angel. She blushed as he looked up to find her staring at him. She suddenly felt inadequate; she came here to bless others, but she had become a burden for them to carry.

Chapter 29 – Ultimatum
Friday, 12:00am August 11ᵗʰ
Beijing, China

President Xi Huang called at exactly midnight from Beijing, and the U.S. Chief of Protocol quickly contacted President Clover. She was expecting his call. She quickly went into the Situation Room and was placed on the speakerphone.

"Good evening, Mr. President," she said as the line went from red to green. "I've met with my cabinet and regret to inform you that we do not have a deal, sir. So where does that leave us?" She wanted for President Xi to lead the conversation and find out what he would offer.

"That is regrettable, Madam President. We had hoped to avert war between our two nations. I appreciate that you have honored my request to speak together again before we engage in any combat. And we still have an opportunity for peace; I ask you to pause, Madam President, and consider the entire cost before you act. We have already done so." President Xi did not offer any change in his position. They were clearly prepared for war, and willing to pay an enormous cost to acquire the Philippine islands.

"I don't need to remind you, President Clover that more than 600,000 American citizens reside in the Philippines. I cannot be held responsible for their safety if we should go to war. The power is yours. You can guaranty their safety, Madam President. All you have to do is *nothing*. We will ensure that no harm will come to your citizens living in the Philippines, and we will help repatriate them." President Clover had been briefed regarding the high number of expatriates living in the Philippines, and she knew that they would suffer greatly if war could not be averted. She was hesitant to sacrifice the lives of trained, battle-tested marines. She had been an advocate for peace her entire life. President Clover couldn't imagine being held liable for the loss of more than half a million innocent American civilians.

"That sounds very much like a threat, President Xi. You are already responsible for their safety. We now hold you personally responsible for protecting their lives and their property. Any attack on American citizens is an attack on our nation. I don't need to remind you, sir, that we possess considerable firepower, all of which will be used to destroy your military, your economy, and your government. We have the means and the will to win, Mr. President." President Clover began to shake as she spoke. She knew that she was threatening all out war with the largest military ever created.

"Please accept my apologies, President Clover, if it even seemed as though I was threatening your citizens in the Philippines. I was merely pointing out that they are plentiful. We do not know where they are, nor do we care. I believe the term "collateral damage" is an American phrase. You must accept that there will be some collateral damage; it's simply unavoidable with modern weaponry." President Xi knew that he had found her soft spot. He could even hear her voice quiver while she spoke.

"Collateral damage is not an excuse I will accept, Mr. President. Confine your strikes to military targets and protect our citizens." This was exactly what President Xi wanted to hear. It was precisely what he had proposed to President Clover in their earlier conversation. In exchange for American inaction, the People's Republic of China was prepared to utilize minimum force, prevent brutality of civilians, and concentrate their military efforts only on military targets.

"There is another important issue that we need to discuss, Madam President, and that is the nuclear option. We will pledge to refrain from using any chemical, biological or nuclear devices if you will pledge to do the same." President Xi was playing hardball now. Even the discussion of using chemical, biological or nuclear weapons made President Clover turn pale.

"You have our mutual understanding regarding such weapons. We will abide by our nuclear cooperation agreement. And we would like your cooperation, sir, in confining the region of combat." President Clover seemed to be grasping for options, as she foolishly uttered what she said.

President Xi laughed and said, "Madam President, we will not confine the fight to a single region. I assure you that we will move quickly to secure the entire coastline of Southeast Asia to protect our naval forces if you engage us in combat. Our operatives around the world will attack your people and your interests. And we fully intend to bring the war to North America. We are not Afghanistan, Madam President. You will be fighting one fifth of the world's population, and our people are resolved to finish the fight."

President Clover decided to take a different approach. "Your military advisors can confirm that our naval forces are moving quickly into position. Our air force is sending long-range bombers into Japan and Okinawa, and our forces in Korea are on full alert, awaiting my orders. We have the means to prevent any additional incursion into Philippine territory, and after we have secured the South China Sea we will destroy the forces that you have already landed on Philippine soil." She knew that it would not be as simple as she had described it. The People's Republic of China now possessed three aircraft carriers and two 'unsinkable aircraft carriers' in the form of man-made islands in the South China Sea containing airstrips capable of landing any aircraft possessed by the Chinese military. U.S. naval and air forces would pay a huge price to drive Chinese forces from the South China Sea.

"You realize that this will be World War III. If you deploy your assets from Korea, you can be quite certain that North Korea will take advantage of the sudden power shift. The same holds true with ISIS in Iraq and Syria; they will move quickly into Saudi Arabia, Kuwait, Jordan, Turkey, and Egypt. Even your beloved Israel will have no option but to fight. Our conflict will embolden Russia to grab more territory, and the feud between India and Pakistan will erupt into bloodshed. The global power shift will not favor your nation or ours. Please consider your actions carefully, Madam President." President Xi wanted to paint the gloomiest possible outcome even if the U.S. prevailed militarily.

"In our previous conversation I offered to forgive your $1.4 trillion debt. I gave you assurances that we will treat the Filipino people with respect and dignity, and we are prepared to invest more than a trillion dollars into the Philippines before the end of this decade to improve their quality of life. You can avoid the deaths of millions, Madam President. You have the power to strengthen America, or to weaken her. I propose that we refrain from any action for another twenty four hours as we consider alternatives to combat." President Xi fully expected a combative retort. His analysts knew President Clover quite well. She always erred on the side of caution. In fact, it was her predictability that made her administration perfect for Operation Zhi. They *knew* that she would opt for a non-military solution.

"I cannot allow your soldiers to remain in the Philippines, President Xi. Our nation is honor-bound to defend the Philippines, regardless of the cost. I accept your proposal to delay combat by another twenty-four hours, and pray that you will retreat from the Philippines. I do not think, sir, that you have correctly computed the cost to your nation. The price your nation will pay for continuing this course will be enormous." President Clover already knew that 'plan B' would be the course of action. And so did President Xi. Twenty-four additional hours for the Chinese to land more troops and equipment in the Philippines would make it far more difficult for America to employ a military option. Even with her threat to take action, President Clover knew that the price of war with China was more than she was willing to accept. And even though Filipinos depended on America to defend them, America would permit the Chinese to vanquish the Philippines.

"I will call you again tomorrow at this time, Madam President, to discuss our options. I thank you, once again, for seeking a peaceful solution." President Xi knew that a 'peaceful solution' would be her course of action. President Clover detested war, and her political history made her position crystal clear, even before her decision was finalized.

"I will await your call, sir. In the meantime I expect to see signs of your withdrawal from the Philippine archipelago." President Clover knew that her staff did not share her viewpoint regarding the best course of action. Even though her advisors had been handpicked, many were far more 'hawkish' and would choose combat over acquiescence.

The phone call ended with no change in the stance of either nation, but the People's Republic of China had gained another day to fortify their position in the Philippines. And they intended to land as many aircraft as possible during that time. America had forfeited the military option, and the People's Republic of China would prepare for the onslaught of diplomatic challenges. There would be sanctions, assets would be frozen, diplomats would be expelled … all of the 'normal' huffing and puffing that takes place by disadvantaged nations. But in the end, the People's Republic of China had gained what she desired.

President Clover asked the six people in the room with her to remain seated. She spoke softly as she said, "I believe that the cost of war against China is too great. There would be far too many lives lost. Our supply chain would be stretched to the breaking point to sustain a war against the People's Republic of China, and, honestly, the outcome of such a campaign is uncertain. We know that the citizens of the U.S. will protest any war, but such a costly war will become highly unpopular. It is my decision, therefore, to accept the terms offered by President Xi."

She continued, "We will announce immediate sanctions against the Peoples Republic of China, freezing all of their assets in the United States and our territories. We will not accept any of their imported goods for at least the next year, and we will announce that the debt they now hold will not be repaid until they have completely extricated themselves from the Philippines. We need to prepare for harsh condemnation, but we must remember why this course of action has been chosen. We are preserving life and maintaining world stability."

National Security Advisor Phil Baker interrupted President Clover. Phil was an astute observer and had uncanny intuition. He had worked with President Clover for more than twenty years and they shared a mutual respect for one another. He said, "Madam President, we can't simply refuse to repay any portion of our national debt, even during a situation like this. Other nations would refuse to hold our debt and may sell what they now hold. Additionally our national credit rating would be at risk. We would suffer most from such a move. I think we need to take the $1.4 trillion off the table."

"We are not refusing to repay the debt, we're merely making it conditional. We will hold all debt repayments to the PRC until they withdraw from the Philippines. If they do not withdraw, we do not release any money to them, so by default it's ours. The interest that we can make on the money we hold back is substantial. I believe the average American will support me on this issue, and it may be the biggest stick we have in this fight." President Clover was resolute; she knew that the amount of debt held by the Chinese was a major policy shift. It was also a monumental mistake.

"The American people are already demanding action," President Clover declared. "They want to see American leadership. This decision will anger many allies, who expect us to remain the policeman of the world. Some will view our inaction as treacherous because we have a mutual defense pact with the Philippines. My father gave me only one verse from scripture to memorize while he was still alive. He said it is something politicians tend to forget. The verse is Proverbs 26:17 and it says: "*Like one who grabs a stray dog by the ears is someone who rushes into a quarrel not their own.*" America has had a difficult time staying out of quarrels between other nations. This time we intend to watch from the sidelines. But we must still appear decisive. Our citizens expect strong leadership."

President Clover was practicing her lines on a friendly audience. Her inner circle sat quietly at the table as she continued her speech. They knew her well enough to know that she was formulating her policy out loud. "Our plan consists of three main tactics. First we will freeze all PRC assets in U.S. banks and institutions. Secondly we will not permit any Chinese made products into our markets. And third, we will not repay any of the debt held by the Chinese government until they completely withdraw from the Philippines. The Chinese are members of the UN Security Council and will veto anything we offer there, but we will put forth a motion in the General Assembly to condemn this act of aggression and demand withdrawal from and reparations to the Philippines."

As she paused Phil Baker interjected, "Do not suggest that we are incapable of winning a war with the Chinese. The press will say that for us, and you will be praised for acting prudently. And make sure to say that we are exploring other options. All our cards should never be on the table; our citizens and allies need to believe that there are some hidden efforts taking place."

"Thanks, Phil. I'll need to announce something to the press today. We will tell them that we have issued an ultimatum to the Chinese leadership, and are awaiting their response before taking the next step. Do not have the military stand down, but keep them at a safe distance – we don't want to get dragged into the fray by a preventable accident. Remind me to ask about Ambassador Stephens and his staff when we speak to President Xi tomorrow. Let's get together again at 4:00 this afternoon to prepare this evening's press statement. In the meantime, let's explore more options. Listen to the press to know what they are saying." They all stood as President Clover made her exit.

As President Clover disappeared through the doors, Phil sat back heavily in his seat. He was still focusing on President Clover's statement "... tell them we have issued an ultimatum ..." The public didn't need to know the whole truth, but an outright lie bothered him. There was no ultimatum. How would President Clover explain her lack of response as the PRC defied her pretend ultimatum? How many more lies would be needed to cover this one? He felt like a crew member on a sinking ship.

Chapter 30 – Disaster Bob emerges
Friday, 3:00pm August 11th
San Luis, Aurora Province, Philippines

Disaster Bob knew he was in deep trouble. He surreptitiously filmed an enemy invasion and posted it online for the world to see. He wondered if that could be classified as an act of espionage. He chuckled at the fact that he could add 'spy' to his resume if he ever got home. But he had doubts that he could escape capture. He was trapped on an island under the control of the People's Republic of China. He decided that Robert Banks could be captured, but Disaster Bob could not; Bob had reported details of the Chinese invasion to the world.

He carefully hid his gear under a huge brush pile near the location of his last transmission. He wiped his fingerprints from each item in the backpack before sealing it tightly. He hoped to recover it when it was safe to do so. He wanted to carry the backpack, but the brand name and conspicuous mountain range logo of the satellite uplink company was printed all over it; it would link him to the equipment. He took only a few essentials from his backpack and carried them in a small nylon bag that he used for his dirty laundry. Soap, shampoo, toothpaste, his toothbrush, his hair brush, two extra tee shirts, a towel, insect repellent, and an extra pair of walking shorts. He took his California driver's license and his passport out of his wallet and left them with the gear he was hiding; the photos looked too much like Disaster Bob. He kept his lone credit card and counted his cash. He had two one hundred dollar bills and the equivalent of three hundred twelve dollars in pesos. He folded his wallet into his only towel and stuffed it deep into the nylon bag. He debated whether or not to carry along his smart phone. It contained too much information, so he reformatted the phone to eliminate all of the photos, notes, and anything else that might identify him as Disaster Bob, and placed the phone with his passport.

Bob's self image included his long brown hair and scraggly beard, but he now needed to change his appearance; he desperately wanted to become Robert Banks again. It was too dangerous for him to be Disaster Bob. With a haircut and shave he could once again look like Robert Banks.

He did his best to shave his beard using a razor sharp pocketknife with a beautiful burled-wood handle. It was not an easy task.

He cut as close to his face as possible, periodically sharpening the blade to make the task less painful. It was an awkward tool for shaving and Bob cut himself three times. He slashed off his long locks without difficulty, cutting his hair to a uniform length of less than two inches. He looked at his reflection using the polished knife blade, and continued cutting until he believed that his haircut looked 'normal.'

Robert gathered all of the hair from his shave and haircut and placed it in a plastic bag. He laughed as he imagined a small, furry animal looking back at him from within the bag. He was surprised at how cool the breeze felt on his neck and face without his beard. Bob made sure not to carry the clothing he wore while filming the videos. Robert didn't realize that his videos could not yet be seen in the Philippines. He felt like a hunted man.

Robert stuffed his pocketknife into the dark blue nylon bag and he threw the bag over his shoulder and began the difficult walk to Baler. He was accustomed to the weight of the backpack with the heavy camera and satellite equipment; it felt liberating to carry less than five pounds. He was glad that he'd spent the extra money to buy the best quality hiking sandals before flying to the Philippines. They were lightweight and dried quickly. Bob believed that he was safe; he was an unarmed civilian with no intention of resisting– why would anyone harm him?

After more than an hour of walking along the muddy path, he came to a fast flowing, muddy creek. He stripped naked, took out his soap and shampoo and climbed into the shallow water to bathe. The water was cool and flowed swiftly. The normally clear water was muddy from the excessive rain from Typhoon Kiko, but it didn't matter at all to Robert, it was wonderfully refreshing. He heard children talking as he rinsed the shampoo from his hair and he quickly exited the water and put his clothes back on. A young woman quickly appeared with three small children in tow as he struggled into his underwear. She was unfazed by his lack of clothing. She spoke rapidly and pointed in the direction she'd come from. Robert couldn't understand a single word, but he clearly comprehended the fervor with which she spoke. She started walking again, talking as she departed, and Robert felt uncomfortable with the encounter. Being discovered naked didn't bother him; what concerned him was the urgency of her warning and the fact that he was unable to understand a word of it.

Robert finished getting dressed, picked up his bag and resumed his trek towards Baler. He knew that it was only a matter of time before he was discovered, and he didn't wish to endure a prolonged period of hiding. The Chinese soldiers would instantly recognize that he wasn't Filipino, thought Robert, and then they would detain him until he could be deported. Robert assumed that, due to his civilian status, that he wouldn't be treated like a prisoner of war. Maybe they wouldn't detain him at all. Robert's optimistic assessment of his situation would soon be shattered by reality.

Robert noticed that the highway was eerily silent as he stepped onto the cemented road that passed through the municipality of San Luis on the way to Baler. There were no jeepneys, no tricycles, no motorcycles, nor any pedestrians. It was like he's stepped into an episode of the *Twilight Zone*. Normally this stretch of road bustled with activity, and the eerie silence made Robert pause. There was apparently a reason that everyone was inside, and Robert felt suddenly exposed. Robert ran quickly to a small cluster of houses only fifty yards away. He knocked on the first door and nobody responded. He saw the faces of two young girls in the second house and knocked on their door. An elderly man appeared at the window and shocked Robert by speaking very clear English.

"What do you want?" the man said.

"I want to know what is going on. Where is everyone?" Robert asked.

"Quickly, come inside. You're not permitted to be outside right now." The old man opened the door and ushered Robert into the home. The mud floor was wet, and half of the nipa roof was missing. It appeared as though Typhoon Kiko had blown off the entire roof and it had been partially repaired. An old woman and two teenage girls sat on a bench built from a split log.

"Please tell me what's happening," pleaded Bob. He knew that the Chinese had invaded, but this family had been given specific instructions to remain inside. Robert needed details.

"Chinese soldiers arrived here this morning with trucks. They've taken all the young men with them and have demanded that everyone remain inside. We're now under martial law; they told us that anyone found outside would be executed. You're lucky that you made it this far. Where are you coming from?" The old man's English didn't contain the normal Filipino accent. He sounded like an American.

"I was on my way to Baler from Dibut. My name is Robert Banks and I'm an American weather observer. I came here to monitor

Typhoon Kiko. I already knew that the Chinese had invaded, but I had no idea that we are under martial law."

"Two men were shot and killed by the Chinese when they arrived here early this morning. They both had tattoos from the Guardian's on their hand and the Chinese were specifically targeting their group. I don't know who else they're after, but we don't intend to test them. They told us that this would be a very temporary situation." The old man held his youngest granddaughter on his lap and he kissed the top of her head. "You might want to consider returning to Dibut."

"What is your name, sir? You speak like you're an American." Robert knew that the man had lived or worked around Americans. His diction was perfect and there was no hint of European or Australian influence.

"My name is Chris Coloma. I served 26 years in the US Navy and returned here to the Philippines about nine years ago. I live in Maria Aurora, about fifteen kilometers from here. I came here early this morning to help my daughter and son-in-law repair their roof, and the soldiers showed up just after we began working."

"Thanks, Chris, for opening your door for me. I don't want to place your family in any danger by being here. What would you suggest that I do?" Robert was hoping for an invitation to stay.

"I suggest that you allow my granddaughter to give you a haircut and finish your shave. You look ridiculous!" Chris smiled as he spoke. "She's the neighborhood barber and will do a good job."

Robert was normally unconcerned about his image, but he suddenly became very self-conscious. His haircut must really look bad for Chris to bring it up under these circumstances. He managed a smile as he spoke, "Yeah, I guess it looks a bit rough. I cut off my hair and beard with my pocketknife earlier this afternoon. It looked good in the reflection of my knife." Bob smiled and asked, "Do you have a mirror?"

The oldest girl walked into the next room and returned with a small, round mirror. Bob laughed when he saw himself. Several patches of beard remained on his face and the 'uniform' length he planned for his hair was anything but uniform. A small patch behind his left ear still fell below his shoulders. "I guess I'm ready for my haircut now. Where should I sit?"

The girl motioned him to the back of the house to a small courtyard invisible from the street. She carried out a plastic chair, a comb, and a double-edged razor blade. Chris picked up a second plastic chair and followed them outside. Bob sat in the chair and the young girl began cutting his hair with the scissors without asking him about style. Bob thought that any style would be better than what he currently sported.

"Where are you from, Bob?"

"I mostly live in the Bay area, but I've been on the road a bit lately. My parents live in Cupertino, California and that's where I grew up." Bob hadn't spoken to anyone in three or four days and having an English conversation was refreshing. "After so many years in the States, what brought you back here?"

"My heart has always been in the Philippines, and home is where the heart is. I moved back here about a month after I retired from the navy, and I live comfortably here. I'm surrounded by family here, and that's what is most important to me." Chris didn't mention simplicity, but that's what he craved the most during his military years. American life seemed too complex; rent payments, electric bill, cable bill, gas bill, water bill, garbage collection fees, internet bill, phone bill, auto payments, health insurance, auto insurance, state taxes, federal taxes … for twenty six years Chris dreamed of returning to a simple life in the province.

With only a pair of scissors and a comb, Chris' young granddaughter transformed Bob into a character you might find in a boy band. She sprayed an oily solution on portions of his face and shaved his entire face. Then she cleaned the back of his neck and around his ears with the razor blade, even trimming his eyebrows before removing the cloth she had placed over him to keep the hair off his clothing. "What do I owe her?" Bob asked, looking at Chris.

"I believe she may have just saved your life, Bob. That's worth fifty pesos, don't you think?" Bob still converted everything into dollars in his head. Fifty pesos worked out to only one dollar and ten cents. Bob reached into his bag and unwrapped the towel. He removed his wallet and gave the girl 100 pesos, and she indicated that she couldn't make change for him.

"It's worth far more than this." Bob spoke to her in English, as he handed her the money. She smiled and said, *"Maraming salamat, po,"* before she vanished back into the house. She returned with a broom made from coconut fronds and swept all the hair into a dustpan and disappeared behind the house.

The girl returned in less than five seconds, speaking excitedly and pointing towards the street. 'The soldiers have returned, Bob, and they are forcing our neighbors out of their houses. They'll be here in just a couple minutes. Let's have our story straight, OK. How do we know each other?" Chris knew that they would be questioned and he wanted to be sure that their stories lined up.

"We could tell them the truth, I was walking by and you grabbed me off the street. That way you're not involved in whatever they blame on me." Bob felt like they might already know about his video and he wanted to protect Chris and his family.

"I'm going to tell them that you came to meet my granddaughter, Lilly. Tell them you met her online and have come to the Philippines to meet her in person." Chris struggled to find a suitable reason for Bob to be in their home.

"She's just a child, Chris. They'll never believe it. They may ask for us to verify the story and there's no evidence to support it." Bob glanced out the window and saw soldiers walking towards the house.

"She's nineteen years old, Bob. Her name is Lilly and you met in an online dating site. That's what I'm going to tell them, please don't contradict me." Chris stood and was already headed to the door to answer it before the Chinese soldiers knocked.

One of the Chinese soldiers spoke in Tagalog to Chris, asking him to step outside to talk. Chris complied and Bob remained hidden inside. The soldiers did not ask to search the home or come inside, and after less than five minutes of discussion they walked down the street towards the next cluster of homes.

"I didn't tell them that you were here," Chris whispered. They said that they are looking for anyone holding a foreign passport. They are under orders to round up all foreigners and bring them to the sports complex in Baler for processing. I don't know what that means or what they intend to do, so I told them that there were no foreigners that live in this community.

"Is Lilly really nineteen, Chris?" Bob ignored what was said about rounding up foreigners. He had been studying Lilly since he entered the home and had developed a fascination with her. She was thin and muscular and her dark skin was flawless. Her brown eyes sparkled and every feature of her face was perfectly situated. "I think I deserve to know more about her since she's my girlfriend."

Lilly understood English and she smiled at Bob as he continued to examine her. Bob said, "I think I like your girlfriend excuse, Chris."

"Pay attention to me, Bob. The girlfriend excuse won't work anymore because I lied to them. I told them that there are no foreigners here and we can't undo that. So we've got to get you out of here as soon as we can. It will be dark in less than two hours and I think we can hide you here until then. I need to figure out where to send you." Chris was now worried because of his lie. The soldiers could return at any time and he knew that he would pay a steep price for his deceit if Bob were discovered in his daughter's home.

"Please tell me honestly, Robert Banks. Do you have a wife or girlfriend back home?" Lilly grinned at Bob as she asked the question. Bob was unnerved by her question because he didn't realize Lilly could speak English. He didn't know what to say. He had no current romantic interest, and the question posed by Lilly shocked him. She was stunningly beautiful and Bob became tongue-tied.

"Would both of you please stop! This isn't the time for this. Get each other's information and 'friend' each other another time. We've got to find a safe place for you. Are you healthy enough to walk ten miles, Bob?" Chris had an idea, but it would require effort and timing.

"What have you got in mind?" Bob asked. He was willing to trust Chris.

"I'll bring you to my place in Maria Aurora after dark. It's a long walk and we're going to need to stay off the roads, so it will take awhile. But you'll be safe once we get there. You may want to take a nap or get some rest because we have a long night ahead of us.

Lilly showed Bob a place where he could lay down in the back portion of the house. And as she turned to walk away she flashed him a huge smile and a half wink. Chris boiled water in a huge kettle in the back yard. They would need it later to remain hydrated as they traveled to Maria Aurora. Bob's mind was distracted by Lilly, which was a good thing. It would have been very easy in this situation to allow himself to be taken to a deep, dark place mentally. Bob closed his eyes to rest and fell asleep in moments, smiling as he drifted off.

Chris whispered quietly to Bob, "They're back. Please stay still and quiet, I'll take care of things." Chris stepped out of the front door and walked towards the soldiers who were approaching his home. He asked them about his son-in-law and his grandson and was given assurances that they would be returned after undergoing a 'registration process.' It was dark and the electricity was still out. The only lights were from the truck the soldiers had arrived in and their flashlights.

Two men walked around, shining their lights into the darkness. A neighbor's dog barked fiercely at them, and one of the soldiers pretended to shoot the dog. The soldiers laughed, and then turned to get back on the truck. The commander of the small group looked at Chris sternly and warned him, "If you cooperate with us, your family will be safe. If you deceive us, your entire family will be punished. Do you understand this?"

"Of course," Chris answered, "We fully intend to cooperate. But I would like to request the swift return of my son-in-law and my grandson." The soldier didn't respond verbally. He nodded, grunted, and returned to the truck, its engine already running.

Chris returned to the house and went immediately to Bob. "It's time," he said. "Grab your bag and let's get moving." Chris kissed his daughter and each of his grandchildren and walked out the door. And Bob took the opportunity to throw a 'flying kiss' to Lilly. She pretended to catch and eat it and they all laughed. The two men slid out of the house and walked quickly to the forest on the opposite side of the highway. They remained concealed in the fields and woods as they headed for Maria Aurora. They hoped to avoid contact with soldiers along the way. Bob and Chris walked by faith, both believing that they would make it safely to their destination.

Chapter 31 – War crimes

Friday, 7:15pm August 11th
Maria Aurora, Aurora Province, Philippines

Unpredictable events frustrated Judge, especially when they jeopardized his mission. A section of the Dikildit Bridge was blown up, rendering it useless. Under normal circumstanced his men would have driven through the Dikildit River, but the river was swollen from the heavy rain from Typhoon Kiko and the current was too strong to cross without risking men and equipment. If everything went according to plan, his men would already be blocking the retreat of soldiers from Fort Magsaysay into the rugged Sierra Madre Mountains. But the quartermasters were unable to distribute weapons and ammunition until quite late in the day. And this unexpected delay at the Dikildit Bridge angered Judge. Civil engineers worked furiously to patch the bridge and make it useable.

More than thirty of the armed four wheelers were already beyond the bridge, guarding various intersections that the convoy would soon pass. Judge sent two men on a small raft across the raging Dikildit River to order his men on the opposite side to protect the Detailen and Malupa Bridges. But minutes after sending his men across the bridge, a large fireball lit the darkened sky. The Malupa Bridge had also been damaged. Judge vowed that someone would pay for this delay.

Judge was the first to pass over the repaired Dikildit Bridge. He raced forward to the damaged Malupa River Bridge and threw his uniform hat on the ground in disgust. The damage to the bridge was significant and would require at least two more hours before their convoy could move forward. Judge ordered thirty men to accompany six silun into the community of Santa Lucia. He instructed them to prevent anyone from leaving the community. He planned to interrogate the entire neighborhood and began to do so at cluster of homes quite close to the bridge.

Judge wanted blood, and everyone who couldn't help him find the bombing culprits would be executed. He burst into the first house and screamed at his interpreter, "Tell them that I need to know what they saw after the explosion on the bridge!" An old woman stood in the candle light of her home and explained that her eyesight was poor. She was shot in the face before the complete translation was finished. Judge dragged her lifeless body from the house by her hair, placing her body in the center of the street.

He then walked to the second house. "What did they see?" he yelled again at his interpreter. An elderly couple calmly answered that they heard voices that moved away quickly towards Barangay Bagtu, but they didn't see anything. Two more shots rang out and Judge ordered his men to pile their bodies in the street. They quickly complied, carrying the poor couple forty feet to the road and unceremoniously dumping them atop their dead neighbor. His men knew that they were also in danger; anyone could be the object of his anger, so they did not hesitate as Judge barked out orders.

A teenage boy, his younger sister, and their mother were dragged from the next home. They offered no information and Judge offered no mercy. He shot them in their stomachs, and had them thrown onto the pile of bodies to slowly bleed to death. The young mother screamed in agony from the gunshot wound and she tried to crawl to her dying daughter. Judge ordered his men to silence her, and she was immediately shot three more times.

The same scenario was repeated seven more times. Every occupant was dragged into the street, interrogated, and then shot. It made no difference whether or not they were compliant and provided him with useful information, Judge wanted blood. This was payback for blowing up the Malupa River Bridge. He wanted potential dissenters to know that a heavy price would be paid for their rebelliousness. And the innocent families of Santa Lucia paid a steep price.

Judge crossed the highway with his men. He ordered every family to stand on the street in front of their homes. He promised to inflict horrible pain to anyone who remained hidden inside, and within a couple of minutes he was given the chance to fulfill his promise. A middle-aged man wearing farmer's clothing was dragged from a pigpen behind his home. He struggled with the two Chinese soldiers who hauled him to the street. One of them hit him on the back of the head with his rifle butt and the man fell to the ground and did not move. Judge made them revive him before he began to torture the beaten man. As soon as he regained consciousness Judge shot him in both of his knees. Judge waited a full minute, and then shot the farmer in the stomach. He never delivered a 'kill shot,' instead allowing the pitiable farmer to suffer and bleed out in front of all his family and neighbors. It was a gruesome sight and parents shielded their children's eyes so they wouldn't have to see their neighbor suffer.

Judge demanded that each child watch the man die. And when one of the women refused to remove her hands from her son's eyes she suffered the same fate. Her young son watched in horror as they threw his mother to the ground and shot her in both legs. The Philippines had not suffered such unspeakable hatred since the Japanese atrocities committed in the Second World War. Judge ordered his men to beat the woman as she rolled in pain on the ground. They didn't like what they were ordered to do, but complied fully out of fear for their own safety. Judge had time to kill – literally. If the bridge had been quickly repaired some of the residents of Santa Lucia would have survived. But the long repair cost the lives of one hundred sixty seven unfortunate Filipinos.

The Chinese soldiers poured into the town of Maria Aurora as soon as the Malupa River Bridge was passable. They quickly commandeered cars, trucks, and vans and rejoined the convoy, which was stretched over several miles of cement road leading into the mountains. It was unwise for the convoy to navigate through the Sierra Madre Mountains at night. Major Yong, Judge's superior officer, was certain that Philippine military forces were now aware of their presence. Helicopter gunship support would help them navigate past ambush locations during the day, but at night the convoy would be easy targets.

Landslides from Kiko covered more than a thousand meters along the alternate route. Judge wanted to 'pacify' some of the communities along the Villa Road, believing that he would become the appointed territorial commander for a period of time. Major Yong was not a fan of 'pacification.'

Judge was ordered to remain in Aurora 'to protect their back door' and Major Yong took control of the convoy. Judge was given command of two hundred marines and provided with only four troop transport trucks and a dozen silun. That would be enough firepower to maintain control of the region until reinforcements arrived. There were no remaining forces in Aurora capable of challenging two hundred trained marines from the People's Liberation Army. Or so they thought.

Chapter 32 – Seventeen seconds

Friday, 6:28pm August 11th
Maria Aurora, Aurora Province, Philippines

Escorted by their Ilongot guides, the missionaries climbed to an altitude of more than three thousand feet. For seven hours they slipped and struggled uphill, covering more than twelve miles of rugged mountain trails. Even Reno, who was the fittest member of the team, showed signs of exhaustion; her muscles ached and she felt weak. The pace of their ascent up the mountain slowed considerably. But the guides, who seemed unfazed by their climb, pushed the team forward to a safe location to spend the night.

Their overnight resting place was perfect. A clear stream emptied into a beautiful pool of water that was deep enough to dive into. An enormous rock overhang provided a dry place for them to sleep. Even with the massive amount of rain that had fallen during Typhoon Kiko, the deeper recesses underneath the overhang were completely dry. Large boulders offered places to sit and the ocean was visible to the east.

The sun disappeared over the horizon and darkness raced at them like a charging carnivore. Then darkness seemed to pause just long enough for the team to gather sufficient firewood to build a cooking fire. Sean and Tyler stripped off their shoes and shirts and dove into the chilly pool, surfacing with surprised looks on their faces. The water was more than cool; it was frigid. They both feigned refreshment as their aching bodies trembled from the cold. They managed to entice Reno to jump into the pool and they laughed when she emerged from the surface of the water and screamed. All three quickly clamored from the chilly pool.

Kelly and Angel lagged many miles behind the team, and Kelly grunted and grimaced as she took each step. Angel knew that Kelly's fuel tank was empty and he asked their Ilongot guides to select a place for them to rest for the night. The earth was soft and moist beneath them when they lay down and Kelly had no problem falling asleep. Angel saw flashes of light in the distance and he hoped that it was from lightning instead of combat.

"How are you holding up, Ashley?" asked Sean. Ashley had been an emotional wreck since Anna and Marilou disappeared. But she had used the hike therapeutically, sorting out her feelings, fears and priorities as she walked. The fire cast dancing shadows that disappeared into the darkness outside.

"Actually, I feel good right now. I feel a bit childish for the way I've been acting, and I'm exhausted." She realized that there was little that she could do about her situation, and she spent much of the day in prayer. And God had answered her prayers by giving her peace.

Ashley asked the same question to Jun and Sean. Jun answered first, "I'm worried about my family. My brother's family lives near the ocean and my parents have a home in the center of Baler. I know that we're not supposed to worry, but I can't help it. Until I see them again I will be worried."

Sean said, "I've been thinking about our new baby. I hope it's a boy. I love my daughter, but want to do things with my son that my father did with me."

Ashley asked, "Like what?"

"Before dad passed away we went camping and fishing a lot. I learned more about my father during those quiet times together than at any other time. He was usually wound pretty tight, and he angered far too easily. But whenever we sat near a campfire or stood by the lake, Dad became contemplative. His tranquility matched the serenity of his environment. The more stressful the situation, the more agitated he became, and he was really quite an ogre at times. But he became a different man altogether during those quiet times. I really miss those times with him." Sean knew that he could also spend time camping or fishing with his wife and daughter, but he craved the same father/son relationship he enjoyed while his dad was alive. Pancreatic cancer took him swiftly from the family and Sean still struggled with the loss.

Reno and Angie cooked the rice, moving away from the smoke every few minutes as they cooked. "I know that you're worried about Sophie, but just place her in God's hands. Everything is going to be okay."

Angie replied, "I'm fine, Reno. I know that God will care for my family, and I will be with them all again whether it's on this side of death or the other." Reno felt a bit uncomfortable with the fact that Angie had gained a sense of peace in her family's death. There's no evidence that they were gone, and it seemed unnatural not to hold out hope.

"Your family is fine, Angie. You'll be playing with Sophie again soon. We just have to figure out what to do with these pesky enemy soldiers." Angie smiled, and Reno could see that she ached from all the worry. She walked around behind Angie and placed her hands on Angie's shoulders. "You are the most important person in my life right now, and I'm going to make sure that nothing happens to you."

Reno listened carefully and heard the sound a second time. It was the phone! Pastor Rod's phone was ringing in his backpack! "Pastor Rod! Your phone is ringing!" Reno ran to his backpack, released the two fasteners and felt around in the bottom of the pack for the phone. She felt it vibrating as it rang and she grabbed it from the pack just as Pastor Rod arrived. She handed him the phone and he answered it. The rest of the team moved close to hear what was being said.

"Hello, this is Pastor Rod." He never answered the phone so formally, but he wanted to make sure that whoever was calling knew that he was the one who had answered.

"Pastor Rod, this is Mike, can I speak with Reno for a moment? How are you guys doing over there?" Pastor Rod seemed stunned for a moment. He couldn't believe that they finally received a phone call! He hoped that it was Gina, but was excited that any of the family members managed to get through.

"Not so good, Mike. You know what's going on over here with the Chinese, don't you?"

"Yeah, we're catching it all on the news. How did you guys do with Typhoon Kiko?"

Before Pastor Rod could respond the line went dead. "Are you there, Mike? Mike, are you still there? Hello?" Rod's hands trembled as he held the phone. The call lasted exactly seventeen seconds.

Reno asked, "Was that my Mike?" Pastor Rod nodded. "He'll call back. I can't believe we have cell phone signal way up here! This is fantastic!" Reno moved closer to Pastor Rod and the rest of the group crowded into the covered area, waiting for the phone to ring again. It didn't.

"Try calling back, Pastor. Maybe we can reach them if we have a signal here." The phone indicated that there was no signal – zero bars. Pastor Rod began walking around with the phone held into the air, hoping to see some sort of a signal. He moved to the center of the opening and turned around in every direction, but nothing changed.

Reno needed Mike. She wanted to tell him that they survived the storm but were being hunted by the Chinese army. She was eager to tell him that a tribe of former headhunters was caring for the team. She didn't want to talk about Anna, but knew that they couldn't avoid sharing her fate if they were given a chance to speak. She missed Mike and had never been quite as homesick as she was at this moment. *Please call back,* she thought. *Please, Mike, call back!*

Pastor Rod could see the questions written across their faces and felt he needed to explain the call to the entire group. "That was Mike West. He asked how we are doing and I told him that things were not so good. But before we could discuss anything, the phone went dead. I'm trying to find a location here that has a signal and we'll try to call back."

Tyler asked, "What will we tell them about Anna?" It was a fair question and was on everyone's mind.

"What should we tell them about Anna?" Rod replied. "We know that she is missing, but we don't know that she is dead. How do you think we should explain it?"

David interjected, "I don't want to extend any false hope to her family or the folks back home. We may not have found her body, but I believe that it is safe to say that she didn't make it. The winds were ferocious and the floodwaters were deadly. We don't have to say that she perished, but let's not seem optimistic about it."

Ashley stared at her boss angrily. "What makes you say that, David? Is there something you know that we don't know?" She spent a great deal of time with David at work and could sense by his demeanor when something wasn't right. And the way he talked about Anna indicated that something was amiss.

David paused as he looked at her. He and Angel had buried Marilou, and he was quite certain that Anna had met the same fate as Marilou. He made a pact with Angel not to share that information, so he looked at Ashley and said, "I'm just being a realist, Ashley. The girls had time to rejoin us, or to send someone to tell us about their situation; there's nothing to indicate that they are alive."

Rod asked again, "If Mike calls back, what will we say about Anna? We may be limited to only a few seconds of conversation, and I'm not sure that's the news we should share."

"We should tell them," said Reno. "We don't know for sure what happened to Anna and Marilou, but they need to know everything that we know."

Reno was right. The team didn't know what happened to Anna and Marilou, so they couldn't confirm that either girl was dead. But all the evidence pointed to their demise. Pastor Ron said, "Okay we're going to explain that Anna is missing, but there's still the possibility that she's okay. Maybe somebody else is looking out for her right now. Let's pray that's the case. The church can begin to pray for her and her family."

Angie spoke up, "Where we're at right now is the border of three provinces. At this altitude we could be getting a signal from Nueva Ecija, Nueva Viscaya, or Aurora. We can't be sure which cell tower we connected to. If we move from here we may not find the signal again."

There was an air of excitement in the group. Everyone anticipated another call at any moment. They could express their concerns, share their love and let the church know where they were going. They could even find out what was being said in the news about the invasion. They wanted to hear that U.S. forces were already driving the Chinese back into the South China Sea. But such news wasn't forthcoming; at least not on this night.

Rod continued to hold his cell phone high into the air and search for a signal. "I'll call you guys if I find a signal. You guys go ahead and eat, I'll work the phone" Pastor Rod didn't want to state the obvious; the battery on his cell phone was quickly dying and they had no electricity to recharge it. Reno noticed it when she looked at the phone. And at exactly 7:51pm Rod's cell phone went black. The battery died, and with it died the enthusiasm that they shared earlier. Their elation had turned gloom. Their situation seemed so hopeless.

After trying unsuccessfully for another 25 minutes to reach the team, Mike West called Gina Franklin with the news. He told her excitedly, "I've made contact with the team! I was able to reach them, Gina. We spoke for only a few seconds, but I spoke with Rod for a moment and asked him how things were going. The entire call lasted only a few seconds, but I got through!"

Gina was thrilled. "What did they say about the storm? Did they know about the Chinese?" Where are they now?"

Mike cut her off, "We didn't get that far in the conversation, Gina, so we didn't learn much at all. Maybe we should text a series of questions to them and they can transmit text messages back. The good news is that they're okay."

"I'll call the others and let them know!" Gina was excited by the news. "Everybody has Pastor Rod's cell phone number, and we can all dial it. Maybe one of us will be lucky enough to get through again. This is such great news Michael, I'm so glad you called me." One after the other, Gina called family members to share the news. Contact! They had made contact! Then she sat on the sofa and redialed Rod's cell phone number every five seconds as she watched CNN. A retired U.S. army general was explaining why the Philippines was now lost. He said, "Our delayed response has allowed the Chinese to land sufficient forces to hold the islands. We will never be able to oust the Chinese military from the Philippine Islands."

As their cooking fire died, so did their energy level and spirits. The team gathered together on the floor of the small shelter and slept. If only they could have had a couple more minutes of conversation. If only the cell phone battery didn't die. If only ...

Chapter 33 – Captured
Saturday 3:40am, August 12th
Maria Aurora, Aurora Province, Philippines

Robert Banks and Chris Coloma struggled through the early evening darkness. Despite his years of military training, Chris was never schooled in escape and evasion. Both men knew the fundamentals of avoiding capture: stay hidden, move quickly, remain silent, and evade the enemy. But neither of them had any experience at hiding. They felt as if they were wild game, being hunted by sportsmen, who might shoot them just for sport.

They moved slowly, unsure of every step in the blackness of the night, fighting with the mud for control of their shoes. Chris worried that their trail through the muddy fields might betray them before they reached his home in Maria Aurora. Chris led the way, with Bob staying only a step behind. They walked around the municipality of San Luis, hidden in coconut groves until they arrived at the community of Balitwak in San Isidro. Balitwak was far enough off the main highway to allow movement over farm roads towards San Leonardo. Once they arrived in San Leonardo they planned to remain a thousand meters away from the national highway where they would cross the Malupa River. From the river they could approach his home near San Jose Elementary School from the rear.

Chris believed that his home would be safe for two reasons; first, he maintained a large supply of rice and grocery items in his pantry. But more importantly, Chris designed a secret chamber between his bedroom wall and the attached storage room outside. The space was small, only four feet wide and eight feet long. But it was large enough to conceal them both from the outside world. He explained to his contractor as the home was being built that the space would allow his dogs to sleep inside. But the contractor knew that the small, concealed doors were intended for another purpose. Especially since Chris installed tiled floors.

Both men instinctively stopped when they heard voices. The voices grew closer and Chris could make out their words. They spoke Tagalog with a distinct accent found only in this region of Aurora. Chris waited until the men were quite close before speaking, and he startled three young men, all in their mid-twenties, moving quickly in the opposite direction.

"Where are you going in such a hurry?" Chris really didn't care where they were going, but he was interested to know where they had already been.

"We're headed to the mountains, sir, and you should go there too. The Chinese have massacred people in Santa Lucia; we saw the bodies lying in the street. They executed children and old women, and there's no way that they would spare our lives if they found us."

"Where have you come from?" asked one of the young men.

"We have been walking from El Pimentel. We went south around San Luis and are headed from Balitwak towards San Leonardo. We haven't seen any Chinese soldiers along the way. What about you; where did you come from?" Chris took careful mental notes as the men shared their ordeal.

"Before it turned dark we walked from Cabiticulan through Bangko and crossed the Malupa river about two thousand meters above the highway bridge. We walked through a small section of Bagtu and took cover when we heard machine gun fire near the bridge. We lay in the bushes for over an hour near the river and watched a Chinese convoy cross the bridge into Maria Aurora. When we were certain that it was safe to move we hurried to get across the main highway in Santa Lucia. That's where we saw the bodies – hundreds of them."

"What's your name, *kaibigan ko?*" asked Chris. The man just confessed to being an eyewitness to a war crime. And Chris wanted to remember his name. Perhaps he could locate others who could testify at a later date.

"You know me, Lolo. It's me, Raulito. *Bunso ni Gloria.*" At first Raulito didn't know who he was speaking with, but things became clear when Chris mentioned El Pimentel. The two men moved close together and hugged.

Chris turned to Bob and said, "This is my grandson! They witnessed a massacre near where we're going and have advised us to head for the mountains.

"Is he related to Lilly?" asked Bob.

"You've got a one-track mind, Bob. But yes, they are related. They have the same father, but different mothers. They share the Montero family name."

"Let me explain our situation, Bob. We have an important decision to make. If we continue towards town we may get caught, and there's no telling what they'll do to us. But if we make it to the house there is plenty of food, purified water, and a secure place to sleep without worrying about being discovered. And if we go with these men to the mountains we may still get caught. But we can likely hide for an extended period of time before we're located."

Bob didn't like the thought of hiding in the mountains. He had just come from the mountains near Dibut and he found them inhospitable. While in the mountains he saw no sign of food, and shelter from the elements was sparse. "Can we make it to your place before dawn?" Bob asked Chris.

"It's less than two hours from here, even if we take the difficult route. We'll be sleeping soundly before the sun comes up." Chris knew that danger was a possibility no matter which direction they went. Like Bob, he also wanted to move forward to his house.

Chris asked Raulito, "We intend to cross the river upstream from the Balete tree. Did you see anyone in that direction?"

He hoped that Raulito would offer encouraging news, but he answered, "They are everywhere, Lolo. We were told that they searched door-to-door in Barangay 4. Come with us, Lolo, we'll be safe in the mountains."

Chris hugged his grandson again, this time holding him close for an extra few seconds then said, "We're going to continue to my place, Raulito. If you need food, you know you can find some at my home. Go with God, son." Chris placed his hand on Bob's back and said, "Let's go."

The hike from San Leonardo to the Malupa River took less than thirty minutes. Dogs barked at them and a woman's voice came from a small dirt-floor hut before the open field to the river saying, "Don't cross the river – death is on the other side."

Bob asked Chris to pause for a few minutes as they arrived at the river. He wanted to lie in the water and cool down. Even though it was nearly 3:00 in the morning the heat still seemed intense to Bob. He longed for California nights, which cooled down even after the hottest of days. As the men enjoyed the cool of the river they were being watched.

"We have two more in the river, headed west, about one thousand meters out." Men sprang quickly into action, donning night vision glasses as they ran towards Chris and Bob. The soldiers carefully watched the movements of Chris and Bob as they closed in on the two unsuspecting men. Within minutes they confronted the two startled men. After hours of walking and hiding in the darkness they were captured only minutes away from Chris' home.

Four men surprised them, shining a floodlight on them from only ten meters away. They yelled instructions in Chinese. Bob and Chris put their hands behind their heads and dropped to their knees in submission, fully understanding the tone of the shouts, but not the words. Neither man spoke. Without warning, Bob was kicked in the side of the head and knocked to the ground. Chris wondered if they would become two more war crime victims, but before the soldier could unleash a second kick, his companion stopped him. A tall, stocky man with a stern face stepped between Bob and the abusive soldier and challenged him loudly. He then helped Bob to his feet and examined his head. Bob sustained a small cut just above his right ear, but there was no serious damage. Chris was helped to his feet, and both men were placed in plastic restraining cuffs.

The men led them towards the Malupa River Bridge, where they climbed the embankment and stepped onto the national highway. Bob and Chris were seated on large square cement barriers that lined the road. Although they faced away from the bridge, Chris glanced over his left shoulder to look across the bridge towards Santa Lucia. He was horrified to see a group of men piling dead bodies into a large, open dump truck. The aggressive soldier saw him turn his head and slapped Chris across the face, ordering him to keep his eyes straight ahead. He required no comprehension of the Chinese language to know exactly what the soldier meant.

"We're in trouble, Bob," Chris whispered quietly as he leaned towards Bob. Bob sat silently, soaking in the severity of their situation. They were indeed in trouble. Just by acknowledging the bodies in the dump truck they could become one of them.

Chapter 34 – The horseshoe

Saturday 7:20am, August 12th
Dianawan, Aurora Province, Philippines

Cockfighting is considered the national sport of the Philippines. Every municipality has a cockpit arena which seats hundreds, perhaps thousands of people who flock to every local 'derby.' Hundreds of thousands of pesos are gambled weekly in each small hamlet as men bet on the cocks that have been bred and trained to fight. Westerners, particularly Americans, view the sport as barbarity. But Filipinos argue that the fighting cocks live a privileged life for an animal; they are well treated and fed a healthy diet that includes vitamins. And, unlike American chickens that are slaughtered in a production line, the fighting cocks are given a fighting chance. Even in death, they die with more dignity than American chickens that have been raised in cages so small that they can't turn around or flap their wings. When they are injured, veterinarians stitch their wounds, administer antibiotics, and do whatever is necessary to permit them to breed or fight again. If they are fatally wounded the roosters are cooked and eaten, including the head, feet, intestines, and blood.

Filipinos find dog fighting repugnant (even though they eat dog.) Bullfighting is also considered cruel because it is interspecies (with one using sharpened swords.) Animals around the world have their teeth cut, horns trimmed, tails removed, ears tagged and rings placed into their noses. Farm animals are routinely castrated, branded and fed whatever makes them grow most quickly into meat. Americans might share a different perspective if they butchered the animals they ate. Who really thinks of a cow when they pitch a shrink-wrapped package of hamburger meat into their shopping cart? Steaks and roasts come from cows. Bacon, ham, and ribs come from pigs. Chicken comes from chickens. And dead fighting cocks are roosters were at least provided an opportunity to survive before becoming stew. Filipinos find it ludicrous that they are judged to be barbarians for cockfighting by a nation that aborts its unborn and sells fetal parts for profit.

Philippine guerillas were trained in the fighting style of roosters. The initial aggressiveness or size of the animal rarely determines the outcome in cockfights. The cocks that shuffle and weave before launching their attacks tend to be more successful. And sustained aggressiveness is typically rewarded only if the animals learn to avoid their opponent's blades while in the air. Braveness is considered a flaw because it causes the gamecock to jump onto its enemy's blade. Guerilla fighters practiced shuffle and weave, or unexpected movement. They needed to avoid head-to-head encounters with the Chinese army now marching towards Pantibangan.

At first daylight Major Yong ordered his men to begin their push through the Sierra Madre Mountains. He knew that they would encounter light opposition and he positioned his forces accordingly. The bulldozers still occupied the front of the column, followed by tanks. His scouts returned quickly to report that another bridge near Baubo had been damaged. Major Yong silently worried about the remainder of the bridges in their path. If they were damaged his men would still be in the mountains after dark; but that was not the case.

Repairs on the Baubo Bridge took less than forty five minutes and the column quickly resumed their trip, but before they had cleared the community of Wenceslao, two bulldozer drivers had been killed by sniper fire, and three other men had been wounded. Even the helicopters providing support for the convoy were unable to locate where the shots had come from. The pace quickened as new bulldozer drivers hurried forward. That suited Major Yong; the faster they moved the better. Communications were still unavailable, so the helicopters, without landing, could provide little information about what lay ahead.

A third bulldozer driver was shot, but this time the alert crew of the first escort helicopter spotted the assailants and quickly returned fire. Three men momentarily returned fire. But their resistance died quickly. A rocket propelled grenade suddenly ripped through the Z-10 as it became stationary. It exploded in an orange fireball, and rolled down the side of the steep mountainside onto the road atop two silun, killing four men. The pilot and gunners became fixated on their target, and failed to realize that the snipers were merely a diversion. The trap had worked perfectly, but it was not over.

The second helicopter gunship quickly located the lone man who had fired the RPG. He didn't get far before the 30 millimeter cannon on the Z-10, which was designed as an anti-tank weapon, ripped him apart. But the second Z-10 did not get far either; a second RPG blew off its tail rotor and it spiraled quickly to the ground, crashing below the road. The People's Liberation Army may have given the Philippine Army too little respect; what they lacked in equipment, the Filipinos made up through superior tactics. Major Yong knew that the trip would be a fight to the other side of the Sierra Madre Mountains.

Major Yong ordered twenty of the silun to the front of the formation. They could easily alter their speed and direction, making them more difficult for snipers to hit. And their heavy machine guns could reach nearly a mile. If fired upon, they could answer with greater firepower. And, section at a time, they secured the road ahead of the convoy. Each silun held its chosen position until the convoy approached, and then leapfrogged in front of the others to hold a new position. The convoy moved more quickly with the silun in the front.

The bulldozers were brought to the front in Dinadiawan to clear nearly fifty meters of road that was covered in deep mud. The road was unstable, and Major Yong worried that the weight of his equipment might cause the entire road to collapse. Once the mud had been cleared, the silun quickly rushed ahead of the convoy to secure more territory.

The convoy passed two small military detachments as they moved through the mountains. Both camps were completely empty. All of the men and equipment had vanished, and even the surrounding houses were empty. The rain from Typhoon Kiko concealed every trace of their departure. It was impossible to tell which direction they went as they evacuated their camps.

Two men on a silun reported to Major Yong that they were nearing 'the humps.' The convoy would be required to drive over two exposed earthen dams several hundred meters long. Engineers restricted the weight of vehicles to 5 metric tons, but vehicles four times as heavy routinely rolled across the top of the dams. The route across the dam consisted of a single cemented lane, with large speed bumps placed every twenty meters. Major Yong moved to the front of the convoy to examine the humps. He observed water on the right of both dams and a steep five hundred foot drop on the left. But a narrow stretch of land extended to the right in the center of the dams. There, in Galintuja at the center of the dams, was a fortified military checkpoint. Major Yong's men didn't see any movement inside the heavily sandbagged shelter, but he wasn't going to be surprised as his men moved into the open. He ordered his tanks to shell the checkpoint, and they destroyed the checkpoint and five surrounding buildings in just a matter of minutes. The tanks rolled forward at the front of the convoy moved over the humps.

Twenty silun followed the tanks and quickly moved in front of them after they cleared the humps. In just a few minutes they entered the town of Alfonso Casteneda, where Brian Roberts, Lisa Stephens, and the rest of the U.S. embassy staff were hiding. They were shocked to see such a large number of enemy soldiers and hoped that they moved by quickly. They were far enough away from the road to be invisible, but would be quickly located if the Chinese opted to search the homes.

Lisa Stephens wondered if it would be wiser to surrender to the Chinese than to hide from them. They were American diplomats, and proper protocol, even during times of war, was to offer safe passage to diplomats. She reasoned that the last thing China wanted to do was to intentionally harm unarmed families of US diplomats; to do so was madness and would bring the condemnation of the entire world. But the invasion itself was also madness.

Lisa turned to Brian and asked, "Can you think of an instance when unarmed diplomats were killed rather than captured and repatriated when war broke out?"

"The U.S. has lost six ambassadors since WWII in: Guatemala, Sudan, Cypress, Lebanon, Afghanistan, and Libya. But many, many nations have had their diplomats murdered during uprisings. I don't know if we're safer as diplomats, or if we might become the only U.S. target that they can easily reach. I suggest we continue to hide. If they find us, then we can play the 'diplomat card.'" Brian was still stunned that the Chinese had invaded without any warning. *How was it possible for them to hide such a massive operation?*

Lisa responded, "I guess Frank never talked much about the dangers of being a diplomat. Until you came to the house and picked us up I really never thought about having to evacuate from the Philippines. I know we have practice drills, but I never thought for a minute that we'd actually have to *escape*. To be quite honest, I was angry that Frank stayed at work instead of being with us during the Typhoon. I guess I underestimated what he does here. I pray that he's okay, and I hope that he doesn't come this way looking for us."

"Frank and James will find a way to reach us. We just need to sit tight and let Corporal Mendez take care of things here. There's no need to panic; we are in good hands, Lisa." Brian trusted Corporal Mendez, but knew that there was a limit to what he could do. Even the corporal was in danger; he would likely be killed if the Chinese soldiers discovered that he belonged to the Philippine Army. But protecting the embassy families was a sacred trust to Corporal Mendez, who would do whatever he needed to do to keep them safe.

The ground shook as the tanks and bulldozers rumbled by. Brian wanted to peek out the window to see if he could get a glimpse of the vehicles passing by, but he was afraid that he might be spotted. The convoy was stretched from where they had lost the helicopters in the mountains near Dinadiawan to the valley communities of Marikit and Cadaclan, a distance of more than twelve miles. They rolled swiftly through the valley region and began to climb towards the horseshoe.

The horseshoe was now paved and widened, but it remained a notable landmark on the road leading to Baler. The horseshoe curves 270 degrees to the left on an uphill grade of more than 32 degrees. A steep cliff drops off to the right when entering the curve, replaced by a thousand foot vertical wall as the curve is rounded. After completing the curve, the left side becomes an abyss, dropping hundreds of feet to the valley floor. As the bulldozers turned left on the steep grade of the horseshoe their steel tracks slipped, sending them to the right, towards the edge of the cliff. But they made it through the curve and the tanks followed them, also sliding to the right as they climbed.

Without warning the mountain collapsed. Elements of the 52nd Engineering Division had been sent to help clear this road after Typhoon Kiko passed through. Instead, they devised a way to detonate enough explosives to bring the entire mountain down on the unsuspecting Chinese convoy. At first small rocks, dirt, and gravel fell. But a moment later the entire mountain crashed across the road, burying the men and equipment in its path and taking everything to the bottom of the valley more than a thousand feet below. More explosions detonated below the horseshoe, obliterating the road, and more than fifty vehicles disappeared over the cliff, bouncing and tumbling to the bottom as the road disintegrated beneath them.

Almost simultaneously eight large explosive charges were detonated inside the Canili Dam. The explosions created a massive gap, and water quickly began to flow through the dam into the valley below. And because the speed bumps prevented swift escape, the final six vehicles in the convoy were swept away in a torrent of water as the remaining portions of the earthen dam melted away. What remained of the Chinese convoy was now trapped between an impassable mountain passage and a destroyed dam that served as the only passage into the Aurora province. Major Yong ordered his men to retreat to the community of Marikit. He ordered silun to the top of every ridge surrounding the convoy, which was still arriving. Like a wagon boss, Major Yong circled the vehicles into defendable clusters and assigned a 'defense coordinator' to each cluster. And just like in the cowboy movies Major Yong sent out scouts to examine their options. Unless an alternative route could be found they might be forced to abandon their vehicles and move forward on foot. Such a move would prove to be very unpopular and lead to grumbling within the ranks.

Lisa Stephens was the first to notice that the convoy has stopped moving. It hadn't passed by, it was still in Castaneda and the engines had been turned off. Soldiers climbed down from the vehicles and began to stretch their legs. Lisa remembered her mother saying, "Idle hands are the devil's workshop," and she thought about all these armed men sitting around with nothing to do.

"Everyone, please stay away from the windows. There are hundreds of soldiers here and they don't look they're going anywhere anytime soon. They look like they are waiting for the road to be cleared so I believe we're safe, but let's make sure that we don't give them any reason to come back here, okay?" Lisa prayed silently for the engines to start again, but they remained silent. And she heard Chinese voices more clearly now. Men were approaching the house!

Corporal Mendez was armed and it appeared as though he was going to do something stupid. Lisa tried to get his attention as he ducked out the back door of the home where they hid, but Corporal Mendez's focus was elsewhere. He apparently intended to 'neutralize' the threat, and Lisa was horrified of the consequences if Corporal Mendez actually harmed any of the Chinese soldiers. Someone would miss them and come looking. She thought about walking out the front door to surrender to the soldiers; perhaps it might help avoid a tragedy. But as she stood up Corporal Mendez returned inside.

"The vehicles are moving again." He said. And as he spoke the sound of starting engines reverberated off the walls of the house.

They had dodged a bullet. Something unpleasant was about to happen and it appeared as though the danger had passed. But as the families would soon find out, appearances can be deceiving.

Chapter 35 – Pity is punished
Saturday 7:30am, August 12th
Maria Aurora, Aurora Province, Philippines

Aida held her grandson's hand as she carried her laundry to the river to wash clothes. Abner was four years old and Aida didn't go anywhere without him – especially to the river. Abner loved throwing sticks and leaves into the current and following them downstream. The river captivated him while Aida washed clothes and caught up on neighborhood gossip. The sun peeked through the early morning clouds, which appeared to be dissolving. Kiko brought several days of heavy rain, and this morning was Aida's first chance to wash and dry her family's clothes and bedding, which were wet and muddy from the storm.

She balanced the large wicker basket on her head and held it with her left hand and held Abner's hand with her right. They walked slowly towards the river as the neighborhood teemed with activity. Young men hammered nails through tin as they replaced or repaired their roofs. The sound of firewood being cut reverberated through the neighborhood. Young girls with long brooms made from coconut fronds swept up leaves and small debris in front of their homes. Others pumped water from wells into buckets and rinsed mud off the small cement path in front of their homes. And the smell of dried fried fish being cooked for breakfast wafted through the air. The rumors of a massacre in Santa Lucia, even thicker than the smell of fish, also floated in the air.

Everyone she passed, in whispered tones, provided information about the massacre. Some said that the people of Santa Lucia valiantly fought back. Others said that most escaped by running to the river. But the only certainty was that heavy gunfire took place across the river, and that people were dead. The neighbors cautioned Aida about going out in the open near the river, but every stitch of clothing her family owned needed to be washed.

She left the narrow cement path and ambled slowly down the muddy path leading to the river. Abner slipped in the mud and Aida caught him as he fell, dropping the basket that was balanced atop her head into the mud. She picked up all of the clothes and resituated them in the basket. After situating the basket back on her head she picked up her grandson and carried him the rest of the way to the river. As they stepped down from the high bank of the river onto the rocks, Aida released Abner's hand. "Stay away from the water," she warned him. "You won't be able to get out if you fall in; the water is moving too fast." She had lived almost her entire life in this same community and had never seen the Malupa River with a torrent this powerful. The noise of the river was normally a trickling sound, but today it roared.

Two of Aida's neighbors greeted her as she arrived at the edge of the river; they were already washing their clothes and talking about the gunshots from the night before. Normally they would talk about some drunken husband from the neighborhood who got caught with another woman, or some young girl who ran away with a worthless man. Lazy, good-for-nothing men seemed to be woven into every story. But today, all of the talk centered on the rumors and gunshots they had all heard the night before. They feared that the rumors were true.

From where they washed clothes they could clearly see two soldiers standing at either end of the Malupa River Bridge with machine guns strapped around their shoulders. There had been no recent gunfire, but they all heard explosions in the distance and were reminded that they were a nation under siege. But rather than sit in their homes in fear, they decided to go about their daily business in fear. What else could they do?

As they washed their clothes eight Chinese soldiers walked toward them along the riverbank. The women had no place to run, so they nervously continued washing their clothes. There was reason to fear because one of the men was Judge, who was entirely unpredictable and ruthless. After a very brief visual inspection of the women, Judge ordered his men to continue forward. Then he reconsidered and asked his Tagalog translator to remain behind with Sergeant Heng to find out what the women knew about the massacre. Judge needed to know if there were any lose ends he needed to take care of. As Judge and the other five walked away the translator asked, "What have you heard about a massacre in Santa Lucia last night?"

The women looked at one another and Aida replied, "We heard gunshots last night – many of them. Afterwards a man ran through our neighborhood yelling that everyone in Santa Lucia had been killed. He moved quickly and I couldn't hear everything he said."

"Did you know this man?" the interpreter asked.

"No," answered Aida. "He moved too quickly in the darkness to see who he was.

"Did you believe him?" asked the interpreter.

"Yes. We heard the shots coming in short bursts, and then there was silence before more bursts. Even last night we thought that people were being killed." Aida added, "We are all accountable for our actions to God, who will judge us. War is not an excuse for barbarity."

"What you say may be true, ma'am. But you must be careful when you speak such words. There are some amongst us who believe that they are above judgment." The two men began to walk away when Li Heng took a close look at Abner. He walked to where Abner was playing and studied him closely. After a full minute of examination, he picked up the boy and began to walk away. Aida and the other women immediately protested. Staff Sergeant Heng walked about thirty paces further then sat down on a boulder with Abner on his lap.

The Chinese translator tried to reassure the women that nothing would happen to Abner. But they were unconvinced; the rumors said that old women and babies were among the massacred in Santa Lucia. Aida walked towards Li Heng to take Abner from him. As she approached him, she noticed tears running down both sides of Li Heng's face. He reached into his pocket and produced a photograph of a young boy that looked remarkably like Abner. In fact, the two boys could have been mistaken as identical twins. The women passed the picture back and forth and marveled at the similarity. Li Heng spoke to the interpreter who told the women, "His only child is now four years old. He apologizes for being overcome with emotion when he saw your child, but as you can see in the picture, they look remarkably alike."

Judge returned suddenly and Li Heng quickly handed Abner to his grandmother. He wiped the tears that were still flowing. Judge demanded to know, "What are you doing playing with children?" He added, "We have a mission to perform, Staff Sergeant Heng, explain yourself!"

Li Heng handed the picture of his son to Judge, then hung his head and said, "I was overcome with emotion when I saw this child. He looks exactly like my son, sir."

Judge tossed the photo onto the muddy ground and stepped on it, saying once again, "Explain yourself, Sergeant Heng!" All the others viewed this tender moment between Li Heng and Abner as a glimpse of humanity in an ocean of hate. But not Judge; he viewed Sergeant Heng's kindness to the enemy as betrayal. Hugging a child would be considered treasonous only to men with a twisted mind; Judge was such a man.

As Li Heng moved to pick up the photo of his child from the mud Judge kicked him ferociously in the ribs, knocking him to the ground. "You are an embarrassment to the People's Liberation Army! I will not have a whimpering coward among my men. Your child is Chinese, Sergeant Heng. He is not the same as children born to these monkey people!"

Li Heng reached again for the photo of his son and he deflected a second kick from Judge as he did so. "These people are our enemies, Heng. Why is that hard for you to understand?" He tried to kick the downed man again, but Sergeant Heng caught his foot and swept Judge's other leg. Judge fell hard onto his side, but managed to remove his pistol from its holster even as he fell.

Li Heng froze, knowing that he was a moment away from death. Judge stood quickly and told him angrily, "I hereby sentence you to death for cowardice during combat." Judge quickly fired three rounds into the chest of his most trusted squad leader.

Judge turned to the interpreter and told him, "Tell these women to bury this coward." He then turned away and went back towards the other soldiers.

The interpreter immediately translated his order to the women, "He has ordered that the three of you bury this soldier. Do it quickly before he returns."

"Is this one of the men you mentioned, sir, when you said that some men feel like they are above judgment?" asked Aida. The interpreter nodded in the affirmative.

What sort of demon possessed Judge? His actions were inhuman, and Aida had never witnessed a more dastardly act. He brutally killed his own companion for showing a moment of compassion. Li Heng had shown the better side of human civilization, while Judge demonstrated an absolute lack of humanity.

Aida calmed Abner, who began crying as Judge first became loud. The two other women lifted the body of the murdered soldier and carried the dead soldier fifty feet to the embankment, where they could dig his grave.

Aida looked around nervously as she picked up the photo of Li Heng's son and placed it inside her blouse pocket. She asked the interpreter to remain with them in case other soldiers found them burying a Chinese soldier. He pointed to the soldiers on the bridge.

"They witnessed what happened. You can tell anyone who challenges you to ask those sentries. They will verify your story."

Their laundry would have to wait until they buried the dead soldier. The women were assigned the gruesome task of burying a murdered man. He stank as his bowels and bladder released when he died. And the amount of blood that leaked from his body overwhelmed one of the women, who vomited near the hole they dug. They used sticks and a flat rock to dig a hole deep enough to qualify as a grave. The mud was soft because of Kiko's rains, but they encountered large rocks as they dug and resorted to digging with their hands. After nearly an hour of digging they dragged the murdered soldier into the muddy hole and covered him with the dirt and rocks they had removed from the hole. Then they returned to the river to rinse themselves off. Black clouds moved in and heavy rain began to fall. All three women picked up their unfinished laundry and trudged back towards their homes in the pouring rain.

Somewhere in China a boy who looked much like Abner would grow up fatherless. His father did not abandon him. His father loved him immensely and died demonstrating his love for his son. But the boy would never know his father or the circumstances of his death. Judge determined that there are inappropriate times and places for fathers to demonstrate their love for their sons. And Li Heng paid the ultimate price for loving his son so intensely at an inappropriate time.

Aida asked her friends, "Do you think it's fitting that we say a few words over this man's grave? We could ask God to accept this poor man's soul and pray for his family. I feel like we need to do something." The other women nodded in agreement and they all walked back to where they buried Li Heng. They bowed their heads and Aida implored God to take care of this man's family. And she also asked the Lord to serve up a healthy portion of justice for his murderer.

One week earlier these same three women laughed about the wedding of Aida's brother. At the age of 62 he had finally found a woman who could tolerate his bad breath. They teased Aida about her new sister-in-law and Aida laughed until it hurt. But today was very different; there was no reason whatsoever to laugh. Their neighbors across the river had been massacred. They witnessed the murder of a kind man, and they couldn't finish their laundry and would carry it home wet and heavy.

They had been so preoccupied with burying the soldier that they didn't noticed two bodies in the bushes on the Santa Lucia side of the river. From more than 70 meters away they couldn't even identify whether the victims were male or female. They couldn't retrieve the bodies to give them a proper burial. Aida felt compelled to pray for them and did so privately and quietly. They grieved for their neighbors and their countrymen. Everything last week had been so right, and everything since Typhoon Kiko arrived was pure horror.

As the women walked homeward with their wet clothing they heard two shots ring out. They quickly picked up the pace and hurried back towards their neighborhood. They walked more easily once they were on the solid concrete walkway, and they were anxious to find out what had happened. Most of the people in this community were related to one another, and everyone knew each other. As they neared Aida's home, she dropped her laundry and ran to the front of her house where a circle of people gathered around her dead son, Marvin. She pushed through the crowd of people, fell to her knees and hugged Marvin's lifeless body.

Marvin was a dutiful son and a hard-working farmer who had never hurt anyone. He wasn't prone to emotional outburst, and had never been violent. He wasn't even political, and he rarely had any disagreements with others. Marvin, in fact, was normally a calming influence when things got out of hand. He was killed only because he was a Filipino male of fighting age. Aida hugged his lifeless body and wailed loudly. Even though she wasn't there and nobody had explained the shooting she knew who killed him.

Cousins took Abner to a neighboring house. Aida continued to hug the body of her precious son until neighbors finally convinced her to stand up. They brought a cart to carry Marvin's body to the cemetery. Normally an extended wake would take place and the family would have time to mourn together. But Marvin's bloodied body was hoisted onto the back of the small wooden cart that was pulled by an aging black water buffalo to the town cemetery. Aida lay next to Marvin on the cart and she hugged him and cried as the entire neighborhood followed the cart to the town cemetery. When they got to the cemetery they discovered hundreds of others burying their loved ones there. Some had died during Typhoon Kiko and some due to the brutality of the sadistic soldiers. No matter the reason, the town of Maria Aurora mourned loudly.

Aida could remember every detail of Judge's face. She wanted to be sure that he would someday stand trial for the brutal murder of her beloved son. She asked her friends to help her identify specific attributes of the cruel man: the rank on his uniform, his hairstyle, the way his eyes narrowed, the thinness of his lips… she hoped to testify against him one day and make him pay for his savage behavior.

Chapter 36 – Foreigners are rounded up

Saturday 8:00am, August 12th
Baler, Aurora Province, Philippines

Every Chinese soldier was given a standing order to secure foreign nationals for deportation. Foreigners were not to be harmed. This order came from top-level leadership, sensitive to world opinion. If they brutalized or killed citizens of other nations it might enrage them, provoking them to join the fight against the PRC. There was no need to foolishly invite other nations into the fray for unnecessary mistreatment of their citizens. The order to detain them included clear instructions to treat their medical conditions, feed them, provide clean water for them, and make sure that they were not mistreated.

Judge knew that Baler was a tourist town. He'd seen many foreigners walking on the streets, eating in the restaurants and frolicking on the beaches the day he arrived. He had even seen the team from Eastside Christian Fellowship and remembered details about their team. He counted seven Americans, three males and four females. Judge expected to find fifty or more foreigners in the area, including the Americans he spied at the beach at Diguisit. There were bound to be a couple dozen expatriates living in the area, and Judge formulated a plan to locate them all.

"When you find any foreigner you must confiscate their cameras and cell phones. Search their homes, their hotel rooms, their backpacks and purses. We don't want to find ourselves on TV in their home nations after they are repatriated. Any recording device must be taken from them." Judge knew these foreigners would carry exaggerated horror stories home as they were deported. But it would all be hearsay, unsupported by any corroborating evidence. Judge even denied them the opportunity to speak with one another while in detention. The less they communicated with one another, the fewer facts that they could agree upon.

The Mayor of Baler ordered all the beachside hotels to close their doors and send their visitors home prior to Typhoon Kiko. He didn't want to be responsible for the death of any thrill seekers. So Judge would find few tourists who remained in Baler. Baler's illustrious mayor had seen to that.

Soldiers were ordered to bring any foreign captives to the Baler sports complex for processing. Bob and Chris found themselves in the back of a canvass-covered olive green truck with five other foreigners found in Maria Aurora. Among them was Larry, an American anthropologist who arrived in the Philippines in the early 90's and decided to stay. His work kept him in the mountains with primitive tribesmen and Larry opted to 'go native.' He abandoned his native tongue and spoke only the tribal tongue of the Ilongot tribe. The people of Aurora laughed at him when they saw him ride by on his sturdy bicycle, always shirtless and wearing only a g-string. On two or three occasions Chris had also seen Larry riding his bicycle. He was quite noticeable as he was nearly naked and sported a long beard and shoulder length auburn-colored hair. Bob didn't know that such people existed. He wanted to interview him and include him on his blog site, but Larry wasn't interested in interviews.

An American known as Uncle Fred to the local population in Baler refused to surrender to the Chinese. He booby trapped his home and detonated an improvised explosive device when the Chinese soldiers entered his home to find him. He then shot two soldiers at close range before he was shot and captured. They made him watch the execution of his wife and two children before Uncle Fred was executed. His neighbors knew that he would fight, and they admired him for it.

Judge generously offered a reward of 10,000 pesos for helping to locate foreign nationals. Ten thousand pesos is a large sum of money to a farmer who toils in the sun all day for less than five thousand pesos monthly. Judge knew that the pesos he offered had no value at all. The Chinese government had printed hundreds of millions of bills in order to bribe local officials and pay for needed goods and services. The Philippine pesos, whether real or counterfeit were worthless pieces of paper. In just a month the Chinese Yuan would replace them all.

Chris spoke quietly to Bob as they bounced in the back of the truck on their way to Baler. He had been cautioned not to talk, and was smacked on the side of his head with a rifle butt when he was caught talking a second time. Chris wanted to assure Bob that they were safe; if the Chinese wanted them dead they would've killed both of them already. Chris said, "We're safe, but don't provoke them."

"Where do you think they're taking us?" asked Bob. Chris answered. "We're headed towards Baler. I don't think they'll take us any further than Baler, there's really nothing up north." Chris wondered why they would be returned to Baler. Was it possible that they would be loaded onto boats?

Judge assigned a team of 100 men to go door-to-door in the town of Baler looking for anyone who was not Filipino. Even if they were Philippine born, but held a foreign passport they would be taken to the sports complex for processing. Judge took his remaining men to Maria Aurora to begin house-to-house search for foreigners.

Judge entered a house in Barangay Ramada and asked about foreigners in the area. The man of the house quickly stated that a team of American missionaries was staying at a nearby church. The man despised Americans in general, but evangelical Christians in particular. And he was quite excited when he learned that he could receive ten thousand pesos for each foreigner found. His family never received any of the gifts the Americans brought with them because he refused to allow them onto his property. His children were jealous of the neighbor kids as they played with new toys brought by the Americans. Now he could make them pay a price for making his children feel left out.

A squad of eight men commanded by Judge followed the man to Ramada Community Church, but the church was empty. Two Filipino families had moved into the dormitories and they confirmed that Americans had been there. They pointed in the direction that they went, and there was ample evidence of their departure. Judge and his men could follow their muddy trail leading into the fields.

The thick mud from Typhoon Kiko made their trail easy to discern, and he followed it to where the Americans had entered the rice field. They followed the trail across the rice field to the tree line and made their way towards the cemetery. As they came out by the cemetery Judge recognized it as the place his men had been ambushed. He quickly jumped to conclusions and blamed the cemetery attack on the Americans. He decided that, because of their treachery, they would take no prisoners from this group.

As Chris and Bob arrived at the Baler sports complex, the seven foreigners were ordered out of the truck and told to sit with twelve others on the floor of the large gymnasium. Seven of them were Australians tourists and three were Americans who lived in Baler. A Korean missionary couple completed the group of twelve. Chris was the only one who was bleeding, and the others appeared to have been treated humanely. This reassured Bob, who was afraid of the unknown.

Bob was made to stand in front of a long wooden table and a

man motioned for him to approach the first station at the table. He was asked, "What is your full name and nationality?"

Bob answered, "I am Robert Banks from the United States." He hoped that the Chinese had not yet linked him to his blog site. He didn't realize that nobody in the Philippines, including the Chinese soldiers, had communications with the outside world. He was directed to the next station.

"Why are you in the Philippines?" asked the next man.

Bob didn't want to be identified as a journalist, so he said, "I'm a tourist."

The man then asked him, "How long of you been in the Philippines?"

Bob answered, "Seven days."

"Are you alone?" he asked Bob, to which he simply replied, "Yes."

Each of the five stations was linked together in a small network, and the soldiers entered the information into a single computerized database. They established a file for each of the detained foreigners.

The next man asked Bob, "Is this your first trip to the Philippines?"

Bob replied simply, "Yes."

Then the man, a pleasant-faced soldier who smiled as he spoke, asked, "May I see your passport, sir?" Bob couldn't produce it and explained that his backpack had been left behind when they were apprehended. Bob was then sent to a desk about forty feet away with a stern-faced corporal sitting behind it, almost at attention. For almost two hours Bob explained to him many times why he had no passport with him.

Over 200,000 foreigners around the Philippines had been apprehended by this time. Most of them were Americans. The U.S. embassy families were not among them yet, but the Chinese were thick in Alfonso Casteneda, and the embassy families would soon find themselves among the foreigners being 'processed' at the Baler sports complex.

Each of the detainees at the Baler sports complex was carefully fingerprinted and photographed. The Chinese also asked each of the foreign detainees to provide a brief narrative on videotape. After stating their name and nationality, each detainee was able to speak freely. The edited versions would be used for propaganda purposes in the coming days. These videos would be used to convince each of their governments that it was important to cooperate to get their people home safely.

Chris laughed when a Filipino couple seated next to him on the bench confessed that had never been out of the Aurora Province. They told the Chinese that they were American citizens because they believed that they would be given preferential treatment. Their English was good enough to convince the Chinese soldiers to include them in the truck. They were fingerprinted, photographed, and they both secretly hoped they would be deported to America. They listed their hometown as Cincinnati, Ohio because their niece lived there.

Bob could smell food being prepared. And at the end of the processing line he saw a water container with paper cups. He considered that, perhaps, being in Chinese custody was the best and safest place he could be right now. He returned to where Chris sat against the wall, and smiled at him as he sat down. It appeared as though he was now fully 'processed.' The next two days would prove to be the longest wait of his life.

Chapter 37 – Embassy staff captured

Saturday 8:40am, August 12ᵗʰ
Alfonso Casteneda, Nueva Vizcaya, Philippines

Lisa Stevens crawled across the floor to where Cpl. Mendez peeked out the slatted window. She tapped him on the leg and asked him to sit down. Then she told him, "You need to change into civilian clothes right away. The soldiers appear to be searching homes, and if they find you wearing a uniform, they may kill you. Put on some civilian clothes."

"I don't have any civilian clothes with me, ma'am. Uniforms are all I brought with me." Cpl. Mendez seemed willing to comply, but needed help.

"Brian, please find some clothes in your bag for the Corporal to put on. They may kill him if they catch him in uniform." Lisa's instincts were correct. If he were found in uniform, Corporal Mendez would have been executed.

"What's your first name, Corporal?" Lisa realized that he needed to change more than his clothes, Corporal Mendez needed to change his identity- and quickly!

"Robert, ma'am," he replied.

Brian reached into his backpack pulled out of pair of khaki hiking shorts and a Boone, North Carolina souvenir T-shirt and handed them to Robert, who quickly changed his clothes in front of everyone in the room. Brian had heard what Lisa asked him, and he repeated to the others, "This is not Corporal Mendez. This is our dear friend Robert, he's Lisa's driver. Do not call him by his rank, okay?"

Brian didn't have extra sandals or shoes to offer Robert, so he asked the others, "Does anyone have a pair of sandals or tennis shoes that you could give to Robert?" A pair of nice leather sandals was handed to Robert and he admired them as he put them on his feet.

"We need to get rid of your uniform; if they search and find any trace of military presence here it could jeopardize everyone in this household." Brian stuffed the uniform pants inside of one of Robert's combat boots. Then he took the uniform shirt and filled the other boot. The two boots were then tied tightly together with the laces and were ready for disposal.

"Listen to me Robert. You are my driver. You are part of the U.S. embassy staff in Manila. All of us are considered to be diplomats and are afforded diplomatic immunity. Now let's lose that uniform." Lisa was worried that Corporal Mendez might try something heroic and get everyone killed. But once he was wearing shorts and a tee shirt he looked more like a tourist than a soldier.

The owner of the house, Robert's uncle, said that he could hide the uniform where it would never be found. His wife, Tessie, was thinking of the same place – the bottom of an open pit toilet just thirty yards behind their house. Tessie picked up the boots and headed for the back door, but Lisa stopped her.

"Robert, where's your gun? I noticed you had a pistol; where is it?" Lisa wanted to make sure that there was nothing left of Robert's military identity.

Robert reached into the waistband at the small of his back and produced a 9mm pistol. Tessie tucked it into one of the boots and opened the door. There were no soldiers visible from the back, so she held the boots to her stomach and walked swiftly to the small open pit toilet. There she dropped the boots into the raw sewage and watched them slowly sink until they were totally immersed. There was little chance that the Chinese would be searching in the cesspool for anything. Robert's aunt stayed inside the toilet for an appropriate length of time and was shocked to find two Chinese soldiers standing at the door as she emerged.

She made a face and held her belly, then smiled. One of the soldiers smiled back and entered the toilet as soon as she began to walk back towards the house. Apparently the two men also felt the call of nature and needed a place to go. She returned to the house and whispered that two Chinese soldiers were now behind the house.

Lisa quickly approached Robert and asked him, "Is there anything else that identifies you as military? Do you have an ID card or anything in your wallet?" Robert reached into his wallet and produced his military ID card. He was embarrassed that someone else had to point it out to him. He dropped the ID card through narrow slits in the floorboards and thanked Lisa for taking care of him. The only thing that made him look military now was his haircut, but so many Filipinos wear military style haircuts due to the tropical heat that his hairstyle wouldn't likely even be noticed.

"Everyone, if you have your passports with you please pull them out now. In just a few minutes we are going to be in Chinese custody and they need to see that you are carrying diplomatic passports." Lisa surprised herself by taking charge. That was Frank's role, but she now felt responsible for the staff and their families.

Robert smiled and asked, "What kind of car do I drive?"

"You normally drive anything that's available in the carpool, but when you drive the Ambassador or his family you drive a black, armor-plated Ford Expedition." Brian knew every vehicle in the carpool, and he had his personal favorite, a silver and dark blue Toyota Land Cruiser. Robert was surprised by Brian's reply because he was only joking, but the reality of detailed questioning took the smile off his face.

Before they could share any additional conversation the back door opened and the two soldiers who had used the commode stood at the door and gaped at them. They didn't expect to find a room full of Americans and they were dumbfounded. One of the men stepped outside and called for backup, and within a few moments the house was surrounded by soldiers who demanded that they come outside with their hands on their heads. The children cried out of fear and their mothers cried along with them. They marched out in a single file line and were led to the shade of a nearby tree.

The soldiers quickly sent for an English translator who arrived about three minutes later. He looked like a boy who couldn't yet be eighteen years old. He introduced himself, but nobody understood what he'd said. Then Lisa took over the conversation.

"My name is Lisa Stevens. I'm the wife of the U.S. ambassador to the Philippines. This is Brian; he's my husband's Chief of Staff. All of the people here with us are either staff members or family of U.S. embassy staff. We have diplomatic passports and we expect to be treated as diplomats. I wish to speak to your commanding officer."

The young interpreter was shocked to discover who he was interviewing. At home he was an English wizard, but he suddenly felt inadequate in the presence of the American diplomats. Lisa had been so assertive that the young man felt compelled to comply with her wishes rather than just translating what she'd said. Lisa made him believe that his unit might accidently violate international law if they mistreated this group, so he quickly said to his superiors in Chinese, "These people are American diplomats and they must be treated in accordance with international standards regarding diplomats." He wasn't translating anything, he was just thinking out loud. He had no idea what sort of international standards applied to diplomats, but he didn't want to be guilty of violating them.

Before launching the invasion the soldiers had all been instructed to treat foreigners with respect. There was no special instructions regarding diplomats, but they instinctively knew that important people required special handling. They were commanded not to brutalize Filipinos; a very different standard than treating people with 'respect'. The instructions were clear - foreigners would be given special considerations. The People's Republic of China didn't want foreign captives returning to their home nation with horror stories of Chinese brutality. But they needed some information. How did the U.S. embassy staff end up here in Alfonso Casteneda? Where was the U.S. Ambassador? What were their official titles? The officers asked many questions, but they were polite and they provided water and food to the families.

Major Yong knew that these Americans needed to return to Baler for 'processing.' He couldn't provide safety for them as his men pushed forward towards Pantabangan. But the Canili Dam had been destroyed and getting back to Baler would not be easy. The water that raced through the gap in the earthen dam created a massive gap. No vehicles could cross to the other side, but it seemed possible to walk down to the lowest level and cross by foot. The water level had stabilized and there was no more flow across the broken dam, but it was muddy and unstable. They could confiscate vehicles after crossing the Canili Dam. But getting across the breach in the dam would be treacherous, especially for women and small children.

Major Yong gave assurances to Lisa that they would be treated with respect and dignity. But he also explained that they would need to sacrifice 'creature comforts' as they traveled and were 'processed' in Baler. He apologized in advance for any lack of food, water or medical care while they traveled. He explained that any discomfort that they might suffer would be temporary. He added that they would all be quickly repatriated to America. "America must cooperate before you can go home," said Major Yong through his nervous interpreter. "But that shouldn't take very long."

The civil engineers under Major Yong's command were unable to repair the Canili Dam. More than seventy-five meters of stone and dirt was completely washed away. A giant crevice that was more than one

hundred thirty feet deep separated the two sides of the road. The only way across the dam was to climb down one side, cross over the mud and stones near the bottom of the breach, and climb back up the other side. Major Yong sent two dozen men across the path and made them secure the way for the American diplomats to walk across. They installed a rope to hold onto, and added stones in the muddiest sections to provide better footing. But that was the easy part.

After they proved that they could get across the massive gap in the dam, they lowered two of their all-terrain vehicles by rope to the bottom. And the soldiers carried them for more than seventy-five meters before hoisting them up to the top on the other side. After they were placed on the road they affixed the machine guns to the back and they quickly raced off to find transportation for their American captives. Major Yong made it clear that only those who held foreign passports would be permitted to go to the processing center. The Filipino staff would remain behind in Alphonzo Casteneda.

Lisa implored Major Yong to permit the rest of the staff to travel with them to Baler. But he was adamant; only foreigners were permitted at the processing centers. All the Philippine staff members would have to remain in Alfonso Castaneda. Reluctantly Lisa agreed to Major Yong's plan for them. She really had no choice, but she believed that the staff members that were left behind would be treated properly. She had Major Yong's assurance of that.

The crossing was slow and muddy. Soldiers helped carry the smaller children and anyone who had difficulty walking through the thick mud. They stepped slowly from stone to stone. Lowering them to the bottom and hoisting them to the top was the most difficult part. It was steep and frightening, and some of the children refused to cooperate. But after only an hour and twenty minutes all of the U.S. Embassy staff and their families stood safely on the opposite side of the washed out dam awaiting transportation. Chinese soldiers brought them buckets of water from below so that they could rinse off the mud. They rinsed themselves as they waited to be transported to the Baler processing center.

Lisa didn't realize it yet, but she had saved the life of Corporal Robert Mendez. Robert was now a driver for the U.S. embassy instead of an AFP corporal thanks to Lisa's quick thinking. Two Philippine soldiers were found near Alfonzo Casteneda after the embassy staff was safely on the other side of chasm; both were immediately executed. Lisa had no way of knowing that the embassy staff presence in the Aurora province would also save the lives of the Eastside Christian Fellowship missionaries.

Chapter 38 – Escape and evade

Saturday 8:50am, August 12ᵗʰ
Bayanihan Aurora Province, Philippines

Just after daybreak Kelly and Angel arrived with their two Ilongot guides at the rock overhang where the others rested. Only Tyler was fully asleep; the others hugged and greeted them as they arrived. Even though she had been carried for much of the uphill climb, Kelly was exhausted when she arrived, and asked to lie down. Ashley was the first to mention the call, "Kelly, we've got some good news. The phone rang and we spoke to Tom West for a few moments."

"Really! What did you tell him about our situation?" Kelly didn't want to mention Anna by name, but that's 'the situation' she was thinking about.

"We didn't have any time to talk; the call was cut off and then the battery died. But there was a cell phone signal, Kelly. That means that we can reach them after we recharge the battery." Ashley was optimistic for the first time during their entire ordeal. The phone call made her believe that things were better than they were. In reality, they were in grave danger. Judge blamed their group for the deaths of his men, and he was now hunting them.

Pastor Rod spoke up, "Since everyone is awake, I'd like to make a proposal. I've been thinking about it all evening. We have very few options right now. We can run and hide for a while, but I believe that we will eventually be captured. We're not trained for jungle survival, and we are not in good enough physical shape to evade capture."

Everyone laughed when Kelly added and emphatic, "AMEN!"

"I suggest," continued Pastor Rod, "that we return to the bottom of the mountain, walk out to the highway, and surrender to the Chinese."

Nobody spoke. They had all considered the same thing, but they feared what might happen to them. Nothing was certain if they continued running, and there was no way to predict what the Chinese would do to them if they were captured.

Pastor Rod added, "I'm told that we can be in Kadayakan this morning and on the highway around lunchtime if we leave right now. We can surrender on our terms rather than getting caught up in some wild gun battle." Still nobody spoke.

Finally Sean spoke up, "I agree with Pastor Rod. I think we would be better off as Chinese prisoners than being hunted in the mountains. It may prevent us from being shot, and sooner or later they'll have to release us."

The Filipino team members were not in agreement with any plan to surrender. Brother Manny said, "I have no passport to show them. Do the Filipino team members get to vote on this also?"

Rod replied, "Forgive me, Brother Manny. I'm speaking specifically to the American team. I think you should discuss your options with Jun, Angel, and Angie. You don't have to do what we do. I know that, as Americans, they might treat us quite differently than they treat you."

Kelly spoke up, "What if America is now fighting the Chinese? Maybe what we'll get is worse treatment."

David voiced his opinion, "We have no food, very little purified water and all we can do is run, not fight. None of us wants to be a prisoner, but surrender to the Chinese might be our best chance to survive."

Reno surprised the team by adding, "Romans, chapter thirteen says that we must submit ourselves to all authority. Whether this new Chinese authority has been forced on us, like the Romans over the Judeans, doesn't matter. As believers we are instructed to submit to *all* authority; we don't have to like or agree with it, but we are commanded to yield. Scripture says, ' …there is no authority except that which God has established.' This may be a test of our obedience."

"I'm afraid, Reno." Ashley expressed her concerns openly. "You and I could be raped. Bad things happen during war. Is there any way that we can just hide until we get the phone recharged? If we can find out what is going on from our families, we can make a decision based on legitimate information instead of rumors."

Pastor Rod believed that they would find the best solution if they leaned on God during this difficult time. He asked for a moment of prayer and concluded his prayer by stating that, "… for those that love God, all things work together for good…" In his own heart, Rod had no clue what good could be found in their current situation.

Tyler was surprised when he woke up to discover that the team was voting whether or not to continue to evade the Chinese military or to surrender to them. He had slept through the entire discussion. He asked, "What if they kill us all?"

"Then we'll be put out of our misery," quickly replied Kelly. "I honestly don't fear what's on the other side of death."

Sean added, "Let's learn from the Apostle Paul. He was stoned, imprisoned, beaten nearly to death on multiple occasions, and he was shipwrecked, but he viewed his trials as 'light and momentary.' We are here as servants of the Lord, and the Lord will see us through this. Let's accept whatever comes our way as 'light and momentary' suffering, believing that God will deliver us home to our families."

"We've heard some deep theology last night and again this morning," said Pastor Rod. We are faced with a difficult decision. We will take a vote and I would like everyone to abide with the majority decision, okay?" He looked at each of the team members, and everyone nodded their head in agreement. "If you believe that we should surrender peacefully to the Chinese soldiers, please raise your hands." Ashley and Tyler did not raise their hands. But David, Reno, Sean, and Pastor Rod created a clear majority, and the decision to walk to the highway to surrender was made.

"What will you do?" Rod asked Manny.

"We will walk to Kadayakan with you, but from there we will leave you and try to find out what has happened to our families."

Angie began to weep, and Reno hugged her. Kelly then hugged Angel; he had shown her enormous kindness. They knew that there might be no time for 'goodbyes' once they headed down the mountain. A sudden separation was more than possible; it was likely. After a few minutes of hugs and tears the group followed their guides, who were already walking down the path that led to Kadayacan. The path was narrow and slippery, but they covered ground quickly as they walked downhill.

Even Kelly, who struggled with every step as she climbed the mountain the previous day, walked down the hill with little effort. The cramps in her legs were gone and her lower back pains had vanished. In little more than three hours the missionaries from Eastside Christian Fellowship arrived at the edge of a concrete road. They could be intercepted at any moment from this point forward.

The four Filipino team members walked ahead of the others to a cluster of homes and located a motorcycle with a sidecar. They offered payment to the nervous driver to bring them to the market in Maria Aurora. He had seen evidence of enemy brutality along the highway, and was frightened to venture out. But he couldn't resist the five hundred peso offer to drive Rod, Angel, Manny, and Jun to the market. After another quick exchange of hugs and tears, the Filipino hosts officially ended the mission trip as they returned to their respective homes.

Their timing could not have been more perfect. The tricycle was able to travel the distance to the Maria Aurora public market without encountering a single Chinese checkpoint. But more importantly, God arranged a divine appointment between the Eastside Christian Fellowship missionary team and the U.S. embassy staff. Just as the ECF team stepped onto the highway they saw a large olive green troop transport truck approaching. The truck slowed, then stopped and several members of the People's Liberation Army jumped out and leveled weapons at them. They already had their hands raised high in the air and, in a matter of moments they were loaded into the back of the truck.

The ECF team was surprised to find other Americans in the truck. And they smiled at God's providence when they discovered that they were in the company of the U.S. embassy staff and their families. Pastor Rod and Reno glanced at one another and smiled when Lisa Stephens introduced herself. They knew that mistreatment of their companions would be highly unlikely. Abuse of U.S. Embassy personnel or their families would bring global condemnation. And now the ECF team would share in any special privilege afforded the U.S. Embassy staff.

Reno leaned close to Lisa Stephens and asked, "Do you know where they are taking us?"

Lisa replied, "They told us that we would be taken to Baler for 'processing.' We have no idea what 'processing' means, but we expect to be returned to the United States after it is completed." Lisa then asked Reno, "Who are you?"

As Reno began to explain their situation, one of the guards interrupted their conversation.

"No talking!" he insisted. And both women complied with his order.

Judge waited as the truck rolled to a stop at the Baler sports complex. He scrutinized each of the foreigners as they climbed out of the back of the truck. He noticed that the missionaries were dressed differently than the others. Their clothing was far dirtier and more casual than the clothing of the diplomatic staff, who wore designer brand shirts and slacks with expensive shoes. Judge asked his men where the 'dirty ones' had been picked up, and after learning that they had come from the mountains, Judge decided to interview them personally. These might be the foreign devils that had killed his men in Barangay Uno near the cemetery. He selected the youngest of the team members, and separated Tyler from the others like a lion might isolate a juvenile wildebeest.

Reno protested as Judge separated Tyler from the team. Without warning Judge sprinted at Reno and punched her ferociously in the stomach. The single punch knocked her to the ground where she curled up in pain. Rod helped her off the ground and moved her into the sports complex to sit down. He didn't like that Tyler was being taken either, but he thought it prudent to remain quiet. They had nothing to hide. They were simply frightened and ran, but they turned themselves in after discussing their options. They had harmed no one. In fact, the opposite was true. They provided medical assistance to dengue victims in Dibutunan and to storm victims in Maria Aurora. Witnesses could verify that.

Tyler didn't realize who he was dealing with. His smart mouth often offended Americans who were used to sarcasm and attitude spewing from their youth. Judge was unaccustomed to such insolence, and slapped Tyler hard across his face when he demanded to be presented with a lawyer. "I know my rights!" Tyler yelled after he'd been slapped. No he didn't. He clearly didn't know who he was dealing with either, and he continued to behave like a spoiled brat. Judge hit him with his fists, and Tyler fell to the ground. His eyes were filled with hate, which fueled Judge even more. Judge took his pistol from its holster. He fully intended to shoot Tyler, but one of his men reminded him that the U.S. Ambassador's wife was part of this group.

His men brought Tyler to a small building near the sports complex. Before the storm it was used as a gift shop, but it had become Judge's temporary office. All of the small souvenirs had been removed from the shelves and piled into a closet in the back of the building. Judge ordered that Tyler be tied up. He then removed Tyler's shoes and began to beat the bottoms of his feet with a rattan rod more than a meter long. Tyler cried out in pain, which delighted Judge. He beat him for more than twenty minutes before ordering his men to, "Clean him up and return him to the others when he can walk on his own."

Chris Coloma was surprised to see so many American families. The typical American tourists were either lecherous old men seeking sex, or lecherous young surfers seeking sex. Seeing families with young children stunned him. Where had they come from? What were they doing here in Baler? He wanted to ask them questions, but he had already been told to remain silent and still. His only chance to find out was if he could use the restroom at the same time and one of the men in the group. So he waited until he saw a man from the group moving towards the restroom. He asked the closest guard if he might also pee.

Chris walked up to the urinal next to Brian and asked him quietly, "Where are you guys from?"

Brian didn't expect such clean English from Chris because he was clearly Filipino. He answered, "We are from the U.S. Embassy. These are staff members and their families. Who are you?"

Chris answered that he was also an American citizen who served in the U.S. Navy. "My companion is a man named Robert Banks, from Palo Alto, California. We were captured before dawn trying to reach my house. We stumbled across a war crime. The Chinese killed an entire community. I don't know what they intend to do with us, but they know that we witnessed their deeds."

"Hey! No talking!" The guard had already added one word to his English vocabulary.

Chris was strangely relieved that the U.S. embassy staff was being held with him. The Chinese would have a difficult time explaining what happened to them if they disappeared. And he felt that he was protected because of their presence. He felt much less alone.

Judge was furious that the missionary team he was chasing had made it to the processing center. There were too many witnesses here to harm them. And these were witnesses that he couldn't simply get rid of. The wife of the U.S. ambassador had met the missionaries in his custody. If they disappeared, Judge would be implicated. He hated being held accountable for their care; he wanted to kill them, not babysit them. He smiled as he watched Tyler limp into the large gymnasium and take a seat near Pastor Rod. Rod put his arm around Tyler, who curled up on the floor and wept. Lisa Stephens noticed Judge's amusement with Tyler's pain. So did Reno. The time would soon come when Judge would be forced to admit his evil deeds.

Chapter 39 – Beaten

Saturday 10:50pm, August 12ᵗʰ
Baler Sports Complex, Aurora Province, Philippines

Reno noticed a pattern within the sports complex; there were periods of calm and quiet, which were shattered every time that Judge showed up. The soldiers seemed tense around him, and there were continuous acts of violence until he left. His very presence inspired cruelty. Reno had witnessed destructive behavior many times before; her high school boyfriend had such a personality. But his narcissism and exploitive nature were quite different from the aggression she observed in Judge. He was evil and clearly enjoyed other people's suffering. In medical school she wrote a paper about violent psychopaths; she clearly understood that such people lack empathy and have no concern about consequences for their actions. Judge displayed all the signs of a violent psychopath: he lacked self-control and was unable to restrain his urges; he responded abnormally to predictable circumstances, and hostility was his primary reaction to ordinary events. Judge's behavior fell into a dangerous category called the 'dark tetrad'. Such people are egotistical, manipulative, distain morality and social norms, antisocial, remorseless, and *sadistic*. Reno knew that Judge was a dangerous man.

The sports complex was uncomfortably hot, even long after sunset. The dull drone of the diesel generator outside the gymnasium doors would have made it possible to sleep, but the officer in charge of processing kept the building as brightly lighted as possible. Tyler was unaccustomed to inactivity; his entire generation entertained themselves with electronic devices during moments like these, but the Chinese officers had seized every electronic device when they were captured. He fumbled around in his backpack in search of something to read and discovered his Rubik's cube. He pulled it out of the bag and scrambled it without looking at it. Then he began to solve its puzzle, aligning the colors on all six sides of the cube. Reno noticed that the cube had captured the attention of two guards, and she told Tyler, "Put that away now, it's attracting attention."

Tyler answered, "I don't care." And he didn't. He had already been beaten on the bottoms of his feet and he felt defiant. He would rather suffer the consequences for playing with the cube than sit idly on the floor for another moment. The two guards approached Tyler and watched him solve the cube for the second time. Then Tyler offered the cube to one of the guards to solve. The soldier took the cube from Tyler and smiled, and then the two guards returned to the other side of the gymnasium to play with it. Tyler stood up to follow them.

"Don't!" Reno admonished him. "Sit back down. You're forgetting who you're dealing with, Tyler." But Tyler didn't even acknowledge her. He ambled slowly behind the guards towards the far side of the gymnasium. His feet hurt him as he walked and he winced. He would soon pay an enormous price for his parent's lack of boundaries. Tyler believed that rules were for other people; he refused to be governed. He followed the men halfway across the gymnasium before one of the soldiers glanced back. The soldier immediately motioned for Tyler to return to where he had been seated, but Tyler foolishly ignored the warning. Several other soldiers stood and walked towards Tyler, who seemed oblivious of an impending problem. Perhaps he thought he would dazzle them all with his cube-solving skills and make friends of them all. Or maybe he was unable to comprehend what was about to happen. But Tyler soon learned the hard way not to challenge armed men who are holding you as a prisoner.

The soldier who held the cube turned around and walked toward Tyler, holding the cube out as he walked. As he approached Tyler he raised the cube over his head and threw it at Tyler's face, scoring a direct hit. Tyler looked shocked as pieces of the cube flew in every direction. The soldier then punched Tyler in the mouth, knocking him to the hardwood floor. The cavernous room burst into laughter as Tyler stood into a fighting stance with his fists balled up. Reno again called out to him, "Tyler! You need to come here! Tyler, drop your hands. Humble yourself, Tyler or you're going to be beaten."

Rod, Sean, Ashley, and Kelly joined Reno as she called out to Tyler. "Stop it, Tyler; you're going to get us all hurt."

Tyler had to understand the gravity of the situation, but he refused to back down. He lunged at the soldier who had punched him, grazing him with a telegraphed roundhouse right hand. The soldier ducked the punch and countered with two left hooks to Tyler's body, and again he went down. Then five more soldiers surrounded him before he could scramble to his feet. They kicked him repeatedly from all sides, and beat him with the butts of their rifles until blood filled the floor. Tyler stopped moving, but the beating continued. Sean stood up, and he was instantly instructed to sit back down. Brian Roberts, Lisa

Stephens and the rest of the U.S. Embassy staff joined in the chorus, demanding that the soldiers stop hurting the unconscious teenager. They finally stopped thrashing Tyler and took turns spitting on him before returning to the gymnasium entrance.

Rod, Sean, and Reno ran to Tyler, picked him up, and carried him back to where they sat. Tyler was still unconscious and was missing teeth. He needed stitches to close a wound on his forehead and more stitches to close a massive gash on the top of his head. Reno reached deep into her bag and found her suturing kit. Tyler remained unconscious the entire time that Reno sewed his wounds. She knew that he had broken ribs and maybe a broken arm and shoulder. He regained consciousness slowly, opening his eyes and then closing them again. He tried to speak, but found it difficult with his broken and missing teeth. His mouth was still filled with blood.

"Take it easy, Tyler" offered Reno. "You've suffered a serious beating, and you have some broken bones." Tyler moaned and rolled onto his side. He groaned even louder as he discovered that it was more painful lying on his side. "Maybe next time you'll listen when someone warns you about something. You're lucky that they didn't kill you!"

Lisa Stephens stood over them. "Is he going to be okay?" she asked. Lisa made her two sons look away during Tyler's beating. She was certain that Tyler was being killed.

Reno answered, "He'll make it, but he's going to be in pain for awhile. We met on the truck, but couldn't talk much at the time. My name is Reno West; I'm a doctor from Charleston, SC. We're here on a medical mission trip."

Lisa replied, "I'm Lisa Stephens, the wife of the U.S. Ambassador to the Philippines. The two boys on the end are my sons, Jamie and Jeffrey. The rest of the group consists of our embassy staff and their family members." Reno still couldn't understand how the embassy staff ended up in Baler.

Lisa could see that Reno was having a difficult time processing the information and she provided a small bit of explanation. "We were trying to get to Clark to fly out before the Chinese invaded, but we were too late. Typhoon Kiko made it impossible to remain on the expressway, so we got off in Bulacan. We were escorted by Philippine military to hide out in a town called Alphonso Casteneda, which is where we were captured. I have been assured that they will be sending us back to the U.S. as soon as possible."

"No talking!" yelled a soldier at Lisa, motioning for her to return to where she was seated. The soldier knew that she was the U.S. Ambassador's wife, and he didn't dare harm her physically. Lisa also knew that she wouldn't be harmed. Major Yong's reaction to her status as Madam Ambassador made that fact clear.

"We're not going to let anything happen to your team, Reno." Lisa spoke with confidence, as if she had some degree of control in this situation. "I'll insist that you go where we go." She smiled at Reno and walked back to her sons. "We'll all be home soon."

Kelly sat behind Tyler and held him in her arms. He was still groggy and in severe pain. She used a handkerchief and wiped blood from his face and arms. "I don't even want to know what you were thinking," she whispered to Tyler. "Don't ever be that stupid again!"

Rod studied the group of soldiers, taking note of their faces and uniform insignias. He counted the number of foreigners being held, including Disaster Bob and Chris Coloma. Rod noticed that the two men stood up during Tyler's beating and yelled at the soldiers to stop. Chris grabbed the back of Bob's shirt and held him to prevent a second beating. The two men were clearly together. Rod hadn't noticed earlier, but the entire gymnasium had been flooded during Typhoon Kiko. The high water mark on the walls was over ten feet high. He wondered about Angie's family and the other families from the church in Baler. How could they possibly have survived such deep and sudden flooding?

A commotion near the door caught everyone's attention. Judge was back, and his men roughly herded a group of Filipinos into the huge room. A gunshot rang out and people screamed outside the door. Then Reno looked in horror as she saw her sweet Angie thrown to the floor near the door. Angie stood up and staggered towards the others. Her clothes were torn and disheveled and her hair was a mess. Angel, Manny and Pastor Mark were with her, but Brother Jun was missing from the group. Why had Filipinos been brought to this 'processing center?' Reno ached to run across the room and check on the others. But she knew that as long as Judge was nearby, any movement might be considered a provocation.

Tyler fell into a deep sleep, which concerned Reno. Drowsiness after any major head trauma was not a good sign, but it was near midnight and the team had been through enormous physical challenges. Ashley was already asleep, and Kelly drifted in and out of sleep as she held Tyler. Rod and Sean had also spotted their Filipino team members;

both wondered the same thing as Reno – *why have they been brought here to the processing center?*

Angie spotted Reno and did not hesitate. She jumped to her feet and ran across the gymnasium. Reno ran to meet her and guards grabbed them both as they hugged one another in the center of the gym floor.

Angie cried out, with teams rolling down her face, "He raped me, Reno! And he just killed Brother Jun for no reason at all." Reno already knew who '*he*' was. Judge walked briskly to the center of the gymnasium and demanded that the women return to their seats. They didn't understand his Mandarin, but his anger made his instructions clear. His eyes blazed with hatred as he grabbed Angie by the arm and yanked her away from Reno like a page being ripped from a notebook. As she was roughly escorted away Angie called out, "I need you, Reno. Please pray for me."

Reno returned to her assigned seating spot on the gym floor and she began to pray out loud. "Almighty Heavenly Father, I know that you're still in charge of all things. Even though we are going through trials, Lord, you are with us. We're going through a powerful storm right now, Lord, and we need you. I pray for my dear sister, Angie, Lord. Protect her from these savage people and give her comfort. Provide her with your peace, Lord. Help heal Tyler quickly, and protect us all from additional brutality. Don't allow us to become like the enemy, Father. Give us your heart and help us to forgive as you have forgiven us. Amen,"

"No talking!" was shouted from the other side of the room. Reno didn't even realize she had prayed out loud. The comment was directed at her. But she didn't stop praying, she merely prayed silently until she fell asleep on the hardwood floor.

Chapter 40 – Who are we?

Sunday 2:00pm, August 13th
Baler, Aurora Province, Philippines

More than a day had passed since Tyler was savagely beaten. His face swelled to the point that he was no longer recognizable. And his breathing became difficult due to his broken ribs. Reno worried that he might have blood in his lungs. The only pain medication available was acetaminophen, which was better than nothing, but couldn't contend with his horrible pain. Judge had been away the entire day, and the guards in the gymnasium permitted people to speak to one another. They even allowed freedom of movement within the gymnasium.

Pastor Rod was accustomed to preaching on Sundays and a particular passage of scripture had been on his mind since he woke up. His Bible had been confiscated, so Pastor Rod guessed at the exact wording. He wanted to share what was on his heart with the others. He planned to share the same message to four different groups so that he didn't cause the guards to be concerned with a large gathering. First he would sit on the floor with Tyler, Reno, Sean, Ashley, and Kelly. Then he planned to join the Filipino team members: Manny, Angie, Angel, and Mark. Next he would speak with half of the embassy staff, and then include Chris and Bob with the remaining staff.

His message began, "I would like to share a short message from the fourteenth chapter of the book of Exodus. First, let me provide a bit of background. God chose Moses to go to the Pharaoh of Egypt, who was the world's most powerful man, and ask him to free the Israelite people from slavery. Moses resisted when God spoke to him, saying, 'Who am I that I should go to Pharaoh and bring the children of Israel out of Egypt?' Moses didn't feel qualified, and even explained to God that he couldn't speak well. *Certainly God could find someone more qualified than me*, thought Moses. That's the first point I want to make: God doesn't always choose the most qualified. God often chooses people who must rely on him; he doesn't expect us to accomplish great things using our own strength.

"Moses did as God requested, and the Pharaoh resisted. Each time he refused to release the Israelites, God sent a plague on Egypt. Pharaoh was stubborn and Egypt suffered through ten plagues that ultimately cost the nation every firstborn son, including Pharaoh's own beloved son. Finally the Israelites were set free and Moses led them into the desert to a place that God had specifically directed him to go. It was a location near the sea that left them with no escape route if the Egyptians came after them, which is exactly what happened. Pharaoh had a change of heart and decided to chase them down and annihilate them. And when the Israelites saw hundreds of chariots and thousands of soldiers approaching they became angry with Moses. But he told them, and I'm paraphrasing here, 'Don't be afraid. Sit still and watch what the Lord does to these Egyptians; he will fight for you. All you have to do is be silent.'

"God opened the Red Sea and allowed the Israelites to escape once the waters parted. Then, as the Egyptians came after them, God closed the sea and destroyed Pharaoh's entire army. God miraculously delivered the Israelites from certain death, showing them that he was their deliverer. And God showed Egypt that he is Lord.

"The reason that I selected this passage of scripture to share with you is obvious. We're in a hopeless situation. There is nothing we can do to gain our freedom. We're not going to get out of this using our own strength, but God will deliver us. Just like the Israelites, we need to sit silently and watch what God will do. Let's all rely on God. We have nothing else to do here, so let's all pray for his miraculous intervention."

Their situation seemed quite bleak. Tyler was seriously injured and needed medical care. He no longer tried to speak, and he drifted in and out of consciousness. Jun had been shot and killed. Anna was likely dead. Angie had been raped. Their phones had been confiscated and they had no way to reach their families. They were all physically exhausted, hungry, dehydrated and lacked proper sleep. And Judge could reappear at any moment, bringing terror and panic with him.

"I've always struggled with situations like this," spoke Sean. "I want so badly to make these devils pay for what they've done. But in my heart I know that we need to rely on God for our revenge. I memorized Romans 12:19 back in high school. I was filled with rage and wanted to avenge a friend who had been attacked by gang members. It says, 'Do not take revenge, my dear friends, but leave room for God's wrath, for it is written: "It is mine to avenge; I will repay," says the Lord.' I know that we can't fight back, but the Lord will even the score with the men who hurt Tyler. We need to encourage one another and focus on staying healthy. God will do the rest."

Reno added, "These men are our enemies, the very people that Jesus commands us to love. I'm struggling right now, because I'm not sure I can follow His command to love them. I know that it's not conditional, and it is meant for times like these, but I need help to overcome what I'm feeling."

Ashley, who seemed to be the spiritual weakling of the group, surprised them as she said, "What good is it if we love only people who love us back? God loves the unlovable and forgives the unforgivable. If we want to share in the nature of God, we need to do the same."

"But how do we do that?" asked Pastor Rod. It was a legitimate question. He wasn't trying to teach anybody; he was also struggling to find a way to translate the abstract concepts of love and forgiveness into action.

Sean responded, "We need to view our captors differently. If we look at them as fathers, brothers, sons, and neighbors they will take on a different appearance to us. Unless we recognize that God loves and values them we'll continue to despise them."

"I understand that, Sean," replied Rod. But when I look at them I see brutality that is undeserving of our love. How do I change that?"

"By understanding that none of us are worthy of God's love," answered Sean. "We're all guilty, yet God chooses to love us in spite of our wicked nature. It's like you told us at the prayer meeting. In fact, you yelled it over the noise from Typhoon Kiko - there are no 10 point sins, 25 point sins or 100 point sins. I think we've assigned a towering amount of points to the sins of our captors, and we look down on them because of it."

Kelly had remained quiet during the discussion. She still held Tyler in her arms and she cried as she spoke. "Look at Tyler. Just look at him! There's a huge difference between a monster who could do this and a man who lies to his girlfriend." She rejected the idea that all sins had equal weight in God's eyes. "Pedophiles, murderers, and these thugs are from the devil!"

"Are you saying that there are unredeemable souls, Kelly?" asked Pastor Rod.

"I'm not sure what I'm saying, Pastor, I just feel in my heart that coveting my neighbor's possessions falls into a very different category than raping Angie or pounding on Tyler after he was unconscious and defenseless." Kelly could say no more; she hung her head and sobbed loudly.

"Your point is well taken, Kelly," said Sean. "We'll let God judge them."

"Let's not attract any attention by bowing our heads and closing our eyes, but let's all pray for God to guide us through this difficult time." Pastor Rod then prayed out loud as he looked around at the sorrow in the room. He prayed for their families back in Charleston and for the Philippines as a nation. Pastor Rod struggled to find suitable words to convey how much they needed the Lord's intervention.

When he finished praying he told the group, "I'm going to visit with the others. Please pray that they will also be able to rely on God. With God's help we'll get through this together." In his heart he believed that God was the 'Grand Conductor' of the universe. *Why*, he wondered, *would God place this group in the middle of this horrid situation?* God would soon provide the answer.

Chapter 41 – Judge misjudges
Sunday 7:40pm, August 13th
Maria Aurora, Aurora Province, Philippines

Judge believed that he was superior to everyone around him, so he treated others as inferiors. He acted with impunity, liberated from consequences of any sort. His sense of self-importance was heightened by his role as a wartime military commander. He was now the ultimate authority in the Aurora province, and began to behave like a true warlord. The Chinese government routinely ignored international law, and Judge knew that he would never be handed over to any international war crimes tribunal. He was untouchable and invincible. His haughtiness overtook his sense of caution, and Judge soon learned that he was, in fact, most mortal.

Believing that all armed resistance in the central region of Aurora had been squashed, Judge no longer traveled with a hundred heavily armed men. Early in the afternoon he whittled his squad of henchmen to only fifteen of his best soldiers. He divided his men into small reconnaissance teams to search each tiny hamlet to locate any police or soldiers that might still be hiding. However, *they* had already located him. Judge led his team nonchalantly, as they walked along a muddy farm road with a massive rice field to his right and a coconut grove on his left. His usual sixth sense betrayed him. There were no barking dogs or startled birds to alert him to possible enemy presence. Nor was there any hint of noise or movement. Without warning the silence exploded into cacophonous confusion.

Four of his men fell in the first volley of gunfire, which seemed to come from every direction. His squad was out in the open and they quickly dove for cover. Three more Chinese commandoes were ripped into pieces by heavy machine gun fire. Judge could see figures running through the darkness towards him under the cover of a coconut grove. His initial instinct was to dig in and return fire, but he quickly realized that there were too many enemies converging on them to stand and fight. Reluctantly he ordered his men to retreat. Judge ordered three men to remain in place to slow the advance of the enemy, while he and four others took cover behind the elevated road and the rice paddy.

Judge momentarily winced as a bullet entered his lower back and ripped out of his left abdomen. Two more bullets found him as he fell, one shattering his right knee and the other splintering his right forearm. Judge lay unconscious, his lifeblood pouring from his body into the mud of the rice paddy. Amidst the confusion and fear his men grabbed his limp body and dragged him as they hobbled clumsily just below the continued spray of bullets.

The shooting stopped as quickly as it began and the shadowy figures that had advanced so quickly retreated hastily into the darkness and dense foliage near the base of the mountain in the community of Debucao. The attackers spotted a counter attack coming from the nearby community of San Leonardo and retreated quickly into the mountains. If fewer Chinese had responded the rebels would have remained to fight, but four teams of Chinese commandos quickly responded to the gunfire and arrived from two directions. They did not engage the enemy; instead they quickly loaded the dead and wounded soldiers on a truck and raced towards Premier Hospital in Baler. A lone medic who looked like a young teenager administered morphine to Judge, who remained unconscious. He inserted an IV containing whole blood, and worked with two other soldiers to reduce the blood loss. They forced gauze into the wounds and hurriedly wound bandages around his arm, knee, and abdomen. Each bullet created both an entry and an exit wound, and Judge's life was draining onto the floorboards of the covered truck bed.

The soldiers were wary of more attacks and sent six silun ahead of the trucks to prevent additional ambush as they drove wildly towards Baler. The men, living and dead went airborne twice during the raucous ride. The medic believed that Judge would be dead before the twenty minute drive was completed, but he was wrong. He had a weak pulse and his shallow breathing quickened as they removed him from the truck.

Four soldiers ran awkwardly towards the hospital door, carrying Judge on a stretcher. But when they entered into the emergency room they were surprised to see that the entire hospital had been ransacked. There were no doctors, nurses, or staff of any kind. All of the hospital equipment had been pilfered, including gurneys and tables, so Judge was laid on the floor as the soldiers ran through the facility in search of a suitable bed. Even most of the light bulbs had been removed from the hospital, so the building was dark. They found a small dining table at a house across the street that was barely long enough to contain Judge's head and feet, and placed him on the table. The medic began a second IV of whole blood and pleaded with his comrades to find a doctor.

None of the military medics were trained to repair such damage; they administered pain relief and could prioritize patients based on the severity of their injuries, but Judge needed more than triage. He needed a skilled surgeon. He also needed God's mercy.

The ranking man, a terrified young sergeant, reluctantly took charge. He sent a truck with six men to the sports complex to fetch the American doctors. He ordered them to gather all remaining medical supplies and bring them to a small medical clinic he had seen on Angara Street. Surely, he thought, a private clinic would have an examination table and medical supplies. And it would be much more sanitary than the ransacked hospital.

The commandos cautiously carried Judge to a passenger van they commandeered, including the driver, across the street from the hospital and laid Judge in the back seat. The young medic held the IV bag containing whole blood, and held Judge in place on the back seat as the van raced to the Angara Street clinic. A kind-faced woman, Doctor Annabelle Basilio, greeted them at the door to the clinic and quickly responded to their emergency. She lived several miles away, but often slept in the clinic overnight. And since Typhoon Kiko struck she had been treating patients almost sixteen hours each day. She held open the door as they carried Judge into her clinic and she pointed them to a full-sized examination table in the next room.

A portable generator provided electricity to the clinic and Annabelle turned on two bright LED exam lights above the table so that she could assess Judge's injuries. She carefully removed the bandages and realized that she wasn't equipped to treat such wounds. Annabelle was a pediatrician, so she pleaded with the men to locate her husband, Bing, who was a retired surgeon. None of the Chinese men who arrived at her clinic spoke English or Filipino and couldn't understand what she was asking for. Her pleading seemed urgent, so they quickly sent for a translator.

A truck arrived outside the sports complex with its horn blaring. Pastor Rod was alarmed as he heard the truck slide to a stop in the gravel outside and saw men rush through the door and run to where they sat on the floor. The Chinese interpreter was out of breath and abruptly, "Which of you are doctors?" Reno and David stood up and the man pointed at them and said, "Quickly, follow me, we need you!" Reno and David grabbed their backpacks and trotted behind the translator towards the entrance to the gym.

They didn't protest because it would have been futile to do so. Despite their circumstances they all remained aware of the fact that they were still 'on mission"; perhaps the Lord might still use them in some remarkable way. Reno knew that Kelly could care for Tyler, and that Rod and Sean would care for Ashley. But she was not going to leave Angie behind.

Reno grabbed the translator's shoulder as they moved quickly towards the door and said, "I need my nurse with me." He nodded his head, expecting that Reno would return for Kelly or Ashley, but he was surprised when she ran towards the small group of Filipinos sitting along the wall and grabbed Angie by the hand. He was about to protest Angie's inclusion, but reconsidered and remained quiet. Reno, Angie, and David were escorted to a waiting van and the driver sped towards Annabelle's pediatric clinic.

"Our commander has been severely wounded. A bullet has pierced his abdomen and the wound where the bullet exited in the front is quite serious. He was also shot in his right knee and forearm. He is unconscious and has been administered morphine for the pain. The medic is providing him with fresh blood, but his wounds need to be repaired and closed. Can you do that?"

"We will do our best," answered Reno. She knew that David, as a dentist was just as experienced as she was at performing combat surgery, but she didn't want to reveal that they were unqualified.

David liked the demeanor of the translator; he felt safe with him and wanted him to remain nearby. He asked, "Will you remain with us to translate if we need anything?"

Their interpreter answered, "Yes. I will stay with you until you are returned to the processing center." The ride took less than five minutes and they were escorted into Annabelle's small pediatric clinic.

The room where Judge laid on the table was far too small to accommodate everyone. Annabelle immediately recognized Angie and spoke to her in Tagalog. "Are these American's surgeons?"

"*Hindi, po,*" answered Angie in the negative.

Annabelle responded in English so that the others could hear her, "Please go to my house and bring Bing here. He's an experienced surgeon, and this patient is going to need his experience."

Angie then turned to the English translator and said, "We need to go to her house and bring her husband here now – he's a surgeon. I know where they live and will go with you." Angie passed by the Basilio family home each day as she went to work in Baler. It was a grand three-storey home with a magnificent front balcony. Angie dreamed about owning such a house, and knew it well. She also knew Annabelle and Bing. They were ardent followers of Christ and helped host Christian training events in Baler. And she frequently encountered them professionally when they visited patients at the regional hospital where she worked.

At first the interpreter balked at Angie's request to fetch Dr. Basilio saying, "I have promised to remain with the American doctors to interpret for them."

Angie responded, "Dr. Annabelle speaks English fluently, and can help them until we return. We can be back here in just twenty minutes if we hurry. Your comrade needs Dr. Basilio! Let's go!"

The interpreter quickly arranged a car to transport them and he jumped into the back seat with Angie as they sped to pick up Bing. Angie navigated, pointing out each turn to the driver as they raced to fetch the experienced surgeon.

Reno spoke up as soon as Angie left with the only Chinese soldier who could speak or understand English, "My name is Dr. Reno West and this is Dr. David Kemp. We are here as part of a church medical team. Neither of us are surgeons, but we will do everything we can to save this man's life. For the first time Reno actually looked at the face of the patient and she gasped when she realized that she would be treating Judge. Reno was immediately filled with loathing. Judge was a disgusting man who deserved to pay for his actions. He was repugnant in every way and Reno felt a surge of elation when she saw him suffering. And then she remembered the words spoken to her by Anna in front of the church after Typhoon Kiko had claimed her, *Do what is right. You'll know what I'm talking about when the time comes.* This was that time, and Reno knew that the Lord was testing her heart. She wanted for Judge to die, but Anna's words made it clear to her that she had been chosen to do what Marilou called *'a marvelous thing.'*

All three doctors scrubbed their hands and donned surgical gloves. Only two surgical gowns were available, and Tom tied them for Reno and Annabelle. All three placed surgical masks on their faces and Reno prayed aloud as they turned to their patient. "I pray, Father, for your mercy on this man. Help guide our hands and our hearts, Lord, as we demonstrate who you are. We give you the glory in advance, Lord. You are the Great Physician, and this man's eternal future is in your hands. I praise you for choosing me as your humble servant. Amen." Tears flowed down her face as she now looked on Judge with compassion.

David did not recognize Judge until after Reno's prayer. He remained silent, but Reno's prayer visibly moved him.

Annabelle asked, "Dr. Reno, would you please examine the abdomen wound? Dr. David can begin to seal his arm wound and I will work on his knee. My husband will join us in a few minutes."

The Chinese medic waited just outside the door and provided clamps, gauze, and a second IV of whole blood. He looked frightened, like a high school student who got caught with drugs in his school locker. He looked into the room every sixty seconds and paced around the remainder of the time.

The bullet that tore through his abdomen had pierced the lower edge of Judge's kidney. His bladder was ruptured and a huge portion of his large intestine would need to be removed. Blood vessels were torn and Reno found it difficult to properly stem the flow of blood. Reno struggled to clamp the largest holes. She was calm as she worked, knowing that God had his hands on this situation.

After only a few minutes Dr. Bing Basilio arrived with Angie. Both quickly scrubbed their hands in the utility sink and put on sterile gloves and masks. There was not enough room around the examination table for five people, so David stepped out of the room and allowed Angie to assist Dr. Basilio with the most serious wound while Reno finished stitching up the damage on Judge's arm. Annabelle was able to stop the bleeding around Judge's knee, but she knew that he would require several surgeries to repair it. It was clear that *Judge would never be the same.*

Reno looked into Angie's eyes and winked. Angie, despite being brutally raped and beaten by this man, felt the same compassion that Reno felt for him. The Lord, who filled them with His love, had touched their hearts. Angie clasped Reno's hand for a moment and then held back torn tissue while Dr. Basilio cauterized sections of the wound to prevent more bleeding. After more than ninety minutes of frying and stitching tissue, the doctors stepped back from the table. Judge was stable and had received an injection of antibiotics to reduce the chance of infection. The Chinese medic wanted to administer additional morphine, but Dr. Basilio advised against it. Morphine can cause bowel blockage or breathing difficulty in some patients. Judge needed recovery time, and as long as he remained unconscious, pain relief was not a concern.

As Angie, Reno, and the other doctors stepped from the treatment room, several Chinese soldiers peered into the room to see if Judge was still alive. Reno spoke to the interpreter and asked him to gather the men together so that she could explain the situation. But what she wanted to do was to pray together with them. She asked the translator to repeat her words to the men.

"Your commander has been severely injured and has lost large amounts of blood. The wounds have been closed and he has been stabilized, but the next twenty-four hours will be critical. He needs fluids, rest, and prayer." The translator looked at Reno, unsure if he should say that prayer was needed, but Reno gestured to him to repeat her words.

"God, the creator of the universe, is sovereign over everything. He gives life and can reclaim it. We will appeal to God on behalf of your commander." Again, the interpreter paused. Reno told him, "This is more important than his surgery – please repeat my words."

As the translator spoke, some of the men removed their hats out of respect. None of them professed any particular faith, but none objected to asking the Christian God to heal their leader. Reno began praying and paused periodically for the interpreter to translate. "Almighty Heavenly Father, we recognize your authority and power and ask for your help tonight. Although we are in the midst of calamity, we recognize that this injured soldier is your creation and belongs to you. We pray that you will heal his body and restore him back to full health. We pray also, Lord, that you will heal his heart, allowing him to practice mercy as you have shown to him. Bless him, Lord. Remove his pain and do not permit him to suffer. Protect his men in his absence, Lord and deliver them all home safely to their families. We have done all that we can do, Lord, and we now entrust this injured man into your care. We pray, Father, that you will prove yourself by doing what only you can do. We pray this in the name of our Lord and Savior, Jesus Christ."

Several of the men were teary-eyed after the prayer. They were overwhelmed that their captives would include them and their families in the prayer. They knew that Judge was not a merciful man, and that karma would dictate that he be shown no mercy. They knew that this team had experienced his brutality, and it was strange to them that they asked their God to be merciful to him and heal him. All of the men were silent, still pondering what had just taken place. The presence of God was an unfamiliar feeling, and they had all just come into His presence.

Reno and Angie agreed to remain at the clinic to tend to Judge. David returned to the processing center with most of the soldiers. Doctor Bing Basilio left behind his medical kit and medications. He returned home and promised to return early in the morning. Annabelle welcomed Reno and Angie into her small room to discuss their plans. They agreed to watch over Judge in three-hour shifts. The translator remained at the clinic and curled up on the floor and slept. Other soldiers remained outside to guard the clinic. Reno asked God for a miracle, and it would soon come. And even Reno would be surprised at God's amazing response.

Chapter 42 – Bob is exposed
Sunday 11:30pm, August 13th
Baler, Aurora Province, Philippines

The drone of the diesel generator outside the sports complex covered the sound of an arriving pickup truck. Seven soldiers climbed from the truck and carried their gear inside. They also carried a large backpack containing a satellite uplink unit that was quickly surrounded by other soldiers. As they unpacked the bag they discovered a passport and driver's license belonging to Robert Banks, a long-haired, bearded 28 year old from California. They also discovered his cell phone and were suspicious because it had been entirely reformatted. What was Robert Banks trying to hide?

Most of the foreigners inside the sports complex were sleeping. But Robert Banks lay wide awake and pretended to sleep. He was horrified when he spotted the huge mountain range logo on the side of his backpack; there was no doubt that the equipment they were inspecting was his. If they had his passport and driver's license they would certainly compare his name with the list of people that they had 'processed.' But they didn't. None of the foreigners being held in the gymnasium matched the appearance of the man in the identification pictures, so they set aside what they had found and laid down to rest.

Robert could not sleep. He knew that most of the men who examined the identification photos could not read English. It was only a matter of time before his passport and driver's license information would be scrutinized more closely. When the men who 'processed' him saw the name they would quickly locate him. What might happen then? He lied to them by saying he was a tourist. He imagined another long interview with the stern-faced corporal and worried about a beating more severe what he'd seen administered to Tyler.

In the absence of other news about Typhoon Kiko, Disaster Bob had become an instant celebrity. Reporters clamored to know more about him. They interviewed his neighbors and found out that he was a prankster. He once froze a frog intended for dissection in his biology class with liquid nitrogen and shattered it on the floor of the principal's office. The school custodian refused to clean up the thousands of shards of melted frog and lost his job. His school never knew the identity of the 'frog freezer' until Disaster Bob made the news. His classmates from high school described him as smart and disillusioned. His professors from college remember him as a gifted writer and speaker. And his bitter ex-girlfriend used more expletives in a single sentence describing him than a professional boxer might use after a bad decision loss. The press exposed everything about him they could find. He dropped out of De Anza College in Cupertino, California one semester before obtaining his degree in journalism. His tax returns indicated that he had never held a job as an employee and he had never been issued a W-2 form.

Bob would have been horrified had he known how much of his life was suddenly being shared in the media. He was an introvert and was intensely private. Unlike other journalists, Bob had no particular political predilection. He wasn't an environmentalist, and had never selected a cause to champion. Nor was he particularly concerned about what people thought about his stories. He worked as a stringer for several publications and was a good enough writer to pay his bills with his writing. But he was fascinated by big storms, so he purchased a great camera and a small satellite uplink system to become a storm chaser. And once he experienced his first big tornado he was hooked. And now, unbeknownst to Disaster Bob, every detail of his life was being scrutinized. The press needed news, and Bob's video of Kiko and the Chinese invasion of Baler had made him famous.

Soldiers arrived with pandesal, juice, coffee, and lugaw to feed themselves and their foreign hostages. And Robert's fears quickly became reality. Two soldiers distributed the delicious, still warm pandesal bread around the gymnasium. Two more carried coffee, followed by two men serving juice. But when the pair scooping the thin lugaw porridge looked at Robert they paused and spoke to each other in Chinese. One of them had helped process him when he was brought to the sports complex.

"What is your name?" he asked.

"Bob Banks," he answered, hoping that the use of 'Bob' instead of 'Robert' might prevent his true identity from being discovered. It didn't.

"Please stand up, Bob Banks, and follow me." The soldier was polite and did not show any signs of aggression. Robert stood up and followed him, carrying his pandesal and a cup of coffee with him.

Robert was escorted directly to the equipment and he knew that it was futile to deny his identity. He only hoped that they had not seen the last reports he uploaded to his blog site. They hadn't.

"Is this yours?" asked the same soldier who escorted him to the equipment.

"Yes, sir. I'm glad that you've recovered it. I hated to leave it behind because the gear is expensive, but I feared that carrying it would expose that I am a journalist instead of a tourist. I came to the Philippines to videotape Typhoon Kiko and ..."

"Silence! Are you now saying that you lied to us during your processing?" The voice came from the ill-tempered corporal who spent the most time interrogating him.

"Yes sir. That is what I am saying. I feared that you might treat me differently as a tourist than as a journalist. Actually I'm a storm chaser, not a legitimate journalist." Bob quickly became silent, thinking that, perhaps, less talk was prudent.

The stern-faced corporal slapped Bob across the face and cursed at him in Mandarin. "You will be punished, Bob Banks. Say goodbye to your friends because your dishonesty has disqualified you as a 'noncombatant alien.' You are no longer under our protection." As he spit at Bob, three other soldiers moved between Bob and the angry corporal. They began to argue loudly. And as they did, Lisa Stephens walked towards them, ignoring their command for her to be seated.

"Who is your commanding officer?" she demanded. The soldiers knew that she was important and made no attempt to intimidate her. They were unaccustomed to such a direct question. It included no term of respect or initial greeting of any sort. The men looked at one another, unsure what to say.

"Major Yong assured me that you would treat us with dignity and respect. You have failed to honor his orders and I demand to speak with your acting commander right now!" By invoking the name of Major Yong she reminded them that their superiors did, in fact, issue specific orders about the treatment of foreign detainees – especially the embassy staff and their families. Lisa walked to Robert and told him quietly, "Stand next to me."

Within sixty seconds a young lieutenant stood nervously in front of Lisa, almost at attention. In English he asked, "For what purpose have you summoned me?"

Just like dogs sense fear, so could Lisa. And she sensed that this young man was sinking quickly in deep water. She asked curtly, "What is your name and rank, sir?"

"My name is Jun An Seng, ma'am." he replied. "I am a second lieutenant in the People's Liberation Army, and am currently in charge of this detachment."

Lisa had him against the ropes and intended to keep him there. "As the detachment commander, Lt. Seng, you will be held personally responsible for the treatment of every person in this processing center. I have witnessed unnecessary brutality," she said glancing at Tyler who lay asleep on the floor, still swollen and in pain. "And unless you want your name attached to my report to the Chinese Ambassador to the United States, it must stop. Do you understand me?"

Lt. Seng searched carefully for the words he wanted to say, but he was unable to find them in English. He nodded his head and said, "I can assure you, ma'am, that you will all be treated with kindness and respect."

It was exactly what Lisa wanted to hear. But she wasn't finished. "Your soldier just slapped and spit on this man, and I demand an apology."

The kind lieutenant looked at Robert and said, "I apologize, sir, for the unprofessional conduct of Corporal Zhu. I assure you that he will be disciplined for his foolish behavior."

The apology was profound and heartfelt, but Lisa wanted more. "I appreciate your apology, sir. I believe what you say, and I thank you for apologizing for the actions of your men. But I think that Corporal Zhu is the one who needs to apologize to Bob, not you."

Lt. Seng bowed slightly and said, "Excuse me, please." He walked swiftly from the gymnasium and returned moments later with Corporal Zhu marching in step behind him.

"Sir," said Lt. Seng to Bob, "Corporal Zhu has something he wishes to say to you."

Corporal Zhu did not look Bob in the eyes and he spoke forcefully as he said, "I acted inappropriately and I ask for your forgiveness. These are difficult circumstances for all of us and I am embarrassed by my childish attitude and foolish behavior. Please forgive me." He extended his hand to Bob, who shook it and said, "Of course. I understand."

Lisa allowed Corporal Zhu to walk away from the forced apology with a smidgeon of dignity. But before Lt. Seng could walk away she said to him, "Bob's dishonesty to your men was inappropriate. I will speak to the others in your care and make sure that we fully cooperate with you and your men. We don't wish to make your job more difficult than it is, Lieutenant. Thanks for your kindness, sir."

Chris Coloma spoke to Bob after he sat back down, "I was just about to rescue you, brother. The name of the dating site where you and Lilly met is called 'Pinoy Cupid' if they should ever ask." He was smiling at Bob, who knew that he'd just dodged a bullet. He smiled back at Chris and asked, "Did she discover me, or did I discover her?" Either way, Bob had every intention of discovering more about Lilly.
He was grateful for Chris and was glad to be his companion through this ordeal.

Reno and Angie took turns sleeping in the back room at Annabelle's clinic. Annabelle had agreed to search for Angie's family as soon as the dawn came. The soldiers outside trusted her and wouldn't restrict her travel. Annabelle even considered asking them for a ride, but she didn't want her neighbors connecting her too closely with the enemy.

Reno admired Annabelle's calm demeanor and her genuine smile in the midst of this horrid situation. She didn't need to show hospitality to the soldiers outside, but she fixed them snacks and boiled tea to serve to them, and they were most grateful. Annabelle took over the task of mothering Angie. As a pediatrician Annabelle loved caring for kids. She remembered treating Angie for intestinal worms and complications from an ear infection when she was a small child. Her parents had no way to pay Dr. Basilio for Angie's medication, so her father brought two live chickens to them in thanks for her care. Annabelle butchered the two chickens and grilled them with soy sauce and lime juice. She cooked some steamed rice and vegetables and carried the food to Angie's home to eat it with them. Angie also remembered that evening well because they rarely had so much meat on the table.

Angie poured out her heart to Annabelle in Filipino, providing the horrid details of the brutality inflicted on her by the man that they now cared for. They cried and hugged as Annabelle explained Angie's options. She could spend her life hating this man and everything Chinese or she could extend forgiveness and let go of her pain. Angie, of course, chose to forgive. She had already done so, but the pain was too fresh to quickly disappear.

Annabelle asked an unusual question, "Can you love him, Angie?"

Angie knew what she was asking and why she was asking it, and answered, "I know that we are commanded to love our enemies, and

God has provided me with a unique circumstance to do so. Yes, ma'am, I can love him." Angie felt the anger inside her dissipate. For the first time since she had been violated she felt whole. Annabelle smiled at her, then hugged her and left the room.

Angie felt God's presence during her three-hour shift as she tended to Judge. She pitied him, prayed for him, wiped his face, and cried over him. God's Spirit filled her the entire time, and she felt uplifted when Reno relieved her in the hours just before dawn.

The military situation changed after Judge was injured. Lt. Seng knew that the men who attacked Judge remained at large. Judge was vindictive and would have hunted the perpetrators, but Lt. Seng opted to change tactics. Judge was no longer in charge, and Lt. Seng felt that his men were already spread too thin as they patrolled the remote communities of Aurora. So he gathered all of his men together in Baler and fortified their position. He believed that communications would soon be restored and he longed for a stronger command and control structure. What he wanted was to have a boss, not to be one.

The helicopters that escorted Major Yong to Pantabangan were supposed to return and provide air cover over the region, but they did not return. What returned, however, was disturbing news of attacks on their convoy somewhere in the community of Cadaclan. Lt. Seng created a tight perimeter around the Baler market and reinforced their position against attack. His men had already accomplished their primary mission, successfully offloading all the men and equipment in Baler. Their mission was now to process and hold foreigners for deportation.

The citizens of Baler, Maria Aurora, San Luis, and Dipaculao quickly noticed that the Chinese soldiers were no longer patrolling their communities, and they were emboldened by the change. Rumors were rampant. Some said that the Chinese had been completely wiped out in Debucao. Some said that they had been driven back into their boats and had retreated into the sea. But the truth was already known to most; the People's Liberation Army was still in control of Baler.

Men began to organize and strategize. The search for weapons had begun. Filipinos are inventive. The adage that 'necessity is the mother of invention' holds especially true for Filipinos. The lack of tools or materials is quickly overcome by innovation. And the lack of resources to fight against the People's Liberation Army presented little problem to people so accustomed to improvisation. Handmade pistols were soon sold openly at the marketplace. An assembly line was started in Maria Aurora to manufacture bombs of various sorts. Even though cell phones didn't currently work, people volunteered them to be used to remotely activate explosive devices. Every type of weapon imaginable was being fashioned: arrows, spears and knives, swords, spiked clubs, and even poison-tipped darts. They would soon be able to confiscate guns, grenades and more sophisticated weaponry from their enemies.

The Santa Lucia Massacre became a rallying cry. Even though the enemy had hunkered down in Baler, the men and women of Aurora knew that the fight would soon return to their communities. But this time they would be ready. They would be organized. And they would show the savage invaders no mercy. Their hearts were as hardened as their resolve. The people of Aurora intended to create as many Chinese orphans as possible. Although 85% of Filipinos identify themselves as 'Christian' they overwhelmingly opted not to 'turn the other cheek.' They would leave no room for God's wrath.

Chapter 43 – Commentary
Monday, August 14th

Editorial in the Washington Post, Monday, August 14th

It's time to recall President Clover – who is with me?
By Dana Parker, U.S. Congressman from the 3rd District of Iowa, August 14th
8:14am

In the past week the Earth began to wobble on its axis. You might not feel it yet because the oscillations are currently light and distant. The People's Republic of China gained mass by annexing the Philippines. And at the same time, the United States experienced unprecedented loss of weight. America no longer carries military weight; we have proven through our inaction that we will not protect our allies if the foe is formidable. America has lost political weight; by ignoring our mutual defense pact with the Philippines we have proven that we will ignore treaties and international obligations if such agreements require sacrifice. And America now carries far less moral or ethical weight. Much of the world already views us as hypocrites because our actions and our policies are incongruent. And our inaction regarding the Philippines has placed the entire world on notice; we no longer promote the ideals of liberty, democracy, or human rights beyond our borders if there is a price tag attached.

President Clover has been in office for less than eight months and through her capitulation she's surrendered our oldest and most fervent ally in Asia to our biggest enemy in the region. China has gained gravity, and the balance of our world is now quite precarious. Brace yourselves for more gravitational wobble in the coming months. Our enemies have observed that our leadership is quivering. President Clover's history as a peace activist is well known, and her inaction in the face of Chinese provocation will embolden the Russians, Iranians, North Koreans, and ISIS to carve as much territory as they can during America's self-imposed 'time out.' We need to throw away our World Geography textbooks because we'll only confuse our students by teaching them an outdated map of the world. The world map is about to change even more, and it will look far less attractive to those of us that believe government should be *"Of the people, by the people and for the people."*

Is President Clover's inaction impeachable? No. She has not committed any impeachable offence. In fact, she's done nothing, which is my point. Can we recall her from office? Yes! And we should. Our constitution provides a mechanism to remove elected officials from office when we realize that we've made a horrible mistake. President Clover is such a mistake. She is attractive, intelligent, and she's a great communicator, which are all reasons America voted her into office. But it's clear that three more years of her incompetent leadership will cripple America and endanger every future generation of American. Join me in the effort to recall President Clover by going to: www.recallpresidentclover.com. Please add your name to the petition to recall President Clover from office, and add the hash tag #overforclover on all your correspondence. The greatness of America rests in your hands.

Editorial in the New York Times, Monday, August 14th

Is inaction really the lesser of two evils?
By Maya McCray, U.S. Congresswoman from the 4th District of NY,
August 14th 8:14am

Everyone likes to hear stories about bullies that whimper and cower when their victims fight back. Experts tell us that we should stand up to bullies, who, they say, suffer from low self-esteem and are just projecting their own feelings of inadequacy. We are told, "Let them know that you are unafraid, and bullies will go away." Maybe that works in the fifth grade in Arkansas, but I was raised on the streets of the Bronx. I grew up in a neighborhood filled with organized bullies that included the street cops. The list of gangs in the Bronx is extensive – look it up for yourself. Go online and you can find at least fifty-five organized gangs there. I learned to cooperate with bullies and it prevented me from becoming a statistic. I've witnessed countless savage beatings, stabbings, and shootings. And I can tell you something about many of the victims - they opted to defy their intimidators rather than cooperate. Street thugs are not simply projecting their feelings of inadequacy; they are ruthless savages who intend to take something from you. We must understand that nations who bully their neighbors are not suffering from low self-esteem. They have weighed the benefits and consequences of military action and have decided that military action is in their national interest.

China is behaving like a bully, but let's not miscalculate in our response to their incursion in the Philippines based on over-simplified psychological advice on how to deal with an individual bully. China has decided that it is in their national interest to invade the Philippines. Their leadership didn't wake up one morning and say, "Hey, I know what – let's invade the Philippines today." They spent thousands of hours devising their battle plan and they have weighed the possibility that the United States might intervene militarily. And they have come to the conclusion that they will prevail, even if America's military is ordered into the fray. How could they think such things? Don't they know who we are? Of course they do!

The People's Republic of China has the world's largest military force. One out of every five people on the planet is Chinese. They currently have more than two and a quarter million front-line active duty soldiers, and they have an equal number of trained soldiers in their reserve forces. More than 19.5 million Chinese reach military age every year, which is five times the number of new soldiers that we can provide if the war becomes a protracted one. When we send our military into combat we seem to have great difficulty extricating ourselves, so a protracted war should be expected, especially since our supply lines will be stretched halfway around the world. Comparing our tanks, ships, and aircraft against those possessed by the Chinese is not a good measure of parity in conflict. Their logistical capacity far exceeds ours. They can produce more weapons each month than we are able to produce and they can deliver them to the front lines in far less time.

But here is the bottom line: China has indicated that they are willing to sacrifice *millions* of men and women to accomplish their objectives in the Philippines. Are we prepared to do the same? Our citizens will lose their appetite for such a war long before the Chinese lose their will to fight. The American press will undoubtedly provide us with a daily body count and gruesome videos of the aftermath of battle. They will share poignant stories about remarkable young men and women whose lives have been cut short due to our government's misguided involvement in a dispute that should have been resolved diplomatically. The heartbreak of war will be poured thickly onto America like syrup on waffles.

Citizens in the People's Republic of China will be fed a steady diet of propaganda portraying their soldiers as heroes. They will read of dazzling victories by their brilliant generals, and the newscasters will provide daily encouragement as they personify valor and courage through 'field interviews'. The citizens will be asked to endure even greater sacrifice, and they will respond to the call.

America has been the policeman of the world for too long. We can't seem to avoid fights, and we step willingly into conflicts we should avoid. I admire President Clover for making the difficult decision to stay out of this war. I'm sure that it was not an easy decision. As much as we love Filipinos and treasure our relationship with the Philippines, the American President is obligated to do what is best for America and Americans. In staying out of this war, President Clover has demonstrated that she is, indeed, fit for office as the leader of our great nation.

Chapter 44 – Overwhelmed
Tuesday, 6:20pm, August 15ᵗʰ
Baler, Aurora, Aurora Province, Philippines

The group of foreigners sat on the floor of the Baler sports complex, totally oblivious to events outside. They had not been permitted to bathe, nor had their movement and conversations had been limited. The past four days seemed like months. The children did not understand and were restless. And their parents feared that their child's crying and misbehavior might bring serious consequences. The only positive development was that Judge was no longer free to terrorize them.

The diesel generator died before lunchtime and remained inoperable at sunset. The heat in the gymnasium was just as oppressive as their captors, and the humidity sapped their strength. Lisa walked to the door and asked to speak with Lt. Seng, who appeared before her in less than a minute.

"I know that your men are also uncomfortable with the heat, but at least they are able to step outside where it is bearable. Will you permit the parents to take their children outside until the electricity is restored?" Lisa was hoping to gain incremental privileges for the group of captives. Her goal was to have the freedom to walk freely around the gymnasium and talk to one another.

Lisa did not expect his response, "That would be no problem, ma'am. We have just learned that all of you may be sleeping in your own beds by this time next week."

"Are you serious?" Lisa beamed as she asked the question, placing her hand on the young Lieutenant's shoulder.

"Yes, Madam Ambassador. Communications with Beijing have been restored and we have been assured that you will be repatriated in the coming days." Lt. Seng smiled at Lisa and he placed his hand over hers. "Please permit me to make the announcement to the others."

"I was waiting for the electricity to return so that I could use the PA system, but the time has come. Please gather your friends and have them come to the entrance." Lt Seng returned to the men near the entrance and informed them that the foreigners would be permitted to walk around outside, then he carried a chair to the center of the doorway and climbed atop the chair.

"For those of you who have not been introduced, my name is Jun An Seng, I am a Second Lieutenant in the Peoples Liberation Army. I am currently in charge of this processing center and I have some good news to share with you. You will soon be going home." The room burst into screams of delight, and the captives danced around and hugging one another. They laughed and cried and the elation finally died enough to permit Lt. Seng to continue his announcement.

"On Saturday, which is only four days from now, you will be transported to the USS Ronald Reagan. The U.S. Navy medical corps will examine your health and assist you with the repatriation process once you are aboard the ship. All of you will be delivered to the Hong Kong International Airport and flown from there to your home counties. Your governments are arranging hotel accommodations and flights for you." The hopelessness that pervaded the building just minutes before had vanished. Everyone was smiling, even the Chinese soldiers.

"Please, let me finish. The liberation of the Philippines is far from complete, so the possibility of attack remains. You may move around and speak freely within this facility, but we ask that you remain only on the cemented steps in the front of the building while outside. We have obtained drums of water that will be placed in the restrooms so that you can bathe. We have soap, shampoo and towels available and we will place them in the restrooms for you. I will provide you with additional information tomorrow morning."

Lt. Seng walked among the elated men and women, who were still hugging and high-fiving one another. The only people who were not smiling were the Filipinos: Pastor Mark, Brother Angel, and Brother Manny. They knew what this meant – America was not coming to their rescue. The Philippines had been surrendered to China.

Angie and Reno were unaware of the announcement at the sports complex; they continued their round-the-clock care for Judge at Annabelle's clinic. Dr. Bing came to check on things every few hours and brought the women food and drinks. He also carried food to give to the soldiers who remained at the clinic to guard their commander. Annabelle went to Angie's home to find out what happened to her family, but the entire neighborhood had been washed out to sea by the tidal surge during Typhoon Kiko. She went house-to-house in another nearby community in search of any information about the fate of the Ampatin family, but nobody could provide reliable information. One young girl, a friend of Sophie's, said that she saw them pass by in a military truck before the storm. She was certain that it was Sophie in the truck. Annabelle continued her quest to locate Angie's family. She didn't want to return to her clinic without truthful information to provide to Angie.

Judge responded well to his treatments and he awakened briefly, looking confused when he saw Reno and Angie. He groaned in pain and tried to roll onto his side, but the two women prevented him from moving, and Reno administered another dose of morphine.

"Do you think he recognized us?" asked Reno. "He was a bit dazed, but he looked back and forth at both of us twice. I could see it in his expression – I believe he remembered us."

"I'm sure that he didn't expect to see us!" She laughed as she spoke. "I'm sure he's never had anyone repay his evil deeds with kindness. Let's confuse him even more the next time he wakes up." Angie spent hours praying for Judge as he lay unconscious during her care. She needed for him to live and was convinced that God had placed him in her care for a reason. He had.

Judge awakened a second time around 10:00pm. He held Reno's hand, looked her in the eyes and spoke to her in Mandarin. Angie ran quickly outside and asked the English speaking guard to translate his words. His voice was weak and barely audible as he spoke. He held Reno's hand the entire time he was speaking to the interpreter, who answered him in a single sentence. Judge then closed his eyes and rested.

"He wants to know why you are helping him. I told him that you are the most qualified doctors available, but he seemed puzzled by that. He asked, 'Where are the Chinese doctors?' He is just disoriented from his injuries and the pain medication." The interpreter knew that Judge was stunned to see these two specific women, but he didn't let on that he knew Judge had mistreated them.

"What is his name?" asked Angie.

"His name is Rong, Peng Bo" came the reply. Both Angie and Reno failed to realize that his name was presented in normal Chinese fashion, with the last name stated first, and they began to call him by his family surname, 'Rong.' Both women were amused that he was 'Rong', but neither mentioned it. The interpreter nodded at the women and told them, "I will be just outside if you need me."

"We will make sure that Rong gets rest," said Reno. "He seems to be recovering quite quickly. His leg wound will require reconstructive surgery, but the wounds in his arm and abdomen simply will simply require time. We'll know more over the next couple days, but it appears as though your commander will survive." Reno smiled at the interpreter as he walked outside, then she sat next to Angie, who was holding Judge's hand.

"Rong held your hand the entire time he was awake," said Angie. "That surprised me."

Reno responded, "Maybe it's just like the interpreter said, he's delusional because of the medication."

"I'm not sure," said Angie. "I think he recognized us both and he held your hand as a sign of his appreciation. He's smart enough, even with the medication, to know that we hold his life in our hands. Rong knows he is alive because we want him to live."

Reno decided to rest for a while and lay down in the small bed in the next room. Angie continued to hold Judge's hand and she prayed for him, speaking the words softly out loud. Judge opened his eyes and looked at Angie. Her eyes were closed as she prayed, and tear streamed down her face. Judge squeezed her hand and Angie opened her eyes to find him awake. Tears also flowed from his eyes. He spoke to her softly in Mandarin and she just listened. The tone of his words and his tears communicated his thoughts quite clearly. Angie wiped his tears and continued to hold his hand. Judge stopped talking, yet wept like a child. Angie wiped his tears and stroked his face until he drifted back to sleep.

Judge awakened two hours later and was in considerable pain. Reno heard him groaning loudly and she joined Angie to see what was happening. He had not been administered any pain medication for several hours and Reno provided another shot of morphine. And as the medication began to take effect he began to speak to the women. Reno started to get the interpreter, but Angie held her back, saying, "Listen to his words with your heart, Reno, and you'll hear what he's saying."

Judge wept, once again, as he spoke softly to them both. He squeezed Reno's hand as Angie wiped his tears. He was no longer agitated or confused, even though the morphine began taking effect. He was clearly communicating his appreciation to Angie and Reno for caring for him. He knew that they were not just caring for him, it was far more than that - they showed him love. Judge was unaccustomed to love because he was not a lovable man, and he knew it. He was clearly impacted by their kindness, especially after his despicable treatment of both women.

"He'll be sleeping for awhile because of the morphine, and I suggest that you also get some sleep," said Reno. "At least lie down and rest. I'll take care of Rong until tomorrow morning." Reno hugged Angie before she went into the back room to rest, then Reno changed his bandages and checked his pulse. He had no fever and nor any indication of infection. His breathing was strong and regular and his pulse was only slightly elevated. His incredible physical conditioning helped him regain his strength quickly.

Annabelle walked into the clinic shortly after dawn. She was smiling broadly and holding the hand of a beautiful young girl. Reno knew immediately that this was Sophie, Angie's baby sister, and rushed to pick her up and hug her. Sophie didn't understand a word of English and seemed shocked at the response of this American stranger. She pushed away from Reno, who put her back down.

Sophie shouted out, "Gi! *Saan Kayo?* Gi!"

Angie burst from the back room and fell to her knees and hugged her baby sister tightly. She shook as she wept and held Sophie in her grip. She had never given up hope, and God answered her fervent prayer to find Sophie alive and well. Reno and Annabelle also wept tears of joy. Angie held Sophie's hand and she returned to the back room and removed a miniature chocolate bar that Tyler had given her while the medical team was still in Dibutunan. Sophie removed the partly melted, smashed candy bar from the wrapper and ate it in a single bite. "I love you, Gi," she said.

"I love you too, Sophie," replied Angie. She was almost afraid to ask the question, but she needed to know the answer. "Where are mom and dad?"

Annabelle provided the answer. "They are outside waiting for you. The government enforced mandatory evacuations and moved your entire family inland to Maria Aurora before the storm. They are all okay."

Angie picked up her baby sister and ran outside to greet her parents. The reunion was sweet, with more hugs and tears. Annabelle asked the interpreter to permit Angie to return home with her family and permission was granted.

Angie returned to the room where she had been sleeping and placed a few lose belongings into her backpack. She felt compelled to remain with Reno and continue caring for Judge, but she also knew that the Chinese soldiers might change their minds and return her to captivity.

She turned to Reno and said, "I thank God for your friendship and I can't imagine going through this life without you. Please continue to pray for me and my family. Every moment you will be in my heart, and I pray that you will soon be reunited with Tom and Lucky." The two women embraced, neither of them could find another word to say. They knew that this was goodbye.

Judge awakened, calling out in a large, powerful voice. Angie returned to the room and grabbed his hand while Reno went to fetch the interpreter, who had heard Judge cry out and was already halfway across the room. He did not grimace in pain this time. His eyes were clear and his voice was strong as he spoke, "These women have saved my life. You must protect and reward them." The interpreter quickly translated the words, and Judge smiled at them as they looked back at him. "I have many questions for you," he said. "Please stay with me so that we can speak."

Angie held his hand and told him, "I must leave now to care for my family. I am grateful that God has healed you. Reno will stay with you and I know that she would be pleased to answer your questions. Perhaps I can return later." The interpreter provided the translation to Judge, who reached out his hand to Angie. She held his hand momentarily, and then he nodded at her, tears welling up in his eyes.

The Chinese interpreter spoke to Judge as Angie and Reno walked outside together, arm-in-arm. Reno greeted Angie's family and was stunned to discover that Angie's mother also looked like a teenager, while her father had gray hair and dark leathery skin. Their reunion celebration was brief as Annabelle asked them to hurry into the waiting jeep. She knew that they were still under the control of the enemy and that they needed to act decisively. Angie was the last to board the jeep. She threw a kiss to Reno as the jeep began to move, smiling beautifully.

Before Reno could walk back inside, the interpreter asked her, "May we speak privately for a moment?"

"Of course" she answered, puzzled by his sudden formality.

The United States government has agreed not to interfere with The People's Republic of China as we liberate the Philippines. In exchange, we have agreed to repatriate all foreigners to their respective homelands without delay. You will be going home on Saturday."

Reno was speechless. She couldn't respond for a few moments, and then she asked, "Do the others know this?"

"Yes. They have also been informed. You will each be permitted a brief phone call early this evening. Our corpsmen will attend to Captain Rong. I will now take you back to the processing center. Water, soap, shampoo, and towels are now available in the restrooms. You will want to get cleaned up."

He laughed as she replied, "Do I smell that bad?" The news of the bath was as welcome as the news of their impending release or their phone call home. "Let me gather my things."

Reno walked back inside to get her backpack. Judge watched her as she came inside and he called out once again while she was inside. When the interpreter came close he said, "Please bring her back to me before she is permitted to leave. I need to talk with her." It was clear that he was grateful for their care, and Reno was eager to explain to him that it was God, not she and Angie that healed him. She was already rehearsing the words in her head. Reno agreed to return, she was eager to hear what Judge had to say.

What a day! Angie and Sophie were reunited, and their family was safe. Reno would bathe, call Tom, and celebrate going home with the other team members. The interpreter asked Reno to climb on the back seat of his motorcycle and he drove her back to the sports complex. The ride took only minutes, and the early morning hues of pink and orange remained in the eastern sky. Reno was elated. She would be going home in just three days! She hopped off the motorcycle and walked hurriedly into the sports complex. The mission team members met her near the door and hugged her as they excitedly provided details about their repatriation process on Saturday. None of them, however, had heard anything about a phone call, so she asked Lieutenant Seng about it.

"Please come with me outside for a moment," he said. She followed him to the far end of the front porch where they could sit in the shade. The early morning sun was already hot. Lt Seng explained his situation politely. "We have been unable to establish cellular communications. Our technicians are currently setting up a new cell phone tower, which should be completed tomorrow. The equipment must be installed and tested, and I have been given no assurances that it will happen before Saturday. That is why I did not share the news of a phone call with your comrades. You will be permitted to speak with your loved ones as soon as the tower becomes operational. Unfortunately, we do not have the capability to do so at this time. It's a technical, not a procedural problem. Please accept my apology for this inconvenience."

Reno was disappointed, but she knew that it wasn't Lt. Seng's fault. He spoke honestly about the situation, and she knew that it was outside of his control. She thanked him for his honestly and let him know that she would inform the others. The others had not gotten their hopes up about the phone call like she had. They would be excited about the possibility of a call rather than disappointed, as Reno had been, when the certainty of a phone call had been taken away.

Reno checked on Tyler when she returned to the gym. He was sitting against the wall. The bottoms of his feet were bruised and sore and both of his knees had been damaged during the beating. He had a couple of cracked ribs, a shattered shoulder bone, bent fingers, a broken nose, and a fractured jaw. His teeth were broken and were sensitive to the air as he breathed. It hurt when he tried to speak, so he remained quiet. Reno still had several doses of morphine that the corpsman had given her to treat Judge. She leaned close to Tyler and told him, "I smuggled some pain medication to give to you, please give me your arm."

Tyler presented his left arm and Reno injected him with the same dosage that she had been administering to Judge. Within moments he felt relief surging through his body, and he smiled through his broken teeth at Reno. She didn't have enough morphine to sedate him until Saturday, but she could help keep him sedated for a large portion of the next two days. And maybe she could ask for more morphine when she visited Judge again.

The morning skies were filled with a variety of aircraft, all Chinese. Three huge transport helicopters landed near the market and pallets of supplies were offloaded and loaded onto waiting trucks. Fighter jets patrolled the region in formation, and appeared to be in complete control of the airspace above Aurora. Massive airlift craft lumbered overhead, moving slowly southward towards Manila. The Chinese were clearly in full control of the Philippines – or at least the island of Luzon. But Reno was grateful for the swift victory; she had no desire to suffer through a protracted bloody war. Her suffering would soon come to an end.

More boats arrived at the Baler fish port during the morning - dozens of them. They began arriving at high tide just before dawn. Hundreds of reinforcements arrived and were immediately loaded onto trucks that brought them directly to the southern front. The same scene was repeated throughout the Philippines as boats and planes arrived every few minutes at each port. No arrivals were permitted for a period of time at the international airport in Manila because men and cargo could not be moved away from the airport quickly enough. Like uninvited picnic ants, they swarmed into the entire nation.

Tens of thousands of paratroopers darkened the skies as they drifted slowly towards the newly liberated nation. Low flying cargo aircraft used parachutes to offload pallets of ammunition and supplies. Even trucks and armored personnel carriers dropped from the sky. There seemed to be no resistance whatsoever – the enemy aircraft operated with impunity and had no fear of being harassed or intercepted. The Armed Forces of the Philippines seemed to vanish into the fabric of society. They were pounded by aircraft, naval artillery and heavy gunfire wherever they stood to fight. All visible elements of the AFP were pinned down and being shredded. But the invisible elements had avoided the onslaught and were organizing their return to combat as guerilla fighters. They would soon practice their 'shuffle and weave' tactics.

Chapter 45– Communications restored

Thursday, 9:00am, 17 August
The Island of Luzon

Hundreds of frequency suppressors shut down programmatically at precisely 9:00am on August 17th allowing communications to take place. Two-way radios jumped to life. Military commanders conversed with their units. Aircraft were able to communicate with one another and with air traffic control towers. Radio and television signals filled the airwaves. But what the people wanted more than anything else was to use their cell phones. The Chinese had disabled or destroyed virtually every cell tower on the island of Luzon over the past week. They were now 'repairing' the cell towers, returning them to service with new transmitters/receivers, transceivers, digital signal processors and control electronics. Only cell phones equipped with specially designed SIM cards could be used with the new equipment installed in the cell towers.

SIM cards, subscriber identity modules, are used to authenticate network subscribers. The People's Liberation Army announced that they would provide free cell phones to anyone who could provide a valid photo ID, and Filipinos flocked to the distribution centers, standing in the hot sun for hours to obtain one. The cell phones were high quality smart phones capable of accessing the Internet, and they were entirely *free*. They required no prepaid 'load' nor were any monthly fees expected. Filipinos are naturally suspicious of anything free, and they had reason to be suspicious of these free phones. The SIM cards were registered to specific individuals and the registry allowed them to locate the owner of each phone. With their new equipment in place the Chinese could monitor every text message or phone call inside the new network. They devised sophisticated software to identify rebellious hearts and thwart treasonous plans. They had programmed it to intercept conversations in all thirteen of the major languages spoken in the Philippines.

The People's Republic of China had effectively used this same software domestically for many years to identify dissidents who foolishly transmitted a 'seditious' text or carried on a 'subversive' conversation. A long list of specific words and phrases were programmed into the software in each language to help them identify troublemakers. Chinese cryptologists teamed up with linguists to identify alternative phrases in case people tried to 'talk around' a forbidden topic. Even abbreviations and shorthand variants were including in the software. In the past Filipinos could purchase a SIM card just about anywhere and install it in their phones and remain anonymous. There was no paperwork to fill out so nothing identified the number to the user. A spare, anonymous SIM card could be used to conceal an illicit love affair, send hate messages to enemies, or make bomb threats without the fear of discovery. There would be no more anonymity.

Each 'Chinese' phone was equipped with a GPS chip that allowed the military to immediately locate the device whether it was turned on or off. Governments around the world, including the U.S. government, have long recognized the benefit of locating mobile devices. Emergency 911 operators no longer need to ask the for a caller's location – the location is already pinpointed for them because of the device. But the more sinister use of the technology tends to escape many people. Government weenies know what you say, download, view, 'like', 'share', tweet, and they even profile your *proclivities*. Revealing their browsing history or even some nefarious activity by someone in their 'friends' list could easily discredit political foes. But Filipinos seemed oblivious to the technological threat that was being provided to them for *free*.

Filipinos embraced the new phones, wondering why their own government had allowed the telecommunications companies to milk them for so long. Filipinos had long been charged ridiculous international long distance fees – ten times the amount that people from neighboring countries paid for the same service. They accused the Philippine government of corruption and collusion with greedy monopolies. They felt that their government received kickbacks for allowing corporations to fix prices and manipulate prices in a supposedly free marketplace. The new phones came with high-resolution cameras, 32 GB of memory, and they were loaded with applications. Filipinos loved them! But what they appreciated most was the incredibly fast Internet speed – the best they had ever experienced. The Communist Party's Central Propaganda Department knew how to win hearts and minds. Providing free phones and fast Internet service to the Philippine public was a subtle first step; why would anyone want to return to the way it used to be?

Electricity, however, was another matter altogether. Seven power generation plants had been obliterated just the week before, and there was simply no quick way to replace the needed 6,400 megawatts from the destroyed facilities. Most of the nation didn't know that radio and television broadcasting had resumed because of the power outage. The citizens needed electricity to recharge the batteries on their new cell phones. And the People's Liberation Army needed to gather intelligence data on the phone users as quickly as possible. Entire communities throughout Luzon remained unaware that the country had even been invaded. They saw the airplanes, but couldn't distinguish a Chinese J11-d fighter jet from an American F-15. They assumed that the aircraft were part of an organized relief effort after Typhoon Kiko. Until power was restored they would remain, literally, in the dark.

The leadership of the PRC acted quickly, delivering tens of thousands of diesel-powered generators throughout the island of Luzon. It was more of a goodwill gesture than a solution to the power problem. But they also sent experts to assemble many medium-sized gas powered generators to boost the supply of power to the grid. Full restoration of the power grid would take months. In the meantime, the PRC would employ the same 'rolling brownout' strategy that had been used by the Philippine government when they couldn't generate sufficient electricity to meet the demand. Each region would receive a tiny portion of the limited supply of electricity each day.

People could at least charge their cell phones, flashlights and fill basins of water. Some would also get a glimpse at the television news provided by a new breed of Filipino journalist, known as 'loyalists' to the PRC, who offered a twisted picture of the current situation. Broadcasts showed the People's Liberation Army cleaning up storm debris, repairing power transmission lines, feeding hungry families and building homes for families displaced by the storm. The absence of a Philippine government response to Kiko was emphasized; Filipino soldiers were shown playing cards while drinking gin and CCTV footage from the airport identified twenty-six politicians and their families departing the Philippines before the storm. There was no mention of America.

Lieutenant Seng walked the length of the gymnasium floor and approached Lisa Stephens with a smile. "I am pleased to announce that our technicians have restored cell phone service. In just a moment we will provide each of you with a cell phone that you may use to call home. We will collect the phones in an hour, so please let your companions know that their time is limited."

"Thank you, sir," said Lisa, now grinning broadly. "That's great news!" She knew that she wouldn't be able to reach her husband, Frank.

But she would call her mother to let her know that they would be leaving the Philippines in just two days. Lisa jogged back to where the embassy staff sat with their families and told them, "We are being permitted to call home!" The news was met with an enthusiastic response. Brian, who was normally somewhat reserved, danced around holding four year old Abby Andersen in his arms. Lisa then walked briskly to the rest of the foreigners in the gym to let them know to prepare for a phone call home.

Lt. Seng motioned for everyone to come to the front door, and as they arrived he said, "We will call each of you by name and you will be handed a phone and given instructions. We have assistance available if you need to look up a phone number. We will collect the phones in one hour. Please be cooperative when we ask you to terminate your calls. I know you are eager to speak to your families, but you have a one-hour time limit." He took a seat at the table and was handed the first phone. "Chris Coloma" he called out. Chris thought it was odd that he should be the first name called. He should not have been the first on their processing list as many people had already been processed by the time he arrived. He wasn't the first alphabetically either. He walked to the table and was handed a cell phone. He had no idea who to call. He decided to call his brother in San Jose, California and went to the assistance table so that they could provide him with the number.

Almost everyone needed assistance finding the proper telephone number to reach their own family members. They relied on the pre-programmed contact list in their cell phone memory when calling; there was no need to memorize numbers. And since everyone's cell phones had been confiscated, they all required directory assistance. Reno thought about how reliant everyone had become on technology. Her name was the sixth name called, and she immediately dialed Tom's cell phone number when she was handed the phone. Tom looked at the phone to see who was calling and didn't recognize the phone on the caller ID. He answered it saying, "Tom West here."

"Hello baby – it's me!" Reno nearly shouted the words because of her excitement.

Tom asked, "Where are you? Are you okay?"

"All of us are sitting on the wooden floor of a gymnasium in Baler. But, I'm coming home on Saturday, Tom. We've been told that we will be delivered by boat to the USS Ronald Reagan, and then brought to Hong Kong before we are flown to the States. I hope to see you this weekend." Reno got excited talking about it. This was the first time that it seemed real to her, and tears began to pour down her cheeks.

Tom said, "We've been going crazy here. There's almost no news about Typhoon Kiko; it's like it never happened. And we're not getting much about the Chinese invasion either. Has there been any combat near you guys?"

"Kiko was crazy, Tom. I've never experienced anything like it. The roof blew off the church where we took shelter and we had to walk through the storm to a dormitory building. The conditions were so bad that we lost Anna and Marilou during the chaos as we walked through the storm at night. We never found them, Tom, and we've heard nothing about them." Reno became choked up and stopped speaking.

"Are you kidding me? That's horrible! Is anyone else hurt?" Tom was shocked at the news and he sat down heavily on the edge of his bed. He admired the way that Anna cared for her disabled parents and knew that they would be crushed by the news.

"Tyler was beaten by Chinese soldiers and he's not doing well. He has broken ribs, shoulder, fingers, nose and jaw and his teeth are a mess. He needs medication and a dental surgeon. The rest of us are sore and mosquito bitten, but we're healthy." Reno didn't want to tell him that Angie had been raped or that Brother Jun had been murdered by Judge. The details would wait, she just wanted for Tom to know that she loved him and that she was eager to get home.

"Should I tell anyone about Anna or Tyler?" Tom was a doctor and was trained and experienced at delivering bad news. He was willing to be the bearer of bad news, but he would rather leave the task to someone else.

"I think Pastor Rod should be the one to speak to the families, Tom. He's the team leader and he can provide them with details that you won't be able to answer. I have so much more to share with you, but most importantly you need to know how much I love you." Reno again struggled with her emotions and paused to find the right words. "I need you eternally."

Tom was still processing the information he'd been given and he knew that Reno had gone through traumatic events. He said, "Me too, baby. I can't wait for you to get home. I haven't unwrapped your gift yet." They both laughed for a moment, then he asked, "Will you arrive at the Charleston airport, or should I plan to meet you somewhere else?"

Reno knew very little about the repatriation process. She assumed that the team would fly directly home to Charleston. The thought of a government debriefing never crossed her mind until now, and she hoped that the flight from Hong Kong would be all the way through to Charleston. "I don't know, baby. I'm sure I will be able to call you from the plane and provide details."

Reno could hear Sean explaining their ordeal to Christi. She missed most of what he said, but clearly heard him say, "….she just disappeared!" The same conversation took place all around her. David helped speak to Tyler's family because of the pain he experienced trying to talk. Tyler was difficult to understand because of the damage that had been done to his mouth. Ashley repeated, "I love you all so much." Kelly told Mark Tucker the same thing. She missed his kisses, and she told him that there would be some changes in their relationship when she returned home. Rod took his phone to the far side of the gym to speak. He didn't want others to overhear what he shared with Gina. He also intended to call Anna's parents. Reno's momentary distraction with other conversations vanished as Tom spoke again.

"Your mother and I have been speaking at least twice each day. She wanted for me to tell you that she loves you. I'll call her in a few minutes to let her know that you're okay." Reno was surprised that Tom was willing to call her mother. Under normal circumstances he would not have answered her call because she was rude and abrasive. Tom didn't like her, but treated her respectfully. Now he was calling her! Tom was such a gem.

"Tell her that I love her too, Tom. She's a pain in the butt, but she's my mother." Reno knew that she needed to spend some time with her mother to strengthen their relationship. Her mother now seemed important to Reno, but nothing was more important than getting home to Tom. But her mission in the Philippines was not complete; she still needed to speak with Judge.

"Lucky also wants you to know that he loves you. He misses you baby. He's lethargic and has lost his appetite and I believe he's lonely." Tom knew she wanted to know more about Lucky, who she called 'the best animal in the history of the planet.'

"If you're at home, please bring the phone to Lucky." Reno knew that he would recognize her voice.

Tom said, "Go ahead, you're on the speaker phone and Lucky is right here."

Lucky barked and spun in circles as they finished their conversation. Reno was eager to see him again. Lucky continued to bark in the background until their conversation ended. She could see the soldiers collecting the call phones and she quickly reminded Tom how much she loved him. As soon as she said "goodbye" the phone was collected from her. Everything now seemed right. Reno was euphoric in spite of the typhoon, invasion, confinement and heat. She had a day and a half to check on her patient and to fulfill the mission that God had placed in her heart.

Chapter 46 – Redemption!
Friday, 7:45am, 18 August
Baler, Aurora Province, Philippines

Oingo Boingo, in their epic song "No Spill Blood," explains that *someone else* makes the rules. Parents make the rules in their household, and children are obligated to obey them no matter how arbitrary they may be. Schools make the rules for their pupils, and the students must follow them, no matter how absurd they are. Governments' make the rules for their citizens, and citizens must comply with them. There are consequences for children who disobey their parents, for students who defy their teachers, and for citizens who defy their nation's laws. We are smothered with *someone else's* rules from the moment we are born.

But men like Judge made their own rules; they defied society's boundaries and norms. Judge behaved as though he was unconstrained by *someone else's* rules. He defied his parents and willingly accepted their punishment. He defied his teachers and suffered their wrath. Yet he managed to conform to the many rules of Chinese society, knowing that his allegiance to the Communist Party and the People's Liberation Army would provide personal benefit. But deep down in his soul, Judge was defiant of all authority.

Everyone is somewhat selfish. This selfishness manifests itself in small ways, such as insisting on specific food that others might not enjoy at social events, or turning up a thermostat to an uncomfortable temperature for others to suit ourselves. Most people would be offended if they were called 'selfish' because they are blind to their own egocentricity. But not Judge. He didn't care what other people preferred – it simply didn't matter. He had always insisted on having his own way.

When Judge punched Reno and raped Angie he didn't care how they felt. In all of the cosmos, only his feelings mattered. It's how he marched through life, ignoring the desires, preferences, and concerns of others. Others lives were not simply less important than his, they were totally *insignificant*. So when he awakened to find Angie and Reno tenderly dressing his wounds, wiping his face, and holding his hands he became confused. How could they possibly do so willingly? He couldn't understand how they could be so compassionate after his despicable behavior. They were thoughtful and they treated him with kindness; Judge could see compassion written on their faces. They didn't treat him kindly out of compulsion to do so; they actually desired to show him affection. Judge struggled for answers because he had never before encountered such people. Why were they so different?

Judge understood mankind's primal instincts. Men instinctively fulfill their primal needs, such as food, water, shelter, or basic survival. But Judge fulfilled more than his primal needs – he fulfilled every whimsical desire and punished those who prevented him from doing so. He couldn't comprehend why these two women would surrender their dignity by serving him. He would never have done so, and he was mystified why they did so without compulsion. He sat upright in his bed as he searched for answers.

Reno was all too eager to provide him with answers. In her mind she practiced what she would say when she saw Judge again. She nervously sat in the back seat of a gray van without air conditioning on her way to Annabelle's clinic. The driver rolled up the black-tinted windows for security reasons, and Reno was thankful that the ride took only a few minutes. The solders outside Annabelle's clinic greeted her as she climbed from the van and walked into the clinic.

Reno was surprised to find Judge sitting up in his bed. And for the first time Reno saw Judge smiling. It was a natural smile that invited her to smile back at him. He seemed happy to see her and he motioned her to sit next to him on the bed. He admired Angie and Reno and he wanted to know more about them. He especially wanted to comprehend their motivation for caring for him as they had done.

Reno was truly astonished to see Judge sitting up in his bed. He had been gravely wounded just a few days ago, but he sat up without grimacing. And even though he had been administered no pain medication he showed no indication of discomfort. He reached out his hand to Reno and she sat next to him on the bed and took hold of his hand. He called for his interpreter, who was standing at the door and immediately joined them and interpreted Judge's words.

"First of all, allow me to thank you for your healing touch and for your loving heart. You should hate me for the things I have done, but I do not sense any hatred from you. I find it remarkable that you don't harbor such feelings and I need to understand why. I want to know more about you and the Filipina doctor; please tell me about yourselves."

Reno replied, "My name is Reno West. I am thirty-six years old and I am married to a magnificent man named Tom. The other doctor you referred to is a nurse from here in Baler named Angie Ampatin. I do not wish to waste any time. Let me discuss why I am here." Judge agreed to listen to what she wanted to say.

She started, "My God is the creator of all things. The entire universe was created by and belongs to him. Astronomers believe that there are more than 300 billion stars in our galaxy, and that the observable universe has more than 100 billion galaxies. The stars are countless! Yet ancient scripture says that our creator positioned each of those stars exactly where he wanted them and he knows them by name. Are you following me so far?"

Judge nodded as the interpreter finished his translation. He did not know why she was explaining this, but he understood what had been said. "The same scripture explains that God created all living things, including you and me. He knows us intimately enough to know the exact number of hairs on our heads. You didn't' create yourself, God did. And he did so according to his design. God planned for you and I to meet. With more than seven billion people on the planet, God placed you and me here together by design. He led you here as a soldier and he brought me here as a doctor; our encounter is due to a divine appointment. God orchestrated every event in our lives, culminating in this moment. And the reason he has done so is for you to receive redemption."

The interpreter paused at the term 'redemption'. He was not just unfamiliar with the word; he was unfamiliar with the concept. He needed Reno to help him explain it. Reno explained, "Redemption is the act of being saved or rescued from our own immorality and evil deeds. God wants to pardon you for the evil things you have done in the past, and he has brought me here to tell you how you can receive his forgiveness."

Reno could sense that Judge was looking for answers. Even during her previous visit he wanted to talk, but was too groggy from the morphine to do so. Before Judge could interrupt her she said, "Let me explain the difference between natural men and spiritual men. A natural man is focused on the material world around him. He follows his animal instincts and, just like an animal, cannot comprehend spiritual truths or anything coming from God. The natural man does not acknowledge God. And the natural man instinctively chooses sin over righteousness." She paused until the interpreter could catch up.

"The spiritual man understands the nature of God and desires to be like Him. God is compassionate, loving, forgiving, and merciful, so the spiritual man strives to practice these precepts. The supernatural work of God is to change the natural man into a spiritual man. And I believe that God has brought us together for this very purpose." Judge's eyes widened as Reno's words were translated. His breathing quickened, yet he remained silent. He also believed that God had sent Reno.

Contemporary culture teaches us to blame somebody else for our behavior. Criminals often blame their actions on others: their parents neglected them, abused them, or mistreated them in some way. The kids at school mocked them, bullied them, or shunned them. Everyone seems to have an external excuse. Their errant behavior is always someone else's fault. Few people willingly accept the blame for their actions, but Judge had already accepted his guilt.

He was guilty of brutalizing and murdering his own men. He had killed innocent people for no reason. He was guilty of raping Angie and punching Reno. He didn't need to be told that he was guilty because the Lord had reached into his heart and convicted him of the things he had done. Judge was ripe for redemption. He was anguished over his treatment of Reno and Angie and struggled to understand their kindness towards him. He was known as a harsh man, and he knew in his heart that he was a cruel, heartless man. The massacre near the Malupa Bridge in Santa Lucia played over and over in his mind. He anguished over the brutal murder of Sergeant Heng, who had been a loyal soldier. He killed him for missing his child! Judge was guilty and he was hungry for forgiveness.

"If I was acting under my own authority you would be dead. But the Lord I serve guides my actions. I do what Jesus asks me to do, and I have been commanded to forgive you, to love you, and to place your needs above my own. Jesus Christ, as an act of love, willingly laid down his life for me. I will explain this to you. You will understand what it means to love sacrificially. And afterwards, you will be given a choice to receive God's grace and forgiveness or to continue life as a natural man.

"But I already know your choice; God has chosen for you to receive salvation today." Reno spoke confidently, believing in her heart that this was, indeed, a divine appointment.

"I don't need to ask this because I've seen it with my own eyes. I know that you are guilty, and you also know that you are guilty. And I don't need to identify your sins because you already know what they are. I believe that the Holy Spirit has already convicted you of the horrible things that you've done. You cannot hide your sins from God. He is already fully aware of your evil deeds. If you want to be forgiven for them, you need to confess them to God. I don't need to hear your confession, but you cannot be forgiven without first admitting your sins to God." Reno was certain that Judge was ready to do so. The first step for an alcoholic to recover is to recognize that they are, in fact, an alcoholic. Drug addicts never recover unless they first understand that they have a problem. Judge needed to take this first step.

Judge did not hesitate. He looked Reno in the eyes, and with tears flowing he said, "There is no question that I am guilty. Yes! I am a horrible man." The Holy Spirit had been telling him the same thing for the past two days and he felt relieved to admit it. He nodded his head and said again, "Yes. Yes. I am most guilty."

Reno quickly responded, "You are correct. And I am also guilty. All of us are guilty. We may sin in different ways, but none of us measure up to what God expects of us. We are guilty of saying things we shouldn't say, doing things we shouldn't do, and even guilty of thinking things we shouldn't think. We are also guilty by our inaction; failing to do what is right is sin. But today, because you have confessed your guilt, God will forgive you. Let me explain how."

For the next three hours Reno, through the interpreter, explained the divinity of Jesus and why He came to earth. She didn't want to leave anything out and explained the entire story. She was uncomfortable sharing just five or six verses from the book of Romans and then asking people to pray the 'sinners prayer.' She wanted to make sure that Judge fully understood that Jesus came as the son of God, was born of virgin, performed miracles, was mocked, ridiculed and beaten, then died for the sins of the world. She outlined the various types of sacrifices required in the Old Testament, and explained that forgiveness required shedding of blood. Jesus, without sin, was the perfect, unblemished sacrifice. And through His sacrifice forgiveness could be extended through faith; Jesus' blood was sufficient to cover all sin.

Reno was surprised at the words as they came out of her mouth. She adeptly tied the Old Testament to the new, explaining creation, the fall of man, and the promise of God to restore all things to their rightful state. She explained the return of Jesus, and wanted Judge to know that His return was rapidly approaching. Both Judge and his interpreter were stunned. They were speechless, both overwhelmed by God's Holy Spirit. Filled with tears of joy, both men eagerly agreed to accept Jesus as their Lord, and follow Him.

Reno had often mocked evangelists who use the 'magic prayer' at the end of their fiery sermons. They would tug at people's heartstrings and engage them emotionally, telling them heart wrenching stories involving: a dying mother, teenagers involved in a horrific car crash, and a stubborn father who suffered a sudden heart attack at the age of 41. And as everyone was choked up, imagining their mother, child, or father dying, such evangelists used the emotion to request surrender to God. The next step was always the 'sinner's prayer.' "Please repeat after me and you will be saved." Very few of their lives were changed by such an experience. Yet Reno surprised herself by repeating exactly what they did; she led Judge and his interpreter through the 'sinner's prayer.'

Afterwards she admonished them, "Today you have been born spiritually. And just like you can't be unborn physically, neither can you become unborn spiritually. But you must follow Christ obediently, and you cannot obey what you do not understand." She urged them both to locate a strong Christian fellowship, and to obtain a Bible and read it. She believed that both men would eventually grow into the people that God created them to be.

Reno had met many pseudo-Christians in her life. They sat all around her at church each Sunday. They were mere spectators who showed up for only an hour each week. They looked and behaved exactly like their pagan neighbors, and sacrifice wasn't part of their lexicon. They were neither doers nor givers. She prayed that Judge and his interpreter, who grinned and wept, would commit to Christ wholeheartedly. She felt judgmental when she categorized other 'believers', and she felt sorry for those who were missing out on God's best for them.

"You said that the name of your young Filipina companion was Angie Ampatin. I must apologize to her and find a way to make restitution. Perhaps I can help her family or make sure that they are protected from any harm. Please express my sorrow to her. I fully understand if she is unwilling to accept my apology, but I want to thank her for the care she has given me. Her care for me has led me to Jesus." Pain was written across his face as Judge spoke of Angie. "God has forgiven me, and I hope that Angie can do the same."

Judge asked Reno, "May I know your last name? Would it be possible for me to contact you in the future? You have changed my life and I'm indebted to you."

Reno requested a pen and paper and wrote down her name, address, phone number, email, her Facebook account name and her username on twitter. She also wanted to remain in contact with Judge. She had witnessed him become a new creation in Christ. She wanted to know about his growth and eventually witness his spiritual maturity.

"I have been told that you will be leaving on Saturday. My heart will go with you. Return home with the knowledge that your efforts here are not in vain. I will remain with Christ." There was no question in Reno's mind – Judge was now an ardent follower of her Lord Jesus. He was now her brother in Christ.

Reno cried as she leaned close to Judge. The tearful translator hugged them both. Angie told them, "Support one another as brothers, because that's what you are." Then Angie explained that she had to return to the sports complex to prepare for her departure. She knew that angels were rejoicing in heaven as she walked outside to the waiting van. Her mission in the Philippines been fulfilled. Reno was grateful that God had used her in such an unexpected and inspiring way. And as she travelled back to the sports complex in the hot van with its windows rolled up she prayed for the two men. She prayed that the Lord would use them to make himself known to their families, their fellow soldiers, and to their neighbors back in China. Today was a glorious and wonderful day!

Chapter 47 – Deported
Saturday, 11:45am, 19 August
Baler, Aurora Province, Philippines

Sean leaned close to Rod after they sat down on the bus and whispered, "Do you really think we're being deported, or are they going to dump us in a huge hole and bury us all?" Rod looked shocked as Sean finished his words. He'd never even considered the possibility that the soldiers might execute them. Perhaps they had been held as hostages and America refused to pay the asking price. Rod looked around at the other passengers on the bus and all were laughing or smiling, clearly relieved at the turn of events.

Rod replied, "Either way I'm headed home today." He smiled at Sean and assured him that there was nothing to worry about. "We would already be dead if that's what they wanted. Lighten up, brother, we're headed home." Sean somberly gazed out of the bus window. Returning home had seemed impossible just a few days ago, and it still seemed too good to be true. Brian Roberts and Chris Coloma, who would later share their fears with the press, had the same concern as Sean. Fortunately all three men were wrong; they were, indeed, going home.

Two buses carrying the 'processed' foreigners sped from the Baler sports complex towards the fish port, arriving in less than fifteen minutes. Everyone was asked to remain seated on the bus until the boats arrived. Nobody complained; they soaked up the air conditioning like a cloud absorbs water. Some slept in the comfortable bus seats while others talked quietly. Reno scanned the horizon for the boats that would carry them to freedom, spying a single small dot to the northeast. The dot doubled in size every minute, until the outline of the USS Patriot could be seen entering Baler Bay.

Larry, the anthropologist who had 'gone native' appealed for his release. He insisted that he had renounced his U.S. citizenship and become a Filipino many years ago. He couldn't imagine returning to life in the U.S. after so many years living in the jungle and pleaded with the soldiers to release him. And, surprisingly, they did so.

The ship anchored about 1500 meters from the shore and immediately sent three motorized rubber rafts towards the fish port. As soon as they arrived ashore Lt. Seng escorted several uniformed sailors towards the busses. One of them stepped onto the bus where Reno sat just behind the driver. "I am Lieutenant Commander Paul Pappin. My men are here to escort you home." Cheers erupted before he was able to continue. "We will begin by boarding anyone who is injured or in need of medical attention. If you require medical assistance, please step forward. Everyone else please remain seated and we'll be with you in a few minutes."

Tyler stood and hobbled forward. So did Walt Summers, the wound on his head was now grotesquely infected. Rod told Sean, "Your dog bites need attention; you should go now." Sean nodded at him, then moved forward and stepped off the bus. Ashley's shin injury had also become red and swollen. She asked for assistance and sobbed, overcome by emotion, as two medics assisted her from the bus towards two waiting Chinese patrol boats. The first boat sped away carrying all of the families and people who required medical assistance. The second boat was loaded only moments after the first one pulled away from the dock. Both boats raced quickly towards the large U.S. Navy ship.

Reno looked back towards the dock instead of at the ship like the other passengers. She wondered if or when she would see Angie again. She prayed silently for Judge. And tears rolled down her face as she thought of Anna, Marilou, and Brother Jun. The joy of returning home to Tom and Lucky was muted by the knowledge that her Filipino friends were still suffering under the control of the People's Liberation Army. She marveled at the beauty of the Philippines as they moved further out to sea. The lush green mountains and unspoiled azure beaches looked so tranquil, but she knew that every household was filled with anguish and dread. Reno prayed silently for the turmoil to end.

Events aboard the USS Patriot were a blur. Only eighty seven had been 'processed' in Baler, including the Filipino couple that claimed to be from Cincinnati. But the ship was crowded with others who had been rescued from other ports. They were a miniscule fraction of the hundreds of thousands of foreigners who were rescued from remote locations around the Philippines. Rather than being brought to the USS Ronald Reagan as they expected, the USS Patriot steamed quickly to the city of Laoag on the northwest corner of Luzon. The trip was over in just a shower, a meal and a nap. Reno didn't even have an opportunity to call Tom from the ship. As they left the USS Patriot they were given an envelope that contained their processing paperwork and were cautioned not to lose or open the envelopes because they were their 'ticket home.'

Thousands of 'processed' foreigners experienced total chaos as they arrived at the airport in Laoag, a secondary international airport that normally handled less than thirty-five flights daily. Throngs of people pushed towards the gates, but nobody knew where they were supposed to go. The group found it difficult to remain together. Tyler and Ashley were placed in wheelchairs, which the other team members pushed. After ninety minutes of pushing forward towards the gates, the group was instructed to step outside onto the tarmac. Filipinos in airline uniforms then pointed the group to a Malaysia Airlines Boeing 737 with mobile stairs in place. Rod helped Tyler up the stairs, leaving his wheelchair on the tarmac. Ashley was assisted by David. They were asked to take the first seat available, and they sat together just behind the occupied first class seating section.

Their arrival in Hong Kong was far more organized than expected after what they had gone through in Laoag. Each departing passenger was asked to present his or her envelope to any 'processing agent', easily identified by his or her yellow vests. The processing agents were helpful and courteous, directing each passenger to specific departure gates for their flights home. "Please present your envelope at your departure gate and they will issue you boarding passes." Strangely Kelly and Rod were sent to a different departure gate than the rest of the team.

Rod was unconcerned, but Kelly seemed perplexed that the team would be split up for the rest of their journey. Rod consoled her saying, "I will be with you, Kelly." She smiled as she recognized the words "I will be with you" from his sermon by that name just three weeks earlier. The team hugged one another and headed for their respective gates.

Reno was the first in her group at the gate counter. She presented her envelope and was directed to board the aircraft. No ticket or boarding pass was required. The flight attendant at the aircraft door told her, "Take any seat you want. We will come around and find out where you want to go and will have your remaining tickets and boarding passes provided to you as you deplane." Most of the first class section was vacant and another flight attendant seated her in seat 3A against the window. Her three companions joked about their first class seating.

"Pardon me, ma'am, Reno asked the flight attendant who had seated them, "Where will we arrive in the States?"

"Atlanta, Georgia, ma'am," she answered.

Reno smiled. Tom would gladly drive four and a half hours to meet her there. "Will we be able to make phone calls once we're airborne?"

"Yes ma'am. You may talk as long as you want courtesy of Uncle Sam. He's paying whatever it costs to bring you home." The flight attendant didn't realize that Uncle Sam had just acquired an extra $1.4 trillion to pay for the tickets. The phone calls could be managed within the new U.S. budget.

Each of the two hundred ten passengers was a 'processed' American returning home. They communicated with friends using the aircraft's Wi-Fi and they spoke for hours with their loved ones using the seatback phones. Aircraft food had never tasted as good. Some drank too much and became goofy, but the flight attendants continued to serve whatever was requested. And, as advertised, each of the passengers was provided with tickets and boarding passes for their continuation flights as they exited the plane.

Reno had no continuation flight; Tom agreed to meet her in the baggage claim area in Atlanta. Few of the passengers had checked luggage, so the baggage claim area would be quiet. They could easily find one another. Her heart beat faster than her footsteps as she followed the signs to the baggage claim area. None of the 'processed' passengers were required to be screened by immigration officers or go through customs inspection. Reno increased her pace after stepping off the Plain Train that carried her from the arrival concourse to the baggage claim area. Tom was less than a hundred yards away. And as she took the escalator down into the baggage claim area she saw him near the door, holding Lucky on a leash. The security officer allowed him inside the terminal with Lucky after he explained the situation, but made him remain near the exit.

He didn't notice Reno running at him from the escalator and she nearly knocked him down when she reached him. Lucky jumped into her arms as soon as the long hug with Tom ended. They couldn't find words to express their relief and their love for one another. Reno said simply, "Let's go home."

Tom smiled and said, "I have a present for you waiting at the Airport Hilton. We're only five minutes away. You deserve to be properly repatriated."

"I hope it's what I think it is," Reno said laughing. They walked arm-in-arm to the parking lot as Reno added, "It's so good to be home, Tom."

Chapter 48 – The new normal
China's 24th Province

Regular class schedules resumed at all elementary and high schools throughout the Philippines on October 9th; just two months after the nation had been invaded by the People's Liberation Army. And the new normal was plainly depicted in the maps and globes displayed in every classroom; the Philippines had become the 24th Province of the People's Republic of China. Mandarin replaced English and the social science curriculum had been modified to glorify The People's Republic of China and disparage western culture. Christian scripture was eliminated from 'Value's' classes. All private schools were shut down. Islamic schools, Christian schools, and International schools were permanently closed to hasten normalcy.

"Normal" is relative. And the Chinese insisted upon their flavor of normal. Conformity is a quality that the Chinese value. People who defy norms are stigmatized, and Filipinos didn't like the smell of Chinese normality. Although considered a 'collectivist' society, where groups of people tend to be loyal and take care of their group, Filipinos were unwilling to surrender their cultural identity to their enemy. Although they belonged to the new Chinese empire, they remained Filipino at heart.

Insurance companies have established 'normal' ranges for height and weight based upon age in order to make 'abnormal' people pay more to acquire insurance. And Chinese society has established 'normal' grooming standards, ostracizing those who deviate from the norm. The flamboyant gay community in the Philippines quickly became a target for the People's Liberation Army. Even though homosexuality was considered legal in the PRC, it had only recently been removed from the list of mental illnesses and was frowned upon. Many of these small cultural differences created conflict.

Chinese believe that punctuality is a virtue and try to practice it, while Filipinos wear watches only for ornamental reasons. The Chinese, like most cultures, are wound far more tightly than the relaxed Philippine culture. Filipinos viewed the expectations of their occupiers to be unrealistic while the Chinese viewed their noncompliance as insolence.

But some of the differences were not small. The greatest social clash came with the introduction of legal abortions and the imposition of

China's family planning policy. Ethnic minorities are exempt from their one child policy within all other provinces, but the PRC determined that birthrates in their new 24th province were unacceptably high, so they imposed a one-child policy on Filipinos, who have historically maintained one of the highest birthrates in the world. Filipinos refused to attend the mandatory family planning lectures or acquire birth control devices that were freely distributed.

The People's Liberation Army acquired a database containing the names and addresses of more than two million registered gun owners in the Philippines. Anyone on the list who failed to surrender a weapon was apprehended.

The Roman Catholic Church was permitted to hold weekly masses. However the highly political *Iglesia ni Cristo* church was immediately banned, creating defiance and violent reaction to the ban. Mosques were surreptitiously monitored, while the armed Islamic groups in the southern Philippines were ordered to surrender their weapons. Their refusal to hand over their arms resulted in a bloodbath, which went largely unreported.

The Philippine press was required to conform to new rules, and many of the familiar personalities remained on the air in the 24th province. There was plenty of news to report as the PRC transformed the Philippines. The Philippine peso was converted to the Chinese Yuan. Filipinos were given thirty days to exchange their pesos for Yuan. The maximum amount that could be exchanged was 100,000 pesos, or about $2,200. The number of millionaires, estimated to be more than forty thousand throughout the Philippines dropped to zero. Politicians holding any ill-gotten gains, at least in pesos, could not circumvent the exchange process that was put into effect and lost their wealth and power.

The Philippine Stock Exchange reopened and immediately collapsed, losing more than seventy percent of its value. Stockholders now held Chinese Yuan instead of Philippine pesos, and the entire board for the PSE was replaced. The rules of the exchange were altered to match those of the Shanghai Stock Exchange. The market would not rebound anytime soon due to the international sanctions that had been imposed on the PRC.

Filipinos had grown accustomed to chronic unemployment and they eagerly filled a surge of new jobs. Manufacturing plants were constructed around the islands, creating fifty seven thousand new construction jobs. Production workers were hired to fill the plants. New seaports and airports were also constructed to handle the planned influx of tourists. Fleets of large fishing boats replaced the small outriggers that fed their communities. Facilities to flash freeze their catch for export were constructed at fishing communities along the coastlines.

New schools, libraries, computer labs, and gymnasiums were constructed creating more than eighty thousand jobs around the nation. Furniture makers were contracted to build student desks, tables, and cabinets. To the poor, the new normal meant jobs, food on the table and the hope of health and prosperity. To the middle class the new normal crushed their dreams and aspirations and lowered their ambitions. And to the wealthy the new normal meant devastating loss.

Parents want their children to become extraordinary, yet, at the same time, desire them to be 'normal.' The goal of most is to thrive within the system. Ordinary efforts produce ordinary results, and the next generation of Filipino was being groomed to become average. They would produce 'normal' music and literature. They would be conventional and predictable. They would prosper a few degrees and find contentment as they lived simple, mundane lives. Or at least that was the hope of the PRC leadership. Filipinos would surprise them with their creativity, industriousness, and their intense love of liberty.

Scoffers mock the very concept of a divine creator. They are too intelligent to believe in an all-knowing, omnipotent, and omnipresent God. But the God they mock, the divine entity who participated in the rise and collapse of thousands of nations, would soon become most visible. The entire world would soon witness the arrival and intensification of prophesied birth pangs.

MAP OF AURORA

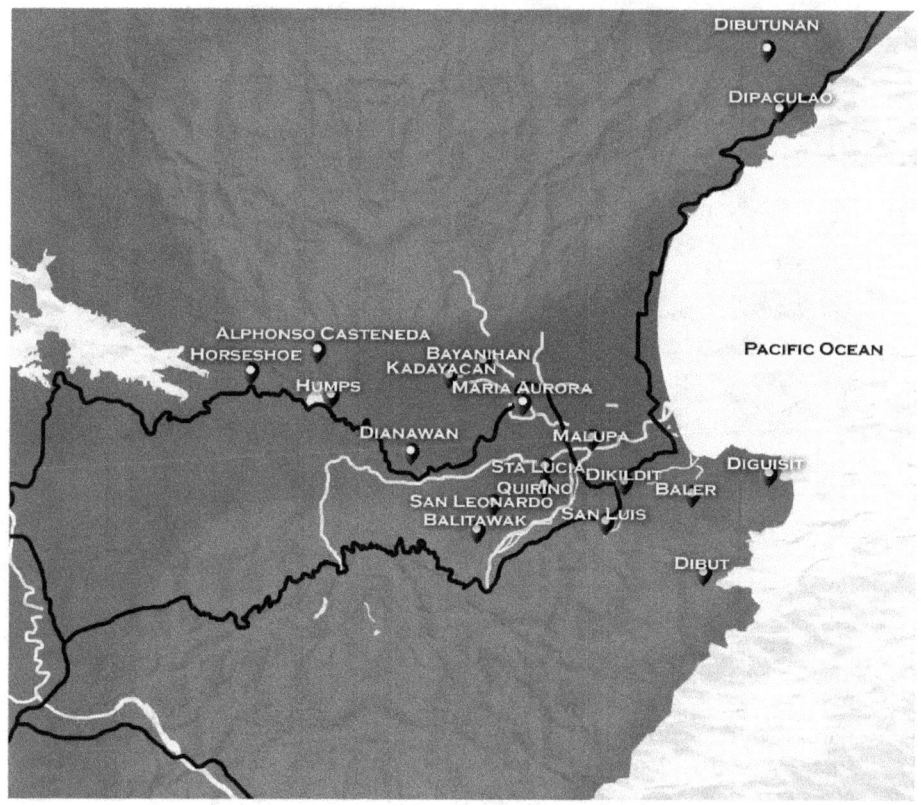

About the Author

Barry Dean Phillips is a full time missionary who lives in the remote Aurora Province of the Philippines. He served twenty years as a US Air Force analyst and has lived in the Philippines for more than a decade. He has been married to Lilia, his Filipina wife for thirty four years. Barry received a BA from Eastern Illinois University; an MSIS degree from Hawaii Pacific University, and an MA in intercultural studies from the Philippine Baptist Theological Seminary. His military background, seminary training and life in the provincial Philippines make him uniquely qualified to write The 24th Province. Barry has written two previous books: "Accidental Missionary" and "I Planted the Seed (and Woody Squashed it)."

Coming soon: *Birth Pangs*

The 24th Province is the first book of a three part series entitled, "*Restoring the Cosmos.*" The second book, planned for release in Q3, 2016 is called "Birth Pangs." Turmoil continues in the Philippines as guerilla fighters organize against their invaders. Nature becomes unhinged as massive earthquakes unleash unprecedented tsunamis in every ocean. A sudden outbreak of super typhoons and massive hurricanes are blamed on climate change. Relief agencies are unable to respond to the demand for their services. Global economic meltdown results in lawlessness as citizens refuse to be governed by failing states. Terrorism, rebellion and war compete with natural disasters for headlines. And in the midst of the turmoil, a deadly new virus emerges and spreads like wildfire. Amazingly few seem aware that what scripture calls "birth pangs" has begun. The world is unprepared for the increasing frequency and intensity of the pain.